Don't Leave Me Behind

Kane Ridge Ranch
Book 1

Bailey Johnson

For Grandma Carol.
I hope the spice is spicy enough for you.

Chapter 1

Leni Fucking Kane

Clay

THERE'S SOMEONE OUTSIDE THE CABIN.

I swear I heard a car door thud. It was quiet, muffled, like someone parked far enough away that I'd be less likely to hear it. This feels like the beginning of a bad joke. I swear to God, if Adler is out there sneaking up on the cabin, I'm going to kill him. Slipping out of bed, I pad to the top of the stairs, squinting through the floor-to-ceiling windows at the front of Leni's cabin. The moon is high and bright, painting the landscape outside, but I still can't see anything that looks out of place.

Picking my way down the metal and wood staircase, I tiptoe over to the entry. It's possible that someone stopped along the highway and got out to take a piss, but I'm far enough from the road that I doubt I'd hear that. No, someone's on Kane land, real close to Leni's cabin. If they're here, expecting to find her asleep in her bed, they're in for a surprise.

A steady cadence of thuds indicates footsteps on the deck. I scan the living room for a weapon, remembering at the last second that I cleaned my rifle when I got home from work

1

tonight. Adrenaline floods my veins as I tiptoe into the kitchen, where my duty rifle leans against a white wooden chair. Moonlight glimmers off the freshly oiled barrel. The magazine sits on the kitchenette table next to it. Five rounds, that's as far as I got before I squirreled my attention away to dinner and left it for tomorrow. I grab the gun and feed the magazine into its slot, hoping whoever is outside doesn't hear the click as it snaps into place.

My fingers pull back the charging handle as a key slides into the lock. *Who the fuck has a key?* No one in the family would sneak in here, not in the middle of the night. They know it would be a bad idea.

So, who is messing with me tonight?

Keeping the rifle ready in my hands, I wait, trying to hear over the sound of my heart banging against my chest. Anticipation coils deep in my gut. There's a pause once the door opens, the moonlight illuminating a silhouette that doesn't look like any of the Kane boys or the ranch hands. I'm about to demand they identify themselves when there's a crash, and the intruder goes flying to the ground.

I shoulder the rifle, ready to defend myself, before flicking on the lights. It only takes a couple of blinks before I can clearly see what's in front of me, and I think my heart stops beating for a second, because here she is.

The girl I've been avoiding since I was twenty-one, only, this is not the eighteen-year-old girl I saw last...*holy shit*. She is breathtakingly beautiful. Air rips from my lungs as I take her in. Long brown hair fans out around her head, wispy bangs hanging on either side of her face. Those big green eyes looking up at me with confusion, her movements slow and apprehensive. The terror in those eyes takes me back ten years. I swore to myself I'd never give her a reason to look at me like that again, but here we are. Her hands are trembling in surrender while I'm pointing a gun at her, in her own cabin. Why...why is she sneaking into the cabin when she's supposed to know I'm here?

"What. The. Fuck?" she snarls.

I move the barrel of the rifle away, aiming at the floor. A sound somewhere between a groan and a growl escapes her as she struggles to stand. *Did I shoot her and not remember? Was she hurt somehow?* I take inventory when she's standing in front of me, checking for injury. Her hoodie hangs loosely on her, the sleeves bunching at her wrists, too long for her short arms. Black leggings hug every single curve and dip of her legs, drawing my eyes straight down to the bright pink running shoes on her feet.

There's no blood or wounds that I can see, and while I want to sigh in relief, I'm too aware of how close I came to shooting her. I can't believe I aimed a gun at Leni. Mercer's little sister, baby girl of the entire Kane family.

My Leni.

I could have shot her.

With that thought, I drop the rifle, stumbling back. Leni tilts her head, her lips moving, but I can't hear anything other than the word *shot,* ricocheting through my brain like a fucking pinball. I'm no longer in the cabin. Even though I can see her, her words don't reach me. Instead, my heart hammers out a steady beat to a volley of gunshots and mortar rounds, to shouts of 'Grenade!' and 'Medic!' I glance down at my hands; they're red, covered in the blood of a fallen Marine, and I can't breathe.

My chest tightens, black creeping at the edges of my vision, every inhale a struggle. It's been years since I've had an attack this bad. I've gone through extensive therapy, done the hard work to get myself out of the dark, and back into something resembling a real, living human again. This isn't supposed to be happening, especially not in front of Leni.

I claw at my shirt, desperate to rip the fabric off, as if that might help me breathe. I watch from a distance, detached, while Leni kneels in front of me. She touches my face, and my hands itch to defend myself from a threat that isn't real. I will not hurt her, no matter how fucked up my brain is right now.

I will not hurt Leni. Not again.

Her lips are moving, but I still can't hear anything past the sounds of gunfire and explosions. I flinch as a mortar round lands too close to us.

Clay. Her lips make the shape of my name, repeatedly, but I can't break through, can't claw my way to the surface to reach her. I want to yell at her to go, will myself to fucking pass out, and be done with this whole thing. I don't want to see her look at me with pity and concern, or worse, fear. She's looked at me with fear in her eyes before. I thought it would destroy me; part of me died *that* day.

I should've known Eleanor Kane doesn't scare easily. She proved that ten years ago, showing up on my doorstep, willing to lose herself to fix me. I should've expected that same look of sheer determination now, as her eyes dart around, searching for a solution. I feel as lost as she looks; none of my usual panic attack exercises come to mind. Maybe the lack of sleep is catching up to me. I should've taken the damn sleeping pills Doc prescribed. This is *exactly* what I want to avoid.

Clay. Those pretty, pink lips, mouth once more. Something like hesitation sparks to life in her deep green eyes. I try to look away, shame gnawing at me, my lungs tightening. She doesn't let me. Soft fingers guide my face back to hers as she leans forward and crashes her lips against mine.

The moment her lips touch mine, it's like someone hit pause, and I remember how to breathe again.

There's no more gunshots, no more screaming; only ragged breathing and jittery hands as the adrenaline seeps out of my body. I reach for her, needing something solid, something real to hold onto, careful not to grip too tight. I'm desperate to make sure she's actually there, kissing me. Her scent of lilacs and vanilla wafts from her undone hair into my nose. A scent so familiar and nostalgic that my chest starts to hurt for a different reason.

Wrapping my arms around her, I haul her into me, crushing her body against my chest, kissing her back. She tenses, muscles locking up beneath my hands. Pain slices through my lip as she sinks her teeth in. It's not a love bite, but a warning. I jerk back, slamming my head into the wall as she scrambles off me. Her chest rises and falls with each ragged breath she takes. Her hands shake, and when she manages to open her eyes to look at me, I gasp. She's angry. Livid. I think I could count on one hand the amount of times I've seen Leni this angry.

The taste of iron fills my mouth, the sting barely enough to rein me in. Leni Kane was in my lap, kissing me. I'm really fucking trying to remind myself why I can't go there with her, but it's so damn hard. Breathing the same air, staring at that gorgeous face. I realize how badly I still want her, even with that scowl.

"What the fuck are you doing in my cabin, Clay?"

I barely suppress the shudder that threatens to overtake me when she says my name. It's been too long since I've seen her. Too long since I've heard her voice, even if my name is dripping with venom when she says it. After a decade of doing my best to avoid her, I deserve that.

"Your parents have those corporate retreat things going on, and I felt like I was getting in the way. Mercer told me he asked you. He said you weren't coming back for the summer, so I've been staying here the past couple of months."

"Oh." Her eyes dart toward the door, then back to me. Fear

and uncertainty fill them. That fear shouldn't be there, and knowing I caused it makes me sick to my stomach.

"I thought you knew." Scrubbing both hands down my face, I try to rein in the emotions I have flooding in and out of my system. "I, uh, I'll head over to Merc's. Come back for my stuff in the morning."

"No!" she says.

I crook an eyebrow at her, wondering, for the first time, what the hell she's doing here in the middle of the night.

"No, sorry...*fuck*." She draws her knees up into her chest, pulling her sleeves down and around her thumbs the way she used to when she was younger. "I don't want them to know I'm here."

"They're gonna know you're here, Len. That's why your dad wanted you in this cabin, so they can keep an eye on you."

"No, I know. I'm not an amateur." She rolls her eyes, huffing in frustration. *Fuck she's cute.* "I've done it before. I park in the trees, keep the lights off after dark. I just...I need a few days to regroup before they get all up in my business again."

I highly doubt they don't know when she's here. It's more believable that they realize when she sneaks back home and figures she wants to be left alone.

My fingers itch with the desire to pull her back into me. To feel the weight of her in my arms. I'd do anything if she'd let me kiss her again, just one more time. It'll never be enough where Leni is concerned, but it would be something. The longer I hesitate, the more restless she becomes, crossing and uncrossing her arms, straightening her legs only to pull them back to her chest. Something's wrong. Something happened, and I want to fix it. Not that I have any right or that I should even be looking at her like this, but I still want to fix it. Leni in pain will never do.

6

Ever.

"Right, I—uh. I'll crash out on the couch until morning and go get a room from the Inn. No big deal."

She looks aghast, like I told some salacious bit of gossip. "You can't go to the inn! Then everyone will know."

"Know what, Leni?"

"Why would you leave here to stay at the inn?"

"I don't know, because you..." *Oh.* She rolls her eyes at me again, and I can't lie, the sass she's giving me is doing nothing to help the situation that has arisen in my pants. I mean, she was just sitting on me, kissing me. It's not entirely my fault.

Okay, fuck, it is my fault, and I feel like a fucking creep right now. Drawing one of my legs up, I try to hide the fact that I am sporting a semi-hard dick.

It's not solely the kiss; it's everything about her. Freckles dust her nose, which still crinkles when she's annoyed. Her hair's shorter than I remember, but it looks good. Natural waves hit right below her shoulders. I want to reach forward, run my hands through it again, wrap it around my fist while I—you know what? Nope. *Down boy.* You are not going there. Not with Leni *fucking* Kane.

The realization of what she hasn't said hits me like a bucket of ice-cold water. Does she really think we can stay here together? "You want me to stay here with you?"

She's been back in my life for all of five minutes, and I've already had my tongue in her mouth. I have zero control when it comes to this girl. I've worked my ass off to stay away from her, so I wouldn't have to deal with this.

Eleanor is all sunshine and goodness, and she deserves someone who can reflect that back. Not someone dark and twisted like me. I won't saddle her with my mess when she has her whole life ahead of her.

"Yeah, Clay, that's the idea."

"No," I snap, the words coming out harsher than I mean. Pushing off the floor, I stomp up the stairs. I need to get my shit and get out of here before I do something even more stupid.

Something I can't take back.

Chapter 2

It Matters a Lot

Leni

W*ELL, SHIT.* T*HAT DID NOT GO THE WAY* I *THOUGHT IT* would.

Not even close.

I chase after him up the stairs, not sure what I'm going to say. *Please stay in this tiny house with me so my family doesn't know I'm a royal screw-up?* Most guys would be happy to stay in a one-bed cabin with me. Hell, most would jump at the chance. Not Clayton Traeger. No, he's practically sprinting to get away from me. The self-righteous prick.

He ghosted me for ten years, then tried to kiss the living daylights out of me. I mean, I know, I kissed him first, but he tried to kiss me back! The least he can do is hear me out.

I follow him into the bathroom, reaching for his shaving kit, trying to pull it out of his hands as he shoves things into it. "Wait, please just listen."

"Uh-uh," he shakes his head, scooping me up and setting me out of the way so he can pull a duffel bag off the shelves that double as a closet. My muscles stiffen involuntarily; I forgot how strong he is. A shaky breath escapes me. This is a bad idea,

9

but I'm out of options. If I don't want to tell my family every-thing, things need to stay exactly as they are. I need him to stay, and I need him to keep it a secret.

"You won't even try to hear what I have to say?"

"I'm not staying here."

He doesn't say it, but the *with you* part of that statement is loud and clear. Of course, he wouldn't want to stay with me. The guy practically ran away from me when we were younger. How did I somehow forget that he ghosted me first? Obviously, I make him uncomfortable.

"Shit, Clayton," I whisper his name, forcing myself to hold back the tears that are threatening to break through. Seeing him, being this close, is bringing back all the feelings I refused to acknowledge. "I'm sorry. Don't leave. I'll go to the inn. Or... or I'll drive back to Benson and stay with Miya for a while."

He turns to me and chucks his bag on the floor with a thud, and the memory of a chair splintering against the wall makes my breath catch. His broad, muscular arms cross over his chest, pulling his t-shirt taut. He's bigger than I remember him. So much more of a man than he was when I last saw him. He's filled out with muscles, exactly like Mom said he would.

"Why are you apologizing? And what the fuck is happening that you can't just go to the main house, or let me stay somewhere else?" His eyes narrow, as if he's trying to read the answer in my body language.

"I—clearly, you don't want to be around me. I'm sorry I kissed you downstairs. I wasn't trying to make you uncom-fortable."

"I shouldn't have kissed you back. You were just trying to help. You don't make me uncomfortable, Len," he scrubs his hands down his face again, drawing my attention to the stubble I'd traced with my fingers only a few minutes ago. I wish I didn't, but I want to touch him again. I wish he wanted me to.

"I don't know how you could be any clearer. I know you don't want to be around me. I'm not trying to make your life harder, I just—" The exhaustion and emotional toll of this past week catch up to me, and I can't help the tear that slips free as I move around him, back into the bedroom. I'm too fucking tired for this conversation. My emotions are too raw, too frayed. It's better to lick my wounds in actual solitude.

Before I can reach the stairs, his strong fingers grip my wrist, the warmth of his skin heating through my plush hoodie. I try to pull away, embarrassment prickles under my skin. *What a fucking joke.* This is supposed to be my one safe haven, the one thing that was mine. Now it's another spot on this ranch that will serve as a reminder that I've managed to turn my life into a total train wreck.

Tears stream down my face. I never let myself cry over him before. Back then, I shook it off and pretended like I wasn't breaking apart when I left.

Pissed at myself and this entire situation, I try to yank my sleeve out of his grasp. But he pulls me in, wrapping his arms around me, tight enough that I can't escape. I fight my body's reaction to being held by him. Every muscle is tight. Every nerve ending is on high alert.

His eyes sweep over me, shoulders tightening before his hands fall away. He grips the back of his neck, those stormy grey eyes filling with grief as he takes a step back, putting space between us again. "Whatever you need, I'll do it. I'm just not sure—I don't love having to lie to our family."

"You don't have to lie. They're not gonna bring it up."

"All Mercer can talk about is figuring out a way to get you home for the summer."

"Fine, but they're not going to assume that I'm hiding in the cabin with you. Why would I?"

Clay rubs his forehead. "Leni..."

"It's no different than you pretending I didn't find you ten years ago." I cross my arms over my chest, one hip jutting out to the side.

"I—what?" He looks confused. "You didn't tell them you found me?"

"No. Did they ever ask about it?"

"No." His brow furrows, eyes narrowing. "I thought...I guess I thought that they knew you saw me, but you obviously didn't tell them all the details. I thought I was getting off easy by them not giving me shit about it."

I snort. "In what world would they not have interrogated you about me showing up to see you? You had to know, had to at least suspect that they didn't know."

He taps his fingers on his thigh, brows drawn close in concentration as he works it out in his head. "You lied. But why? Mercer said you got hurt on your way back home. I assumed he knew—"

"Right," I cut him off. My throat tightens, chest constricting like a boulder pressing down on me. Sometimes, I forget what really happened on that trip. I've told the lie so many times, I've started to believe it. The panic always takes me by surprise when the memory tries to break through, looking for purchase. *Do not go there, Leni. It's in the past.* "Listen, I told Merc on Monday I wouldn't be back this summer. I don't see why he'd even bring me up. It's not like you, and I have talked recently, and you barely see the others during the week anyway, right?"

Clayton hesitates, like he's not quite sure that will be the case, then sighs. "Yeah, okay. How long are we talking, though? Because lying by omission to Merc is one thing, but Ma..."

I chuckle, letting myself relax and take in the space. It's the same cozy cabin I left behind, minus the unmistakably hot guy scent that is clearly coming from him. Like one of the spicy, earthy candles you'd purchase at the store.

"A week? So, only one family dinner. You could pretend to be sick?"

He backs up across the loft, dropping that big body onto my bed, the *only* bed in the cabin. His upper body bends forward, elbows resting on his knees as he rests his head in his hands. "You know damn well if I play sick, she's coming straight over here to spoon-feed me soup and clean the cabin." His voice comes out muffled from behind his palms. He sounds exhausted.

"True. You'll have to figure it out, I guess. Or maybe you'll get called out for work?"

"Not a chance. Mercer gets calls twenty-four-seven, but for those three hours on Sunday evening, his phone never rings. I think Ma put the fear of God into Patsy, and she literally calls anyone else but him, and by extension, me, during family dinners."

I laugh at the idea of my five-foot-nothing mother marching into the Sheriff's office to threaten Patsy within an inch of her life. Clay's head snaps up, his gaze locked on my face. When the smile fades from my lips, his shoulders slump, and his hands come up to cover his face. The heels of his palms resting in his eyes.

"Fine, second option, how often do you duck out early cause you're not sleeping well?"

He slowly brings his gaze up to me, eyes wide like I caught him with his hands in the proverbial cookie jar.

"Don't look so surprised. I can see the bags under your eyes. You're clearly exhausted."

He sighs, veins bulging in his forearms as he runs his fingers through his black curls. He can't deny that he isn't sleeping well. Clearly, that hasn't changed since I last saw him.

"Yeah, that's what I thought. Just tell them you need to go

get more sleep. Ma won't be offended by that, and it should keep the boys off your back."

"So how does this work then?" Clay eyes the one bed in the loft, an eyebrow raising so high it disappears behind a curl on his forehead.

"I...uh...I'll sleep on the couch."

"Not gonna happen. I'm not making you sleep on the world's most uncomfortable couch after you drove five hours to get here."

"Fine." I shrug. If he wants to sleep on the couch, who am I to stop him? I'm too tired to argue. I don't care if he sleeps on the floor, as long as he doesn't tell my family I'm here.

"Great." Clay sighs, one hand scrubbing down his face. His shoulders stoop more, like they're too heavy to hold up. When was the last time he slept well? Was it ten years ago? Shouldn't he have figured out a way to sleep by now?

"You could—" My voice catches, the weight of what I'm offering makes me pause. He *could* sleep in the bed with me. It's a queen-size mattress, not huge but big enough for the two of us to sleep without being on top of each other. I bring a finger to my mouth, gnawing at the nail bed as I think it through.

"It's alright, Leni." Clay gives me a tired smile, walking toward me. Or probably, the stairs behind me. "I'll be fine on the couch."

"Are you going to actually sleep?"

He shrugs. The look on his face tells me he won't be getting any sleep.

"Stay," I whisper. Even though I'm practically cringing internally. "You can sleep in the bed, Clay. It's fine. We're grown-ups."

"I'm not sure that it is fine."

It's not. Not really, but I lie to myself when I say I don't care. Clay is the one person I will never be able to bring myself to not care about. He's a freaking Sheriff's Deputy; he needs sleep. He can't be driving around in a patrol truck, barely conscious because he didn't get enough rest. That's not safe for anyone. So, while the idea of climbing into bed with him again makes my skin feel itchy, it's kind of the only acceptable option.

"It's fine. You need sleep. Maybe having me here will help." I glance at him through my lashes, fighting to push back my anxiety. "Like it used to."

"It might." He shrugs. "But I don't want to make you uncomfortable in your own home."

"You'd rather sleep on the couch?" I'm about to rescind the offer. If the idea of sleeping next to me is that abhorrent, he can have the couch. Ugh...no, I'd take the couch. He needs sleep.

"Of course I'd rather sleep next to you." Clay massages his temple like I'm giving him a headache.

"Great." I roll my eyes, making my way to the bathroom. I keep it stocked with the basics because, aside from summer trips, I'm not usually prepared to come back here. I take my time with my nightly routine, pushing back memories of the last time we saw each other. That was ten years ago; neither one of us is the same person now. I don't need to be afraid of Clay. I need to get through this week and figure my life out.

Slipping into a fresh pair of dusty pink boy shorts, I scan my top options. None are remotely appealing for sleep, so I grab a charcoal grey t-shirt from the side of the closet he's claimed. Soft, comfy...and a quick sniff confirms the hot guy smell comes from him. A second inhale has me taking in a hint of vanilla, cinnamon, and something woodsy. Like Christmas, only better. The shirt doesn't cover everything, but he's seen me in less clothes, so what does it really matter?

Apparently, it matters a lot. When I step into the bedroom portion of the loft, Clayton takes me in, wearing his t-shirt. His eyes darken, his throat bobs ever so slightly. Maybe the issue isn't that he doesn't want me. Maybe it's something else, because right now, it looks a lot like he does.

He mumbles something unintelligible before tossing his phone onto the nightstand and flopping onto the bed. I'm stuck standing by the bathroom door, painfully aware he's in my bed, and I'm going to have to sleep next to him for the foreseeable future.

This feels like a really bad idea.

"You comin', Leni girl?"

I shiver at the way he says *Leni girl*. As if no time has passed. Like we're still the same, Leni and Clay. "Mhm," I manage, before slipping into my side of the bed.

"Is this a terrible idea?" he whispers, before he flicks off the light on the nightstand.

"Probably." There's a reason we've avoided each other for the past decade. "Just get some sleep. We can reassess in the morning if we need to."

"Sure," his voice is already growing deeper, thick with sleep. "Whatever you want."

My hand flies to my mouth as I choke back a tiny sob that's threatening to escape. He said that to me that night, too. One minute, it was, "whatever you want," and the next, my whole world flipped upside down. My heart races, and I know, despite Clay already finding sleep, I won't be doing much of that lying next to him.

Maybe I should have picked the couch.

Chapter 3

Stupid Fucking Hat

Clay

FOR THE SECOND TIME IN LESS THAN TWELVE HOURS, I'M jolted awake. My heart pounds almost as violently as whatever is beating on the door downstairs. A muffled yell follows, then a groan from the bed beside me. Leni's curled into my side, her hair fanned out behind her. Looking down at her, I realize I didn't wake up once from the time she lay next to me until now.

"Make it stop," she grumbles, and it's adorable.

While Ma Kane has enough attitude to keep all five of her boys in check, Eleanor is all sugar, with a sprinkle of spice. She's about as threatening as a kitten, and I love that about her. Reaching back to my nightstand, I grab my phone, and jolt upright when I realize it's nine o'clock.

Holy shit. I slept through three alarms and am two hours late for my shift. I'm usually the first one at the office.

"What is going on?" Leni sits up on the bed, wiping sleep from her eyes.

"I'm late for work, like, *really* late."

"Clay." Her eyes widen. "Who's at the door?"

"Fuck," I groan, stumbling down the stairs at the exact

17

moment someone is turning the lock. I manage to kick Leni's purse and hot pink shoes behind the door before coming face to face with her eldest brother, Brooks. There aren't many people who make me feel small, but at six-foot-four, Brooks is an inch taller and way more confident. His hair is dark like Leni's, beard always trimmed and clean cut. I've looked up to him for half my life, for the way he always seems so sure, so put together.

"Hey?" he says it like a question. He glances behind me for signs of, I don't know, struggle maybe?

"Hey, man, sorry. I was still sleeping." Rubbing my hands over my eyes, he stands there and blinks at me. "I didn't sleep much last night."

"Is he okay?" Mercer's voice comes muffled through the phone in Brooks's hand. Brooks jabs at the screen like its very existence offends him, and suddenly Mercer's on speaker. "Hello? Brooks? Ah, hell, Patsy, I think they're both goners."

"I'm right here dickhead," Brooks grumbles. He's a man of few words and even less emotion. I'm honestly surprised he got all four words out before cutting himself off and scowling.

"Well?" Mercer chirps.

"I'm fine. Sorry, Merc. I didn't sleep well last night and didn't hear my alarms going off."

"It's fine, nothing going on right now. I just wanted to make sure you were okay. Do you need the day off?"

"No." My answer is a bit too forceful, causing Brooks' eyebrow to arch at me in question. *Fuck.* I'm not trying to be suspicious, but the last thing I need right now is a full day off to spend with Leni. "Nah, man, I'll come in. I need to finish that supplemental report for the State Police anyway."

"Alright, see you soon then. Thanks, Brooks."

Brooks grunts an acknowledgement and jabs his thumb at the red button to end the call. He cocks his head, studying me.

Brooks doesn't say much, but he's good people, and no one cares more about his land or his family than Brooks Kane. I always figured he'd make a good father someday, if he ever took enough time away from the ranch to find someone.

"You good, brother?"

"Yeah." I squeeze the back of my neck. "I'm good."

"Good."

He heads down the small deck, snatching up the reins where his palomino gelding, Whiskey, is ground-tied. With a grace I envy, he swings into the saddle. At thirty-one, most days I feel like a grandpa moving through my various aches and pains. Brooks is thirty-five, and after working every day of his adult life on the ranch, he moves like a well-oiled machine. Taking one last look at his phone, he smirks at me and rides off toward the main house.

By the time I make it back up the stairs, Leni's sitting on the bed, my phone in her hands, squinting down at it with a Brooks-worthy scowl. Notifications are pinging nonstop, which can only mean the group chat is going off.

"Is he gone?" She gets out of bed, stretching her hands over her head. My shirt is riding up higher on her thighs.

"Did you expect him to stay and chat?" I drop my head back, looking at the ceiling so I don't stare as the shirt rides up over her hips. She snorts. We both know Brooks isn't the type to stick around for small talk. Another notification pings on my phone, Leni's nose wrinkling with annoyance.

"Take it before I kill it." She tosses the phone at me and disappears down the stairs, the globes of her ass peeking out from under the hem of my t-shirt.

She's always been a knockout, but I never would have guessed she could get more attractive. Yet here we are, my dick twitching in my pants while I think about my best friend's little sister. I squeeze my eyes shut, trying to erase the image of Leni in my t-shirt, but trembling hands and tear-filled eyes flash in my head. My gut churns at the memory, a timely reminder of why Leni Kane and I can *never* happen.

When I glance down at my phone, the guys' group chat is still blowing up. These assholes are supposed to have real jobs, the kind that shouldn't leave time for gossiping like a bunch of old hens.

KANE BROS GROUP CHAT
MERC D

He's alive!

E-MAN

I told you he was fine

TOBES

Yea bro we told you to chill out

ADDY

You need a woman. Leave the rest of us alone dude.

To no one's surprise, Mercer ignores everyone else in favor of interrogating Brooks.

MERC D

How'd he look Brooky?

BROOKY

I told you asshats not to call me that anymore.

ADDY

Yea that's not going anywhere

TOBES

Absolutely not

E-MAN

Agreed. It's here to stay man. Unless Leni ever comes home and gives you a new nickname.

MERC D

Answer the gd question

BROOKY

Fine. He looked fine.

ADLER

Why was he late then?

E-MAN

Why are we talking about him like he's not in this group? Why were you late man? You good?

TOBES

Yea you good Traegs?

MERC D

Said he didn't sleep well

E-MAN

Does he ever?

ADDY

Does anyone?

BROOKY

Fucker looked like he slept just fine to me

That bastard. Of course, Brooks would notice that I'd slept okay. For the second half of the night, at least. *Damn it,* now they're all going to be on my case, assuming I'm seeing someone. This is exactly why I told Leni it wouldn't be a good idea to have me lying to them. They're a bunch of nosey bitches, and it won't take them long to figure out I'm hiding something.

ADDY

Excuse me! What are you insinuating?

TOBES

Ooh insinuating...thats a big word for you Addy. Did you hurt your noggin pulling that one out?

ADDY

Fuck off Teabag 🫖

E-MAN

I too would like to know what's being hinted at.

BROOKY

Said what I said. Run along and fuck off now

I put the phone down, knowing damn well they'll keep this nonsense going all day.

They're stubborn like that. Normally, I don't mind, but I'm generally not the center of attention or interrogation. I reply with a quick middle finger emoji before I quickly brush my teeth and get ready for work. Normally, I don't bother with my hair; the curls do what they want. Today, I work a bit of pomade throughout. Attempting to give them some kind of structure. Taming them as best I can. I pull on a pair of light wash Wranglers, tucking my tan polyester uniform shirt into the waistband. Slipping a leather belt around my waist, I secure my handgun in its holster, then shoulder my vest. Everything else I carry on duty is strapped to the vest. Handcuffs, taser, extra magazines, all of it gets stored on the vest itself. It's a bad habit, but I don't wear it unless I'm on a call or running traffic, keeping it stowed in my vehicle when I'm on shift.

Another message pops up from Mercer, this one in our private thread. I smile at his name. Years ago, Mercer got hold of my phone and changed everyone's contact name into some ridiculous nickname. He put his as *Sexy Cowboy*. I changed it to Merc D because it makes him mad, but also Leni calls him D. Another little piece of her that I can't seem to let go of.

> **MERC D**
>
> We'll definitely be talking about this when you get here. I've instructed Patsy not to call me out

> Good luck with that.

> **MERC D**
>
>

The scent of coffee fills my nose the closer I get to the first floor. There's a skillet of fluffy scrambled eggs on the stove, and my travel mug sat by the coffee maker like always. Leni is already tucked into her breakfast at the small dining room table. One foot propped on her chair, cheek resting on her knee between bites. An arm draping around her leg in a half-hug.

"Still sitting like a gremlin?" My eyes catch a tiny stripe of pale pink cotton fabric that I hadn't noticed before. One small scrap of clothing between me and whatever heaven she's hiding between those thighs.

"My eyes are up here, Traeger."

"Yeah, but your panties are on full display right there." I jab a finger toward her lap.

The leg she had propped up slips back down, crossing over the opposite knee. My eyes find hers, a fire burning in them. Leni might've been all sugar once, but I got a feeling she's adopted more spice in the years since I last saw her. "You gonna tell me how I can dress in my own home?"

"Technically, I think the cabin still belongs to your parents."

Her eyes widen, steam practically billowing out of her ears

23

as her nostrils flare. *Yup, that was the exact wrong thing to say.* "Don't you have a job to be at, or something?"

"Sure do. Don't you have some explaining to do about why you showed up in the middle of the night and don't want to tell your family?"

"It's not really any of your business, is it?"

"Come on," I roll my eyes and scoop the rest of the eggs onto a paper plate to take on the road. "You guys tell each other everything. What could be so bad you can't tell them you're home?"

She snorts, a mirthless laugh scraping out of her. "Yeah, okay. Whatever, Clay."

"No, seriously," I stammer. "I haven't been gone that long. You guys tell each other everything. This isn't you."

"You don't know me anymore, Clayton." She spits my name out like a curse, shaking her head. Definitely spicier than I remember. I used to know everything about her; now I'm left with the scraps her brothers have told me over the years. She's changed, we both have, but there's so much I don't know about her. I don't know this version of Leni...but I want to. I want to unravel all the pain she's holding onto and fix it to make her the same girl she was before *that* night.

"Well, I'm here to talk, if you need someone to listen."

She grunts, turning back to her food, tucking that same leg back under her chin.

"Thanks for the coffee. I'm gonna take the eggs to go."

A wave of her hand dismisses me. Her eyes flick back in my direction for a second, but I hold myself back from walking over, like I might kiss her goodbye. The truth is, I *want* to kiss her goodbye. Good thing I've spent the past decade *not* acting on the things I want to do to her. She deserves someone better, someone who doesn't make her flinch when they walk by.

"Need anything from town?"

"No—ooh, yes! Coffee creamer, please."

I groan, throwing my head back to look at the ceiling. "You know, Bertie is just going to text Ethan and tell him that I'm buying coffee creamer, right?"

"I read the group chat, might as well perpetuate this idea that you're sleeping with someone." She wrinkles her nose when she says it, like she doesn't quite like the idea of it. I don't either, to be honest.

"Easy for you to say when you're not the one they're interrogating."

Leni sticks her tongue out at me, little brat that she is.

"You're going to be the death of me, you know that?"

Slipping my Stetson onto my head, I make my way to the door. The piercing sound of glass shattering sends my pulse into my throat. I reach for my pistol, pivoting on my heel, my upper body tucked low. Leni's coffee mug lies on a broken breakfast plate; her shoulders hunched to her ears. She doesn't look at me, shoving off the table to grab a towel from the kitchen.

I'm about to ask if she's okay when I hear her mumbling, "Stupid fucking hat with the stupid fucking uniform."

"You kiss your mama with that mouth?" I couldn't keep the cocky smirk off my face if I'd tried.

I never let myself really look at her before. Back when we were kids, four years felt too big an age gap to consider her as more than a friend.

I can't seem to keep myself from looking now. *Damn*, she looks good. Long lean legs with curves in all the right places. I still haven't seen her without a baggy top on, but something tells me it's going to hurt when I do.

"Fuck off, Traeger! You're late for work."

I send her another wink before tipping my hat at her and making my way outside. Warm spring air brings me back to myself. Teasing Leni like an older brother is one thing. Flirting with her, after I went out of my way to make sure, she never thought twice about me, feels cruel.

I need to get my shit together. Falling for Leni isn't an option. It never was.

Chapter 4

Cute Little Traeger Babies
Clay

LINES ON PAVEMENT BLUR AS I MAKE THE TWENTY-minute drive to Hillcreek. I can't stop thinking about Leni. My mind compares every little difference from the girl I knew at eighteen to the woman who crashed into my life last night. She is all woman now, the girl I once knew stuck in a past neither one of us wants to return to. Even the way she holds herself is different. There's a guardedness to her that never used to be there. Before that night.

I bring my hand up, dragging it down my face when I catch a hint of lilacs and vanilla. Her scent calls back a memory so vivid; I have to stop on the side of the road.

I fly out of the driver's seat, breath coming in ragged and painful as I try to think of anything but that night. My hands grip the grill guard of my pickup, knuckles turning white as I'm swallowed whole by the day that changed everything between us.

. . .

I FIND Leni standing outside the barracks, somehow there without any of her brothers. She snuck away, told her family she was with Miya, and crossed the country to see me.

I think my chest would swell with pride if I weren't so damn worried about her family blaming me. She put herself in unnecessary danger, and for what? Me? A broken man who could never be right for her? I lay beside her in the hotel room, counting her breaths as they deepen with sleep.

Muted light filters from the street through dirty polyester curtains. The run-down motel was a practical choice on my part. Trying to make this visit as uncomfortable as possible for her, so she has no desire to stay. Or come back. It's probably a giant waste of time, considering how stubborn each of the Kanes are.

Leni shifts in her sleep, her arm wrapping around my chest. Her head tucked into the crook of my shoulder. My chest expands as I take a deep inhale of her scent, trying to memorize it. I'm sending her home tomorrow, I have to. She doesn't belong here; she belongs on the ranch. Finishing high school, going to college. Not piecing me back together.

Slowly, I feel myself starting to drift off, the usual barrage of gunfire and screaming replaced by her soft, quiet breathing.

"No!" I growl, backhanding the soldier beneath me. He's not getting away this time. He's going to die. I watch, detached from my body as my hands wrap around his throat, thumbs digging into his trachea, crushing his windpipe. Fingernails dig into my skin, drawing blood as he fights me off. I ignore the pain, pressing harder as his lips beg for reprieve, his eyes wide and full of fear. I blink, trying to clear my doubt. He will kill me if I don't kill him. That's how war works. The soldier before me gasps when my hands loosen a fraction. Enough to take a breath. I bear down on him again, fingers tightening their hold. I watch in horror as the soldier's face shifts, and it's no longer an enemy fighter, but Leni. Her

lips turning blue beneath me, tears streaming from the corners of her eyes.

"Clay," she rasps. *I try to pull my hands back, but I'm stuck. My muscles locked, unable to release the hold I have on her. More tears stream down her face, her eyes pleading. No! Not this, not her.*

"Clay." *I hear my name, like she's speaking into my mind. It's syrupy and muffled. Her mouth isn't moving, her hands aren't fighting me, and her eyes go dead beneath me.*

"No!" *I hear myself scream this time.*

"Clay!" *Warmth radiates on my cheeks, soft fingers brushing tears off my face.*

"Leni," *I cry, unable to open my eyes, worried I'll find a corpse beneath me.*

"It's okay," *the sweetest voice in the world whispers to me.* "You're okay, Clay. I'm here."

"Leni. Leni. Leni," *I chant, choking between sobs that rack through my entire body. I killed her. I fucking killed her in my dream, and it felt real. The whole thing felt so fucking real.*

I finally manage to open my eyes, hands gripping her face harder than I mean. Pulling her away from my chest so I can see her, I move her head left, then right, checking her neck for bruising. For any signs that the dream might not have been a dream.

She's quiet, with gentle eyes, studying my face as she lets me assess her. Never once complaining about how rough I'm being. How insane I must seem to her right now.

"You have to go," *my voice cracks as I jump off the bed and start packing her bag.*

"What? No. This is why I'm here. You need help, you need me."

I chuckle, a dark twisted kind of sound coming from my chest. "I need you? What the fuck is a high schooler going to do to help me?"

"Clay," she whispers, tears glistening in her eyes.

I turn my back, shoving down the lump in my throat as my head begs me to take it back. To tell her, I don't mean it. That I do need her. That she's the only person I have ever needed. I'm too full of adrenaline; the image of her dead, lifeless eyes under my hands floods my mind.

"I'm not going," her voice floats across the room. It's hard and stubborn, the same voice Ma uses when she digs her heels in.

"Yes, you are!" I roar, whipping around to face her. The bag flies from my hand, slamming into the TV.

Green eyes widen, her pouty bottom lip trembling.

Rage fuels me. I saw my mom look at my dad that way. Scared. I'm scaring her, but I don't know how to stop. I don't know how to pull it back.

"You have to go."

"No, Clay. You're just scared." Tiny feet walk toward me, her hand raising outward, like she's approaching a scared horse.

"You don't get it. I am not meant for you."

"Please," her voice wavers when she begs. Tears streaming down her face now.

"GET OUT!" I scream. Wood splinters as I haul the shitty wooden chair up and smash it into the wall.

Leni's hands fly up, covering her ears, her body shaking. My fingers grip her elbow, spinning her around to flatten her back against the wall. Her eyes squeeze shut when she makes impact, a whoosh of air puffing into my face.

"I. Don't. Want. You. Here." I grit the words out through clenched teeth. Plaster dusts across her freckles when my fist finds the wall beside her head. Her eyes open, a cry loosening from her lips brings me back into my body.

"Leni," I half sob, half beg. Stepping back from her, I stare at the broken chair, the hole in the wall, the way her body is shaking, eyes overflowing with tears. She gathers her things, franti-

cally shoving the rest into her backpack before she sprints toward the door. I reach for her, my brain freezes when she screams, green eyes full of terror.

My chest tightens, lungs stop functioning as I drop to my knees and watch her leave.

I don't know how long I sat there, staring at the empty doorway. My lungs burned as a panic attack ripped through me, stealing all the air. My vision started to blacken, my body collapsing under the weight of it. I knew she'd leave eventually, like my mom did. Running from the shitty DNA stuffed into us, Traeger men. I wasn't born inherently good or well-adjusted like the Kane siblings. I tried to tell her, tried to warn her, and still I'd chased away the one person I ever truly felt at home with. Scared her so bad she still flinches when I move near her.

I tried to call her the next day, when I woke up in a hospital bed, my CO was standing over me, shaking his head. She never answered. I learned pretty quickly that she got a new phone; I found hers smashed under the bed. She'd rushed out of there, in the middle of the night, without having a phone on her. I'm a bastard, and I will never deserve her.

I thought the family knew what happened, figured she called them to come get her. Now I'm questioning if she told them anything. They've never treated me any differently, never asked about that night. No one asked why I stopped sending her letters, no one except Mercer. He never lets me forget it. You'd think he would take more of the classic big brother stance, where they freak out if their best friend had a thing for their sister, but Mercer is a romantic at heart. He told me once that I looked at Leni the way his dad looks at his mom, and that had to mean she was my soulmate. That I was stupid for pushing her away like I did. He still thinks that, and every chance he gets, he brings her up in conversation.

Rubbing it in my face when she goes on dates, or who she

dances with at the bar when she comes home for a visit. Telling me when she's had bad days, when she calls him crying because she's lonely. I've gotten daily updates on Leni for the past ten years, but she thinks Mercer wouldn't bring her up. She has no idea her brother has been playing matchmaker for most of our lives.

I suck in deep lungfuls of air, shaking out fingers that ache from gripping the grill too tightly. I need to get my head screwed on and figure out how to survive the next week. Need to get her out of my brain, erase the memory of having her in my lap yesterday.

The way I sleep like the dead when I'm near her because she is safety for me. Leni is home and so fucking off limits. I can't risk it, hurting, scaring, watching her leave me again. I wouldn't survive it. Never mind the risk of losing her entire family. The only family I've ever known.

Fuck. I'm in such deep shit.

Pulling into the back parking lot of the county courthouse, I brace myself for a Mercer interrogation. He's taken on the role of Sheriff a little too seriously, like having a badge gives him the right to snoop even harder into our lives. He's the youngest sheriff in Halfor County's history, but that's not saying much considering the last one retired after working here for forty years. He was a decent sheriff, but a little forgetful there at the end.

No one local wanted to campaign, so the only name officially on the ballot when it came time for the election was some big-shot oil company CEO who wanted to play wild west. Ethan started a write-in campaign in Hillcreek, and it caught on pretty quickly throughout the county. One night, Mercer went to bed a ranch hand and woke up a sheriff. He had no idea that Ethan had even started the campaign. Mercer went to school for criminal justice, but I didn't think he had any desire to use his degree.

I swear, there's nothing the Kane brothers can't do. It's a major part of their appeal. A mix of old and new money, they're humble and some of the best people I've ever met. The whole town is in love with them, and I'm pretty lucky to be lumped in with them.

Scanning my key fob at the back door, I let myself into the Sheriff's office. We're tucked into the back of an old stone courthouse. Over the years, they added new additions, like the Halfor County Jail, housing up to thirty inmates at a time. It's not much, but it's bigger than the four cells they initially started with. One tiny courtroom on the third floor, and a handful of county employees with offices upstairs. During renovations, the previous sheriff said he liked the basement, so they came through the ancient sublevel and modernized things.

I walk past Mercer's tiny office, not surprised when he jumps into the hallway to follow me with Ethan close behind him.

Ethan isn't technically a county employee, but he is the unofficial town lawyer, and his office is upstairs. Most mornings, you can find him down here, shooting the shit with his brother, stealing our coffee and pastries, the bastard.

No one says anything as I make my way into the deputy's room. It's small for the amount of workstations crammed in here, but it does the job, I suppose. Taking a seat at one of the stations, I log into the computer, then sit back in my chair. I need someone else to start a conversation, so I don't start talking about how gorgeous their sister is. That'll just lead to them asking questions I'm not supposed to answer. Ethan leans against my desk, his broad chest giving his tailored suit a run for its money. He dresses like a big city lawyer, with fancy shoes.

His dark brown hair always slicked back and shiny. Mercer, on the other hand, is a lot more rugged. His Sheriff's uniform hangs off his torso like it's made for someone twice his size, and he exclusively wears cowboy boots. His wavy hair tousled in an 'I just took my hat off' sort of way.

He picks the furthest chair from us. Turning his back to us, he shoves off the ground, rolling his way across the room to us in big, dramatic rows.

"Fucking child." Ethan whacks Mercer upside the head. "Kate's in town." He crosses his arms, his signature resting bitch face coming out to play.

"Okay," I drag out the word, a little confused. This was not the direction I saw this conversation going. Kate is Brooks' ex-fiancée. They were high school sweethearts until Kate discovered she liked alcohol and drugs more than life with Brooks. Brooks nearly tore himself apart trying to fix her. He hasn't smiled since.

"Are we worried about it?" Mercer pulls a beef stick out of his pocket, like that's a totally normal thing to be carrying around on your person. Ethan rolls his eyes at me, and I smirk. *Fuck*, I missed this, missed them.

"Yeah, we're worried. Last time she came to town, she fucked around and left with ten K from our brother." Ethan's voice rises with a passion I envy. I'm surprised when he doesn't start pacing like he does in the courtroom. "I don't see how Kate being in town can do anything *but* worry us."

"Well, you're a worrier, so you're always worried." Mercer kicks his feet up on the desk near where Ethan is leaning, dirty cowboy boots a little too close to his expensive suit. Ethan grumbles, scowl burning holes into Mercer's badge. Bringing a knee up, he shoves Mercer's legs back down to the ground, boots thudding against the floor.

34

"So what? We need a preemptive intervention?" Mercer asks around a mouthful of beef stick. The man is constantly eating.

"Brooks is a big boy. If he wants to get tangled back up with a toxic mess, who am I to stop him?" I sip my coffee.

"You two are hopeless. You could at least pretend to care that Satan incarnate is going to try to get her hooks into our brother again."

"Yeah, yeah, I care. But it's been, what? Eight years since she's been around? Brooky knows she's bad news. He'll steer clear. What I really think we need is a plan of action for... Leni."

I nearly spew coffee out of my mouth when Mercer says this. "Wha—what? Why do you say that?"

Ethan quirks an eyebrow at me as I clean the coffee that did manage to slip onto my uniform shirt. Thank God, my uniform color matches the coffee. Patsy will kick my ass if she has to order me anymore.

Mercer throws his head back and groans, "Because of you, dickhead."

"Me?" I splutter. Jesus, how do they already know she's here? Or that I'm hiding her? Do they know I kissed her? That I slept in the bed with her?

"Yes, you! I told her you moved back, and now she's not coming home all summer. She's a teacher, summer is our only chance to see her, and you're fucking it all up."

He's being dramatic, I know this. I know he doesn't mean it, and yet, I can't help but feel a little pang of hurt at his words. That's me, though. Clayton Traeger, the boy from the wrong side of Hillcreek who is bound to fuck up everything he touches. *Damnit.*

"Leni is an adult." Ethan narrows his eyes at Mercer. "She

makes her own choices. It's not anyone's fault if she doesn't come home."

"It kind of is." Mercer glares back. "If Traeger would just get his head out of his ass and tell her he loves her, then we wouldn't be having this conversation. Leni would be living on the ranch, popping out cute little Traeger babies."

I inhale coffee straight down my windpipe, full-blown, choking on it as the mental image starts to take place in my mind. Mercer stands up to slap my back while I hack my lungs up, trying to clear the coffee out of my airway. I'm gasping for air by the time I sit back in my seat. Try as I might, I can't get the image of a pregnant Leni standing barefoot in that tiny cabin kitchen out of my mind. It does something funny to my chest, and I shake my head to clear the thoughts away.

"Jesus, Merc, are you trying to kill him?"

Ethan rolls his shoulders, trying to keep from shaking as he stifles a chuckle. Bastards, all of them, I swear. It's obviously not a big secret that I had feelings for her, but most of them think Mercer is razzing me. I don't think they know how on the nose he actually is most of the time.

Mercer shrugs. "I'm serious, though. I cannot go a whole year without seeing our Leni girl. Remember her freshman year?" He turns to Ethan, knowing that I don't remember because I wasn't here for it. Ethan screws up his face, a snarl forming as his hands come up to crack his knuckles. There's definitely a story there. One I'm not sure I want to know.

"Fix it." Ethan jabs a finger at me, then turns on his heel and marches off.

"I hate you," I mumble to Mercer.

"No, you don't. You love me, and you love my sister. So, whoever you're secretly banging, you can send them packing and figure out a way to get Leni home this summer."

I flip him the bird before pretending to ignore him in favor of writing my supplemental report for the state police. But really, I'm thinking about the woman with soft brown curls and bright green eyes currently sitting in a cabin on the ranch. Just a few miles away from the main house.

Fuck.

Chapter 5

How Many is a Few

Leni

MY LIMBS FEEL HEAVY, PULSE POUNDING IN MY HEAD. I don't think I slept a wink last night. I lay there, replaying the night over and over in my head. Thinking of the last time I saw him. He doesn't know, no one in the family does, how bad that night was for me. Running scared from that hotel room, trying to figure out a way to get back home with the limited resources I brought. Baby Leni thought Clay would welcome her into his life. That he would choose and want me.

I groan, mentally cringing at how fucking naive I was, on so many counts. I ruined my life by chasing after him. I'm still trying to pick up the pieces, still a mess with no clear direction or way to move forward.

I'm desperate to roll back over and get some sleep when my phone starts to vibrate.

BEST BITCHES GROUP CHAT
PEPPER

Excuse me.

ELEANOR

> Care to tell me why I just got turned away from your HOUSE by a married couple in their thirties??

MIYA

> 🙄 Why are we yelling already Peps?

> ...

> Maybe because I got kicked out...?

MIYA

> EXCUSE THE FUCK OUTTA YOU

> WHAT?

PEPPER

> Now who's yelling?

> It gets worse...

> Video chat?

I've barely sent the text before my phone rings with an incoming video call from Pepper. She's wearing a white crop top, long legs pulled up into her chest as she paints her nails. Her long blonde hair is braided off to one side, and her eyes sparkle, because she always sparkles somehow. Miya and I met her in a bar during our senior year. She was a sad little freshman that night, drowning her sorrows when she spilled her life story, and we just sort of adopted her into our friendship.

"Hey, Lenibeni!" She chirps her greeting, that megawatt smile of hers making it impossible for me not to return it.

"Pepperoni! I miss you!"

Miya's face pops up next; her smooth black bun is styled perfectly, and if you didn't know her, you wouldn't know how tired she is. I can see it, though. It's mostly in her eyes. They look exhausted and maybe a little lonely. I miss her so much. I know I only left Benson yesterday, but it's been months since our schedules aligned for us to see each other in person. I might video call them often, but we hardly ever get to hang out.

"Mimi!" Pepper squeals. "I forgot how much I miss your face."

Miya, to her credit, laughs. She's not much for squealing or girl talk; fast-tracking your way through medical school will do that to a person. "Hey, Pepper, miss you too."

"What about me?" I whine, faking offense.

"So needy, Len." She rolls her eyes, but her face softens with a smile at the same time. "I think I might actually be dying from withdrawals. I miss you so much."

"Much better," I croon. Rigging up my phone on the nightstand, I lean against my pillows, getting comfy.

"Alright, spill." Miya leans forward, eyes widening when she sees where I am. "What happened, and why are you home?"

I blow the bangs I panic-cut on Tuesday off my face before deciding how to answer. I'm the one who called this little 'meeting,' but I find that I'm nervous to talk to them about everything. Why is being an adult so hard? Couldn't we have someone tell us what we're supposed to be doing?

"The bangs were a choice," Miya jokes. Her way of buying me some time when she can tell I'm stalling.

"I think they're cute!" Pepper grins as I try to push the too-short curtain bangs back behind my ears.

"They were a terrible choice." I grin. "Honestly, I've thought about cutting them off completely pretty much every second since I cut them."

They laugh, and a little more of the tension I'm carrying melts away.

"They cut my teaching program at school," I sigh, feeling justified in my anger as Pepper's nostrils flare, her eyes flashing with the promise of violence. She might be cute and little, but Pepper would go to war for her people. "Actually, they cut a ton of programs at the school, mine just happened to be one of them."

"I'm confused," Miya cuts in. "How does this translate to a different couple at your place? Didn't Edna renew your lease?"

"Oh, she did." My poor, sweet elderly landlord. "Her son sold the house, then moved her into a nursing home. She was supposed to tell me weeks ago, but I guess she forgot."

"Oh my God." Pepper stifles a laugh.

I don't take offense to it, though. Only my life could be such a cluster fuck.

"What are you going to do then?" Miya covers a yawn with her mug.

"I don't know. I was thoroughly unprepared for moving houses or careers."

"You could try to get on at my school!" Pepper grins. "They're looking for a pre-school teacher."

I shudder, my eyes bugging out of my head. "No, thank you."

Pepper shrugs, nonplussed by my refusal. Teaching pre-k would be bad enough; doing it after years of teaching high school? Hard pass.

"That's not all," I groan. "It gets worse. Here I thought losing my job would be the worst thing, and then I thought having to move back home was the worst, but then..." I pause for dramatic effect. "A few months ago, Mercer told me that Clay was moving back."

Miya gasps while Pepper sits up a little straighter.

"Who's Clay?" Pepper asks at the same time Miya says, "Where is he staying?"

"He's no one," I mumble, wishing I could take it back.

Pepper doesn't know about Clay. Miya is the only one who knows what happened between us.

"He's the one that got away." Miya winks at Pepper.

Pepper's eyes widen as she leans forward, tipping the nail polish over as she does it. Thank God, she already put the cap back on. Her landlord would not be happy about that.

"We were just friends." I narrow my eyes at Miya.

She snorts into her phone, sipping from a steaming mug of what I can almost guarantee is chai. "She was obsessed with him when we were growing up. He lived with her family for a while and left to join the Marines. When he came back, he was a mess. Our girl Leni here patched him up."

"Ohhhh." Pepper practically has hearts bulging out of her eyes, giving me a dreamy smile. "What happened next?"

"I ran away at eighteen to go see him."

Pepper gasps, clutching her hands to her chest. She might be dramatic, but she is the best person to tell a story to. I've seen her listen to audiobooks. This girl doesn't know how to hide a single emotion around us.

"He...we...I don't know. It didn't work out."

Miya gives me a sad, understanding look. The pity in her eyes makes my skin itch.

"That's it? That's all I get?" Pepper's voice rises an octave, hands picking at the ends of her braid.

"He had a night terror and got scared. Said he was going to hurt me. He didn't, not really, but he did smash up the hotel room and scared the living shit out of me."

"Holy fuck."

I nod, hoping that's enough to appease her. I've worked my fucking hardest to bury the rest of that trip. To box it up and keep it tucked far, *far* away.

"So?" Miya raises a brow. "Where's he staying then?"

"Here." I bury my face in my palms. "As in my cabin, here."

"Oh my God. Oh my God. Oh my God!" Pepper is screaming as Miya says, "I'm sorry, what?"

"I literally showed up in the middle of the night and scared the crap out of him. He had a panic attack. Like, a bad one. His lips were turning blue, Mimi. I thought he was going to pass out."

"What did you do?" Pepper's eyes widen, her hand flailing off to the side, pulling a bag of pretzels into her lap. Never once taking her eyes off the screen. *Oh, yeah, she's fully invested in wherever this is going.*

"Well, I don't know how to stop a panic attack—"

"Generally, you'd want to stay calm and distract them. Most people can be talked through them." That's Doctor Park coming out to play as Miya lists the ways you can help someone with a panic attack.

"Right, well, I distracted him."

"Oh my God." Pepper grins like the devil. "Did you flash him?"

"What? No! I didn't flash him! I...kind of...maybe...kissed him?"

Miya looks contemplative as Pepper bounces up and down like an excited puppy, trying to keep her thoughts inside.

"But was it effective?" Miya finally asks. She leans toward the phone, like she's asking a colleague about an important medical finding.

"That's your question?" Pepper looks deeply offended now.

"What else is there to ask?" Miya shoots back.

"I don't know...everything? Like, was it just a little peck? Did you make out? Did he kiss you back? Did you have sex? Was it as good as you remember it? Is he the best kisser, and everyone else will forever be subpar, or was it a total letdown?"

"I defer." Miya sits back, cupping her tea to warm her

hands. Mimi almost always runs cold. "Those are much more important questions."

"Ugh, you guys. You're supposed to tell me that this was a terrible mistake, and I shouldn't have kissed him."

"Fuck that." Miya grins.

"Traitor," I mumble. "Like I said, I didn't know what I was doing, but he clearly needed something to happen. He was on the ground, so I just sort of climbed into his lap and kissed him." Pepper bites back a squeal. Miya's one eyebrow raises in surprise. "It worked. He started breathing again and tried to kiss me back."

"What do you mean, tried?" Pepper tips forward, nearly falling out of her seat.

"I panicked and bit his lip."

"Oh my God!" Miya snorts. "Of course you did."

I hide my face in a pillow, wishing I could end this conversation and pretend none of this happened. "He ended up sleeping through his alarms. Mercer sent Brooks over to see if he was okay."

"How did *you* sleep through his alarms?" Miya looks like she can't quite believe it.

"I barely slept all night. I was exhausted."

"Did Brooks catch you?" Pepper interjects.

"No, he didn't see me. Don't think he suspected anything either. But that's not all, this morning, he came downstairs all fresh from the shower, with wet curls and his deputy uniform on and then—"

"There's more?" Pepper squeaks.

I lean in to whisper conspiratorially, "He had the audacity to put a cowboy hat on."

"No," Pepper gasps while Miya ducks behind her mug, trying to hide her smile.

"Yes!"

"Well, shit, if you weren't fucked before..." Miya can't control her giggles now, with Pepper joining in. I was born on a ranch, cowboys do it for me, and they know it.

"Stop laughing at my expense, you two! This is terrible! How am I supposed to figure out my life when I can't stop imagining him in that stupid uniform?"

"I mean, you could imagine what he looks like with just the hat on."

My jaw drops at what Miya said. I'd expect something like that from Pepper, but Miya? She doesn't have a romantic bone in her body.

"Where the hell did that come from?" I stare at her in shock. Pepper is cackling now, her laughter dissolving into tears.

"What?" Miya gives me a mock look of innocence. "You've been in love with him your whole damn life, Leni. You think it's a coincidence that you both moved home at the same time, and ended up in the same cabin with, how many beds is it? Oh, right, *one*."

Pepper is absolutely no help as she's wheezing in the background. The mention of a popular romance novel trope sends her back over the edge.

"I didn't *move* back home. I'm...*re-grouping*."

"So, you're not sitting there spiraling, pretending he isn't the reason you've never had a real relationship?"

I'd like to punch Miya in her smug little face at this point. How dare she point out the obvious when I'm struggling to accept it? She's right, of course. I have been sitting here spiraling.

I dated here and there, tried my best to get over this crush, but I think it's pretty safe to say that I never did. That Clayton Traeger is so deeply ingrained in my bones, I'm not sure I'll ever get over him. I never gave my heart to anyone else, because despite everything that happened between us, it has always belonged to him.

"You know it's not that simple." I hate the way my voice sounds small and wounded.

"Well," Pepper cuts in, finally sobered from her laughing fit. "Nothing in life is ever really simple. Maybe you were sent back to the ranch at the same time for a reason."

"Agreed." Miya sets her tea down on a side table and looks me straight in the eyes. "This is a chance to figure out what happened, Leni. You walked away and never gave him the chance to explain himself. Maybe this is an opportunity to see what could have been. You're not eighteen anymore, and from what I've heard from Ethan, he's grown a lot, too."

"Wait," Pepper butts in, "you talk to her brothers?"

"Just a few of them."

"How many is a few?"

I narrow my eyes at Miya in surprise. I had no idea she talked to any of my brothers.

"It's not all the time. Ethan was in town a couple of months ago and asked to get lunch. That's all."

"What do you mean, that's all?" I demand. "I live in the same town! Why didn't he ask me?"

"He did. You had that overnight field trip with tenth grade that weekend."

"Oh." I scrunch my face up, still trying to wrap my head around Miya having lunch with Ethan.

"Next question." Pepper bites her lower lip, giving me the face that gets her all the free drinks at the bars. "How do *I* get their numbers? Your brothers are hot."

"Ewww." I shake my head, trying to ward off the mental image of Pepper with any of my brothers. "Nope, not happening, Peps, you're mine. I will not share you with any of my nasty brothers."

"That's so not fair!" She whines.

Miya chuckles, and I give her a disapproving glare.

"What? It's an objective truth, Leni. Your parents made beautiful babies, and those babies just so happened to grow into some fine-ass men. And you, of course, you're a bombshell, too."

"Ugh, you guys are the worst."

Pepper giggles before hanging up to head to her first shift at her new summer job. She's always doing crazy stuff to supplement her income during the summer months. While I tend to come home and mooch off my parents and brothers, Pepper finds the zaniest odd jobs to keep her busy and the rent paid. This year, she's working at a new tiki bar. Complete with a coconut bra and hula skirt uniform.

"I mean it," Miya uses her doctor voice on me before she lets me hang up the call. "At least think about it, Leni. Maybe it's time you two talked about what happened. About *everything* that happened."

"I don't want to talk about it," I mumble, dropping my eyes like a chastised child.

"Babe, you need to tell him. You need to tell *them*."

"I can't even tell them I'm here, Mimi. How would that go, exactly? Hello family, it's me. Remember when you told me I was too immature and irresponsible to leave and that I should stay on the ranch because I wouldn't make it in the city? Yeah, that's exactly what happened. Also, I wasn't really mugged all those years ago. I lied about that so you wouldn't go all maximum security on me, but whoops, you all did that anyway."

Miya sighs; she'd pat my cheek if she were here right now. A trait she picked up from her mom. "You need to work through it, Leni. They went all lockdown crazy on you because you got hurt...because they care."

"It was so disproportionate to what they thought happened, though. I wasn't a kid, Mimi, and I'm not a kid now."

"Would it have been disproportionate if you'd told them the truth?"

Her work phone pings, saving me from having to tell my childhood best friend to fuck right off.

"Think about it." She blows me a kiss, then ends the video chat.

"Sure." I roll my eyes. "I'll think about it."

Everyone But Leni and Clay Group Chat

MERCER

Ok. I need help

ETHAN

No

MERCER

You don't even know what I need help with

ETHAN

The chat name kind of gives it away

MERCER

Ok but come on.

THEY ARE MADE FOR EACH OTHER

MA

I happen to agree with you dear but some things are best left to themselves.

MERCER

They don't even talk to each other though

ADLER

I really think it's time to just move on bro.

TOBY

Yea just let them live their lives man.

MERCER

I hate you all

BROOKS HAS LEFT THE EVERYONE BUT LENI
AND CLAY GROUP CHAT
MERCER

None of you have a single romantic bone in
your bodies.

Except you ma

MA

Speaking of romance... did you all see that
new cowboy romance Leni recommended on
the instagram?

ETHAN HAS LEFT THE EVERYONE BUT LENI AND
CLAY GROUP CHAT

TOBY HAS LEFT THE EVERYONE BUT LENI AND
CLAY GROUP CHAT

MERCER HAS LEFT THE EVERYONE BUT LENI
AND CLAY GROUP CHAT

ADLER

Yea actually.

That scene in the barn... 🔥

MA HAS LEFT THE EVERYONE BUT LENI AND
CLAY GROUP CHAT

Chapter 6

Lady Friend?

Clay

I'VE BARELY STEPPED OUT OF THE MERCANTILE BEFORE MY phone starts to vibrate in my pocket. I already know that it's going to be the group chat. Bertie looked like she was bursting with a secret when I asked her which flavor of creamer women were into these days. I hadn't made it to the door before I saw her pick up her phone and tap away on it. Once I'm in my truck, I fish my phone out and open our thread, named by Mercer.

> KANE BROS GROUP CHAT
> E-MAN
>
> I have updates on our Clay situation
>
> > There is no situation
>
> ADDY
>
> Finally! I've been waiting all day for this
>
> TOBES
>
> It better be good. I'm having a shit day

ADDY

He means that literally. Tello bucked him off into a steaming pile in the round pen

MERC D

BROOKY HAS LEFT THE KANE BROS GROUP CHAT

MERC D HAS ADDED BROOKY TO THE KANE BROS GROUP CHAT

BROOKY

ADDY

Everybody shut up! E...dude...what's the update?

E-MAN

I have it on good authority

TOBES

whisper shouts he means Bertie

E-MAN

As I was saying...

good authority that our brother was in the mercantile asking for advice on coffee creamer

BROOKY

Who the fuck buys coffee creamer?

TOBES

I think...

I think that's the point big bro.

Maybe I just wanted to change it up? Ever think of that assholes?

E-MAN

I might have bought that but Bertie said you were asking which one a lady friend might like

ADDY

snorts milk Lady friend? How old are you Traeger?

I'm not that fucking old asshat.

And shut up Ethan. Tell Bertie to mind her own damn business

MERC D

I don't suggest that. Last time I told her that she trespassed me from the bar...

FOR A MONTH

E-MAN

Yea...won't be doing that

TOBES

Wait. So who are you fucking then? Didn't you move back two seconds ago?

ADDY

I have similar questions...

I'm not fucking anyone! Leave me alone

BROOKY

Good luck with that

MER D

Didn't we just talk about this?? You can't be secretly screwing anyone because we need you to get Leni back home.

TOBES

groans

E-MAN

😊

ADDY

Not this again Merc. Come on.

MERC D

No you come on. Do you guys not remember the massive crush she had on him? Or the way he used to watch her when he thought no one else noticed?

E-MAN

That sounds...

TOBES

Kinky

ADDY

Creepy

BROOKY HAS LEFT THE KANE BROS GROUP CHAT

ADDY HAS ADDED BROOKY TO THE KANE BROS GROUP CHAT

BROOKY

Goddamn it. leave me alone assholes. I do not care who Clay is or is not fucking and I do not have time for this shit

TOBES

...

ADDY

You know you can just put your phone down right?

Maybe turn off the ringer

Or throw that bitch on do not disturb

BROOKY

I'm going to throw it in your fucking face the next time I see you

ADDY

Sheesh. who pissed in your corn flakes
big bro?

MERC D

I feel like we've lost focus here

E-MAN

Leave him alone Addy. Brooky just put the
phone down

YOU HAVE LEFT THE KANE BROS GROUP CHAT

MERC D HAS ADDED YOU TO THE KANE BROS
BROS GROUP CHAT

FML

Taking Adler's advice, I switch my phone over to *Do Not Disturb*. I'm nervous enough, knowing that I'm going home to Leni. It was bad enough staying in her space, where every little thing reminded me of her. Now I'll have the actual Leni in my face and after that kiss last night...I don't know how I'm supposed to act. Do I pretend it didn't affect me? Do I pretend I didn't sit at my desk for half the day, replaying the entire night over and over again in my head?

Any other night, I'd take the long way home. Swing by the main house to see if Marcy had any leftovers or take Mako out for a ride. Maybe see if Brooks had any last-minute things he needed help with. I'm worried, though, that Marcy will take one look at me and figure everything out. The last thing I need is Leni thinking I can't keep my word.

So, I suck in a deep breath and head home to the ranch, a cinnamon coffee cake creamer in my front seat.

I WALK into the cabin to find the living room rearranged. The sofa and coffee table are pushed off to one side, while Leni lies on the floor in front of her laptop, a yoga video playing on the screen. She doesn't notice me coming in right away, so I stay there in the entryway, watching...like a creeper.

She's wearing a white sports bra, her tan skin seeming darker next to the light-colored fabric. Her back muscles are flexed, shoulders bunching together as she pushes her upper body away from the floor into a cobra pose.

I'm trying to convince myself to look away.

Leni is Mercer's little sister.

Leni has been put through enough of your shit.

Leni deserves better.

Keep it in your pants, man.

"And now we transition back into our downward dog." The woman on the screen moves, but I can't take my eyes off the woman in front of me. Leni shifts her weight from the tops of her feet to her toes. As her hands press into the yoga mat, her upper body moves backward, hips push up toward the sky. Annnnd...there's her ass. Right there, looking fucking edible in those tiny beige shorts.

A strangled groan comes from my lips, causing Leni to yelp. She loses her balance, toppling onto her side. Sitting up, she swipes the sweat from her brow and glares at me. I cock an eyebrow, giving her a *what the fuck did I do* look. She huffs at me, snapping the screen of her laptop down as she gathers her things.

Brat, I almost snap at her. Clearing my throat, I kick my boots off and head into the kitchen, only now realizing the mouthwatering aroma that's coming from it. A crockpot sits on the counter, some kind of spicy meat marinating on low heat inside. As much as I want to open the lid and sneak a taste, I learned long ago not to mess with shit in a Kane woman's kitchen.

Leni crosses the cabin as I'm putting the coffee creamer into the fridge. "What kind did you get?"

I pull the bottle out for her to inspect, hoping she'll like it. "Bertie said it was good."

"Oh my God! You asked Bertie?" Her eyes dance with amusement, lighting up the little flecks of gold in her irises. She's radiant when she smiles.

"I know," I groan, struggling to hide the way I want to stare into her eyes. Maybe lose myself in them. "Rookie mistake. I've already heard about it from the boys."

She stifles a laugh, biting into her lower lip, drawing my eyes down to her mouth. *Fuck,* that kiss. I can't get it out of my head. I've kissed a lot of women since leaving the ranch at eighteen, but nothing ever came close to the way Leni kissed me.

The way she tastes. The way she feels in my arms. Leni was my home, and I'm starting to wonder if I'm in a losing battle trying to keep my distance.

"Clay?" Leni breathes my name, making me realize that I've drifted closer toward her. Too close.

She's leaning up against the counter, big green eyes looking up at me. I lean down, placing both hands on the counter on either side of her hips. I want to run my nose up the length of her neck, breathe her in, maybe press a kiss to her pulse point. Taste her skin. I don't do any of those things. Instead, I stand there, staring into her eyes, breathing in the air that she breathes out.

I shouldn't be here, staying in her cabin or standing in her space. I spent years trying not to think about her. Trying to convince myself that I don't want her.

Looking down at her, being this close to her, I can't help but think that if anyone is worth total annihilation, it's Leni Kane.

Her eyes dart back and forth between mine, like she's trying to read me, to figure out what it is that I want. Good luck, sweetheart. I'm not sure what it is that I want right now.

I lean further, attempting to close the distance between us when she stiffens. Her body tips away from me. *Fuck.*

I move back, running my fingers through my hair. I want to tell her she doesn't have to be afraid of me, but what I blurt out is the question I haven't been able to shake since last night. "Why don't you want your family to know you're home?"

"Because I don't," she snaps, defiance shimmering in her eyes.

"They'd be thrilled. You should see the way they talk about how much they miss you. They want you home."

"What they want is to micromanage my life," she spits, eyes narrowing.

"What the fuck happened?" I haven't seen the whole Kane family together since that summer before her senior year. It certainly was never like this. The way the boys talk about missing her, I never would have assumed she was staying away on purpose.

"What do you care?" She moves toward the stairs, hard eyes staring back at me, challenging me to answer.

"I care," my voice dips low, a bit of my father's temper rising to the surface. "I never stopped caring."

"Could've fooled me, Traeger."

I want to throw up, my stomach rioting as I watch her ascend the stairs. Little pieces of my heart going with her.

Is that what she thinks of me? That I didn't care? If I didn't care, I would have let her stay. I would have let her ruin her life as she tried to piece me back together. I don't know how to fix this. I don't need things to change with us. She can hate me for the rest of our lives if she wants to, but this rift between her and the family?

That needs fixing.
And I'm going to be the one to fix it.

Chapter 7

You Could Call Me Baby Again

Leni

I DON'T KNOW WHAT I'M DOING.

I don't know what I'm doing.

I don't know what I'm doing.

I keep repeating the phrase over and over in my head while I take the world's hottest shower. I think Clay was going to kiss me down there. There's a part of me that wanted him to. The other part of me could feel the icy fingers of panic starting to grab hold. Logically, I know Clay would rather pluck his own eyes out than hurt me, but logic doesn't always win in the moment, does it? The way he had me backed up against the counter, cornered...

I don't like feeling like I'm trapped. Like I can't get out. Every single relationship I've had in my adult life has been with men who are soft. Less athletic, more bookish. The ones who prefer manicures to working with their hands. The ones who I could defend myself against if I had to.

When my skin is red and hot to the touch, I finally get out of the shower. I'm not sure how long I've been in there, but I'm impressed with my little water heater. What a good investment.

Avoiding the elephant in the room, I plant myself on the floor, looking through nail polish colors. Maybe if I act like he's not here, he'll take the hint and go...anywhere but where I have to look at him. Because right now, I'm not sure I could look at him without either cringing, crying, or jumping his bones.

As messed up as our history is, I still can't help but desire him. Clay was my first and only love. I'm no longer angry at him for what happened. He scared me, and I took off. I know he had a dream. I didn't ask what it was, but I know that's what set him off. It wasn't me being there; it was him being afraid he would hurt me.

I'm angry because life served me a shit sandwich that day, and I am not the same Leni because of it. I'm not the Leni he fell in love with. I'm no longer the girl who once chased after him. Everything changed that night. Not just our relationship, but *everything*. Maybe he doesn't know it, but I do.

Several more minutes go by before there's a knock on the bathroom door.

"Leni?" His deep voice comes muffled through the wood.

I revert back to being a toddler and stay silent as a mouse.

"Baby? I know you're having a moment in there, but I'm starving, and whatever you have in the slow cooker smells like it's going to change my life. So, maybe, you could come downstairs and we can eat and...talk."

Baby, I mouth the word. Holy shit, did Clayton Traeger just baby me? *Fuck me*. It's worse than I thought. There is no coming back from this. Why is he doing this to me?

"I'm going to need a sign of life in there."

"Yeah," I squeak, clearing my throat to bring my voice back to its normal vocal range. "Yeah, fine, I'll be down in a minute."

"Are you okay?"

"Yeah," I squawk, glad he can't actually see my face right now.

"I—I'm not gonna hurt you, I swear."

Tears prick my eyes, the air whooshing out of my lungs. I hate that I keep hurting him when I flinch away. I want to say I'm not afraid of him, but I think there might be a little part of me that's afraid it's a possibility. My brothers have tempers. I've seen angry men, but I had never seen that kind of rage before. Never been so close to the damage it can do. The last time I saw him, he destroyed a hotel room. My heart knows he would never hurt me, but my brain hasn't gotten the memo.

"I know," I whisper it first, clearing my throat so I can repeat it loud enough for him to hear.

"Okay, take your time. I'm not going anywhere."

I sit a moment longer, waiting until I hear his footsteps receding before I stand and look at myself in the mirror. "Get it together, Leni. It's Clay. Just get down there and serve him supper."

I start to leave, then turn back to the mirror, pointing at myself for good measure. "In case you get any ideas, Clayton Traeger does *not* want you. You are serving Quesabirrias for supper, hoe. Not yourself."

SINCE MY LITTLE meltdown and emergency shower, Clay has righted the furniture in the living room and taken off his uniform shirt, leaving him in a white tank top, Wranglers, and socks. The tank top clings to the muscles in his chest, with bulging biceps on full display. His shoulders are broad, his body tapering down to a slim waist. I wonder what he's hiding under that cotton fabric. I look, but only for a second. Long enough to feel my cheeks heat in embarrassment all over again.

Why does he have to be so good-looking? Couldn't he have slacked off some? Gotten fat, or grown grey hair? This is...it's too much. I'm about to turn back up the stairs when my gaze snags on his, and he seems to relax. As if he was sitting there holding his breath, worried about me and if I would come down. It makes me pause and pull my big girl panties on. *I can do this.* It's just dinner. I'll only be here for a few days. It doesn't have to be awkward unless I make it awkward. Straightening my shoulders, I march into the kitchen.

"Fuck," I practically moan. "You weren't lying. That smells so good." I may not be as good of a cook as my mom, but there are a few dishes I can crack out when I need to. That's why I keep the ingredients for them stocked.

It's not hard to do when there are only three recipes I've perfected, but whatever. "I hope you're ready, cause my tacos will knock your socks off."

"I fucking believe that." He gives me a toothy grin, leaning against the doorjamb between the kitchen and the entryway. I pause for a second, allowing myself to fully take him in. He's aged like a fine wine. Somehow, thirty-one-year-old Clay is even hotter than twenty-one-year-old Clay. I want to explore every inch of his body, even though I know I never will. Can't blame a girl for looking, not when a man looks like that.

I feel his gaze on me, the sensation making my skin tingle. I ignore it. I was just eye fucking him. It'd be stupid to call him out on doing the same. Moving towards the fridge, I start setting out my toppings. Clay steps into the small kitchen with a bit of hesitation. I can't blame him. I've seen my mom chase the boys out of her kitchen with a rolling pin before. He's smart to be timid in a Kane woman's kitchen.

"Anything I can help you with?"

You could call me baby again, my traitorous brain thinks. "Uh, yeah. You could start shredding the roast if you want."

"Sure." He reaches past me. And that spicy, woodsy scent wraps around me as he grabs a cutting board from where it hangs off the side of a cupboard. He sets it down next to me, then goes to get a knife from the block next to the fridge.

"No, do it over by the stove and the cooker." I nudge the cutting board toward him, noticing the hesitation and... is that hurt in his gaze? "I'll be over in a second." I try to reassure him. "We're going to dip the tortillas in the juice from the crockpot before we add the cheese and meat to fry them up. Trust me, it'll be easier to have it all in one place."

Clay gives me a soft smile, it's one I've never seen. I've seen cocky Clay, and happy Clay, even flirty Clay has made an appearance, but soft Clay? That's a new one for me. An unfortunate one, it turns out, considering the butterflies his smile unleashes inside my belly.

Between the two of us, it takes a measly ten minutes before we're sitting at the table, Quesabirrias and ice-cold Coronas sitting before us.

"Where did you even find all of this food?" Clay waves his hand at the spread of tacos and toppings.

"The chest freezer in the basement."

He whips his head toward me, so fast I think he might have cracked his neck in the process. He rubs a spot under his skull. "There's a basement?"

"Of course, there's a basement." I roll my eyes. "Where do you think the water heater and furnace are? Not to mention, the freezer."

He sits back like he's trying to decide if I'm fucking with him or not. The boys would, and maybe that's what makes this whole thing so damn funny. "I swear to God, there's a trap door in the pantry."

He gets up, food forgotten as he saunters to the pantry, and back. "Huh." He sinks back down into his chair, looking genuinely puzzled.

"Some deputy you are," I tease, picking up my first taco and moaning a bit when the flavors hit my tongue.

Clayton blinks at me, his mouth dropping open ever so slightly as he watches me tuck into the food.

"I hate to break up, whatever fantasy is happening inside that head of yours, Traeger, but I make no promises not to finish off all of these tacos if you don't start eating."

He shakes that headful of messy black curls, before giving me a sheepish grin and turns his attention back to his dinner. It's been a long time since anyone has tried my cooking for the first time. I love getting people's reactions to the foods I make.

He eats half of a taco in one bite, sinking into his chair as he groans. It takes him one more bite to finish off the rest of it, that guttural sound making another appearance as a zip of electricity heads straight between my thighs.

So that's why he'd been staring earlier; food groans are inherently sexual, noted.

"Leni." The way he says my name this time is downright sinful. He's loading up his plate with four more tacos, talking between bites. "Where did you learn to cook like this?"

"Ma, obviously." I shrug, trying not to show how affected I am by his praise. But holy lord, am I affected. Like, head-to-toe body shivers affected. The way he's enjoying his tacos is not helping my case either. I gulp down half my beer in one go, chugging like my life depends on it.

"Seriously, these are incredible."

"Thanks." I look down at my own plate, suddenly overwhelmed by having his full attention on me.

Dinner finishes faster than the time it took to assemble the tacos, as we forgo the small talk and simply eat our food. I have to say, I don't mind. The tacos are to die for, and I usually never get to finish my food on a date. Opting to get to know the person instead. Not that this is a date. I'm just enjoying being able to eat my food the way I want without worrying if the person eating with me will judge me for it.

We clean up supper together, Clay shooing me away when there's only the slow cooker left to deal with. It's not quite dark enough to trek over to my car for the rest of my stuff, so I head for the front room to settle into my reading nook when a flash of metal precedes the rumble of my dad's old pickup.

With the front of the cabin being all windows, I'm limited to where I can hide to keep from being seen. I opt for the most obvious answer and throw myself down on the floor, unable to stop the little yelp from escaping when my hip slams into the hardwood.

"Leni?" Clay pops out of the kitchen area, looking at me with concern, when a knock sounds on the door. His eyes widen as he peeks around to see who's outside. "Hey, Pa," he says, opening the door wide enough to not be suspicious, but not far enough to show me in the living area.

"Clay, how's it going, son?"

A little ache slices through my chest at the sound of my dad's voice. I haven't realized how much I missed seeing him in person until right this second.

"I'm good."

"Settling in, okay?"

"Yeah, I think so. Though I'm sure Leni will be happy when I find somewhere a little more permanent. Mercers on a campaign to find some way to lure her home this summer."

Another stinging pain cuts through my chest at the thought of Clay not being here permanently. Somehow, this place feels more like home with him in it. My dad laughs; I can almost see him shaking his head at Mercer's antics. He's kind of like the class clown of the family.

"Well, I won't take any more of your time, Clay. I just stopped by cause Brooks said he couldn't reach you by phone."

"Oh, shit." I hear some rustling, likely Clay pulling his phone out of his pocket. "I put it on *Do Not Disturb* after work. The group chat was out of control."

"This is why I don't have one of them fancy phones," Dad grunts. I can almost guarantee his white, Tom Selleck-style mustache twitches when he frowns.

"Yeah, well, not all of us can be as cool as you, Orson."

"Ain't that the truth?"

"Should I call him back then?"

"Oh, nah, he's taking a personal day tomorrow." I scrunch my face up in confusion. Brooks doesn't take personal days. He doesn't know the meaning of rest. "Was wonderin' if you could help pick up the slack a little. Half the guys took off the weekend for the first rodeo of the season."

"Yeah, of course. Everything okay?"

"You know, Brooks," Dad says. "He didn't say much, just said he needed the day. Possibly the weekend."

"Got it. Well, I'll be there."

"Great." There's a brief pause before my dad sniffs loud enough that I can hear it. "Whatcha cooking up in there, Clay? Smells like Leni's tacos."

"Oh, uh, yeah. I found a bag of stuff in the freezer."

"Damn, you find any more, you let me know."

"Will do," Clay promises.

"Alright, see you in the morning then, kiddo."

I stay down on the floor, listening as Clay closes the door and my dad's old pickup starts up. The familiar rumble fading away into the distance. I turn over on my back, groaning a little as I peel myself off the floor. Clayton is leaning a shoulder into the door frame; one ankle crossed over the other, a hand tucked into his jean pocket. "You good over there?"

I give him a weak thumbs up as I struggle to my feet. That's three times now, in two days, that I've crash landed on the floor, and my body is hurting. I need to take a hot ass bath tomorrow when Clay is gone.

"Kate's in town," Clay says as if he's talking about the weather, but my entire body freezes up at the statement. I don't make a habit of hating people, but I *hate* Kate McGinnity with the passion of a burning sun. The way she wrecked my brother is unacceptable. I'd like to take her little heroin addicted face and stomp it into the ground. "Easy there, killer." Clay moves to stand in front of me, turning me around so he can work his thumbs into the solid rocks where my shoulder muscles are.

It takes Herculean effort not to make any kind of sound as his fingers work magic through the knots in my shoulders. I don't want him to stop, but I'm pretty sure any moaning on my part, and he'll bolt to the other side of the room, so I'm doing my best to keep quiet. Enjoying the fact that he's touching me, and I don't want to run away from it. "Do you think that's why he's not working tomorrow? I don't think I've ever heard of Brooks taking a day off."

"I'd hardly call it a coincidence. The only time Brooks has taken any time off from work, since dumping her sleazy ass, was when he had pneumonia. We had to sneak sleeping supplements into his drinks to get him to stay inside."

"Do you think he'd get back together with her?"

"He better fucking not." Clay wraps an arm around my collarbone, supporting my body as he digs into my right trap. I lean into him, fairly certain at this point, he's supporting more of my weight than I am. "I'd be more worried about her conning him out of some money or something. Not to mention all the bad feelings she brings up every time she rolls into town. Brooks needs to find someone else."

"She'd have to be a veterinarian or something. How else would he meet someone?"

"True," I snort. It takes me a minute to realize that he's not massaging me anymore, but he's holding me. I snuggle deeper into his chest, pleasantly surprised when his other arm comes around me. His chin resting on the top of my shoulder.

I feel his chest expand and contract behind me, pushing into my back before it recedes, like he's breathing me in. I want to turn around and bury my face in his chest, wrap my own arms around him, and maybe shake him a little to ask him why he never called me. Ask him why he never checked on me. How he could just let me go. I don't want to move away or break this moment of surrender and silent confession between us either.

Chapter 8

You Can't Fix Me

Clay

BY ALL ACCOUNTS, MY HANDS ARE IN RESPECTABLE PLACES. You just wouldn't know it by the thoughts racing through my head right now. We're standing in the living room, fully clothed, nothing remotely sexual happening, and I can't shake the image of spinning her around and taking that sassy mouth of hers with mine. Claiming her once and for all.

My dick responds every time I inhale her sweet scent. Whatever perfume or body wash she uses always has an underlying smell of lilacs to it, I want to lose myself in it. I didn't expect to have such a visceral reaction to her. Where the hell did she come from? Barging into my life after I'd worked so hard to put up walls between us. Where do we go from here? Is this something she even wants? Could it be that easy for her to forgive me for everything?

I don't have any answers where Leni is concerned, and that scares the hell out of me.

She deserves the fucking world, and I don't see what I have to offer her. Maybe this is enough, for now at least. Maybe we can take this time to get to know each other again. I don't know everything about her anymore, but I want to know every little detail there is to know about her and make up for all the years we've spent apart.

She sighs, letting her head loll back into my shoulder. I can see her pulse beating out a steady rhythm, and I can't help but press my lips to it, wanting to savor the feeling of her wrapped up in me. Hating the way, she tenses when my lips meet her skin.

"Do you hate me?" I whisper, my lips brushing the shell of her ear, using every single ounce of control not to kiss her again.

"Sometimes I wish I did. I think it'd be easier to hate you."

I tighten my arms around her and nod. I know exactly what she means. "I think I might hate me a little."

For the first time since the hug started, she moves to reciprocate, letting one hand sink into my hair, the other wrapping around my neck. Pushing her hips into mine, she buries her head into the crook of my neck. Her right hand squeezes my neck while the nails on her left scrape my scalp.

"I think we all hate ourselves a little."

"You don't hate yourself, do you?" I tighten my grip on her, a possessive kind of protectiveness swelling up inside of me.

"Sometimes," she breathes, her voice barely audible after what feels like the world's longest pause. I tuck her in closer, dropping my head to her shoulder.

"Talk to me. What's going on with you?"

She stiffens in my arms, her back going ramrod straight, arms fighting to come down. I go to pull away, every fiber of my being repelled at the thought of making her uncomfortable. She grips my wrists, keeping my arms around her, loose enough that she can turn in them. "You're gonna have to hold me through this, if you can." Her sweet voice is muffled by my chest.

"I can." I tighten my hold on her, one hand pressed against her back, pulling her close. "I won't let go."

"I lost my job...and my housing."

"Lost your job?" I rear back, looking down at her. She keeps her face pressed into my chest, nodding. "How? Didn't you build that creative writing program yourself?"

It's her turn to rear back, pretty green eyes widening as she looks at me. "How did you—"

"You realize you're the only exciting thing your family talks about, right? They were so proud of you for creating that program."

She shakes her head, pressing it back into my chest.

"You seem surprised."

"I am," she sighs, letting her hands wander up my back. This tank top is not nearly enough fabric between us. I can feel the warmth emanating from every one of her fingertips. The heat of them branding my skin, making me want more.

"At the risk of sounding like a broken record, what happened with you and the family?"

"You," she whispers.

"Me?" I pull back, sliding a hand onto the side of her face, forcing her to look at me.

"I went to see you. I...I didn't have a phone when I was on my way back, and something...happened." A shaky breath leaves her lips, her eyes squeezing shut.

A moment passes, her silence killing me. I know she got hurt, but I need to hear it from her. "What happened?" I beg. The eagerness in my voice snapping her eyes up to meet mine, fear creeping back in.

I'm about to apologize, worried she won't continue now that I've interjected. But she sighs, her shoulders deflating as she continues. "I was mugged." Her head drops, then lifts back. Her eyes meet mine with something hidden beneath them.

"I had to call my dad to come get me. No one trusted me after that. I was basically kept in lockdown." She takes a deep breath, shoulders slumping. Her backs tense beneath my hand. There's something she's not saying. Her words are too rehearsed. I want to call her on it, dig until she tells me the truth, but at least she's talking. I don't want to ruin whatever truce we have tonight. Hoping that maybe, down the line, she'll be ready to tell me everything.

"The only reason they let me leave for school in Benson is because they had no legal grounds to stop me. They tried everything else to get me to stay. Ethan told me I wasn't ready. Brooks said I'd never make it on my own. And mom," she chokes on a sob. My heart shatters at the thought of her going through this without me. "She told me if I disobeyed them and left, they'd cut me off. Told me not to bother coming back."

"Jesus." I tug her back into me, wrapping her in my arms like a shield.

"She was just scared," she justifies. "She called me a few days later to apologize, but the damage was done, you know? I didn't come home that summer. Miya and I stayed in Benson. She went to school year-round, and I worked a shitty part-time job. Tried to keep busy. That's the longest I'd ever been away from the ranch, from all of them."

"Oh, Leni." I cradle her head, stroking her hair, trying to comfort her. "Have you tried talking to them? Do they know you feel this way?"

A sharp, sardonic laugh shakes her shoulders. "Yeah, because that will help."

Her voice is brittle with a bitterness I've never seen in her before. Leni was the glue that held the family together. The boys were always using her as a personal therapist. There was no problem, bad day, or argument that Leni couldn't fix with her eternal optimism.

"How do you know, if you haven't even tried?"

She scoffs, pushing out of my arms. "You're hilarious, you

know that? Coming in here after ten years of acting like I don't fucking exist, and now you want to be a part of my life? Now you want to tell me how to fix things? Why Clay? Why do you want to fix things?"

"Because it's not right. I broke something between you all that night." My fists clench at my side, shame filling me when her eyes track the movement. I force myself to stretch my fingers out, grinding my molars together.

"You don't want to feel guilty anymore. News flash, not everything is your fault."

It's your fault. My dad's voice echoes in my brain. The feeling of his fists ramming into my ribs over and over sends my shoulders up toward my ears. *It's your fault she left. You're weak. You're nothing.*

My heart thunders in my chest, lungs suddenly starved for air. What the fuck is happening to me? I've had my panic attacks under control for years. I've never even had one connected to my dad before. They've always been about my deployments, this is...this is fucking stupid.

"Clay," Leni's voice comes out hard and commanding. "Hey." She grips my face, her hands pressing hard on my cheeks. Her eyes bobbing back and forth. "If you want to kiss me again, just say it. You don't have to be so dramatic about it."

I gasp out a laugh, disbelief coursing through me as she beams at me. I want to scoop her up into my arms, hug all the air out of her, and tell her how goddamn much I've missed her.

"There you are." Her smile softens, eyes sweeping over my face as she slowly pulls her hands away from me.

"Fuck," I sigh, dropping onto the world's most uncomfortable sofa. "I don't know why this is happening. I haven't had an attack in years. I got better." I look at her, knowing my eyes are pleading for her to see I worked on myself and I *am* better.

"I know." She gives me a gentle smile, plopping herself onto the oversized chair in the corner. "Mercer told me all about his trip to knock some sense into you."

"I thought he did that because you told them what happened."

"Nope." She leans back onto her palms, her chest arching out towards me. It takes everything in me to keep my eyes on her face. Leni has the most perfect tits. Teenage Leni did not have the same chest back then. *Knock it off,* I chide myself. This is not the time to be ogling her. "That was all you, bud."

"Huh." I sink down further into the sofa, trying to remember what happened when Mercer came out to babysit me. I called him when she didn't answer, told him I was in the hospital, that I was being investigated, and potentially going to be court-martialed for trashing a hotel room.

"What did you tell them?"

"That I didn't find you," she sits back up, looking down at her hands.

"Why didn't you tell them the truth?" The words come out more harsh than I intend. Leni never lies. She was never mean, but she would always give it to us straight.

Green eyes burn into mine, some of that fire banking in them again. "I wasn't going to turn them against you."

"Maybe you should have," I mumble, gripping the back of my neck.

"You don't mean that." She leans forward, her eyes wide.

"I do. Because maybe if you'd have turned them against me, you wouldn't be pushing them away. Punishing them for caring."

"Fuck you," she forces out, her voice more water than venom.

"Leni." I reach for her, my heart shattering when she recoils, her eyes full of fear. I pull my hand back, curling my fingers into a fist. I'm starting to wonder if it wasn't just me that scared her. She says she's not afraid of me, but her body is. I would never physically hurt her. "What happened to you?"

"You fucking happened," she cries. The brokenness in her voice rips me in half. "I thought you wanted me. How stupid is that? You ghosted me, and I still thought you might want me. Need me even. So, I ran to you. I came to help you, and I've been paying the price ever since."

"What price, Leni? Tell me what happened, what *really* happened. Tell me how to fix it." I collapse off the couch, begging on my knees. My voice is desperate, pleading.

"You can't fix this." She takes a step backward, a chasm opening between us wider than that night, wider than the ten years we've spent apart. "You can't fix me. You were right not to want me," her voice cracks at the end, eyes overflowing with tears.

I try to reach for her, but my arms are too heavy. Helplessness glues my knees to the floor below me.

I've felt this dark, hopeless anguish twice before in my life. Tonight makes it the third time that a woman I love has walked away from me, and like with my mom, I know it's my fault. She doesn't trust me. Not with the truth, and not with her heart. I made sure she knew that I'm not built for love. It's not in my genes. I know, my mom knew, and Leni...

Leni knows it now, too.

I wanted this. I wanted her to realize I wasn't the right one for her. Only I didn't realize it would hurt so damn bad.

Chapter 9

Why Do You Keep Doing That?

Clay

"I think Leni's seeing someone," Mercer says, first thing in the morning, before anyone's had coffee or even talked about the day's assignments. The hired hands who are there excuse themselves to go get some caffeine before having to deal with the crazy family drama. The rest of us left standing around the breakfast table that's set out behind the main house.

"What?" Adler asks, his voice muffled by half a muffin he shoved into his pie hole. He's wearing a backwards baseball cap over his dark, wavy hair. A grey tank top on his torso, black combat boots gaping at the tongues where he's neglected to tie them up.

"Why else wouldn't she come back at all for the summer?"

Toby shakes his head, long hair dusting his shoulders beneath his cowboy hat. He should pull it back or cut it. I can't imagine how hot it'd be to run around with so much hair. "I thought you said she wasn't coming back because he's here." Toby hooks his thumb over his shoulder at me.

"Thanks," I deadpan.

"*Obviously.*" Mercer rolls his eyes, taking a sip of his

coffee before continuing. "But what if that's only half the story? What if she's secretly hooking up with some guy and they're running off to do naked time on a beach or something?"

I choke on air, slamming my fist into my chest, willing myself the ability to breathe again. What the fuck is wrong with this family, and why do I now have the image of naked Leni on the beach burned into my mind?

Ethan gives me a hearty pat on the back before muscling Adler away from the table where Ma put out some breakfast burritos and pastries.

"Why do you keep doing that?" Mercer puts a hand on his hip, his eyes narrowing at me.

"Swallowed wrong? Sue me." I rub my chest, throat burning from the coughing fit.

"Maybe I will." Mercer looks at Ethan, who rolls his eyes.

"You can't sue someone for choking dipshit. So what if she's seeing someone?"

"Well, did she tell any of you assholes about him?"

That gets all the boys standing a bit straighter. Generally, if Leni likes a guy and knows he'll fit in, she'll tell at least one of the boys about it. The news spreads through the grapevine, and the boys make plans to go 'meet' the new boyfriend. On the other hand, in the past, when Leni started a relationship and didn't tell anyone, it was usually because she knew he wouldn't fit in. Guys who ended up with their faces rearranged because no one ever treated her right.

I rub my jaw, imagining Brooks taking a potshot at my face. I watched that dude drop my dad with a single punch to the jaw. I have no intention of finding out what that feels like for myself.

"Shit," Adler sighs. "There's too much going on. I do not have time to drive to Benson and spy on Leni. Then cover for

Brooks while trying to stake out Clay to figure out who he's fucking. This is getting ridiculous."

"I'm sorry, what did you just say?" I feel my eyes bulge out as I stare at the youngest Kane brother.

He presses his lips into a straight line, eyes widening as he realized how badly he fucked up.

"Adler James, did you just say you're spying on me?"

"What? No, I never said that." Adler shoves the rest of his muffin into his mouth before turning back toward the table.

"He totally is." Toby jumps up to sit on the tailgate of the side-by-side. "Said you slept on the couch for some reason last night."

"Jesus H Christ." I rub my hands down my face and make a mental note to tell Leni that her brothers are up to no good. "Jefferies!" I call the ranch hand I gave stall duty to. "Change of plans. You're gonna work the sevens with Toby here. AJ is going to muck stalls."

"Wha?" Adler turns and groans. "Come on, man! I've done my time in the barn. There's like, eighty horses out there now!"

There's fifty, and only twenty or so were in their stalls last night. So, it's an easier job than running the fence lines and fixing wires, but I don't tell him that. I twiddle my fingers at him in a fake wave and send him on his way. Adler's shoulders stiffen, a muscle in his jaw ticking when he bites back whatever insult he's thinking. Flipping me the bird, he grumbles past us, and I avoid the temptation to kick him in the ass as he walks by.

Mercer smirks at me, grabbing his to-go cup. "I'm so glad I'm the boss at our real jobs."

I flip him the bird, and we head for the big barn to grab our horses.

My blue roan Mako is kept here in the stables. Everyone used to keep their horses here, but now the boys mostly keep theirs at home. All of them, except Adler, have their own little patch of dirt to call home. I have my own plot across the highway. Someday, I'm going to build a little cabin there. Maybe get a dog, keep Mako nearby so I can ride whenever I want.

Mercer saddles up Leni's old horse, Calypso. He's old and fat and has not been worked nearly enough. A big step down to the younger buckskin he favors. Fabio has a lot more pep than Calypso does, but for riding pastures and pushing a few cows, he's still got it. I wonder if Leni misses him.

"How you been, Clay?" Mercer tips his hat a little lower on his brow, blocking what he can of the sun as it begins to peek over the horizon. Deep purples, blues, and fiery hues of orange and pink paint the sky.

"Okay," I breathe, hoping I don't crack like an egg and spill everything.

Twisting at the waist, Mercer's saddle creaks while his weight adjusts. He tips his head off to one side, one eyebrow disappearing beneath the brim of his cowboy hat. From the moment we met, we were best friends. He's the reason I moved into the Kane household and was given the chance of a better life. I owe him everything, and the best I can repay him with is some fucking trauma and lies.

"It's gonna be like that then, huh?" He tucks his tongue between his back teeth, leg bouncing twice in the stirrups before he squeezes Calypso and rides off.

Fuck.

I lift my reins out to my left, leaning forward in the saddle to push Mako toward Mercer. He follows, chomping at the bit to do some running. He loves the roping pen and a good cattle drive. Even when he's out in the field, he's always working. We happen to have that in common.

"I've had a couple of panic attacks since being back." I offer the most truth that I comfortably can, without betraying Leni's confidence.

"Shit, how bad were they? Is that why you were late Thursday morning? Were you lying in that cabin unconscious? Because I swear to God, Clay—"

"No, I wasn't unconscious in the cabin. I really did sleep through my alarms."

"Damnit, you *are* seeing someone, aren't you?"

"Also, no." I narrow my eyes, flicking my wrist over the saddle horn. I give Mako his head, and he's off like a fucking bullet. The wind is nearly ripping my hat away as we tear across the grassy pasture.

Mercer curses behind me, shouting obscenities at Calypso, who was perfectly content to walk wherever we were headed for the day. I lean forward, moving my hands up Mako's soft neck, giving him permission to move however he'd like. As long as we're headed to what Pa calls the sevens. The Kanes rotate their herd through the ranch's pastures, letting the land regenerate stronger between grazings. The fields are laid out in a grid formation, so it's easier to know where to move them to.

The sevens make up the grids numbered through the seventies, and some of my favorite spots on the ranch are here. Our biggest challenge is that a large portion of this grid borders the highway. In a perfect world, that wouldn't be an issue, but it isn't. Our fences are constantly being torn down by drunk drivers or kids who shouldn't be out so late. We've even had a few run-ins with cow tipping. They sure don't like to get caught, not when Sheriff Mercer puts 'em to work landscaping his yard as community service.

Mako is huffing by the time we reach the cattle guard between the grazing field and the open land. Mercer and Calypso follow behind, slowly but surely. I lean down to open the pass-through gate and stand waiting for Mercer. Calypso steps into the pasture looking like he's ready to croak. White foamy sweat froths from beneath the saddle pad, his body heaving as if he can't get enough air.

"Goddamn, he's out of shape," Mercer whines, reaching to pet Calypso's neck, then thinks better of it.

"Nah, Mako's just that fast."

Mercer's face contorts, like he might want to disagree with that statement, but he knows it's true. "So," he huffs, putting his hands on his low back, stretching his torso backward. As sheriff, he doesn't have enough extra time to be in the saddle. He and Ethan are gonna be hurting tomorrow. "What're we doing about the panic attacks then?"

Sleeping next to your sister. My brain unhelpfully supplies. *Daydreaming about her tits.* My dick adds its own commentary. *Fuck.* I need her to woman up and tell her family she's here. This is torture.

"Woo-woo breathing exercises," I lie. Because that's what I do now. I'm a pathetic liar. Might as well sit here and set my goddamn pants on fire.

"And those work?"

"Sometimes." At least that's a truthful answer.

"Huh...too bad you can't call Leni up and have her sneak into your bed."

My mouth drops wide open. Mako rips the reins straight from my hands and lunges forward to get a drink from the stream.

Mercer cackles, sliding out of his saddle as he leads Calypso closer to the water. Calypso's a good horse, but he's never been a fan of the water. Brooks tried to train it out of him, but Leni took a lunge whip to his ass when she didn't like his trainings. Brooks never touched Calypso again.

"Did you think we didn't know?" Mercer's green eyes glint with mischief when he looks at me. "Why do you think I push so hard for you two? You haven't slept well since that summer you spent sleeping in her bed, like she's some kind of comfort item. Shouldn't that tell you something?"

"Give it a rest, Merc. Your sister deserves to find her perfect someone."

"She does, and she has," he grunts, swinging himself back up into the saddle.

I cock my head, giving him a scowl. I look down at my reins tethering Mako to the ground. Mercer winks, moving Calypso toward the fence line. "Bastard!" I call after him. Jumping to the ground, I snatch my reins, then snap a picture of Mercer riding away from me on Calypso. I think about sending it to Leni, but I bet she's still sleeping. Bet she doesn't want to hear from me. She hasn't even given me her number again. The only reason I have it is because she's in the family group chat.

There used to be a sibling chat too, but when it was clear Leni and I weren't responding to any joint messages, the boys moved everything over to the bros chat. Ma refused to accept it, so on occasion, we text in the family group chat. All of us but Leni.

"I'm just saying," Mercer picks up the conversation, like I wasn't two minutes behind him. "I don't get why you guys can't be with each other."

"She really never told you?" I'm still trying to reconcile the idea that she lied. That they aren't as close as they used to be.

Mercer sits back in his seat, head whipping to glare at me. "Told me what?"

"About the night she came to see me." Picking at the leather on the pommel, looking for anything that might keep me from having to look my best friend in the eye.

"What night?"

"Right after she turned eighteen." My eyes meet his, waiting to see the light turn on as he puts the pieces together.

"That trip she took when she was mugged?"

I jerk my chin, acknowledging his answer.

"She said that she didn't find you."

"I'm just piecing that together." Cows lowing in the distance draw my attention away from him.

"Why would she lie?"

I nudge Mako into a trot, a sinking feeling starting to settle into my gut.

"She was protecting you, wasn't she?" Calypso, to his credit, keeps pace with us. Mercer moves him alongside me as we make our way toward the herd.

I give a tight nod, trying to fix my breathing before I lose it completely. I shouldn't have said anything. *Fuck.* I'm so fucking stupid.

Mercer is quiet as he works the details out in his head. We get closer to the noise from the cows, but they're not lowing anymore. Now, they're screaming.

Something is wrong.

"She was in that hotel room you trashed. Wasn't she?"

I turn to my best friend, eyes darting over a mask of indifference as his own drill through me. I give another jerk of my head, watching the muscles in his jaw tick.

He opens his mouth, ready to read me the riot act, no doubt, when a car horn blares. The sound of rubber skidding on pavement assaults our eardrums. We drop the trot, urging both horses into a full-blown gallop.

Chapter 10

Fast as Fuck Boi

Leni

ROUGH HANDS GRAB MY SHOULDERS, GRIPPING SO HARD I CAN *feel fingernails dig into my skin. I try to break free, but it doesn't work. Instead, I'm shoved back into the sink. Fire bursts out across my back, pain searing me as I scream. A fist grabs my hair, dragging me across the bathroom toward the wall. Shoving me against it and slams my head into the concrete as he pries my legs apart, pushing between them.*

"No!" I scream, throat burning as my voice scrapes out of me over and over. He's not trying to keep me quiet. His hands rip at my dress, frantically touching my skin. Then he reaches for his jeans.

My heart is pounding in my chest, every breath I heave burning as it leaves my body. I slam my forehead into his face, pain blooming in my temples as it connects with his nose.

Cold, dead eyes look down at me, his lips curl into a wide, bloody smile. One tattoo-covered hand grabs my neck, anchoring me to the wall, his other circling my wrist as he pulls my arm out to the side. I watch, helpless as he clamps those bloody teeth down into my arm.

I scream and scream and scream.

I WAKE UP, drenched in sweat; the nightmare I just had makes it hard to breathe. I never have nightmares anymore. I've moved past this; let it go. This is why I can't talk about it, because when I do, this is what happens.

My head is swimming with the lack of oxygen, as I continue to hyperventilate. I pat my nightstand, desperately seeking my phone so I can tap out an SOS text to Miya.

I don't realize I've texted our Best Bitches Group Chat until a FaceTime call from Pepper flashes on the screen. I hit decline. My phone rings, Pepper's bubbly face lighting up the screen again. I know she's not going to stop unless I answer.

"I'm okay," I rasp, sounding like I ran a marathon.

"I think that might be a lie, considering the text you sent the group says, 'Please help me.'"

I let out a sob. Pepper doesn't tell me to stop or demand I tell her what's wrong. She listens, occasionally telling me that she's here, that I'm not alone. Tears still stream down my face, shoulders shaking as my breath hiccups out of me.

"I'm so sorry," I whisper.

"Leni, don't ever apologize for needing someone. You can call me and cry any time, girl, you know that."

I do. I have the best friends. I just wish I didn't need them like this.

"Are you going to be okay? Should I come down there? I can be there in three, four hours max."

A laugh bursts out of me. It's a poor imitation of my real laugh, but it's a laugh all the same. "Pepper, it's at least a five-hour drive."

"I'm fast as fuck, boi," she scoffs.

"You'd get arrested driving that fast."

"Nah, I'm too pretty, baby, I'd end up with a sexy escort. Hey, isn't your brother a cop? The sappy romantic one?"

I gag. "Please, for the love of God, forget I even have brothers."

Pepper giggles, and my cheeks feel tight and swollen as a smile tugs at my mouth, despite the tears still damp on my skin. "Thank you for calling."

"Of course," her voice softens. I can almost see that warm, caring look she uses when speaking about her kindergartners. "Do you want to talk about it?"

"Clay brought up some stuff from the past."

"Oh." I hear her sit down. Pepper's personal signal that she's ready for the spilling of tea. I never planned on telling her. Most days, I regret telling Miya. I know Pepper's story of growing up in foster care. So, if anyone can understand this anxiety and bad memories, it's her.

"That night, when Clay lost it and trashed the room, I left. I didn't realize until I was off base that my phone fell out of my backpack. I didn't have enough money or my ID to get a plane ticket either. So, I got on a bus in the middle of the night. It was going to take me three days to get home, but on the second night, I got stuck at the bus stop. The next bus was coming a few hours later, so I sat there and waited. I stayed locked in the bathroom, but had to come out and check occasionally. Since I didn't have a phone, and there was no clock in there..." I pause, swiping an errant tear, keeping it from tracking down my face. "That last time I went out to check, someone shoved the door into me. He tried," I choke on my own words, unable to say it out loud. "He didn't," I manage to get out. "He didn't—"

"But he did hurt you, right?" Her voice is quiet and steady, exactly what I need to focus my breathing on.

"Yeah," I whimper.

"Oh, Leni, I'm so sorry. You were so young."

"Yeah." I rub both my eyes, dropping the phone onto the bed as I try to stem the river of tears gushing down my face. My eyes are going to look horrendous for the next couple of days. "I told my dad that I was mugged. I still haven't told them what really happened. I was so dumb. I made one stupid decision after another that trip."

"Leni, you know that wasn't your fault, right? What he did to you, the way Clay acted that night, none of those things are your fault."

"I chose to be there, Peps. I left myself vulnerable."

"No, Leni. That was not your fault. No matter the reason for being where you were, that shit is on him. *He* chose to hurt you. *He* is the one at fault here." Her voice is hard, like she's trying to impress upon me how strongly she believes it wasn't my fault.

"I shouldn't have been there. I never should have gone to Clay."

"Maybe not," Pepper says, softer, more contemplative and warm. "But maybe you wouldn't have gone to school then. Maybe you never would have come here and created that program. Maybe some of the problem kids who went through your classes might not have made it to graduation. Maybe you wouldn't have met me."

I chuckle, Pepper once again, working her contagious enthusiasm on me.

"You can't change the past, Leni, but you can decide how you let it shape your future. You can talk about it, heal it."

"I could..." My phone vibrates in my hand, a smile tugging at my lips when I see Adler's name. "I'll try Pepper."

"Good, I mean, I say that you can, but I still have my own shit I've never worked through. So, you do you booboo."

"God, I love you."

"I love you too, Leni. Take care of yourself, okay? And call me if you need to talk. Just, you know, at a reasonable hour of the day. I work at a bar, you know."

"Yeah, yeah. I'll call you later. Miss your face!"

"Miss yours more!" She smacks her lips with a playful *mwah* sound before ending the call. I inhale sharply before opening my phone. Noticing that for once, I feel a little bit lighter.

THE BABY BROS GROUP CHAT
ADLER JAMES

Brooks is taking a personal day.

Someone put Clay in charge.

I AM DYING.

TOBIAS RUSSEL

WE NEED LENI

ADLER JAMES

Please come home

I know Mercer keeps begging you...but can you really deny me? I'm adorable

That's debatable

What do you mean he's taking a personal day

ADLER JAMES

We don't know. No one will tell us anything!

TOBIAS RUSSEL

Ethan knows something. But he's not saying

And what exactly do you expect me to do about it?

ADLER JAMES

fix it

TOBIAS RUSSEL

Fix it. Please. 🙏

> I told Mercer I'm not coming home this summer

ADLER JAMES

Booo

TOBIAS RUSSEL

Reconsider. Even if only for our sakes Sis

Merc is driving us crazy things are weird and you never come home.

ADLER JAMES

Do you even like us anymore?

> Shouldn't you two be working?

ADLER JAMES

See?

TOBIAS RUSSEL

You don't love us

ADLER JAMES

And you never did

> You are the whiniest bunch of men I have ever met.

ADLER JAMES

At least you called us men this time

TOBIAS RUSSELL

She actually answered too. That's new.

A weight drops into my stomach when I realize how long it's been since I've texted my brothers. I answer their calls, but only because I know if I don't, they'll jump in a truck and come find me. I learned that the hard way my freshman year of college. I never call them, and always avoid it until I absolutely can't anymore. I love them, and I miss them so bad it hurts sometimes. But I can't live with everyone hovering over me all the time, smothering me worse than a Texas barbecue.

> I miss you guys. Be good.

ADLER JAMES

Who us?

TOBIAS RUSSEL

We're always good Leni.

MERCER DUANE

We'd be better if you were here though.

ADLER JAMES

Goddamn it Mercer!

TOBIAS RUSSEL

How the fuck is he in every group chat?

I stg

MERCER DUANE

I cackle. The fog from the nightmare lifts as I stare down at my screen. When I left, I swore I'd never move back here. That I would never miss being so close to the family, but I do. I miss them more as each year goes by. The trouble is, I don't know if it's them I miss, or the way it used to be. We've all grown and changed. Who's to say they wouldn't drive me off again? Overreacting and overreaching as they 'protect' me.

Scooping up my laptop, I search the online job boards back in Benson. The sooner I can find something, the sooner I can get back to life as it was. Not how I wish it could be.

I GAVE up half an hour into filling out applications and took a long, hot bath. Letting my weary bones soak, scrubbing my skin raw. I always feel so dirty after those nightmares. He might not have raped me, but his filthy hands were all over me. Strike number one thousand against myself: I'd only brought dresses to wear. Teenage Leni was hoping Clay would take advantage of the easy access, not some stranger.

By one thirty, I can't sit alone with my thoughts any longer. Hillcreek is the epitome of a small town; even driving my Jeep around is a risk. Leaving my options of wandering excessively limited. If I can sneak over to the big house, I might be able to get some of my old books and find those letters Clay wrote me. I bring my phone out to check the family group chat, trying to figure out where everyone is.

KANE FAMILY GROUP CHAT
MOM

> I'm bringing lunch out to the boys in the sevens. I understand that half the herd is out on the highway and Brooks is taking personal time. NO ONE is to call him. Understood?

TOBIAS RUSSELL

> Understood

ADLER JAMES

> Suck up

HE WHO SHALL NOT BE NAMED

> We're verging on 3/4 of the herd. Not enough cowboys

MOM

> Pa's on his way

HE WHO SHALL NOT BE NAMED

> There's a fence down between block 77 and 79. Think that's how they made it all the way over here.

ETHAN TODD

Got it. On our way

TOBIAS RUSSEL

You know... I almost forgot what Ethan looks like without a suit on

ADLER JAMES

That was Ethan?!

MOM

Back to work boys

ADLER JAMES

Jesus one day without Brooky and the whole place falls to pieces

Perfect. If everyone is out in the field, trying to wrangle cows, then I should be able to sneak into the main house. I used to do it all the time as a kid. Miya and I would sneak out to parties, but we weren't nearly as sneaky as we thought. One or more of my brothers usually ended up at said parties and escorted us home. At least they had the decency to let us sneak back in, instead of ratting us out.

Searching my closet, I select a matching leggings set. It's a pretty taupe color that I'm hoping will help me blend into the landscape as I hike the mile and a half up to the house. There's no way I could drive my Jeep over there. Even if most of the hired hands are off at a rodeo, there's still plenty of employees wandering around at the barns and main house. I'll have to be extra careful not to get caught.

My family will hear about me being back on my terms.

I curse myself when I realize all I have are boots, flip flops, and my bright pink tennis shoes. The rest of my shoe collection is still in the Jeep. Guess I'm wearing cowboy boots with leggings. My fuchsia-colored trainers would act like a homing beacon for anyone within eyesight.

Squaring my shoulders, I tie my hair back into a ponytail and set off into the pasture. I feel ridiculous, keeping my body crouched low, inching my way through the empty field. The only thing that could possibly make this better is some war paint, and my brother's hiding out there somewhere, trying to catch me. *Stealth* was my favorite game growing up; I happen to be the reigning champion. Or I was...I wonder if they ever play games anymore.

Chapter 11

Robbing a Bank?

Leni

THE TREK UP TO THE MAIN HOUSE WAS INCREDIBLY uneventful. I didn't even need to crouch as much as I did. I wait at the side door, listening for the telltale signs of my mom in the kitchen.

Once I know she's not inside, I slip in through the door, the scent of home immediately knocking the wind out of me. I barely make it to the kitchen island before I stop, fingers gripping the back of one of the bar top chairs. Nothing has changed. Warm, hardwood beams and rustic furniture welcome me. Creamy, off-white cabinets with dark iron accents give off an industrial farmhouse vibe.

I can't recall how many meals I've eaten at this kitchen island, how many family dinners we've all sat around the big oak table Grandpa Kane built. It never seems to matter how often I make it back; every time I'm here, the memories creep back in.

Turning toward the living room, I can't help but smile. We used to sit on the floor, in front of Pa's chair, listening to him tell wild stories. Some made up, others about the ranch. About how

Kane Ridge came to be. My personal favorites were the ones he told about him and Ma. How she played hard to get, and how it was love at first sight for him.

I used to pretend that that's what happened with me and Clay. From the first moment he walked in the door with Mercer, I was smitten with him. Of course, I was the annoying kid sister back then. Fifteen felt so old, so far away. Looking back now, it's funny, thinking he was so unreachable back then. Little Leni would be absolutely horrified by the way things shook out.

Moving into the living room, I run my fingers along the back of the leather couch. Warmth and longing flood my chest. I loved growing up here, out on the ranch. Most summers, Miya would come stay with me, at least twice a week. We ran as wild as the boys did, causing mayhem, stirring up trouble.

I look around the room, and all those happy childhood memories disappear under the more recent ones. Memories where one or more of my brothers and I got into a screaming match because our opinions differed. I could see Ma biting her tongue, too afraid to speak her mind because our relationship was tenuous at best, like on Christmas two years ago. The one time I brought home a boyfriend I actually liked.

"REALLY, LENI?" Mercer hisses in my ear at the island. "This guy?"

"What?" I look across the living room where Aspen is sitting next to the fireplace, talking to Brooks. I begged him not to come, but he wouldn't hear of it. He insisted on meeting my family, even though I haven't met his yet. I wondered if he was regretting it. After all, Ethan manhandled him out of the cabin, escorting him into the main house. When I snuck into the guest

room to see him, he told me to leave, his face white as a fucking
sheet.

"This guy cannot be serious about you," Mercer continues.
"He hasn't even held your hand or given you a hug."

"Because Ethan threatened him with bodily harm after dragging him out of my cabin." I feel my eyes widen, nostrils flaring
wide.

Toby snorts, approaching my other side. "Yeah, I'm with both
of them, Leni. This dude is not it."

"There is nothing wrong with him." I throw my hands up,
aggravation boiling inside of me.

"There's nothing right about him either." Adler reaches over
my shoulder, grabbing a cracker off the charcuterie board.

"What do you know? You're barely an adult."

"I'm twenty." He puffs his chest out, like that makes much of
a difference. Twenty years old, and he's never spent any signifi-
cant time off this ranch. Nor had to fend for himself or pay his
own bills. I roll my eyes.

"He's a fucking desk jockey," Mercer sneers.

"And you're a glorified mall cop," I bite back.

Toby's eyes widen, and even Adler takes a step back, shaking
his head.

Mercer sucks in a breath, his jaw clenching before he looks
toward the dining room, giving Ethan a nod.

I watch, in abject horror, as my three older brothers surround
my boyfriend. The conversation is over before I can make it back
over. When I do make it over to him, Aspen is shaking. He looks
like he's about ready to shit his pants. I reach for him, and he
jerks his hand away, like the contact might actually hurt him.

"Sorry, Eleanor, I just..." He looks around at my brothers, all
of them towering over him. "I think this was a mistake. I wish
you all the best."

· · ·

97

I never saw him again after that. He blocked my number and left a note on the kitchen island asking me to move out before he came back from his New Year's vacation with his parents.

That's how I ended up moving into an upstairs bedroom with my elderly landlord. I don't think they knew I was living with him, not that it would have mattered. They probably would have still run him off, then come back to Benson with me to pack my shit and force me to move back here.

Every single time I've left to go back to my life in Benson, Ethan pulls me aside, fingers digging into my elbow, and gives me the same spiel. *"You've made your point. Congratulations on not falling on your face. Time to stop throwing a tantrum and come back home."* Every single time he does it, it reinforces the idea that this place is no longer my home or where I want to be.

I sigh, trying not to let myself get swallowed up in the past. It's meant to stay there for a reason.

Circling back to the kitchen, I find a bag of cookies Ma has hidden in the mixer. She thinks she's tricky hiding her sweets in the mixing bowl, but we learned at a very young age where to find them. I take the whole bag, unable to resist the little taste of home they'll offer. Twenty bucks says Adler or Mercer gets blamed for taking it. The thought makes me giggle.

Ma's laptop is open on the countertop like she set it aside to work on lunch. Wiggling the mouse, I wake up the screen, her retreat website pulled up into a blog post that she's working on.

I sit in front of it, nibbling on the world's most delicious brown butter cookie, reading through her half-written post. It's a mess. I'm not sure if she's trying to encourage people to come back, or if she's writing an expose on how hard it is to run her business. Either way, this isn't usually her job. Last I knew, there was an employee who wrote the blog posts and ran her socials. Staring at the screen, I let my brain wander, rearranging sentences and writing new ones. Giving a more eloquent spin to what I think Ma might be trying to say.

I'm tempted to put the words into the post, but instead, I navigate to her social accounts. There hasn't been any interaction in months. Some people have asked basic questions, and there's no reply. Not even an automated one inviting them to message for more information.

I chew on my fingernail, itching to write out a basic reply. If only so it doesn't look like the business is going under.

The sound of a car door has me scrambling to set the computer screen back to how it was. Bursting out of the kitchen, I slip down the hall toward the family rooms.

The Main house is more of a mansion. Great-Grandpa Kane called it a lodge, and I guess it is, but it's massive. There are eight family rooms on the East wing. Twelve guest rooms in the center of the house, and well, there used to be another seven on the West wing, but Adler has taken that over. I don't know what he's done to it, probably stuffed it full of arcade games and Sports Illustrated posters. Actually, they're probably half-dressed cowgirls, but whatever, my point stands.

The second my feet hit the worn-out boards of the hallway, I pause. When I came back the first time, I had one condition: I wouldn't stay here. The compromise was the cabin because you can see it from the main house. So, everyone could still "keep an eye on me," but it also meant I got to avoid the main house for the better part of ten years. When I am here, I tend to stick to the kitchen area for meals and holidays. It feels easier that way, more detached.

I slip into my bedroom, avoiding the memories of playing hallway hockey with the younger boys. Ethan stomping down the hardwood planks, a serious lawyer look on his face, before he tells me all the shit I'm doing wrong. God, if only they weren't omniscient and *soooo* smart.

I roll my eyes.

My room looks mostly the same. There isn't a single speck of dust, and no dirty clothes are strewn about the floor. Overall, it's barely changed. The same wildflower comforter with soft pink sheets underneath. I wonder...walking around to the head, I stick my hand under the pillow, grinning when I pull out a soft brown horse. Even as a teenager, I kept Speckles close. He does, in fact, not have a single speckle on him, and yet, I couldn't be convinced to change his name. No matter how much the boys teased me.

Pa gifted him when I was seven. I never took him out of the house, and I always slept with him. I set him on the end of the bed, fully intending to take him with me. I doubt Ma does much with the linens; she won't notice.

Across from my bed is a vanity, which is white with little pink flowers decorating the edges. The mirror is streak-free. Old makeup and knick-knacks scatter across the vanity counter. I used to keep my diary in the side drawer. Miya helped me build a false bottom to it, so I had a proper hiding spot. I took the diary with me when I left, one hundred percent aware that the boys would go through my shit once I wasn't here to monitor it.

Nosy bastards.

I catch my reflection in the mirror, taken aback. I haven't seen myself in this room in nearly a decade. Whenever I'm here, looking at that bed, I can't help but remember Clay. The first night he snuck in, the bed shook with his tears before he finally fell into a restful sleep. That memory always leads to the next, which was the last time he was here. The time he kissed me, then snuck away and pretended I didn't exist afterward. That should have been my first sign he didn't want me.

Pushing those thoughts back, I consider that I've never seen adult Leni here. You'd think the differences would be subtle, but they're jarring.

Where a flat-chested, little twig of a girl should be, I see a woman. Thick thighs, the flare of my hips accentuated by my workout clothes, and man, my tits look huge here. I didn't get a chest until after high school. Not sure why they didn't come in with puberty, but the second I moved out, I suddenly looked all grown up.

Another thing that the boys probably hated was me coming home after a year, looking nothing like the scrawny kid they said goodbye to.

I shake my head and walk in the opposite direction, toward the bathroom, perks of being the only girl in the family. I had my own ensuite and walk-in closet.

The shower curtain and rug have changed to a soft sage green. It looks much better than the black and white zebra print I had chosen. The counter has little hotel toiletries, like Ma was hoping I'd come back. She has a million other guest rooms; I know they don't use this for visitors.

The closet, to my memory, is also the same, stuffed full of outfits I wore in my teens. I pick up a pair of denim shorts that look like they're made for toddlers. Double zero. Holy shit. Was I actually that tiny?

Holding them up to my hips in the full-length mirror, I have to smother a laugh. Oh my God, these wouldn't even make it up one thigh now. I turn to the side, running a hand down my leg. I used to be self-conscious about the weight I gained once I moved out. Now, I kind of like my curves. I like the swing of my hips and the power I wield when a man shows interest.

I might not be the perfect picture of mental health, but at least I like my body now. It helps on days when I don't particularly care for the rest of me. I should probably consider scheduling a video therapy session soon. Being here, seeing Clay, it's bringing up a lot of old shit that I thought I dealt with.

Moving down to my knees, I shuffle the shoe rack, cringing at the multiple pairs of platforms I have. I should sell these online; I bet I could call them vintage and make a decent little chunk of change.

I feel around by memory, finding the little hole in the wall where I stuffed a narrow shoebox. Pa would probably have a heart attack if he knew I butchered the drywall, but it's hidden enough that no one will ever find it. Unless they clear everything out.

I run my fingers over the lid of the box. A light and warm feeling consumes my belly. To anyone else, these letters would be boring. They're mostly Clay talking about his day. One of them is about the time he broke his toe while on a march. Another about how the pears are always crunchy and never fully ripe. Little details that made me smile and made me think I was important to him.

How wrong I was.

My shoulders droop, the lightness replaced with a heavy weight I can never quite shake. He stopped writing after that summer. I offered to go back with him. To help him sleep better. I realized then that I was in love with him. That I'd happily give up any kind of future, if it meant I could help him not hurt so much.

When he left, it was the first time I realized that maybe he didn't want me to. When the letters started coming in for Mercer or the others, but never for me, I realized I was losing him. I wrote him through the fall, until I turned eighteen and went to find him.

Somehow, I convinced myself that he did want me; he was just being noble. Being honorable because I was still underage. Turning eighteen was the catalyst I thought would bring us together. Clearly, I'd been wrong. Shoving the box back into the hole, I shake my head. There's no use pining for something that was never going to happen. For someone who was never going to let himself want me back.

I do a slow circle, standing in the middle of the closet, looking for something to do, some reason to stay. Dark blue sequins peek out of the back corner. Running the scratchy material through my hand, I pull the body con dress off the hanger.

I wore this on my twenty-first birthday. Miya and I got a small group of girls from college together and decided to hit up a couple of nightclubs. I was drinking, obviously, but not enough to impair my decisions. Some of the girls were getting tipsy, but Miya wasn't drinking at all. We made a pact at our first college party that one of us would always stay sober to make sure both of us got home safe.

We were having a good night, the best night, actually. The five of us were dancing with each other, paying no mind to anyone showing interest in us. We were being safe, responsible even. It was shaping up to be one of my favorite nights, until it wasn't.

Brooks and Ethan showed up and physically removed us from the club. They hauled a screaming Miya out of that bar with me, making such a scene that the bouncers came over to check if we were okay. Ethan gave them one look, lied to say I was his underage sister, and they let them haul us out.

None of the girls talked to Miya or me again.

They drove us back home, not to our dorms. They didn't say anything on the car ride, not even letting us stop to pee.

Brooks waited until we were parked in front of the main house before assuming an intimidating position, with big arms crossed over his chest. The first thing he did was let us know how stupid we were for dressing the way we did. When I asked what they were even doing in Benson, he said they came to celebrate my birthday with me. Which is bullshit, because fall on the ranch is a busy time of year. The prep for winter is intense and fast-paced. Brooks wasn't there to celebrate. He was there to make sure I didn't have too much fun. That's the kind of shit they pulled, over and over, until I threatened to move across the country and never come home.

They conceded a little bit after that. They might not drive to Benson to insert themselves into my life anymore, but it certainly doesn't stop them from running commentary about the choices I make whenever I am home. From the clothes I wear to the state of my Jeep is apparently fair game. It's maddening.

Shaking off the memories, I bring the dress with me, wondering what sequins look like when they burn. I snatch up two random books off my bookshelf and Speckles, heading for the door when footsteps come down the hallway.

I listen to the steps make their way down the hall. They keep going, and the breath rushes out of me when I finally can't hear them anymore.

I'm about to celebrate my victory when my phone starts to ring. *Loud.* In my panic to shut the ringer off, I accidentally swipe to answer it. Mercer's voice comes muffled from behind my palm as I try to listen to the background. Checking if anyone is around now, or if they heard the phone.

I don't hear any footsteps, but I can hear someone banging around in the kitchen. Probably Ma, which limits my options for escape. Thank God, this part of the house is all ground level.

"Uh, hello?"

"Hey," I whisper, wedging the phone between my ear and shoulder as I ease the old wooden window open. I peek my head out, checking to make sure the coast is clear before I step one leg through the opening. I set my foot into one of Mom's prized peony bushes. "Oh fuck." I keep my voice quiet, trying to right the stems while staying out of the kitchen window's line of sight.

"What the fuck are you doing, Leni?"

"Hang on, D, I'm a little busy."

He's quiet on his end. The sounds of cows come through. Well, that's good, at least I know the guys are still out. It takes a ridiculous amount of effort to coax the window back down, the wood swollen with humidity.

"Goddamn, fucking thing." I rip my finger back, disgust churning in my gut when I see the inch-long splinter embedded in my index finger.

Mercer snorts into his phone. "You have the loveliest mouth on you, Sis."

I can't help but chuckle, still trying to keep quiet.

"What *are* you doing? Robbing a bank?"

"No," I gasp. "That would be way cooler! Edna fell asleep in the living room. I'm trying to be courteous."

"Courteous? That woman can barely hear with her hearing aids in, Leni. I doubt you'll wake her up by talking."

I crouch down, trying to keep my steps quiet, so Mercer won't pick up on the gravel crunching beneath my feet. Hopefully, the cows are loud enough that he won't hear anything at all. Counting to ten in my head, I sprint across the driveway between the main house and the big barn, cursing internally when one of the brood mares in the paddock whinnies at me.

"Was that a horse?"

"Yeah, I definitely heard a horse on your end." I try to play it off, talking in my normal voice now.

"Why are you out of breath now?"

"I ran up the stairs." I shrug, even though he can't see me.

"Jesus, I thought I was out of shape."

I scoff at him, indignation burning a path up my throat. This is why I don't initiate contact. No matter which brother I talk to, they always have something to say to me. Something to point out that I'm doing wrong, as if making one mistake in high school makes me incapable of ever growing up and learning.

"Did you call me to insult me, brother?"

"No, I meant what I said in our text this morning. Life would be better, nay, perfect, if you would get your ass back home."

"My ass is currently sitting in front of my laptop, watching old westerns all summer."

"So, you're just content to sit and rot for the summer while we languish away missing you?"

"Has anyone ever told you that you're dramatic?" I glance up at the clear blue sky, my chest swelling with a peace I haven't felt in a long time. I love the skies out here.

"Of course, it's part of my charm."

"None of you assholes have char—ahh!" I squeal as my toe sinks into the top of a gopher hole. One arm flails, the other arm gripping my phone tighter, trying to keep myself from eating dirt.

"You good?" Mercer sounds amused on the other end, if not a little sad. I bet he's working too hard. I don't know much about law enforcement, but I'm not sure Mercer has taken any real time off since he started four years ago.

"Yeah, almost fell off my bed." It occurs to me how easily I can lie to him. I never lied to him growing up. Mercer was my best friend. We were inseparable before he met Clay, and I started spending every spare second with Miya. Guilt settles onto my shoulders, making me hate myself a little more.

"You know you can tell me anything, right?" Mercer's voice goes soft, the one he reserves for weaseling out information.

Mercer is a master at getting people to talk about exactly whatever it is he wants to know. It makes him a great sheriff, but it's annoying as hell being the gullible sibling.

"I know, Merc, but there's nothing to tell."

"Is it money?"

"Hmm?"

"Do you need money to get back home?"

"No, Merc, I don't need money," I sigh, picking up my pace to the cabin. I want to get home.

"It's just...I know you don't want to take any from Ma and Pa, but if that's why you're not coming back, I could help."

"No, Mercer, I...I don't know. I'm not ready to be home, that's all."

"Because of Clay?"

"I don't know, maybe. It was ten years ago; we're both adults now. It shouldn't be this hard, but I can't force myself to rip the band-aid off yet."

I'm going to hell, lying through my teeth like those bastard mechanics who up-charge you because you're a pretty girl. That's the level of hell I'm headed for.

"Then let me come see you." The earnestness in his voice makes me pause.

"I—what?"

"Come on, Leni. You didn't come home for the holidays. I haven't seen you since last summer. Let me come visit. Edna won't mind. She loves me."

I can hear the smile in his voice. It's true, Edna loved Mercer the one time she met him.

"I don't know D..."

He sighs into the phone. "You know, now that the idea is in my head..."

He won't drop it. I know that. We're nothing if not consistently stubborn, the whole lot of us.

"Might as well pick a day, Sis. It's gotta happen now."

I groan. "That's not how it works, Mercer. You can't just—"

"Hey! Hey, hey, hey, hey, hey!" Voices boom in the background, chaos erupting on Mercer's end of the line.

"Gotta go, Leni!" He doesn't wait for my reply.

I sigh, looking out across the open field between the main house and my cabin. Blowing my bangs out of my face, I force my legs to move as I keep my mind focused on my pulse throbbing in my index finger. Grounding my thoughts in the weird sensation to keep my mind from wandering too far. I have a habit of assuming everything my family does is for some ulterior motive. The chances that Mercer does miss me are more likely than him wanting to visit to get information out of me.

He has no reason to think I'm hiding anything.

He just misses me.

That's all.

Chapter 12

Just Pull It Out

Clay

BROOKY

Please tell me you fuckers didn't burn down my ranch today.

> Nope. Ranch is still standing.

BROOKY

Thank fuck for that

> I am curious as to why I've suddenly been put in charge?

BROOKY

...

You're kidding right?

> No really. WTF man?

BROOKY

Who the fuck else am I supposed to put in charge? Adler?

> I mean...he actually works here...

BROOKY

That's not fucking funny

I'm not laughing

BROOKY

He's a fucking idiot. Speaking of...he still alive?

Yea. He's not a child anymore Brooks.

BROOKY

He might as well be.

...

You good bro?

BROOKS, TO NO SURPRISE, DOES NOT RESPOND. WELL, AT least whatever he has going on, I know he's himself. Unlike Mercer, who could barely even look at me after I told him about Leni's visit. That whole debacle in the sevens was a complete shit show, made worse by the fact that my partner wouldn't look at me long enough to catch my cues, or bother to see where I was in all of it.

I could have been hit by one of the trucks screaming past us at highway speeds, and he wouldn't have even looked my way. That's not true, he would have, but fuck, man. In the twenty-plus years we've been friends, we've never fought. Not about school, sports, or women...probably because I was constantly fantasizing about his sister. Still, I don't think he's ever been genuinely mad at me...it's fucking miserable.

Finalizing the assignments for tomorrow, I get up from behind Brooks' desk in the big barn and make my way to my truck. Toby is kicked back on his tailgate, a beer resting on his thigh, his head tipped toward the sky. He's the quiet Kane, not in a brooding kind of way, but more like a quiet observer.

He doesn't see the attack coming. Adler strolls up behind him, pure chaos gleaming in his eyes. Before I can even utter a warning, he strikes with perfect precision. Sliding up beside Toby, he taps the bottom of his beer bottle to the top of Toby's. White foam instantly spills over the top. Toby's curses echo through the ranch yard as he bolts after a cackling Adler.

A smile tugs at my lips, exhaustion keeping it from taking hold. Toby saunters back, looking a lot like he pissed himself, his eyes promising revenge as he stomps to his truck and climbs into the cab. The slam of the door rings in my ears.

I crawl into my own truck, my body weary. Wrecked from the physical labor of the day, not to mention the adrenaline. Nothin' quite sets your blood on fire like watching a big rig turn one of your beef cows into red mist. *Fuck*, that's an image I won't be erasing from my brain any time soon. I drive the long way to Leni's cabin, taking the highway. Trying to kill more time, hoping she'll be upstairs, or already in bed by the time I get home.

I'll have to sneak through her room to grab a shower, but that might be worth it to avoid any potentially awkward situations. My phone buzzes when I finally get to the cabin, giving me an excuse to stay outside a little longer, avoiding confrontation like the pussy I am.

KANE FAMILY GROUP CHAT
MA

Thanks for the help boys. looks like tomorrow will be a busy one again. Brooks won't be back until after next week. Will pack family dinner to go tomorrow.

ADDY

What do you mean after next week?! IS HE DYING?

TOBES

I'm going to go check on him

MA

No you are not Tobias Russel. You will go back to your house and mind your business

ADDY

Ma this is insane. Brooks doesn't take vacation he doesn't take personal time

E-MAN

Just give him some space dude. He'll let us know what's going on when he's ready

TOBES

What do you know

ADDY

WHAT DO YOU KNOW?!

MA

Clayton worked out a schedule for tomorrow to reinforce the fences in the 7s. Looks like someone mighta driven through it.

ADDY

Now Traeger's doing paperwork? we are literally falling apart

I do paperwork at my day job. Dick

ADDY

Oooh mister big shot police man.

You know what Addy? I think the troughs need cleaning tomorrow and I know just the guy

ADDY

You wouldn't dare

Wouldn't I though?

LENI ROSE

Wish I could have been there to help looks like you're in good hands though boys. Let me know what's up with Brooks.

ADDY

Holy shit. Leni in the CHAT!

LENI ROSE

☺ Dramatic much?

MERC D

I have a theory on Brooky

MA

No theories. Everyone go to sleep. The cows wait for no man or woman. Leni dear, I miss you.

LENI ROSE

Miss you too ma

My body is screaming for a hot shower and a bed. *Shit.* I forgot that I've been relegated to the couch because I'm an asshole. The thought of sleeping on that tiny piece of cardboard makes me want to stomp my feet into the gravel like a toddler. What will Addy say tomorrow if he spies and sees me sleeping on the couch again?

"Goddamnit, you fucking little pussy. Just pull it out!" Leni's voice immediately assaults my ears as I walk through the door. I peek into the kitchen, taking in the scene before me.

Her brown hair is tied up in a knot on the top of her head, bangs held back with a red bandana. She's perched on the kitchen counter, legs crossed, tongue peeking out between her teeth as she concentrates on whatever task has her attention. I can't stop myself from wishing I could go over and free her tongue. Set it loose from her teeth so it could tangle with mine. I watch, completely entranced. Tonight she's wearing tiny silk pajama shorts and a loose cotton bralette that barely contains her breasts. The swell of their underside plays peekaboo with me as she moves. My dick hardens the second I see the soft, plump flesh.

"Clay?" A mellower Leni speaks my name. Snapping my eyes back to her face, my breath catches when I see her looking at me, her big, glassy eyes meeting mine through thick eyelashes. "I got a sliver," she whines.

There's a pause before a laugh that I can't help bursts out of me. Leni has always been a baby when it comes to slivers. She could fall off a two-thousand-pound animal at high rates of speed, and nothing. Burn her hand on a hot dish in the kitchen? Barely a tear. Tell her you need to dig a sliver out with a needle, and she'll run for the hills. *Every damn time.*

"Glad to see some things don't change."

Her eyes narrow, hands dropping into her lap as she considers her options.

Toeing my boots off, I keep my eyes on her, walking into the kitchen to assess her wound. "Fuck, that's a massive sliver."

"I know!" she shrieks. The scowl melts from her face as she clutches her finger to her chest.

I wash my hands, then return to where she's sitting. Using her knees to turn her body toward me, I step into her space. "Where the hell did you get this?"

I inspect the sliver closer; it's *definitely* coming out in parts. Glancing at the counter, I notice the tweezers, needle, and peroxide she must have grabbed.

"Climbing out of my bedroom window."

"What?" I drop her hand, looking her in the eyes. "You went to the main house?"

"I checked the group chat, and I knew everyone was out."

"Why am I not surprised you used the group chat for evil?"

"Evil?" she scoffs, indignation lighting her voice as I work the wood out. "I'd hardly call walking through my parents' house evil."

"I mean, who's to say you weren't putting hex bags under their beds?"

She gasps as a jagged edge of the window frame scrapes across her skin. "I only did that one time."

"Uh-huh." My eyes meet hers, letting her see the humor in them.

"You would have too if Mercer kept eating your favorite cereal. He didn't even like it. He only did it so I couldn't have it."

"That does sound like Mercer." I wet a paper towel with peroxide, hoping I got most of the sliver out. I wrap it around her finger, my eyes meeting hers as she lets out a sharp gasp.

"Dick." Her free hand reaches out to punch me in the shoulder.

"I'm sorry about last night." I shift my hand to hold hers, keeping the paper towel pressed between her fingers. "I have no right to tell you what to do or how to live your life. I hate seeing you like this."

She ducks her head, heat rising in her cheeks, and attempts to draw her knees up to her chest. I shake my head, pressing my palm against them to coax her legs back down to the counter.

"Not like that, Leni. You're not a failure. Having to come back home and figure things out isn't a bad thing. You're lucky to have this place to fall back on."

"I know," she bites back, defensive.

"I hate seeing you distance yourself from the family. That's all I meant."

She stares at me, her gaze so intense I have to look away. I should go upstairs, shower, and make my peace with another night on the atrocity she calls a couch.

"I'm going to tell them. Just not everything," she corrects, gently taking her finger from my hold to inspect it. "I just need a little bit of time. I filled out a couple of applications back in Benson. I just have to find the right one. You know?"

My chest aches at the thought of her leaving, going back to a life where I won't see her, hear her voice, or feel her touch.

"Do you not want to teach anymore?" I shake out the thoughts, reminding myself that Leni isn't mine to keep. Gathering the sliver extraction equipment, I put it back into the correct spots in her first aid kit.

"I don't know."

"If you didn't teach, what would you do instead?"

"Write, maybe?" She brings a finger up, chewing on her nail, eyes searching mine, waiting for me to judge her.

"Like, books?" I turn back to her, barely containing the yawn that's trying to rearrange my face.

"No, I don't think books. Articles, maybe? Social media posts? I don't know, that's probably stupid." She slides off the counter, heading for the electric kettle. "Tea?"

Chapter 13

You Saved Me

Leni

"Tea?" He stares at me, dumbfounded.

"Yes, Clay, tea. Would you like a cup? I could make some while you shower and bring it up for you."

"Bring it up?" he repeats. I feel my eyebrows raise into my hairline as he stands there, blinking at me.

"Dude." I turn to face him fully, putting one hand on my hip. "You clearly need a shower and some fucking sleep. I'll bring the tea up to the bedroom; you can have the bed tonight. You need it more."

"Oh, yeah." He looks at me a second longer, his grey eyes unfocused, then yawns so wide his jaw cracks. "Sorry, I'm fucking beat. Tea is great."

"Sleepy time?" I call after him as he's already halfway up the stairs.

"Sure, doesn't really matter, it won't help." He turns at the waist, offering me a sad smile before continuing up the stairs. I shouldn't care that he's not sleeping, or if he ever sleeps again. Clayton Traeger is *not* my problem. Nor does he want to be my

117

problem. Still, my chest aches a little at the thought of him suffering alone.

Helping him is easy. He literally needs nothing more than my presence to sleep better, to relax. I've yet to meet anyone who needs me the way he does. And yet, he doesn't want to need me. I think he might actually loathe the idea of needing me.

I've thought about what it felt like to press my lips to his again. Thought about the fact that Clayton Traeger could be my first and last kiss, how perfectly we could wrap up our story. Together.

Then I remember that he's already been claimed by my brothers as their own. The same brothers who annoy me and habitually get up in my business. Yeah, nope, I don't belong here anymore, but Clay does. He'll find someone else, someone who helps him sleep at night, someone he wants to be with.

For now, maybe I'll use this time to figure out how to be around him without secretly pining, even as my body flinches every time he moves. If such a thing is possible with him. Maybe part of me will always want him. Maybe that's part of growing up. Acknowledging there will always be something and still finding a way to move forward. That's possible, right?

I'm sitting on the bed, twisting my hair into braids, trying to convince myself it's possible, when Clay stumbles out of the bathroom. Judging by how long he took, I'm nearly certain he dozed off at least once while getting ready for bed. His eyes find mine when he finally looks up, widening for a moment when he registers I'm sitting on the bed in my pjs.

"Your tea is cold," I offer, but what I want to say is, *let me help you.*

"Okay." His head dips, damp curls bobbing with the motion. He stands there, fingers flexing in and out as tension slowly draws his shoulders up to his ears. *Jesus Christ.* Is he for real right now?

"Tell me to go," I say at the exact same moment he says my name, a little of that broken boy shining through.

"Please don't." He scrubs his hand down his face, eyes pleading with me. "I mean, you can, if you want...you can go, but please don't. I'll stay on my side of the bed. I just—*fuck.*" He pulls his fingers through his wet curls and sighs.

"What do you need?"

"Sleep," he laughs, a broken sound that guts me. "You," he adds. "I don't know why, but somehow you're the only thing that has ever helped and I'm sorry."

"It's okay," I whisper. "You don't have to be sorry."

"Well," he sighs, finally making his way over to the other side of the bed. "I am."

"I'm not." I shrug, slipping under the covers on my side. "Get some sleep."

"Hmm," he hums, his eyes closing the second his head hits the pillow.

I lay next to him, unable to sleep, like the night before, too aware of how close he is, and how warm it would feel to sidle up and be held by him. "Clay," I whisper into the darkness, unable to stop myself.

"Yeah, Leni?" My name escapes on another yawn.

"Did you ever..." I trail off, cheeks heating with a blush I'm grateful he can't see in the dark. This is so stupid. I'm twenty-seven years old. *I don't care,* I try to convince myself. Only I do, and I care a lot.

"You can ask me anything." Clay's smooth, deep rasp coasts over me, settling into my bones.

"Did you ever miss me?" I don't turn to look at him. I stay on my back, staring up at the ceiling, wishing it didn't matter.

"Only every fucking day," he whispers. "All three thousand

four hundred and ninety-two of them." The sheets rustle as his hand slides through them. His pinky brushes mine before wrapping around it. My stomach swoops as we lie there, listening to each other's breath, fingers locked in a promise.

What we're promising, I don't know. But I think I'd like to find out.

ROUGH HANDS BRUSH MY SKIN, flashes of blond hair and dark brown eyes streak through my mind as I'm pulled under. The dream begins to take shape: grungy tile walls, a metal door with a deadbolt looming in front of me. Teeth flash, and I whimper, curling in on myself as if I could ward off the memory. Warm, calloused fingers pull me backward. I want to fight it, but I can never outrun these dreams. A scent fills my nose—warm, spicy, and familiar. I burrow into it, breathing it in, letting the warmth wrap around me.

Safe.

I'm safe here.

HOURS AFTER MY ALMOST NIGHTMARE, a blaring alarm rips me from a soft, dreamless sleep, and Clay's warmth pulls away from me to silence the alarm. His arm wraps back around me, pulling me even deeper into his chest as he mumbles into my hair. "Five more minutes."

I don't argue. I could sleep for ten more hours. My body melts as I inhale the warm vanilla and cinnamon scent of him. Yeah, I could do ten more hours of this. *Please.* This is bliss. What feels like only seconds later, the alarm shrieks again. Clay's soft curses whisper over my hair before he eases himself from my hold.

"No," I mumble, trying to reach for him. I can't open my eyes, or rather, I have no desire to open them. I want to stay like this a little longer. Clay chuckles, then plants a soft kiss on my temple before he climbs out of the bed for the day. I sigh, clutching his pillow to my chest, a poor imitation of holding him again.

I know we don't have a future together. I can't be with someone who actively works against whatever he might feel toward me. But I can imagine what it'd be like, waking up to Clay every morning, kissing him goodbye, and pulling him back into bed with me for five more minutes. I squeeze my eyes shut tighter, willing my heart to remember that we missed our chance. Clay is not mine, and I have to be okay with that.

By the time I'm up for the day, it's after ten o'clock. Clay has the coffee ready for me to start a pot. A blueberry muffin is sitting next to it. If I didn't know any better, I'd say he snuck back to the cabin and left it for me. Mom's muffins are top tier, and blueberry happens to be my favorite.

I scroll the job boards for Benson as the coffee maker begins to sputter, filling the tiny kitchen with warm, cozy notes of hazelnut and vanilla. There are a few teaching gigs open, but most of them are in early childhood. The thought of sitting in a room full of seven-year-olds has me shuddering in my chair. That's too many little kids.

I want kids someday. Badly enough that when Miya suggested going and getting our ovarian reserves tested, I signed up. We went to a fancy medical spa where they gave us freshly squeezed juices and then drew our blood. Turns out, I'm a *Fertile Myrtle*. Miya, on the other hand, was diagnosed with a diminished reserve. They suggested she go through an egg retrieval cycle to freeze them, in case she wanted kids down the road, but she never told me if she went through with it or not.

Miya is the kind of person who needs to be the best at

everything she does. Secretly, I think she might want kids eventually. I also think it broke something in her when she got the news. I didn't push; having kids is such a deeply personal topic. I figure, if she wants to talk about it, she will.

We haven't been as close as we once were. My family dynamic wasn't the only thing that changed the night of the attack. We're still best friends, still talk all the time, it's just more superficial. I hate that there's such a big space between us now. I need to get back to Benson so I can fix things and see my girls.

Reaching for my phone, I'm about to text Miya and Pepper when I notice several messages waiting for me. I open Clay's first. Seeing his name on my screen does something strange to my stomach. He's inching his way back into my life, and it's getting harder and harder to pretend that there's nothing between us.

HE WHO SHALL NOT BE NAMED

> heads up Adler's been spying on the cabin.
> he knows I slept on the couch the other night

Of course, he was. Swiping out of that conversation, I move to Ethan's because I'm not prepared to deal with Clay's until *after* I've had breakfast and some coffee.

ETHAN TODD

> You should come home.

Oh yea? Why?

ETHAN TODD

> Brooks is going through something

I heard something about that

Care to share?

ETHAN TODD

...

Client confidentiality and all that

> Well I doubt anything is so bad you need me home for it.

ETHAN TODD

Fuck you're stubborn

> I mean... you've met my family right?

ETHAN TODD

Just come home Leni. What else do you have to prove? You went off and did the thing. Time to come back and be apart of the family again.

> I'm not doing this with you

ETHAN TODD

Fine. Who will you do it with then? You're needed here.

You don't leave your family

> You're just mad that you were wrong

ETHAN TODD

I'm never fucking wrong.

> Bullshit.

You told me I'd never make it out here but look at me now. Making it just fine without all you overbearing pricks watching every move I make.

> Eat glass Ethan

My phone buzzes with another message, but I toggle my notifications to Do Not Disturb. This is why I moved away. Everyone thinks I'm incapable of taking care of myself and making my own decisions. Having five brothers is a lot. Once they deem you too weak and fragile to fend for yourself, it becomes impossible to live in the same town. Much less on the same ranch. Hell, it's bad enough being in the same state as them. Brooks and Ethan are the worst. They have absolutely zero chill when it comes to letting me be my own person.

I can still hear Brooks' deep voice when I told them I was moving to Benson. *"That's just plain stupid, Leni. You'll never make it without us. Look what happened last time you tried to do something on your own."* He acts like he's never made any mistakes, as if he weren't engaged to a drug addict who stole from him and almost burned down the big barn. Twice.

Fucking assholes.

Putting my newfound anger to work, I decide to rage-clean the cabin. Clay kept it nearly spotless, but there's always something to clean when you're mad. I focus on the bathroom, scrubbing the toilet and sink, then move on to the tub.

Once it's sparkling on the inside, I move to the outside of the tub. The plastic gets kind of grungy, with dust bunnies and dirt clinging to the bottom. As I come around to the far end of the tub, my fingers brush something that feels like canvas. I manage to hook my fingers into the material, pulling a small black shaving kit out from between the tub and the wall. Strange, I definitely didn't put that there.

My breath catches when I open the zipper. A black spider webbed phone screen stares back at me, the bright pink case a stark contrast to the bag. Holy shit. He kept my phone, the one that fell out of my bag that night.

Shaky fingers pull the phone out. I turn it over in my hand, staring at the case and the Polaroid behind it. I bend the plastic case back to remove the picture and my driver's license. God, I was such a baby when they took that picture. My cheeks still had baby fluff on them, hair twisted back into double braids, much like the ones I'm wearing now.

I don't know why he would keep this, but my phone isn't the only thing in the bag. I find letters, hundreds of letters, all of them with my name on them. Most of the envelopes are sealed. I dump them all out, inspecting each one until I find one that isn't. Carefully, I pull out a bundle of papers and unfold them. Clay's blocky, all-caps handwriting greets me.

SEPTEMBER 9TH
45 DAYS WITHOUT YOU

DEAR LENI,

I TOLD MYSELF I WASN'T GOING TO WRITE YOU ANYMORE. THAT YOU'D BE BETTER OFF WITHOUT ME, BUT I DON'T THINK I'M BETTER OFF WITHOUT YOU. I'VE BARELY SLEPT SINCE GETTING BACK TO BASE. I GOT NEW ORDERS TODAY, LOOKS LIKE I'M SHIPPING OUT TO THE MIDDLE EAST AGAIN.

I'M SCARED, LENI. THAT LAST TOUR REALLY FUCKED ME UP, AND I'M SCARED THAT I'M NOT GOING TO COME BACK AS ME. OR WORSE, I WON'T MAKE IT BACK AT ALL. MY UNIT CAME HOME INTACT LAST TIME, BUT WE SAW TOO MANY THAT DIDN'T. AND THE PEOPLE THERE, LENI. THE PEOPLE WE HAVE TO DEFEND OURSELVES FROM, SOME OF THEM ARE KIDS. I SWEAR, I SAW ONE THAT LOOKED JUST LIKE ADLER. HE WAS STILL SMILING, LYING THERE ON THE GROUND, FLIES BUZZING AROUND HIS HEAD. FUCK.

I SHOULD HAVE STAYED ON THE RANCH. BECOME BROOKS 2.0 OR SOMETHING. I'M IN IT NOW, I GUESS. I WOULDN'T BE ABLE TO LOOK ANY OF YOU IN THE

EYES IF I LEFT NOW. PLUS, I'M PRETTY SURE DESER-
TION IS A CRIME NOWADAYS. OR IS IT STILL? FUCK, I
DON'T KNOW, LENI.

ALL I KNOW IS THAT WHEN I CLOSE MY EYES, ALL
I SEE IS DEATH AND DARKNESS. AND I HATE MYSELF
SOMETIMES BECAUSE THIS SUMMER, WHEN YOU HELD
ME? I DIDN'T SEE IT ANYMORE. I JUST SAW YOU. YOU
CHASED AWAY THE DARKNESS FOR ME. DID YOU KNOW
THAT LENI?

DID YOU KNOW THAT YOU SAVED ME?

I MISS YOU
—CT

JUNE 1ST
676 DAYS WITHOUT YOU

DEAR LENI,
I RE-ENLISTED TODAY. I WASN'T GOING TO. I TOLD
EVERYONE THAT I WAS DONE WITH THIS LIFE. THEN I
CAME HOME THIS SUMMER, LOOKING FOR FAMILY AND
SUNSHINE, AND YOU WEREN'T HERE.

I FUCKED EVERYTHING UP, DIDN'T I, LEN? I FEEL
LIKE I'M DROWNING. LIKE I'VE LOST ALL SENSE OF
DIRECTION. I DON'T KNOW WHICH WAY IS UP OR DOWN.
I DON'T KNOW WHAT I'M DOING OR WHERE I'M
GOING. THE ONLY THING I KNOW IS THAT I MISS YOU.

I MISS COMING IN FROM THE FIELD AFTER A FULL
DAY OF RIDING AND SEEING YOU. I MISS HEARING YOU
LAUGH. I MISS THE WAY YOU LISTEN. I MISS SITTING
ON THE DECK IN SILENCE. I MISS THE FEEL OF YOUR
HAND IN MINE.

I MISS YOU. I MISS YOU. I MISS YOU.

I'M SO SORRY, LENI.

—CT

1,135 DAYS WITHOUT YOU

DEAR LENI,
I DON'T WANT TO BE HERE ANYMORE. ~~IT'S TOO HARD TO LIVE LIKE THIS.~~ I'M SO TIRED, ~~LENI.~~ I WISH THAT YOU COULD HOLD ME ONE MORE TIME.

—C

My heart hammers in my chest. All these letters, these moments where he needed someone, and he never sent them. Never called me. I was a phone call away, and still, he never reached out. I waited for him to call me after that night, for him to at least check in and make sure I was okay. But the silence was louder than any words from him could have been.

My fingers itch to open the other envelopes, confirm this growing suspicion that maybe Clay lied. Maybe he did want me. Maybe he never stopped wanting me. So, why? Why didn't he say anything?

Why wasn't I enough?

Chapter 14

Please Don't Ruin Smut For Me

Leni

Four o'clock, on the dot, my phone rings for my weekly call with my mom. I bought her Bluetooth headphones a few years back, and now we chat every Sunday while she prepares family dinner. It took a few years, after our big fight, to rebuild our relationship. It's okay, but it has been better.

"Hey, Ma." I settle into my reading nook, enjoying the feeling of the sun shining through the windows. I might not be a cat person, but I can one hundred percent respect their predisposition to napping in the sun.

"Hello, sweet girl, how are you?"

"I'm good, enjoying some time off for the summer."

"You seeing anyone?"

I groan, stretching my legs out as much as I can in the over-sized chair. "Ma, this is not what Sunday chats are about. You're supposed to vent about the boys and remind me I'm your favorite child."

She tuts at me, and I can hear her opening cabinet doors. "You are my favorite daughter." I roll my eyes. It goes without saying that I'm her only daughter, and it's such a copout. We all know Adler is her favorite anyway. She was supposed to be done after having Toby; the doctors told her it wasn't likely that she'd have any more, and then Adler came along. She's had stars in her eyes ever since.

Youngest, am I right?

"What're we making today, Ma?"

"Oh, nothing special, all the boys are out in the fields, and Brooks is busy with...stuff."

"That's not vague or ominous at all."

"All will be revealed in time," she says, like I'm a fantasy character on some wild quest and she's the wise old Sage. "That's why it's just some sandwiches and veggies."

"Brown paper bagging it, I like that. Tell me, are you cutting the veggies into shapes and making the world's most bougie cold cuts?"

My mom was born to be a hostess. She has a heart for serving others, and her favorite way to do it is through food. I can't remember a single bad day when she didn't cheer me up with something beautiful and tasty.

"What am I supposed to do? Slap some cold meat and plastic cheese on it and call it food? That won't do, Eleanor, and you know it."

She goes through all the ingredients she has for sandwiches, like pickled onions, fresh tomatoes, and horseradish mustard. My mouth is watering hearing her describe them, and I'm half tempted to march my way over to the main house to steal one. I wonder if I'd be testing my luck by trying to sneak over a second time.

"One of the guests here, on that retreat last week, asked if we had a newsletter describing the goings on at our events. She said it would make for good visibility on the internet."

"Oh, yeah, a newsletter, or even posts on your website, would be great. Testimonials, too."

"Like reviews? I think we have one of those Yelp pages, and I've seen a few happy commenters on the Facebook app."

I smile. No matter how many times we tell her she can call it internet, Facebook, or Google, she always adds in *the* to the title. It's adorable, and I love her for it.

"Yeah, testimonials would be kind of like reviews, but there could be little pop-ups on your website pages. Just so people can see snippets of what clients think of their time with you. Do you have anyone fill out surveys after they stay?"

"I think Annie was setting something up on the website before she left."

"Oh, Annie left?" I knew there was supposed to be someone running the pages.

"She did. Went and fell in love with one of them hotshot firemen and moved closer to the mountains."

"Oh." I'm surprised; Annie was one of the most introverted people I've ever met. I never would have pictured her with the type of person who can run toward danger. "Wow, good for her."

"Yeah, very," my mom says, her voice dropping into a conspiratorial whisper. "He's delicious, Leni. I've never been attracted to muscle heads, but he is one hunk of a man."

"Oh, God. Mom!" I burst into laughter. I can't believe she's talking about a man who's likely younger than most of her sons. Good Lord.

"I've been reading some of those books you review on the Instagram." My eyes bug out of my head, mouth dropping open in horror. I'm not a book reviewer by any means, but I enjoy tracking what I read with a quick little review on my Instagram stories. I had no idea my *mother* was following them and *reading* them. "They're very...enlightening."

"No, stop. Please, I beg you. I do not want your take on my books! Please don't ruin smut for me."

"Is that what they call it these days? Smut? We used to call them Harlequin novels, and the covers were always the same half-naked man with long flowing hair. Now they're so adorable. You think you're picking up a cute little love story, and the sex hits you out of nowhere. I've had to ask your Pa to help me figure out how some of the things they do work out in real life."

"Oh, God. Yup...you've officially ruined it for me. Now I can't post any of the books I read because I'll be worried that you're reading them!"

"Don't worry, honey. The fantasy stories aren't for me. I prefer the cowboy romances."

Burying my face into the cushion of the chair, I scream. What have I created? My mom is reading cowboy romances, while her sons are out working on a cattle ranch. Good God, this is what nightmares are made of. I glance at the new cowboy romcom on the side table and make a mental note to put it away immediately. No more cowboy romances for me.

"I'm getting distracted. I brought up Annie because I wondered if you'd be willing to take a look at what she set up. I know you have your program in Benson, but maybe you could write some posts remotely? I can have someone take photos during events and give you a synopsis that you could put a pretty spin on. I'd pay you, too. It'd be an easy little side gig for you." Ma's voice gets quieter, and I can hear the silent aching behind it, the hopefulness in her tone. Anything to get me closer to home, and closer to her.

"Ma, you know I don't want your money."

"I'm not giving it to you like some kind of handout, Eleanor. I pay my employees."

"I don't know that I want to be your employee, Ma."

There's a pause on the other end of the line, no shuffling or sandwich making, just one deep breath into her lungs as she processes. We haven't had a fight in almost seven years now. I didn't talk to her from the beginning of my freshman year to the summer between my sophomore and junior years. I stayed in Benson year-round and worked my ass off to afford school and the shitty little apartment I subleased for the summer. I worked odd jobs throughout high school, but I never knew what it meant to struggle until that summer. I missed my mom. My family. It was hard working through that fight with her, letting her back into my life when she left it so easily.

Weekly therapy sessions helped. It was the one thing I let them pay for, and I'm fucking glad I did.

"You're right, that wouldn't do. I need a partner. I'd like to slow down some. Maybe take on a few less responsibilities. You could—"

"Ma," I stop her. "I have a full-time job." Yup, absolutely going straight to hell. "I don't have time to be a partner in your business."

"I suppose not," she sighs. Not the condescending kind, but the kind of sigh you feel down into your bones when you're weary.

"I should let you go, Ma." I know where conversations like this one end up, and I'm not willing to go there tonight. She wouldn't guilt-trip me directly, but I know she misses me. I miss her and my dad so much. I just...I don't see how anything has changed. "Love you."

"I love you too, Leni dear."

IT'S dark out by the time I hear Clay's pickup rumble up the driveway. Glancing at the clock, I realize it's already nine o'clock, that's basically the middle of the night, ranch time. He must have been up and out of the cabin by four a.m., at least.

Clay comes up the stairs, dirt coating his clothes and face. He gives me a soft smile before heading toward the bathroom. "Gonna grab a shower."

I follow him, leaning against the door frame of the bathroom before he can close the door. He quirks an eyebrow, hands going to his hips as I raise one hand and pick at my nails.

"What is this?"

"You wanted me." I feel the fire stoke in my belly. Years of suppressed anger finally making it's way to the surface.

"What?"

I take my cracked, decade-old brick of a cellphone out of my pocket and cross the bathroom. Shoving the old device into his chest, I glare at him. "You wanted me."

He looks down at the phone, cradling it to his chest as his hand rises. I move mine before he can take it. Soft grey eyes meet mine, a yearning I've only ever dreamed of burning deep within them. "Of course, I wanted you."

His voice comes out quiet, fingers gripping the device a little tighter.

"You never called," I say, voice shaking a little as I back away from him, unable to keep up the courage to stand toe to toe with him. "You never said so, you said..." I cut myself off, turning on my heel to march back into the bedroom. The air in the bathroom feels too hot and charged to breathe.

"Leni..." He follows me out, keeping space between us.

"No! Clay, you lied! You told me you didn't want me. You let me think that none of it was real."

"That's not true. I told you I didn't want you there. I never told you I didn't want you."

"You might as well have! I know Mercer told you about the mugging. I know you knew and you never once—"

"I did," he grits out, one hand running through his curls. He looks around the room, frantic. "I tried to call, but I had your fucking phone. Three days," he growls. "Three days after you left, I called again, and your number was disconnected. You never called *me*. You left *me*."

His voice comes out broken as he stares at me with wide, pleading eyes, begging me to see him. To understand something, I'm not sure I can.

"I told you I wasn't good for you. I told you that you deserved someone better. I knew you would, but part of me hoped you wouldn't go and stay away."

"I was eighteen." My defenses start to rise, old wounds piling up on top of each other, festering.

"I know. Fuck. I know that. I fucking hate myself for what I did to you that night. For the way it changed everything here." Both hands reach up into his hair this time, fingers pulling at the ends of his curls. His eyes are wide and glassy as his chest heaves in breath after breath.

"Clay." I start towards him, jumping back when he puts his hands up to stop me. They fall back to his sides, chin tucking into his chest, defeated.

"Jesus Christ, you're terrified of me. How can I stand here and tell you that I want *you* when you're scared of me?"

"Want?" I breathe, my vision tunneling onto him, because it's always been him. "Not wanted?"

"Yes, Leni. *Want*." Clay backs up, bracing himself against the wall as his hands drop to rest on his knees. His head lifts, enough to take me in. "You're the only thing I've ever wanted. I never stopped wanting you. How could I? You're my home."

"Then why did you let me go? Why didn't you come after me? Why did you write me all those letters and never send them? Why—"

"Because you were dead!" His voice explodes, spittle flying from his mouth as he sinks to the ground. Head in his hands, he takes in a shuddering breath. "You were fucking dead. I watched my own hands kill you in that nightmare." Shaky palms turn up to me; tears streak down his face. "I killed you. I know—I know it wasn't real, but I watched it like it was."

"Clay," I croak, voice sounding foreign to my ears. Dropping down next to him, I pull his open palm to my face. I press a kiss to the heel of it, then press it to my cheek, shifting my gaze back and forth between his.

"I can't risk you. Anything but you. Anyone but you."

I nod, squeezing my eyes shut to try and stem the tears welling in my eyes. "I'm not afraid of you."

He snorts, wiping at the moisture on his cheeks. "I think the evidence proves otherwise. It's okay," his voice softens as he runs his thumb along my cheekbone, tucking a loose wave behind my ear. "I don't blame you for being scared."

"It's not you," I reiterate. Pulling my knees up into my chest, I wrap my arms around them, fisting my hands so tight that I can feel my nails dig into my palms. "I lied," I whimper. "About everything. I wasn't mugged." My voice cracks, all the bravado from earlier gone. Clay sits up straighter, his eyes never leaving mine as he gives me the time to find the words. "My ID was in my phone case."

Reaching back, I pluck the little plastic card out of my pocket and toss it at him, watching his eyes widen.

"I couldn't take a plane, so I got on the bus."

"You took a bus? In the middle of the night?"

I turn my face away, shame burning my cheeks.

"Sorry." He squeezes my ankle gently, leaving his fingers there, wrapped around it like an anchor. "What else were you supposed to do? I'm so sorry. I shouldn't have let you leave. I should've gotten you a new room, made sure you got back safe."

"It's not your fault." I turn back to face him, dropping my head down to rest my cheek on my knee. "It wasn't a mugging. I told them that to make up for having no phone and no ID. I even threw my backpack away in the hospital to sell the story."

"Why?" He looks at me softly now, no judgment, no disapproval. His eyes full of an understanding no one else would ever give me.

"I didn't want them to know. I didn't want anyone to know because then they'd all know how stupid I am."

"Leni..."

"No, it's okay. I know it was stupid. I did so many things wrong that trip. So many things that should have ended so much worse than they did. I'm not afraid of *you*. I'm afraid of the way men move sometimes, not you. I just...I know the kind of violence some men are capable of now. I've felt it."

All the color drains from his face as he takes in my words.

"I was in a stupid little dress," I mumble, talking into my hands so that I don't have to look at him. "I fought him off as hard as I could. Bought myself enough time that he didn't finish what he started. Fought back hard enough that he forgot to lock the door, and someone happened to walk by and hear me scream. I got lucky."

Clay is quiet. When I tip my face up to his, I see a fury like I have never seen before. Sure, Clay throwing a chair at the wall was scary, but this? This is an anger that supersedes any I have witnessed in my lifetime.

"I'm alright," I offer halfheartedly.

"It's okay if you're not," he whispers as his face softens. His fingers flex in and out, going through the motions of cracking his knuckles, like Ethan does.

"But I am," I insist, even as my bottom lip starts to tremble. The pressure in my chest is too much. The weight of everything I've been keeping secret spills out of me as the tears fall like rain. "I'm okay."

"No, baby." He spreads his legs wide so he can pull me into

his chest. "You're not, but that's okay." Settling my legs on either side of him, I fit perfectly around his body, burying my face in his chest as I sob.

I don't know how long we sit there, but Clay never complains. He holds me while I soak his t-shirt, practically washing it as I drain every last drop from my eyes. He continues to hold me, even after I stop crying. Deft fingers smooth my hair back, letting me sink even further into him as exhaustion washes over me. As I'm about to fall asleep, he slips his fingers into my hair, pulling my head back a little.

"Leni," he whispers, one hand reaching up to smooth the hair away from my face. I wait for him to continue; the intensity on his face steals my breath away. "I really need a shower."

I grin, a little laugh huffing out of me as I start to push away from him.

"Wait." He grabs the side of my face. His warm fingers spread across my cheek as he darts his eyes back and forth between mine. "I'm so sorry that happened to you. I'm sorry you feel like you have to keep that buried. Thank you for telling me."

I nod, not trusting my voice to answer him. His thumb moves over my bottom lip, light enough to make it tickle. Fire licks up my skin where he's touching me.

"I'm dying to kiss you."

Butterflies unleash in my stomach. A bolt of something raw and needy shoots down into my core when I realize how badly I want him to kiss me. "So kiss me," I breathe, leaning back as my eyes flutter closed. He tips his face toward me, and soft, warm lips press a gentle kiss to the tip of my nose.

"I'm still not sure I should." His breath is hot on my face, while his words feel like a dagger to my heart. I can't fucking do this with him. The back and forth. The not knowing if he'll choose me one second and change his mind the next.

"Right," I growl, scrambling off him. I flee to the other side of the room as fast as I can.

"Leni..."

"No. It's fine." I'm too exhausted to cry anymore. All my tears are gone, and this rejection isn't new. It's another chapter in what he's dealt me before.

"Leni, it's not that simple. It's..." He sighs, gripping the back of his neck as he stands in front of the bathroom, swiveling at the waist like he's trying to figure out what to do. "No, you know what?" Something sparks in his eyes, a hunger I've never seen from him before. "Fuck it."

Chapter 15

Sounds like you do, Sue

Clay

I MARCH ACROSS THE BEDROOM, CLOSING THE GAP between us in three long strides before I have her face in my hands. My thumbs press into her jawline, tilting her face up toward mine.

"Are you sure?" My voice comes out rough, gravel in my throat, my body vibrating with the sheer need I feel for her. She nods, and that's all it takes for me to snap. One last look into her eyes, and I crash my mouth into hers.

She surges into me with an intensity I feel burning me from the inside out. She's so fucking beautiful, so fucking perfect. Her hands glide over the stubble on my face before sliding back to sink into my hair. I moan when her fingernails scrape my scalp.

I'm fucking lost to her. Gone. Died and found myself in heaven. Kissing Leni feels like taking my first real breath in years. She's the feast after a famine. An oasis in the desert. She is life itself, breathing oxygen into my starving lungs. I want her like I've never wanted anything in my entire life. She—this—is everything.

My right hand slips into her hair, fisting it, taking the kiss deeper. She gasps, her lips parting enough for me to sweep my tongue inside. Without hesitation, her tongue meets mine stroke for stroke, like she needs me just as bad. As if she wants this as much as I do. She arches into me, the front of her body pressing into mine, rubbing against me as my left hand drops to her lower back. Hauling her even closer, wishing there was nothing between us. No space. No clothes. No past full of wasted time and second-guessing.

Leni pulls away, and I groan, holding myself back. Big green eyes look up at me through her dark lashes, her soft, pillowy lips curving into a smile.

"Hi," she whispers, her hands slipping from my hair to rest on my chest.

"Hey, pretty girl." I smooth her hair back, tucking wild strands behind her ears. Bouncing my eyes between hers, I keep one hand on her face, the other on her hip. "You're so fucking beautiful."

Her cheeks are already flushed from the kiss. She turns away, hiding her embarrassment, teeth sinking into that juicy bottom lip of hers. I want her mouth back on mine, fingers in my hair. As if she can hear my thoughts, she glances at me, fire in her eyes. The twin flame to mine.

"Kiss me again." She steps onto her tiptoes, her hands sliding up my chest and around the back of my neck, pulling me into her.

"Yes, ma'am," I breathe into her mouth. Her lips part, body arching into mine. This kiss is slower, more intentional. I take my time, memorizing every hitch in her breath, every gasp and moan as I explore her. My hands take on a mind of their own, wandering down her sides, over her hips, exploring every inch of her they can reach.

I grab her ass with both hands, squeezing hard enough to make her squeal.

"Fuck," she giggles, her voice breathy and light.

"Yeah," I mutter, my lips brushing hers again.

"Go." She gives me a nudge. The motion is so halfhearted, I'm not sure she means it. "Go shower."

"You gonna be here when I'm done?" I don't ask her what I want; I'm not sure if I'm ready to know if she regrets kissing me.

"Where would I go?"

"I don't know, just...don't."

Her lips quirk into an amused smile, eyes dancing with humor. "I'm not going anywhere, Cowboy. Are you going to go in there and overthink this?"

"Probably," I admit. My thoughts are already swirling with a million questions. A million reasons why that kiss was a bad idea. And why it can't happen again.

"Hmm." She settles back onto flat feet, taking a step back. Her hand still resting on my chest, an index finger tapping on my pec, as her eyes turn toward me, concern written across her features. "I won't chase you again. If you want me, you're going to have to prove it."

I cover her hand with my own, running my thumb up and down her index finger. "Yes, ma'am." Picking her hand off my chest, I bring her finger to my mouth, pressing the tip to my lips.

"Now be a good boy and go take a shower so we can go to bed."

Leni Kane, standing in her bedroom and using the phrase "good boy," is downright diabolical. My dick twitches in my jeans, bringing my attention down to the uncomfortably hard erection I'm sporting. Her gaze shifts down. A smirk plays on that sinful little mouth of hers when our eyes meet again.

"Take your time." She winks, turning around to give me an eyeful of her perfectly shaped ass before she disappears down the stairs.

Well fuck.

～

I WAKE UP FEELING HEAVY...LITERALLY. Somehow, Leni ended up nearly on top of me; her left leg draped across my midsection while her upper body practically covers my chest. Soft brown waves tickle my chin, and if my alarm wasn't blaring, I'd take the extra time to lie here and savor the way her body feels on mine. She stirs, grumbling about the noise as the obnoxious ringtone continues to get louder.

We're in the middle of the bed, too far away for me to reach my phone. I slip out from beneath her. "No," she grumbles, blindly reaching for me as I get out of bed. "Come back, you're warm."

I chuckle as I silence the alarm and lean forward, kneeling on the bed next to her. I plan to kiss her temple, like I did yesterday, only Leni has plans of her own. When I'm close enough to kiss her, she flips herself over and grabs my face, pulling my lips onto hers.

Goddamn, this woman can kiss. The second my lips open, she takes control, exploring my mouth, pulling my body closer as she surges up to meet me. I'm off balance, barely managing to straddle her body with my limbs, so I don't end up crushing her.

Warm hands slide beneath my shirt, her skin searing mine as she traces them around my chest, then down my abs. My cock jumps, growing harder as her fingers get closer to my waistband. I groan, nearly coming in my pants when she crooks her leg and rubs her knee into my groin.

"Fuck," I breathe into her mouth, lips brushing hers when I do.

"Have a good day at work," she says in such a sweet voice. Her eyes look anything but innocent and sweet right now.

"You're going to kill me," I mutter.

She leans forward, pecking me on the lips one more time before she sinks back into bed. "Hopefully not any time soon, Cowboy. There are things I'd like to do to you first."

I groan into her collarbone. My dick's practically weeping in my pants. "So mean," I whisper.

"I think you'll survive. Now get. I'm going back to sleep."

I shake my head into her shoulder, stopping to press a kiss to the hollow of her neck. "There's no surviving you, Leni girl." I wink, push off the bed, and make my way to the bathroom and get myself ready for work.

I call dispatch from my truck and clock in on my phone, debating if I'm going into the office or if I'll start patrolling right away instead. Mercer still wouldn't look at me yesterday, and I don't feel like continuing the silent treatment at work. On the other hand, I should go talk to him and make him work this shit out. I don't like being on the outs with my best friend. I came back here to set things right, not let our relationships get rocky.

Fuck. I try to clear my head of all things Leni as I make my way into the Hillcreek Courthouse. I don't need to lay all my cards out on the table for the boys, but I do need to settle things with Mercer so we can get back to normal.

I scan my badge to let myself into the Sheriff's office. Removing my hat, I send a wink to Miss Patsy, who, despite being nearly sixty years old, blushes like a schoolgirl whenever a deputy smiles at her. I head for the break room when I hear Mercer call my name. He's across the hall with Deputy Nathan Clark, his other best friend. He doesn't wave me over, so I wait until he's done.

"My office," Mercer mutters as he shuffles past me. I follow behind him, biting back a "yes sir." Automatic from my time in the corps, but dripping with sarcasm, I've seen Mercer get stuck in a tunnel slide at the park. It's hard to take him seriously. "Sit," he commands when we enter, walking around his desk to take his seat on the other side.

I do as I'm told, putting my cowboy hat on my knee, trying not to let my leg bounce. I knew he'd have things to say; knew he'd be mad at me. I'm a big boy. I can take a little verbal sparring from my boss...I think. Mercer taps his fingers on the desk before pulling something out of his shirt pocket. He tosses it down onto the surface.

It's a photograph. But not just any photograph. It shows Leni's soft brown waves, her ears, her neck, but her face? My stomach churns. My hand balls into a fist as I struggle to swallow the rage threatening to spill out. One eye is swollen shut, hair in disarray, the other eye wide, wild. Her lips are split, the bottom one torn, a bruise blooming across one cheek, the other cheek sliced open as well.

"Did you do that to her?"

My head snaps up, eyes searching his in disbelief. "The fuck did you just ask me?"

"Did you..." He leans forward, pushing up from his chair, looking down at me with the wrath of God on his face. "Do that?" His finger jabs at the photo of Leni. My whole body coils underneath me as I let the weight of his question sink in.

"Are you serious? Do you really think I could—"

"Answer the goddamn question, Traeger. Did you do that to my sister?"

"No! Jesus, Mercer."

Mercer flops back into his chair, his shoulders slumping as he breathes out a harsh breath. One hand scrubs down his jaw as his gaze settles on me, the friend I've known since junior high, finally peeking through.

"Do you seriously think I could have done something like that?"

"You?" He quirks an eyebrow. "Hell no. Twenty-one-year-old you with an axe to grind and night terrors plaguing you...I don't know, Clay. Felt like shit to ask."

"Damn right it did, you asshole. I would never lay a hand on her." My teeth grind together, fingertips digging into my jeans, temper barely at bay.

He sighs, resting his elbows on the desk, head in his hands. "I know—I know that. Fuck. Why did she lie, though? It was messed up enough that she lied about where she was, but to lie about finding you?"

"I don't know, Merc. Maybe she thought she was protecting me. She was there to help me. I don't think that desire changed after I scared her."

"You didn't hurt her?"

I look down at my hands, trying to shake the image of my fist buried in the drywall, inches from where Leni's head had been. "I was rough," I sigh. "More than I should have been, but I swear to God, Mercer, I'd rip my own heart out before I ever did that to her. Or anyone."

He nods. His eyes still holding some of that heat. The Kane boys are fiercely protective of their loved ones, and none more than Leni. There wasn't a boy in town who broke her heart and got away with it. They were lucky if they only ran into one brother, much less the pack of them.

"No more secrets." He jabs a hand my way. I flinch. "Motherfucker, you're hiding something else! What is it?"

I shake my head, rising from my chair because if I stay, and he keeps talking, I will tell him everything, and there are some things that aren't mine to tell.

"Sit your ass back down!" he hollers from behind me. "Clayton Sue Traeger! Tell me your secrets!" He's screaming as I make my way out of the office. Deputy Clark quirks an eyebrow as I pass.

"Don't have a middle name." I grin.

"Sounds like you do," he grunts. He's quiet, more reserved, like Brooks. A couple of years younger than Mercer and me, and probably closer to Toby's age. I don't know that much about him, but I know Mercer has mentored him. I know he plays one hell of a poker game. Last time we played, he cleaned house. Toby was furious.

"Nah, the Kane boys didn't like that they all got triple-named, and I never did. They gave it to me."

"Like I said." He gives me a wicked grin. "Sounds like you do, Sue."

"Fucking goddamn it," I curse as I get into my cruiser. My phone vibrates in my pocket.

MERCER

I swear to God

if I have to camp outside the cabin to learn your secrets...I will

> You have to have better things to do with your time

> Sheriff

MERCER

I. Don't. Like. Secrets

> Yea well I don't like nosy little bitches

MERCER

Watch it. Or I'll take this to the group chat.

I'll get there Merc. There are some things I know that aren't mine to share

MERCER

Fine. Have your secrets.

Let them eat you alive

evil laugh

asshole.

Chapter 16

What I Want is Fried Pickles

Leni

I wake up with my arms wrapped around Clay's pillow, his spicy rustic scent flooding my senses. It must be mid-morning, seeing as the light is pouring in through the front windows, leaving my room warm and cozy.

My phone dings once, alerting me to a new voicemail. I assume it was the missed phone call that woke me. Heaving a sigh, I roll myself over and reach for my phone that's charging on my nightstand. The missed call is a number I don't recognize, but it's a Benson area code. I open the voicemail app, hit speaker, and stretch out across the bed as I listen.

"Hello, this message is for Eleanor Kane. My name is Daniel Riley, and I'm calling from Rosemont Prep. We have reviewed your application and would love to schedule an interview with you sometime next week to see if you would be a good fit for our students and teaching program. You can reach me at this number. I have also sent an email to the one you provided on your resume. Feel free to email back at your earliest convenience. We look forward to hearing from you."

I wait, willing my heart to leap for joy, or at the very least a smile to crack my face. But nothing happens. Teaching was my life, but I think I enjoyed it because I did what I wanted. I created the program, the curriculum that I taught, and I never had to go off of what someone else wanted. It was exactly what I needed in my pursuit of independence.

With a sigh, I scroll through my social media, looking for something inspiring to do. With riding and hiking out of the question, I'm stuck inside the cabin. I brought my Kindle with me, but every time I pick it up, I can't focus. My brain's too busy wondering what it would look like to let Clayton in.

Like...all the way in. Not just a couple of stolen kisses, but actually into my life. Would he want that? Would it work? I'm seconds away from spiraling into a deep dive of feelings when I scroll past an advertisement for a writing competition. It takes me three tries to find my way back to it.

"Modern Ranch Life wants to hear your stories. Your successes and failures, what you do to keep your ranch going, and how you infuse new life into your business." I stare at my screen, tugging one sleeve down over my thumb before lifting it to my mouth and chewing on the soft cotton sleep shirt. I could write about my dad, or even my grandpa. How they turned this place into an empire. There've been a few articles written on my family, but none from our perspective, nothing that shows the little details of how we're still ranching on this scale.

I might be out of the loop about how things run now, but I know the stories we grew up on, and I know how it all started.

Opening my laptop, I type out a rough outline for the story of Kane Ridge Ranch.

I'm four pages deep when I hear the pounding of hooves approaching the cabin. This place is a prototype for future guest cabins. It's an A-frame cabin; the entire front is windows that see into the front room, kitchen, and bathroom. Lucky for me, the one room that isn't completely visible is the bedroom on the second floor. I run a mental checklist through my head and wonder if I've left any clothing or shoes out for someone to see.

Shit. I hope Clay locked the door.

"This is so stupid." I hear Toby's deep voice.

"What are you doing here then?"

"I'm bored. Brooks isn't here to yell at me."

"Fair enough." Adler's voice comes muffled through the door. "Fuck, it's locked."

"Locked? Who locks their door on the ranch?"

"I don't know? Clay? Think it's something he picked up in the city?"

"Maybe...seems weird. Did you bring the key?"

I feel my heart jolt. Of course, there's a million spare keys to the cabin, even if it is unofficially mine.

"No," Adler hisses. "Why would I bring a key? It's not supposed to be locked."

"Jesus Christ, you dragged me all the way out here, and you didn't even bring a key?"

I shove a pillow over my face to muffle my laughter. These two are ridiculous. God, I miss them.

"How was I supposed to know he locked it? He has to be hiding something. Do you think she's in there?"

"Who?"

"I don't know. Whoever he's fucking."

"How should I know?"

"Let's go get the key."

"Nah," Toby sighs, his voice growing softer. "I have actual work to do."

"But you just..." Their voices trail off as I hear hoofbeats moving away from the cabin. Holy shit, that was close. I reach for my phone and text Clay.

> The boys were here snooping around

HE WHO SHALL NOT BE NAMED

Who this?

> Fuck off Traeger

HE WHO SHALL NOT BE NAMED

Did they see you? Are we finally not
hiding you?

> No. I told you

> I'm no amateur

HE WHO SHALL NOT BE NAMED

Right. You're just really good at hiding.

> Pretty sure you never saw me coming in
> Stealth

HE WHO SHALL NOT BE NAMED

Or we let you win to make you feel better

> bullshit

HE WHO SHALL NOT BE NAMED

Wanna find out?

> Yea actually I do.

HE WHO SHALL NOT BE NAMED

Deal

I'll text you when I'm on my way home

$20 says I find you in ten minutes

> Hmm. Keep talking.

HE WHO SHALL NOT BE NAMED

Fine

I'll bring burgers from the Rail.

Winner gets fried pickles

Oh you're on Cowboy

What are my parameters?

HE WHO SHALL NOT BE NAMED

You have to be within 1 mile of the cabin

No running off and hiding in the outbuildings or in the big house

I know you like to cheat

I am deeply offended by the insinuation sir.

Fine. Text me when you leave

You better not forget my pickles

HE WHO SHALL NOT BE NAMED

Would't forget my pickles for the world

This is what Clayton Traeger reduces me to: a simpering little girl who smiles at electronic devices. Ugh. I need to get out of here. Picking up my phone, I call Daniel Riley back and schedule an interview.

HE WHO SHALL NOT BE NAMED

I'm heading your way. Clock starts when I park.

I DON'T REPLY, I've been spending way too much time overthinking a hiding spot all day. The copse of trees where I hide my Jeep is too obvious. But then, would he know it was too obvious and check the one on the opposite side of the property instead? Hiding in the cellar would probably work. The point of stealth isn't to hide in one spot; it's to run the timer down without being caught. One year, I followed Toby and hid in the first place he looked, so he wouldn't think to circle back and check again.

It used to be all about knowing your opponents and fucking with them. I don't know how Clay will play now, but I'm sure he's already running scenarios through his head. I'm still not sure which direction to go; limiting my parameters to a mile around the cabin makes it hard when the cabin is surrounded by a wide open space.

Throwing open the cabin door, I decide to let my feet direct me. I'm not surprised when they carry me toward the Jeep. The trees out here are small; they never progressed past pole trees. This whole plot used to be pastureland, so big groups of trees weren't a priority. It's my luck that there's a downed pile of trees with enough space between them and the ground for me to hide underneath. I toss some loose branches on top, hoping it looks natural and not manmade, before I wiggle under the tree and wait.

I hear Clay drive by, wheels churning up gravel as he slows to a crawl past the copse of trees. Fucking asshole is cheating. He's not supposed to look before he parks! I can't call him out on it because he'd know I was here. Sneaky bastard.

HE WHO SHALL NOT BE NAMED
Ready or not baby girl

A thrill shoots through my body. My shoulder shivers in anticipation. It isn't long before Clay's footsteps pound through the tree line. He circles my Jeep, whistling in a high-pitched, creepy voice. I've heard the whistle before. I'm struggling to remember which horror film it might be from before I realize I no longer see Clay, and I can't hear him either.

That's when I realize he was being loud on purpose. He

wanted me to know where he was, so he could distract me. *Shit.* I sit up on my elbows as quietly as possible, trying to peer around the branches I tacked across the top of these trees.

"Where the fuck—" Big, strong hands grip my waist, hauling me backward as I scream. It's the only logical thing to do when an unseen entity pulls you backwards out of a hiding spot.

Clay's laughter fills the grove, his breath hot against my ear as he manhandles me away from the tree. I can't fight my own giggles as I kick my feet in the air, realizing he's got me completely off the ground. I halfheartedly pound on his arms; I'm not even sure I want him to let me go.

"It's cute you think that will work," he huffs into my ear, his arms tightening like a vise around me.

"I'm not trying to hurt you." I grin, tipping my head back to look at him. The smile he's wearing takes my breath away. It's beautiful the way his eyes are lit. He's alive, happy. I reach back and rest my palm on his cheek, running my thumb along his cheekbone. Clay's eyes flutter close, his head tilting into my hand.

Lowering my feet to the ground, he spins me around. His hands cup my face. "Hey, beautiful." That soft, unguarded smile takes over his face.

"Hey, Cowboy." I bite my lip, feeling giddy when his eyes dart away, distracted. Shoving his chest as hard as I can, I watch him topple over the downed trees behind us. He hurls obscenities as I haul ass back toward the cabin. "The pickles are mine!" I shout over my shoulder, and his laughter echoes after me.

"Not a chance in hell!" He's gaining on me, booming footsteps crashing through the underbrush behind me. I'm nearly at the cabin when a giant body slams into mine. The force of it knocks me right off my feet. Clay spins us, catching the brunt of the fall as we collide with the ground.

"Oh my God!" I can't stop giggling, looking down at him as he realizes how hard he hit the dirt. "You are going to feel that tomorrow."

He gasps, struggling for air as I press my body against his. "Fucking right I will." He gives me a goofy grin. "Worth it. I won those pickles fair and square."

My eyes widen as I glance up at the deck, spotting a bag of food from the Rail sitting outside the door. I look back down at him, grinning like a madwoman.

"Uh-uh." He flips me over, his big body pinning me to the ground before I have a second to realize what's happening. His hand rests behind my head, keeping my skull from smacking into the driveway.

I'm breathless, chest heaving from sprinting to the cabin, his proximity not exactly helping either. When he looks down at me, something carnal and hungry sparks in his eyes. I feel that spark all the way down in my core, lust and need surging through my blood.

"Fuck it?" I ask, my eyes dipping down to his lips.

"Fuck it," he breathes, his mouth crashing down into mine. I moan when his tongue sweeps in. My body is losing all ability to hold still as my insides are set on fire with need. He commands my mouth, tipping my head to the perfect toe-curling angle. Clay presses his hips forward, pinning his erection into my abdomen. I wish I were a little taller, wish that monster he's got tucked inside his Levi's was hitting between my thighs, rubbing the ache that's building up in my core.

I'm panting harder, my body writhing by the time he pulls away. He rears above me, using his elbow to stabilize himself. His hand still protecting my head. His eyes drag over every inch of my face. They move lower, taking in the way our bodies are pressed together from the waist down. I feel him grow harder between us. His heated gaze comes back up to my face.

"Your body is insane." His muscles shift, the left side of his body digging into mine as his right hand glides along my side, the warmth of his skin bleeding through my thin leggings. I gasp when he reaches higher, touch grazing my ribs, his big, rough hand coming up to cup my breast. "So goddamn perfect," he mutters when his thumb brushes over my nipple, hips bucking beneath him.

"Clay," I breathe a quiet plea, my voice breathy and full of need.

Stormy grey eyes come back to mine, his lips tipping up into a smile. "You can have the pickles. I'm hungry for something else."

I groan, my whole body aching for this man. "Are you gonna do something about that hunger?"

"Not tonight." He grins, swiping his thumb over my nipple one more time.

"What?" I pout my lower lip.

"I'm not going anywhere. Let's have dinner. Catch up, talk some."

"Then you'll eat me?"

Clay's eyes widen, before one side of his mouth tips up into a smirk. "If that's what you want." He leans forward, nipping at my pouty lip.

"What I want is fried pickles."

He chuckles, hauling me off the ground. Once I'm on my feet, he gives me a little push toward the cabin. "I ordered two sides of pickles, Leni. You can have them both if you want 'em."

"Now you're just flirting with me."

He tips his head to the side as he holds the door open for me. "Is it working?"

"Might be, yeah."

Chapter 17

All Mine For Now

Clay

Leni settles at the kitchen table while I grab a couple of beers from the fridge. A sexy little moan escapes her lips when she bites into the first fried pickle chip. I want to lean down and capture it with my mouth, devour all her little noises so I can keep them for myself. Keep her, for myself.

Leni's little two-seater table has a chair on either end; it's big enough to seat four, but she has one side pressed up against the wall. I bring my chair to the long side, putting myself in the middle, closer to her. Her gaze meets mine, emerald green eyes peering out from beneath long, beautiful lashes.

I lift her chin with my thumb and fingers, pressing a kiss to the corner of her mouth. Now that I've kissed her, I don't think I can stop or keep myself away from her.

"Sit down. Before I eat your burger."

"So bossy." I grin, settling into my chair. I take a swig of the cold beer, watching as she digs into her food, eyes rolling back at the first bite. *I am not jealous of a burger,* I repeat to myself, trying to believe it. But it's not true. She's enjoying her food way too much and sitting too far away from me.

Reaching over, I grab the bottom rung of her chair and pull her into my lap, one leg on either side of her. She squeals, lettuce falling off her burger as I spin her around. When her eyes meet mine, a fire blazes within her. One I want to stoke into a frenzy later. I nuzzle into her neck instead, running my nose upward until my lips brush her ear.

"I've wasted enough time with you. I'm not wasting anymore."

She gulps, wide-eyed, and nods. "Okay."

"Okay," I repeat, settling my hand on her thigh before I turn to eat my burger one-handed. "What'd you do today, Leni? Other than pick the most predictable hiding spot?"

"Shut up," she mumbles around a mouthful of fried pickles. "It wasn't that predictable!"

"The branches were a nice touch, I'll give you that."

She smacks my arm, shaking her head as she swallows back some beer. "It was a perfectly acceptable hiding spot. If we had been playing in the dark, you never would have found me."

"I'll always find you." I tuck a stray hair behind her ear, my eyes searching hers.

She glances away as a blush works its way over her cheeks. I lift her chin, guiding her eyes back to mine.

"Tell me if it's too much, Leni. Tell me if I move too fast, because now that I've tasted you, you're the only thing I can think about."

"It's not." She offers me an earth-shattering smile. The kind that lights up her eyes and reminds me that she is the most beautiful woman I have ever met. "I'm all yours."

For now.

She's going to leave me again. The thought makes my gut churn. We've kissed. That's all. I shouldn't expect anything more from her, but for some reason, this feels like more. Leni Kane isn't the kind of person you can work out of your system. Hell, I've been trying to avoid this for ten fucking years, and look at me, tucked in around her like she belongs here. Like I have any right to keep her here and call her mine.

"I scheduled an interview in Benson for next week."

I nod, chugging half my beer in one go as reality sets in. Leni didn't just move on from me ten years ago. She moved on from this whole place, and until she fixes things with her family, there's no point in asking her to stay. I need to figure out why she won't tell them, or consider moving back. Maybe if I can figure out how to fix what I broke, I can convince her to stay. Convince her that she doesn't have to live five hours away in order to live her own life.

"What's the interview for?"

"A teaching position at a prep academy."

"Huh." I cock my head at her. She doesn't seem enthusiastic about it. "Not your cup of tea?"

"Not really." She picks at the breading on a pickle, peeling it back piece by piece. "I wrote something today."

"Oh?" I rescue the pickle she's defacing and drop it in my mouth before she can protest.

"Modern Ranch Life Magazine asked for stories. I wrote one about the ranch."

That makes me perk up. "Can I read it?"

"What?" She looks surprised, and my heart aches for her. She's so stuck in this mindset that no one believes in her. She has no idea how much her family has championed her successes. I thought they were like that all the time, celebrating with her. Now I wonder if they did it in the family group chat as a way to try to show her. To reach her when she wouldn't let them in. "You actually want to read it?"

"Hell, yeah, I do. I love stories about the ranch, and if you wrote it, it has to be good."

She rolls her eyes. "You haven't read a single thing I've written."

"Bullshit." I push away from the table and lumber up the stairs. Searching through my bags until I find the bundle of her letters I kept from all those years ago. She's standing at the kitchen sink when I get back, leaning against the porcelain as she watches me move toward her. "I read all of these." I hold up the envelopes. Her eyes widen when she realizes what they were. "Multiple times, actually."

"Clay." She reaches for them, but I hesitate. These were all I had left of her after that night. They kept me from losing my mind while I was struggling through the panic and PTSD. They were the lifeline I needed to remind me it was worth fighting. Leni must read it in my eyes, because she tucks her hand over mine, letting me keep the letters.

"You can read it, of course, you can. They probably won't pick it for the magazine anyway, but it felt good to write it."

She squeezes my hand, then walks around me toward the living room. We settle on the small couch. I place the computer on my lap when she offers it.

"Leni." My voice breaks when I finish the article, eyes meeting hers in awe. "This is really good."

"It is?"

"Yeah, baby. It's really fucking good. If they don't publish this, someone else will. Holy shit." I skim back through the document, my eyes finding the lines about her brothers continuing the legacy. About how her mom has done everything to preserve the authenticity of their buildings and way of life. She might not think she needs her family, but this article is proof that they are a huge part of her identity. The way she wrote it, there's a longing in the words here. She's homesick, and I wonder if she even knows it.

"It's really fucking good, Leni girl." I set the laptop on the coffee table and haul her into my lap. "When do you turn it in?"

"I sent it already." She bites her bottom lip, glancing down at me. "The deadline was tonight, so they should start going through submissions in the next couple of days."

"I'm proud of you." She snorts, rolling her sassy green eyes. "Listen here, brat." I slip my hand up into her hair, squeezing a handful at the roots before I pull her face down toward mine. "I'm fucking proud of you, and you're going to accept that fact without putting yourself down. You're not rolling over, boohooing about your situation. You're here, figuring out what comes next and putting yourself out there while you do that. Stop acting like no one believes in you, Eleanor. Because I do."

Her eyes turn glossy, and that pouty bottom lip of hers trembles.

"Fuck," I whisper, kneading the back of her head with my fingers, attempting to lessen the sting. "I didn't mean to make you cry. I—"

Her lips slam into mine, a leg straddling me on either side. She tips my head back and kisses me deeper. Harder. Our teeth clack as she claims my mouth in aggressive, needy kisses.

My hands settle on her hips, staying in a "safe" spot as she wrecks any notion of who I thought I was and what I thought I wanted. I thought I was fine without her. I thought I wanted her to find someone else and live her life without me. Now, if she asked me to go with her, to chase whatever dream she finds for herself, I would.

"Thank you," she breathes into my lips, pecking me once more before she pulls her face back. Her head tips down to look at my hands, a smirk pulling at her lips. "You can touch me, you know."

"I know," I breathe. Not sure that that's true. Once I touch her, I won't be able to stop. I'm already looking for any excuse to get my hands on her. If this is all she wants from me, if she's planning on leaving without me, I'm not sure I'll survive if I touch her more.

I stare at my hands on her hips, giving her a gentle squeeze before I bring my eyes back to hers. "How are you not taken already?"

She huffs a laugh and takes my wrists, slowly dragging them around her backside. I swallow back a groan. She has the most incredible body. "I had this insane crush when I was younger."

"Oh, did you?"

"Mhm." She winks, nudging my hands to move up her back. "No one else really measured up."

I sigh, hands trailing up her back and over her shoulders. Goosebumps appear under my fingertips as I drag them down her arm. Her nipples pebble in her thin workout top. My mouth waters at the sight.

"What about you?" She drapes her arms over my shoulders, the tips of her fingers playing with the curls at the nape of my neck. "Why are you still single?"

"I never really looked," I answer honestly.

"How come?" She sits back, her head tilted to the side, eyes assessing me.

"Who would I be good enough for? The insomniac veteran who comes from a shitty family and occasionally has panic attacks."

"First of all, the man who fathered you and the woman who abandoned you are not your family. Second, me...for starters."

I chuckle, rolling my eyes. "I'm really not good enough for you. Not even close."

Leni grabs my chin, lifting my gaze to meet hers. She stares into my soul, stripping me bare with the weight of her eyes. "You were raised by the best man that I know. I've seen your heart, the one that aches for anyone or anything in pain. I've seen your kindness and your generosity. Ten years away didn't change that. You deserve everything you want in this life and more."

"What if the thing that I want risks all the other good things in my life?"

"What's life without a little risk?"

"Safe. A life without risk is safe."

"Is that what you want?" She pulls away, pressing down on my shoulders to stand. "You want to play it safe? For the rest of your life?"

"No." I'm scrambling. The thoughts in my head rush through faster than I can organize them. She sees the pause as hesitation, more indecision, when that's the furthest thing from what this is. I'm trying not to prematurely tell her I love her. Trying not to get down on my knees and beg her to stay. To let me fix what's broken between her and the family so that everything can go back to the way it's supposed to be.

I see the disappointment dim her eyes, shoulders stooping with a sigh as she walks away.

"Leni," I launch myself at her, spinning her around and cradling her face in my hands. "I want you. You're all I've ever fucking wanted."

Her eyes bounce back and forth between mine, nodding once. "Then stop pretending you don't, Clay. I can't do the 'will they, won't they' bit with you. Either have me, or don't have me. It's that simple."

"It's not that simple, and you know it. Us being together and falling apart affects more than just us. Your family is my family. I have no one without them. I already lost you once, and it nearly destroyed me. How do I pretend that the risks don't matter?"

"You don't pretend anything. You choose to take a chance

on us and stop planning for the worst-case scenario. You choose me over the fear. You let *me* be enough."

"You are," I whisper, my hands slipping back into her soft hair. The strands move through my fingers like silk. "But what if *I'm* not?"

"You are more than enough." She whispers the words I've so desperately needed to hear my whole life.

I kiss her tenderly, pouring all the words I didn't say into the kiss, hoping she can feel them. Hoping she understands how much I mean it.

Chapter 18

Who Buys One Condom?

Clay

THERE'S A MOMENT WHEN I WAKE UP, AND I DON'T KNOW where I am. I tighten my arms instinctually, pulling something warm and soft deeper into my embrace. I open my eyes to a headful of brown waves tucked below my chin. Lilacs and vanilla flood my senses as I bury my face in her hair.

Home.

I'm home.

Leni gives a little sigh, one that has my morning wood straining against my boxer briefs. I slide my hands down to her hips, intending to rub her ass into my erection, when I realize how little clothing she's wearing. I swear she went to bed wearing more than this. There's skin everywhere. She's soft and warm, and the more I let my calloused hands explore, the more receptive her body is to my touch.

I trail my fingertips up her thigh and over her ribcage, taking note of the way her whole body shivers into me. I trace my way up to her shoulder, down her collarbone, and in between her breasts. A breathy gasp escapes her as her back arches. Continuing down her center, I trail my fingers along her stomach, pausing to toy with the little bow on the waistband of her panties.

When I slip a finger below that waistband, I pause, asking a silent question. Leni hums her approval, rubbing her tight little ass into my crotch, giving me the best kind of friction. I let my fingers explore her further, brushing over her smooth mound, into the warmth between her legs.

"Jesus, Leni," I breathe into her hair, barely able to contain the groan that's trying to rip through my chest when I feel how wet she is. "Is all this for me?"

"Mhm." She arcs again, putting more pressure into my groin, swirling her hips.

Fuck. Me.

I need to see her. All of her.

Pulling my hand from between her legs, I rip the covers back, baring her whole body to me. She pouts at the sudden loss of warm blankets, but I hardly have it in me to look at her face right now. Not when her perfectly curvy body is splayed out before me. She's wearing a light pink bralette, the material so sheer I can see her nipples. A matching pair of underwear covers her mound, the little triangle of her thong wedged up between her pussy lips. Her long, tanned legs are thick at the hips and thighs, her calves toned and muscular. God, I want her squeezing my head between those thighs.

When I glance back at her, she's watching me with the same desperate intensity in her gaze. Her eyes drift down my face, to my chest, and then lower. The way they darken with arousal makes it hard for me to breathe.

"Leni," my voice breaks. I have no fucking words to describe everything I'm feeling right now. She is perfect. "So fucking pretty." I let my hand wander down the same path from earlier, stopping at her hip as I give a gentle squeeze.

"Clay," she whines, squirming a little under my gaze.

I hook a finger under her chin to bring her face to mine. Her lips part when my hand lowers to her chest, thumb grazing over her nipple. I take the opening and claim her mouth with mine, swiping my tongue against hers with aggressive, needy strokes. She kisses me back, bringing her hands up to my hair, fingernails scratching deep into my scalp. Closing the space between us, she rubs herself against my leg, needing more from me.

I flip her onto her back, lining my body over top of hers to press my leg into her core. She grinds on my thigh, her arousal soaking my skin, and I'm going out of my mind with how badly I want this girl.

"I need you," I murmur as I kiss along her jaw, taking a minute to tug at her earlobe. As my kisses draw further down her neck towards her chest, I shift my weight further down her hips, my leg moving from between hers, drawing out a whimper.

"So needy," I suck a nipple into my mouth, sheer fabric and all. Her gasp is all I need to keep going. With the tight little bud between my teeth, I bite enough to sting, but not to hurt her. By the time I switch to give the other side attention, she's writhing underneath me, breathy little pants coming from between those perfect pink lips of hers. They're puffy from my kisses, her hair a tangled mess up on her head.

I pull away to drink her in. This is how I want to wake up every morning from now on, with Leni underneath me, hair a mess, body wild with the need building up inside of her.

"Clay, please," she begs. And fuck if that doesn't do exactly what I need it to. I slide off the end of the bed, pulling her thighs with me so that her pussy is right where I want it. I kiss her inner thighs, light teasing touches that have her squirming. Starting at her ankles, I make my way past her thighs, hooking my fingers into her lacy thong, and I drag it back down her legs, my eyes never leaving hers. Her chest is heaving, breaths coming in quick and uneven.

I take my time exploring her, using my fingers to spread her open. She has the prettiest pussy I've ever seen, and she is soaked for me. My fingers glisten with her desire when I pull my hands away. She withers, her thighs clenching to give some much-needed friction to her clit.

I'm done playing, now, I need to taste her. Gliding my hands beneath her, I cup her ass and bring her center right up to my face so I can give her entrance an experimental flick of my tongue. Her head drops back down to the mattress, fingers sinking into the sheets in a death grip. I take my time, figuring out where she wants me and what she likes. Her body responds to the slow, steady pressure I give her clit while I undulate my tongue against it.

She's so damn responsive to me. Every little flick gets a moan from her. Her hips buck off the bed when I hit the right spot. I shift my hands so that I'm holding her in place, reaching to play with a nipple when I feel her muscles start to tense, coiling beneath me, but she doesn't let go.

"Clay." Her fingers leave the sheets to twist around my hair. "I need more. Please."

"So fucking polite. What do you need, baby? Do you want me to fuck you with my fingers while I eat this perfect little pussy?"

"Oh, God, yes. That—that, Clay."

"Yes, ma'am." I give her nipple one last pinch before I trail my hand back down her body and slip my finger inside her tight, wet heat. Bringing my lips back to her pussy, I suck her clit between my teeth, making her buck as she starts to ride my hand and face. Her muscles clench tightly around me, breath coming in shallow pants now. I slip another finger inside of her and lick her exactly as she liked it earlier. When I curl my fingers inside of her, she cries out.

"Yes, Clay!" She jolts into me, her back arching as her hips take over the rhythm she set. I snap my own hips forward, finding the edge of the bed exactly where I need it. The more she builds herself up, the more her body shakes with the need to come. I curl my fingers inside of her, using deep pressure on my fingertips while I suck her clit. My mind spins as she shatters around me, chanting my name when she comes. I keep my eyes on her, watching as she falls apart, my own release spilling into my boxers.

She rides out the waves of her orgasm, pulling my hair tight enough that it stings, but I don't mind the pain. Watching Leni come apart at the seams is what dreams are made of. Kissing my way back up her body, I bring my lips to hers, taking my time to memorize every little thing she does.

I pull away, my own chest heaving now. Glancing at the clock, I groan. "Fuck." I plant a final kiss on her lips before I shove off the bed and head for the bathroom.

"What about you?" Leni whines from the bed.

I turn to face her, pointing at the wet spot in my charcoal grey underwear. Her eyes widen, a feral grin taking over her face.

"Clayton Traeger, did you..."

"Come in my pants like a teenager? Yeah, I might have done that."

"Holy shit." She flops back down onto the bed, curling up with the sheets. I want to stay and revel in the fact that I'm the one who did that to her, but the clock is ticking, and it looks like I might be late to work again.

I expect to find her on the bed when I rush out of the shower and toward the stairs. Only the bed is empty, and my girl is waiting at the door for me with a travel mug of coffee and something wrapped up in a paper towel.

"Goddamn, you're perfect." I slip an arm around her back to haul her into me for another slow kiss.

She smiles, a blush painting her cheeks. "Be safe, Cowboy. I'll be waiting for you to get home."

Slipping into my boots, I grab the breakfast she has ready for me and head into town. I'm trying my best to wrangle my face into something passive, but my cheeks are starting to hurt from smiling so much. If I can't get things under control, I will never hear the end of it from Mercer and Ethan.

WHEN I ARRIVE at the Sheriff's office, Ethan is hanging around in the break room, talking to a few of the other dayshift guys.

"Hey." He nods, making room for me near the coffee pot. "How you been, brother?"

"Good." I pour myself a cup of black coffee and head back to the deputy's room. I wonder if Mercer is hanging around there, seeing how he's usually here in the mornings.

"You talk to Mercer recently?"

"Uh, yesterday, during shift," I offer, surprised that he's not somewhere in the office already.

"Something's up with him." Ethan leans against the cubicle wall, a scone in one hand, coffee in the other. I try to keep my face neutral, it's bad enough I brought up that night to Mercer, telling Ethan would be much worse. Ethan is the bruiser of the family. Addy might like to pick fights, but that's only for entertainment. Ethan enjoys kicking people's asses, and I don't need mine to be one of them.

"What do you mean?"

"He's doing that thing where he fixates on something. He's

on some sort of trail, but he won't tell me what it is. You guys running something undercover?"

"Nah, not that I know of." A stone drops into my gut because I have a feeling, I know exactly what Mercer is looking into, and it's not going to be good for anyone.

KANE BROS GROUP CHAT
E-MAN

My sources tell me our boy who may or may not be fucking someone came in and bought a value pack of condoms

> JFC are you kidding me with this shit

ADDY

Value pack huh? Got some big plans there buddy?

> She didn't have any smaller packs!

TOBES

That's not true... you can buy singles at the counter

MERC D

First question

Why do you know that Tobes?

Second... who buys one condom?

TOBES

Totally... yea... who does that?

E-MAN

I also heard he took home two burgers yesterday.

ADDY

That's really not that impressive. I can eat
three... easy

E-MAN

Correction

Two full meals

TOBES

Yea... I'm still not getting the correlation....

E-MAN

Jesus. It's suspicious with all the other
evidence

MERC D

Is it?

FUCKING HELL. I swear these guys are trying to run me off
again. Goddamn small towns with their busybody gossip tree.
If Bertie weren't best friends with Ethan, I'd probably go tell
her off. As it stands, she's been around the Kane family longer
than me, so I don't think that would go over well with anyone at
this point.

No wonder Leni didn't want anyone in town to know she's
home. There is no way it'd stay a secret for long. I forgot how
little privacy you have in a place like Hillcreek.

I'm about to respond to the group text when dispatch calls
my number over the radio.

"2799, Halfor SO."

"Halfor SO, 2799."

"2799, we have reports of a domestic at Cross Point, lot
twenty-two. Unknown injuries at this time, ambulance and
backup have been dispatched, Halfor SO."

"Copy SO, you can mark me en route."

"Copy that."

Dispatch wouldn't know this, but Cross Point is the trailer park where I grew up.

As far as I know, Caleb Traeger is still rotting in lot fourteen. I haven't seen him since the Kanes came for me when I was fifteen, nearly sixteen. Brooks and Orson came crashing in through the trailer door when they heard him screaming. He might have killed me that time if they hadn't shown up. Brooks hauled him off me and dropped him with one right hook to the jaw. I'd never been so in awe of someone in my whole life. He took me out to the truck, and when Orson came back out, he had a bag of my stuff and some kind of understanding with my dad. He wasn't to contact me, and I never had to go back.

"2799, Halfor SO, we are unable to get a clear idea of the suspect and the number of victims in the home. RP is a ten-year-old girl. Unknown of any weapons at this time."

My chest squeezes as I reach for my radio, pulling it close to my mouth. "Copy SO, I'm arriving in the area."

"Copy that."

"2799, 2700." Mercer's voice comes across the radio as I navigate the little roads to find lot twenty-two.

"2700, go ahead." I lean forward, watching the lots as I pass by.

"2799 wait for backup to arrive before entering the premises."

"10-4, I'm on scene."

I get out of my truck, listening for the telltale signs of a domestic violence situation. In my own personal experience, there's generally a lot of yelling and smashing going on. It's quiet for a moment before I hear the screaming. Their shouts are muffled through the trailer walls. It takes everything in me not to rush the door. Domestics can turn deadly in a matter of seconds. Whoever is getting beaten inside that trailer might not have the minutes it will take for backup to arrive.

"Help!" A high-pitched voice calls from the front door. A little girl appears, with long skinny arms and legs. She stumbles, tumbling down the stairs. I run to catch her, my strides eating up the distance. "My mom...he's going to kill my mom." She's shaking when I reach her, a bruise blooming across her cheek, one eye already swelling shut.

This fucking piece of shit hit his kid.

"Please," she whimpers. "My mom."

"Go get behind my truck, sweetheart, okay? More deputies are coming, wait for them behind the truck."

She nods, tripping over her gangly limbs as she makes her way toward my truck.

Chapter 19

Bold of You to Assume

Clay

I REACH FOR THE RADIO ON MY SHOULDER, MOVING IT closer to my mouth. "Halfor SO, 2799, I'm entering the house. Juvenile RP is outside by my truck," I say in a slow, low tone.

"10-4 2799, units are less than a minute out."

"2799, 2700, you need to stand down and wait for backup."

I don't answer Mercer. I'll take whatever consequences he wants to give me later. Right now, there's a little girl's mom in there, who might not make it out alive. Pulling my duty weapon from its holster, I square my shoulders and make my way inside the trailer. It's a fucking disaster, reeking of stale beer and old food.

Trash litters the walkways. A puppy is sitting in the corner of one of the rooms, shivering. Another child pokes his head into the hallway. He points toward a closed door, where all the screaming is coming from.

I can hear the blows landing. The sound of fists thudding into flesh calls back one too many memories in my head. I kick the bedroom door open, finding a man straddling a woman. You can barely make out what she looks like; he's hit her so many times. Her face beaten to a bloody pulp. He rears his fist back again, and I see red.

Putting my gun back in the holster on my vest, I slam into him, expecting more resistance, but he clearly didn't see me coming. He topples like a house of cards, taking me to the ground with him. While he had an easy enough time beating the woman on his bed, his drunk, sluggish movements are easy to bat away.

Flipping him over, I get one hand snapped into a cuff. He tries to buck me off, but it's easy enough to wrench his other arm back and put that wrist into the cuff. He's screaming obscenities at me, but the sound of sirens outside drowns him out.

"Traeger!" I hear Nathan Clark's voice booming down the hallway.

"All good," I call back, hauling the asshole up onto his butt.

"Traeger?" The balding man mumbles, his eyes barely able to focus because of how drunk he is. "You Caleb's boy?"

I don't respond, making my way to where the woman still hasn't moved from the bed. Her chest is rising and falling, but her pulse is weak. "She's going to need medics asap," I bark at Clark, who gives me a curt nod. He steps out of the room, talking into his radio.

"Yeah," the drunkard continues. "You're Caleb's. You got his curlicues, didn't you, boy?" He tips his head side to side, like he's flopping around a mop of curls.

"2799, 2700, what's your status?"

"2700, 2799, all good here."

"Roger that, bud." Mercer signs off in the least official way possible, and I know he won't come over for this. Monitor the radio a little closer? Definitely. But there're bigger fish for him to fry. I can handle a domestic, especially when it's as clear-cut as this.

"I thought he hauled off an' killed you, way you disappeared." I'm sifting through the wallet on the nightstand, looking for Mr. I-Hit-My-Wife-For-Fun's ID when he continues running his mouth.

"Not dead," I mutter back, holding the ID card up. Jerry Benedict. His ID's been expired for years. When I run it back through dispatch, it turns out he's wanted in a couple of states over for domestic abuse and child support.

Jerry laughs, a gross gurgling sound before he spits at my feet. "Shoulda done away with you like he did your mom."

I feel, more than see, Clark enter the room again. A steady presence behind me as I haul Jerry up to his feet.

"The fuck did you say to me?"

"Didn't you know? He went after her. Used to joke about it at the bar. Made her scream when he caught up to her." He laughs in my face, spittle and stale alcohol churning my stomach into something hot and acidic. I shove his chest, head slamming into the wall, hard.

"Shut your fucking mouth."

"Go ask 'im," Jerry cackles. "He's probably over there rotting in a pile of vomit since his good-for-nothing son couldn't bother to come check on him!"

He's shouting at me as I leave him with Clark and stomp my way out of the trailer. I don't bother getting in my truck. I already know I'll have to come back here to get statements.

My feet carry me through the streets, boots pounding pavement as I haul ass to lot fourteen. A weight drops into my stomach. My breath catches in my throat when I see the trailer. It looks the same, only worse. It's fallen into a state of disrepair, so bad I'd almost think it was abandoned, if my dad wasn't sitting right there, nursing a beer.

"Did you kill her?" I storm up the little sidewalk that leads to his front door, my fists itching to pound into him.

"Son?" He looks up, bewildered. I grab the collar of his shirt, slamming him into the side of the trailer, the smell of beer and cigarettes wafting into my face when the air rushes out of him.

"Did you kill her?" I grit out, my voice low and lethal. *I'm going to fucking kill him.*

"Who? Your mom? I didn't fucking kill her. She left us, remember that? She left. Couldn't handle your whiny little—"

I wind my arm back, about to rearrange his face, when I'm jerked backward by my vest. A strong tattooed hand shoves my chest toward the street.

"Leave him," Nate's voice is low, menacing. "He's not fucking worth it."

My chest heaves, fingers flexing and contracting, making fists at my side. My heart is pounding. Hot, demanding blood pounds in my ears, *his* blood.

"Leave him to rot here, Clay. He doesn't deserve any of your time or hatred." Nate's in my face, his wintergreen-scented breath blowing over me, centering me.

"Yeah, Clay," my dad's voice grates out. "Run along like the little pussy you are."

I lunge for him, already knowing Nate won't let me get any closer than I am. I need to put the energy somewhere.

"He wants you to hit him, Clay." Nate shakes his head, looking at me with eyes that seem to know, like he's been here before. "You are not him, so walk away."

He gives my vest another shove before I turn around and head back to the call. To the other asshole who doesn't give a shit about anyone but himself. I might not have been able to do anything about my dad, but I can lock this motherfucker up and make sure he can't hurt his wife and kids again.

At least not today.

~

I'm finishing up my supplemental report when Mercer finally makes a physical appearance. He rolls an office chair over to the desk I'm sitting at, scrubbing a hand down his face when he plops down into it.

"You're a dick." He pins me with a glare, fingers tapping on the armrest of his chair. "I told you to wait."

"She would've died," I mumble, not even looking at him as I finish typing the last sentence into my report.

"You don't actually know that."

I take the report from the hospital and toss it at him. I've already scanned it into my case file. The ER determined she was minutes away from succumbing to her injuries. If we hadn't shown up and gotten her help, she would have died. Leaving those two kids with their abusive father or foster care as their only option.

"Well, shit." Mercer closes the file and puts it back on the desk, waiting until I turn to him. "I trust your judgement, Clay, I do. But stupid shit like this is how good cops die. I don't know about you, but I'm not ready to bury you yet."

"I get it, Merc. I was waiting. I waited outside until that little girl came stumbling out with a bruise on her eye, saying he was going to kill her mom."

"Fuck," he breathes. "Why's it always the kids?"

"Fuck if I know." I shake my head, leaning back in my chair. trying to let my body decompress. My dad's words ring through my head on repeat. *I'm the reason she left.* I know that. I've always known that. He beat that shit into my head. There's no escaping it. Mom knew I'd end up like him one day; it's the curse of all the Traeger men. I wasn't worth bothering with.

"You okay?" Mercer brings me back into the present, head cocked to the side. "I know it must have brought shit up, being in Cross Point, dealing with a domestic."

I nod, my eye catching Nate's as he leans around his desk to look at me. I can see the question in his face; he's wondering if I'm going to tell Mercer about my dad. About Jerry goading me into a fight with him. I will, eventually, but tonight, all I want to do is go home. Forget about all this shit and pretend I never came from that place.

"I'm good, Merc. Swear."

"Good." His eyes narrow slightly, fingers tapping on the top of his knee. He's looking for something, trying to read me. "Poker on Friday, if you're not too busy with all your secrets."

I roll my eyes, turning back to my computer.

"You're coming too," Mercer says to Nate before he leaves the room.

The deputy room falls silent, except for the keys of our keyboards tapping as we finish up our case reports. I log the rest of my photographic evidence and sign out. I stand pausing as Nate comes up next to my desk.

Nathan Clark is a big dude. I'd probably be a little intimidated by the guy if I didn't know him. Big square jaw, every inch of skin showing in his short-sleeve Sheriff's uniform, covered in tattoos. He's got to be around my height, maybe even six foot four, but he's got muscles stacked on top of his muscles. I don't even want to know what he can bench.

"Grab a beer with me?"

"I don't drink much," I offer. It's not that I don't like the guy, but I don't feel like hashing out my trauma with someone I'm still getting to know.

"So, sip it," he mutters, turning around to walk out the door. "I'll be there in ten," he calls over his shoulder, making his way out the door. I want to argue. It's not a good look to park my patrol unit outside of the bar and go drink in my uniform. Though I doubt anyone in Hillcreek gives a damn. They probably wouldn't be surprised, seeing another Traeger sipping a drink in uniform, like father like son.

I debate it back and forth on my way to the Rusted Rail. Bertie's bar has all the charm you'd expect in a small country town. She's renovated the whole place, installing a dance floor and new wooden tables. Her kitchen is state-of-the-art and the best place to buy a burger. If you want cheap beer and soggy fries, then the biker bar on the other side of town is for you. I park in the back, near Bertie's old truck, and shuck my uniform shirt off. Normally, I'd have a t-shirt underneath, but with summer fast approaching, I prefer a tank top.

Now I really look the part of my father, stomping into a bar wearing a wife-beater tank and jeans.

Bertie whistles when I walk by her. "Got a hot date, Traeger?"

I flip her the bird, finding a table along the far wall that faces both entrances. I watch Clark enter the bar, every single female head turning to the door when he enters. Even Bertie checks him out when he saunters up to order a drink. She points in my direction after handing him two bottles, then turns crimson with something he says. I don't know if I've ever seen Bertie blush before. She's got to be a good ten years older than him; looks like the kid might have some charm after all.

He sits across from me, painfully oblivious to all the attention he's drawing with his gym shorts and cut-off t-shirt. The sides of his shirt ripped all the way down to the hem, combat boots hanging open at the laces. He's like a bigger, stockier version of Adler.

"It's NA." He hands me a beer and tips his back to take a swig. "Bertie said you'd probably like it. Said she keeps it stocked for your brother. Didn't know you had a brother."

I sigh, shaking my head. "She means Brooks."

"Ah, I see." He tips his head to the side, considering.

"I met Mercer in high school, grew up a couple counties over before that. The Kanes took me in when they figured out how my dad *parented*." I wrap air quotes around the word parented. What he did was technically child abuse. Tomato, tomahto.

"I know. Mercer told me," he says, the side of his mouth tipping up into a smirk.

I narrow my eyes and cock an eyebrow.

He raises his hands, then drags one over his cropped blond hair. "Figured you might want to talk, is all."

"Bold of you to assume." I sip my beer, letting the cool, crisp liquid coat my tongue before I swallow it down.

"I killed mine," he says, setting his beer down as his voice drops low, growing cold and emotionless. My back straightens, eyes widening a little as I try to wrap my head around what he just admitted. "Got big enough to fight back and pushed a little too hard. He hit the coffee table just right and broke his neck. Now my therapist tells me that it wasn't my fault. The court found me not guilty; it was an accident brought on by self-defense. But I can't tell you how many times I thought about it. How badly I wanted to end him and me to be the one to do it."

The wooden chair beneath me creaks as I sit back in it. The front legs rock off the ground as I drum my fingers on the table between us.

"I stopped havin' nightmares about him coming after me and started dreaming that I didn't stop with him. That I was worse than him because I killed a man, and all he ever did was beat his kid."

Air whooshes out of my lungs, chair slamming down onto the ground with a heavy thud. "Jesus, man." I look at him, and I think I can see it. The way he's hiding behind a Sheriff's badge and combat boots. He's so fucking young, too. That couldn't have happened more than ten years ago. "Jesus," I repeat, unable to find anything else to say.

"I'm not looking for your pity, Traeger. I thought you should know the problems don't go away when they do. You seem like a good dude. I've heard a lot about you from the Kane boys, and everyone in this town respects the hell out of you, man. You don't seem like the type that would go off half-cocked. I just wanted you to know that I've been there. I get the anger. I get wanting to make him pay, but it's not worth the stain on your soul. He ain't worth it."

I lean forward, my eyes never leaving his. "Are you secretly twenty years older than you look?"

"Fuck no." He grins. "But I've seen some shit."

"Clearly." I lean back and offer my beer for him to cheers. He taps the neck with his own, and we shoot the shit about our fucked up pasts and non-existent parents. Guess I'm not the only one scared that it's written in my blood.

Chapter 20

I Certainly Do Not

Leni

I AM NOT ASHAMED TO ADMIT THAT I WENT STRAIGHT back up to bed once Clay left for work. No more schools have reached out about jobs, and while I could have been surfing the job boards, I'm sure the listings will keep coming. At least for a few hours. I wish I could say I went back to sleep, but that has eluded me ever since this morning.

I thought a bath might clear my head, water being cleansing and all that. But no, I'm stuck here thinking about the way Clay's hands felt on my body. The way he looked with his head between my thighs. The way it felt to come crying his name. Wondering, for the first time in a decade, what it would be like if I stayed.

Which is fucking crazy, because I can't stay here. This is a bump in the road, a little stopover as I figure my shit out. Kane Ridge Ranch hasn't been my home in a long time. Until now, I truly believed it never would be again. One weak moment with Clay, and now I'm questioning everything.

BEST BITCHES GROUP CHAT

> I fear I might be losing my mind...

PEPPER

Please tell me this has to do with a certain hot cowboy

> ...

> Maybe...?

PEPPER

OMG. You boned. Didn't you?

MIYA

snort Who the fuck says boned anymore?

PEPPER

Me. Obvi

Soooo how was it?

> We didn't bone...exactly

MIYA

how does one not bone exactly...?

> It didn't go that far.

> That's not the interesting part anyway

PEPPER

I beg to fucking differ

MIYA

I'm with Peps on this one

How is your hooking up with CLAYTON TRAEGER not interesting?

> Oh ye of little faith.

MIYA

Fine. I'll bite....

What has our dearest Leni losing her mind?

I'm sitting here

In my soaker tub

PEPPER

Just rub it in for the rest of us poor folks

And I'm wondering…what it might be like if I stayed.

PEPPER

Gasp WHAT?!

MIYA

Noooo. Shut your face right now. You can't leave me!

Like I said…losing my mind!

MIYA

I'll say!

PEPPER

Wait. I still don't fully understand why that would be so weird? I mean…other than you've lived here for so long…Why don't you want to move back?

Because my family is insufferable.

PEPPER

Even the hot brothers?

Especially the brothers

PEPPER

I don't get families.

MIYA

Are you for real Leni?

Yes?

No.

Definitely no. Could you imagine?

Ugh. The things he can do with his tongue...

PEPPER

Hell yea! Now we're talking!

MIYA

I stg Leni. When I said you needed to figure
out what happened with him I didn't mean
you should move in with him.

I know. I know. The sooner I can get a job in
Benson the sooner things can go back to
normal.

PEPPER

Fuck normal.

Save a horse and ride off into the sunset on
your cowboy.

MIYA

You mean with her cowboy?

PEPPER

I certainly do not

I hate you both

Normal is good. Normal is what I need, not this confusing
pull to Clay and his incredibly skilled tongue. Nope, what I
need is to get my head on straight and get back on track. I don't
need my family. I don't need any help, and I certainly don't
need Clay. Maybe, though, it wouldn't hurt to explore things
while I'm here? That might satiate this sick and twisted part of
me that keeps insisting that getting tangled up with him is a
good idea. Work him out of my system and out of my head. It's
possible, right?

Apparently, I have learned nothing in ten years, because the longer the day goes on, the more I start to miss Clay. He's still not home by supper time, and when I check my phone to see if I have any messages from him, I don't see anything. So I set the table and wait. The smell of the chicken dish I threw together makes my mouth water. When seven o'clock hits, I can't wait to eat anymore. I forgot about lunch, too wrapped up in my own thoughts that I haven't eaten since breakfast. I scarf down a plateful, waiting to hear something from Clay. Even if it's just a hey, I'll be home late.

I know calls can go long, that you don't always get a say in when you're done for the day as a deputy, but I really thought he would let me know if he was going to be coming home late.

By eight fifteen, I'm starting to get nervous. There's nothing in the group chat about him being hurt on the job, but if he wrecked on his way home, would anyone know? When I dial his number, it goes straight to voicemail.

Fuck. I'm pacing the entryway, trying to decide if I should go out and look for him when I hear gravel crunching down the lane. His headlights flash across the front of the cabin, momentarily blinding me. I blink away the stars and put my hands on my hips, blowing air through my nose as I try to collect my temper. He doesn't look harmed, doesn't even look like he had a hard day.

"You didn't call or text. I was starting to worry."

"Stopped at the Rail to have a beer with one of the guys." He shrugs, like it's no big deal. Like I wasn't sitting here about to blow up my life by calling Mercer to see if he was alive.

"Oh." I feel an unreasonable amount of something ugly twist in my gut. "Since when do you go out and drink?"

"I drink when I want to. Didn't I just have a beer with you?" His arms cross over his chest. The look on his face lets me know he's unimpressed by this conversation. "Why is this a big deal?"

"You didn't even call. Didn't text, either." I tap my foot on the ground. Impatient, annoyed for no reason other than the fact that I made him dinner. I expected him to come home to me. To spend his evening with me. So now I'm...what? Jealous? Jesus, what is happening to me?

"Was I supposed to?" He cocks his head, one eyebrow lifting into his hairline. This motherfucker. Now I'm jealous and pissed.

"You're kidding, right?"

He shrugs, leaning back against the door of his pickup, ankles crossed over one another, like he doesn't have a damn care in the world.

"What the fuck, Clay?"

"You're not my girlfriend. I don't know what we're doing, but does it even matter? You're just going to leave again. What's the point?"

"The point, Clay...is that I'm not your fucking mom. I'm not abandoning you."

His eyes snap to meet mine, a challenge in them.

"I was barely older than a kid. I wanted you, and you pushed me away. You kept me at arm's length. *You* did that."

"Jesus Christ." He glances toward the night sky, one hand squeezing the back of his neck. "It's always me. Isn't it? I already told you...I'm not good enough for you. I wasn't good enough for her either. How many times do I have to tell you I'm not fucking worth it?"

Oh. I'm stunned. Silence weighs between us. I rewind my words through my head, wishing I could take them all back. Wishing there was a way to unsay them, rephrase them, anything other than reaffirm the belief that he isn't worthy. That he's the cause of all his heartache.

"Clay." I close the gap between us, wrapping my arms around him. He doesn't say anything, and it takes me a minute to realize that he's standing there. His arms hang stiff by my sides. His eyes glassy, that faraway haunted look taking them over. "Clayton," I whisper his name. "Clay." I touch his cheek, his chest suddenly inflating, eyes flicking down to meet mine.

"Leni." He barely gets my name out before he's crushing me to his chest. His arms wrap around me so tight it almost hurts. "I'm sorry, baby. I'm not mad at you. I don't even know why I'm trying to pick a fight. I'm sorry."

"It's okay." I run my hands up and down his ribs. It's the only motion I can really manage with the anaconda hold he has on me. "I started it, I'm sorry. I don't want to fight either." He sighs into me, heavy and wounded, like the weight of the world is on his shoulders. "Are you okay?"

"No." His voice is muffled, face buried in the crook of my neck.

"Talk to me. What's going on?"

"I saw my dad today."

"What? Why?"

"Got sent to a domestic," he exhales, leaning back against his truck again. Long fingers spear into his curls, tugging at the roots. "The guy I arrested knows my dad," he scoffs. "Guess everyone in Cross Point knows him. He said he thought my old man killed me, like he killed my mom."

I rear back, my heart skipping a beat. "But you said that she left."

"She did. Guess old Caleb Traeger couldn't handle that, though. He told everyone he took care of her." Clay's hands ball up into fists on his thighs, squeezing so tight his knuckles turn white. "I went over there to kill him. I wanted to, Leni."

"What happened?"

"Nothing, one of the guys followed me. He pulled me out of there; made sure I didn't do anything stupid."

"Okay," I breathe out a sigh of relief. If nothing happened, then there's nothing to worry about. "That's good."

"None of this is good." He looks at me, his eyes burning with rage. "Every time I see him, every time I think about him, I realize that that is where I'm heading. Don't you get it? It's in my fucking DNA. Why do you think I never looked for something serious? Why do you think I worked so hard to keep you away from me? I came from that asshole. I was raised by him. Look what I did to you that night."

Clay's eyes widen, his breath growing more and more rapid with each passing second. I know he's heading for another panic attack, so I pull his face into my hands and look him in the eye.

"Breathe, Clayton. Breathe with me." I take a slow, deep breath, then push it out through my lips, loud enough that I know he can follow it. Once his breathing is slow and even, I tuck myself into him again, wrapping my arms around his waist. "You are not your dad."

"Give it ten more years," he sighs, his arms still hanging awkwardly down at his side.

"You are nothing like him." I tighten my hold around his waist, willing him to hear me. To really hear me. "And you never will be. You know how I know?"

"How?" He finally pulls me closer, leaning his head down to rest on mine.

"Because you care. You're worried about becoming him. He wouldn't be worried about that; he'd relish it, because he likes to hurt people. But you—you're scared, you don't want to hurt people. You are not him."

"I might not have hit you, but I'm the reason you got hurt.

I'm the reason your relationship with your family is broken. I hurt you, and I will never forgive myself for that."

"None of that was your fault."

"It is, though. This is what I'm trying to tell you. All I do is hurt the people I'm close to. You deserve someone better, someone who isn't broken. Someone who can give you the world."

"I don't want the world." I want to scream. My voice shakes with rage. "I never wanted more. I wanted you. You're all I've ever wanted. I never cared about your past. I never saw you as something that needed to be fixed. I just wanted you."

"I'm not the boy you fell in love with back then."

"Good, because I don't think he could handle me anyway."

Clay's lips tip up into a smirk, and his hand caresses my face. "No, probably not." He presses a gentle kiss on my lips, resting his free hand on mine. We stand there, breathing each other in for a few more minutes.

"Come on, let's get you cleaned up." I slip my hand into his and interlock our fingers, not surprised when his tightens around mine. Clayton is on the verge of floating away, of letting himself sink back into that dark place where he doesn't have to feel his feelings or think about the bad things he's seen. I don't want to lose him to that place, so I squeeze back, hoping it's enough to keep him here with me.

When we get to the bathroom, I twist the handle to get the water heating. Clay brings his hands up to the buttons on his shirt. His fingers fumbling, unable to remove them with how bad they're shaking. I cover his hands with mine, holding them until they stop trembling. Steam starts to billow out of the shower. I finish unbuttoning his shirt, but I pause because the buttons are fake.

"Zipper," he whispers, his voice barely audible over the stream of the shower. I narrow my eyes, not trusting the false buttons on his shirt before I find a zipper under the collar. The tricky bastards hid a zipper under the button placket. It's kind of genius, actually.

I slide the uniform shirt from his shoulders, and it drops to the floor before I move onto his belt. He sucks in a breath after I pull his undershirt out of his pants and slip my fingers beneath the hem so I can pull it off him. He bends forward to help get it over his head.

When he straightens, I can't help but look at the tattoo that covers his chest. It's a mountain scene. The sun is peeking over the top of the mountains, trees, and a river sitting at the base of them, and to the left of it, a separate tattoo sits. They didn't cover it or incorporate it into the chest piece, but worked around it.

"A rose," I whisper, letting my fingers trace the older tattoo on his left pectoral, right above his heart. This is the tattoo I caught a glimpse of when he was home that summer. Clay flattens my hand out on his chest, his thumb stroking along the tops of my fingers.

"Look closer." His voice is so soft and tired that I wonder if I'm hearing things, but when I shift my hand, I can see the whole rose. I realize that there, in the center, one line of the smallest petal isn't actually a line, but...my name.

A tear finds its way down my cheek as I reach to kiss the spot where I'm forever etched into his skin. His Eleanor Rose.

Chapter 21

I trust You

Leni

I PULL AWAY FROM HIM, ENOUGH TO LOOK UP AT HIS FACE. There's warmth in his eyes, but he's still standing in front of me, looking lost. Stuck in a past he doesn't think he deserves to leave behind.

"Come on." I pop the button on his Wranglers and slip my thumbs into the sides. "The water's hot now."

"I got it." He pulls my hands away and steps back from me, shucking his jeans and boxers off in one go before stepping into the shower. If he thinks I'm going to let him disappear, he's got another thing coming.

Stripping out of my clothes, I step into the shower behind him. His back is to me when I get in, but I can see the jerky motions as he washes his hands. Scrubbing them, like he's trying to scrub away years of dirt and grime.

"Let me help you," I whisper.

Let me in. I want to scream.

Instead, I grab his shoulder and turn him around toward me, pushing him back under the spray as I take the soap from his hands. I start to knead it, gently scrubbing every crack and groove, soothing my fingers over his calluses. His head drops, water beating against the back of his neck as his chest rises and falls in long, heavy breaths.

When his hands are clean, I travel up his wrists, soaping his arms, then his shoulders, and down his chest. He doesn't say anything, but I can feel him watching me. The weight of his gaze makes my skin itch. I'm washing every square inch of his body, and somehow, I'm the one who feels exposed.

I drop to my knees in front of him, lathering the soap up his legs. My hands shake as they go. The silence feels like a weighted blanket, one that's filled with yearning and tension and all the words we haven't said. I glance up at him through my lashes, and the look on his face steals my breath away.

There's a fire in his eyes, lust and longing etched into every taut line of his face. His chest is heaving with every breath, and still, he doesn't speak to me. It would be so easy to reach forward and take his cock in my hand, to stroke his rock-hard erection that's practically reaching for me. The things I would do to that dick with my mouth, I don't think I'd even be able to take him fully, not in my mouth at least.

This isn't about sex, though; this is about making sure Clay knows he's not alone. That he is not the product of his circumstances, and I am here for him.

I stand, nudging him back under the spray so he can rinse the soap off. Turning to the side, I grab his shampoo and squeeze a bit into my palms. He leans forward, letting the water beat down on his shoulders. I sink my fingers deep into his hair and begin to massage his scalp, making sure I don't miss a single curl.

A guttural moan comes from him, so I take that as a sign to keep going. I scrub until my fingers ache, and I worry he's going to get a crick in his neck from leaning forward for so long. "You can rinse," I say, my voice coming out a bit hoarse.

My hands drop, and I suddenly feel awkward without something to do with them. He can either read the awkwardness I'm feeling, or he doesn't want me to stop touching him because he grabs my hands and puts them on either side of his ribs, before tossing his head back to rinse out his hair. I move closer, resting my head on his chest as my arms snake around him.

Clay moves a leg around mine, pivoting us so that I'm the one under the water now. Leaving my arms around his waist, he tips my head back before he runs his fingers through my waves, separating the layers to get them wet.

He pauses for a second, looking at the hair products I have lined up along the shelf. "The pink one," I say, still not wanting to let go of him. He squeezes a generous portion into his palm before lathering it between his hands. His fingers begin to rub the shampoo in, returning the scalp massage tenfold. My eyes flutter closed as I lean into his strong hands. *God, this feels so damn good.*

"Which one's next?" Clay's voice startles me a little. It's the first time he's spoken since we stepped into the shower, and I don't expect all the gravel it's laced with.

"Blue bottle." I point at the smaller bottle of conditioner on the shelf. "It only goes on the ends."

"Copy." He gives me a small smile that heats my core, fire lancing through my bloodstream. *Yeah, he's going to be the death of me.* Once he's done working the conditioner into my hair, he washes my body. When he gets to his knees to soap my legs, I nearly fall to the floor with him. His hands steady at my hips, a knowing smirk tilting the corners of his mouth. While he's washing my legs, he peppers my abdomen with kisses. They're soft and sweet, with no bite or urgency to them. It's almost lazy, the way he gently presses his lips to my skin.

After a slow, torturous cleaning between my legs and backside, Clay stands and nudges my head back under the water to rinse my hair out. The water is significantly cooler than when we started, but I am once again impressed that my little water heater lasted this long. Clay reaches behind me to turn the water off, then steps out of the shower to grab us a towel.

They're warm to the touch because I'm bougie and I splurged on a heated towel rack. It's a luxury I didn't get in my everyday life before.

We dry off our bodies, and Clay stands behind me, hands on my hips as I blow-dry my hair. I don't have it in me to dry it completely, but I know I'll regret it if I don't at least get the hair on my scalp dried. It really doesn't take that long, but it feels like ages as I keep eye contact with Clay the whole time. Normally, I'd flip my head over and get the bottom better, but the way he's looking at me has me rushing to be done.

When I set the blow-dryer down, he leans forward and sinks his teeth into the little slope between my neck and shoulder. I gasp, the bite is hard enough that I know it'll leave a mark, but the sting is soothed when he smooths his tongue over it. I lean back into him, letting him take some of my weight as I find it harder and harder to breathe.

He kisses up and down my neck, sucking on my earlobe as his hand snakes up and loosens the knot at my chest, letting my towel drop to the ground. He does a slow perusal of my body in the mirror, eyes taking in every single inch of me. When his stormy gray eyes find mine watching him in the mirror, he leans forward and whispers into my ear.

"Look at you. Look at how gorgeous you are." Dropping his own towel to the ground, he pulls my hips back into his. "Look how well we fit together. You were made for me." His hands start to wander, tickling my skin. I whimper when a finger dusts over my clit, his other hand gripping my thigh so tight, I don't doubt it will leave a bruise. "Mine," he growls into my ear as he thrusts two fingers inside of me.

"Clay," I moan. My back arches deeper into his chest as he strokes his fingers inside of me. My whole body is buzzing with need, muscles clenching around his fingers, hips bucking.

"Ride me. I want to watch you come on my hand." He dusts kisses down my neck, watching what he's doing to me in the mirror. I feel so exposed to him, with my body on display. My breasts bounce as he thrusts his fingers inside of me. I feel vulnerable in a way that I've never felt with anyone else, *ever*. Spreading my legs further apart, I shift my hips back, swiveling them, exploring what feels good.

Finding a rhythm that suits me, I tip my head back onto his chest and reach up with my hand, gripping the back of his neck, holding on for dear life as I do exactly what he asked and ride his hand.

Clay's free hand reaches up from my thigh, leaving red finger-length marks where he was holding me. Those same fingers find a nipple to play with. He twists and pulls until my nipple hardens into a peak, giving me a little pinch before moving onto the other side. I moan into him, his fingers crooking up at the perfect angle for me. My legs begin to shake, my orgasm so close, but still out of reach.

"Do you need more, Leni girl?" Clay's voice skates over me, making the hair on my arms stand up, pleasure shooting deep into my already needy core.

"Yeah," I whimper.

"Show me how you touch yourself," he pauses what he's doing with his fingers and looks me straight in the eyes through the mirror. "I want to see how you come when you touch yourself thinking about me."

"Oh God," I cry, circling my clit with my free hand. I couldn't tell you how many times I did this, wishing it were his hands on me instead of mine. How many fantasies he starred in, even after everything, it was always him that came to mind when I came. Now, having him here, his fingers inside of me, mouth on my neck, I can hardly breathe. It's too much.

I press a little harder, rubbing that little bundle of nerves at the same time he crooks his fingers inside of me, and I'm a goner, incoherently sobbing his name over and over again as my orgasm barrels through me so hard it's almost painful. I don't even know how I'm holding myself up, or if I am holding myself up. It's more likely that Clay is keeping both of us upright. My legs feel as stable as a freshly born foal's. I'm gasping, riding the waves as I come back down from the pleasure, my body jolting as Clay takes his fingers from inside of me. I watch, unable to look away from our reflection, when he brings them to his mouth, cleaning off my arousal.

"Mmm," he breathes, letting his free hand trail around my stomach, up to my chest. "So fucking sweet. You taste so fucking good."

My body feels like Jell-O, limbs loose and limp as he lifts me into his arms and carries me to the bed. Lying me out beneath him, he toys with my neck and collarbone. Lips, tongue, and teeth tracing fire across my skin. Before I know it, I'm aching again, mindlessly writhing beneath him, eager for another release.

"Fuck," he grumbles. "I left the condoms in the truck."

"You bought condoms?"

"Of course, I bought condoms. I've been dying to be inside of you since the moment you kissed me."

Smoothing a curl away from his forehead, I bite my lip, considering. "I'm on the pill. I had my annual a few months ago and came back clean. I haven't been with anyone after my check-up."

He goes still above me. "Leni." His voice is anything but

calm as his eyes dart back and forth between mine, like he's trying to decide if I meant what I said.

"I've never *not* used a condom, but I want you to be the first one. The only one. I need to feel you. All of you."

He makes an anguished noise before dropping his forehead to my collarbone. I can feel the tension in his shoulders, his desires warring inside of him.

"I trust you," I whisper, lifting his face back to look into my eyes. Those must be the magic words, because in an instant, he's kissing me in slow, deep, breathless strokes.

My entire body ignites with electricity.

Bringing his hips in line with mine, Clay trails the head of his cock over my pussy, teasing my clit with a gentle pressure that sends my hips bucking off the bed. I take his shaft into my hand, giving it a slow stroke before I line him up with my entrance, taking a deep breath so I don't tense my muscles.

He's big, probably the biggest I've ever had, and I'm going to need to relax if he's going to get it all the way seated in me. His arms shake with effort, holding himself back as he slowly pushes in.

I watch as inch after inch sinks inside of me. Marveling at the way we fit together, the way we look joined like this. When he seats himself fully inside of me, I gasp at the fullness of him. He's stretching me more than I knew was possible, hitting a spot so deep inside of me that I've never felt anything like this before.

"Oh God," I cry, fingernails digging into his shoulders as I hold on for dear life.

"Don't move." His voice comes out strained, arms shaking in earnest now. "I need a minute. Holy fuck, baby, you're so goddamn tight."

I lie still for him, bouncing my eyes back and forth between his face and where our bodies are joined together. It feels too good to be true, to have him like this, feeling every ridge and vein on his cock inside of me. I give a little squeeze, testing how my muscles react to him, grinning when I feel his dick twitch in my pussy.

"Jesus," he drags the word out as he starts to move. It's a slow exploratory pace, one that stokes a fire inside my core. "Are you going to come again?"

"Yes," I pant, stars painting my vision as my second orgasm threatens to take me.

"So greedy, aren't you, baby?"

"Mmm." I'm beyond speaking words at this point, the way he's rocking into me, taking me back to that place of pleasure and connection. I shatter around him, my pussy clenching painfully as I arc off the bed, his name spilling from my lips.

His strokes are slow and sure, a gentle rhythm guiding me through the aftershocks of my orgasm. "Can you take more?" He pauses, looking down at me with eyes full of wonder and desire.

"Yes," I whisper.

Clay grabs his pillow and tucks it under my hips, angling me just right as his hands grip my hips tightly. I gasp at the new depth he's found inside me. How is it possible to feel him even deeper?

"You tell me if it hurts, and I'll stop. Okay?"

"Mhm." I'm too distracted, grinding my lower half into his like a dog in heat. Clay pinches my chin between his thumb and forefinger, dragging my gaze to meet his.

"I need to hear you say it, Leni." His hand moves down my jaw, thumb stroking my skin, back and forth.

"I'll tell you if it hurts me."

"Good girl," his voice rumbles. And I have no time to delve into the way my body reacts to that phrase when he pulls out to the tip and slams himself back into me. I scream, not in pain, but in mind-blowing pleasure. I have never had sex like this before.

Clay commands me, taking what he needs as my own pleasure starts to build up again. He must be able to feel my muscles tighten because he releases one hand on my ass and presses his palm into my clit.

"Oh God." Tears are streaming from my eyes; it's too much. *It's all too much.*

"Let go."

"I can't," I sob. "I can't, it's too much."

The hand on my pelvis moves lower, his fingers slipping in between my thighs to circle my clit, applying pressure with his fingertip. I cry out, breath shaky as I barrel toward release.

"I've got you, baby. Let go."

He slams himself into me at the same time his fingers circle my clit, and I am thrown off a cliff, hurtling down, down, down as I unravel again and again and again.

I feel the moment his release hits him, hot ropes of cum branding me on the inside as his thrusts begin to slow. A grunt pulls from his lips as he stills above me. His chest is heaving, sweaty muscles quivering through the aftermath of his own orgasm.

I'm dizzy from the lack of oxygen, sweat dripping off my brow. My body aches in the most deliciously sore way. When he lowers himself back over my body, his lips find mine for a slow, lazy kiss. We're locked like that for a while, Clay only pulling away when he's gone soft inside of me. Without a word, he goes to the bathroom, returning with a warm washcloth. He presses it between my legs, using gentle strokes to clean me up.

I want to whimper when he takes that warmth away, but I am fully spent. My limbs limp, body sated and sleepy.

It's seconds before he's back in bed, but I'm already half

asleep when he pulls my body into him, his arms and legs wrapping around me.

"I love you." He buries his face into my shoulder, pressing his lips to my sweaty skin.

"Yours," I murmur. "I'm yours, Clay."

His arms relax around me, a sigh slipping out of him.

And I fall asleep to the sweetest sound I've ever heard, as Clay whispers into my ear one last time.

"*Mine.*"

Chapter 22

She's It for Me

Clay

Leni is still boneless when my alarm goes off in the morning.

I'm sore from time in the saddle, but not sore enough that I don't plan on having her again. I'd set my alarm for earlier than normal, in case she was up for more. Once I got a taste of her, I knew she was perfect, and I wouldn't be able to stop. Now that I've been inside of her? There's no place I would rather be than in this bed, tangled up in our sheets, my body joined with hers.

I don't know how I lived without her for those ten years. Fuck I wish I hadn't. I've never had sex like that before.

I knew it when she kissed me the first night she tumbled into the cabin, but last night solidified it. I will never be able to go without her again.

Pulling the covers down, I lift her hair off to one side as I take her in again. Her body is incredible. She's all toned lean muscle, with the right amount of curve to her hips. Leaning over, I take in the tattoo on her shoulder that I somehow missed before. It's so small it's nearly microscopic, one tiny heart. It could almost be mistaken for a freckle if you weren't looking

204

closely enough. I wonder when she got it, or if she has any more hidden surprises I don't know about.

"When did you get this?" I ask as she starts to stir.

"Mimi and I got them right when we turned eighteen."

I mock gasp, before pressing a smiling kiss to the ink. "You rebels."

She grins, the same smile that used to stop me in my tracks when we were kids. It still makes my heart skip a beat, seeing the way she loves me so openly. I might not have seen it for what it was back then, but I can see it now. She loves me, and always has. The same way I've always loved her. I'm not afraid to admit it now.

Leni reaches up above her head, chest lifting off the bed as she stretches. My eyes want to linger on her bare breasts, to stare at the naked perfection that is Eleanor Kane, but something else catches my attention. I reach for her arm, taking in her upper bicep, at the scar there. A scar that looks a hell of a lot like a bite mark.

"Leni." My voice cracks. "What is this?"

"It's nothing," she whispers. Her voice is small, distant over the rushing of blood in my ears.

"It's not nothing." I look up at her, my eyes tracking down to the deep purple-red marks peppered along her collarbone. There's a bite mark on her shoulder, *my* bite mark. *Fuck.* I'm no better than the guy who tried to rape her. I fucking marked her. "Baby," I whisper. I touch the spot where I bit her, but draw my hand away, terrified I might hurt her again.

Her head shifts off to the side, baring her unmarked shoulder to me. "Do it again."

"Leni." I say her name like a warning. I can't. I won't do it again. I shouldn't have done it in the first place. I should have asked last night. I should have double and triple-checked that she wanted that. That she wanted me. "These are bruises. I don't want to hurt you. I shouldn't have—"

She shakes her head, those pretty green eyes begging me. "Please. I want your marks."

"Fuck, baby, don't ask me to hurt you."

"Not hurt," she whispers, her hands framing my face. "Replace. He took my choice; he took my safety. I need you to give it back. Make me forget about him."

I rear over her, taking one last look at those marks on her skin. My marks. Gentle fingers tip my chin up, bringing my eyes to hers. Her emerald green eyes shimmer with tears, a vulnerability there that I've never seen before. I don't know what it cost her to ask me. To put that trust, that power, into my hands, but I won't take it for granted. I won't leave her with the memory of him. Not if I can give her a new one. "I can't say no to you."

Her eyes brighten, soft fingers sink into my hair. I moan into her, breath catching when her hands trail down my neck, fingernails scraping down my back.

This is going to go much faster than I want if she keeps doing that.

Snapping my hips forward, I seat myself fully inside of her with one powerful thrust. She cries out, head falling backward as her back arcs beneath me. I lace one hand through hers, intertwining our fingers as I drag it over her head.

"You're fucking incredible," I whisper into her neck. She whimpers when I drop my mouth to her collarbone, teeth nipping down her chest until I make it to her breast. Taking one of her nipples into my mouth, I lick and suck until it's a hard little bud. On the next thrust, I sink my teeth into her nipple and give it a sharp tug.

"Clayton," Leni moans, eyes closing as her head tips back into the mattress.

"Look at you. Look how well you're taking me." Her eyes snap to mine, slowly drifting down to where our bodies are locked together. Heat flashes through them, her nostrils flaring the tiniest bit when she sucks in a deep breath. She's panting, eyes drifting closed again as she tries to think her orgasm into existence. She probably could, women are wild like that, but I know how to help, so I might as well.

Shifting up onto my knees, I grip hers and lift her legs, wrapping them around my hips. She takes the new angle, tipping her pelvis back so that her pussy practically sucks me in.

"Holy fuck," I breathe, trying my best to hold it in. I want to make her come before I blow my fucking load.

"Oh God," she whispers. Her pussy starts to flutter around my dick. Thank God, because any more squeezing from her and I'm going to lose it. Slipping my hand between us, I put pressure right on that tight bundle of nerves, right where she needs it.

I wait, feeling her muscles bunch up, one by one, building with the pressure of an impending orgasm. When I can feel her muscles baring down, I lean back down and sink my teeth into the spot she offered earlier.

She cries out, hips bucking into me as I ride through my own orgasm with her. We're moving slowly, bodies still joined together as we come down from the high.

Tremors rack my body when I collapse into her, teeth still sunk into her shoulder. I force my jaw open to pull away from her. Soothing the spot with my tongue, I revel in the way she chants my name, over and over again like a prayer.

I lay with her until I absolutely can't waste any more time. It still takes monumental effort for me to pull away from her, but I do. I clean her up before I wash myself and get dressed for work.

My dirty uniform is still in a heap on the floor, and I make a mental note to make sure it gets cleaned tonight.

"Holy shit." I hear Leni squeal from the bedroom. "Clay!"

I rush over, my thoughts racing with all the bad things that could have happened to her in the five minutes I've been gone. Maybe the pain was delayed. Maybe I hurt something inside of her. I swear I was slamming into something solid at the end there.

Leni is sitting, staring at her phone, fingers flying across the keyboard, fast. "Your phone," she says without even looking up. "Family group chat."

Rounding the foot of the bed, I reach for my phone and swipe open to the group chat, which is flooding with messages from everyone. At the top of today's thread, there's a selfie of Brooks and a tiny little girl. She has a thin face with rosy, red cheeks, a shock of auburn hair on the top of her head, and a giant pink pacifier stuck in her mouth. I do a double-take, because last I checked, Brooks didn't have any small children hanging around him.

> KANE FAMILY GROUP CHAT
> BROOKY
>
> I will not be answering questions via text. Should you choose to come and visit you will be put to work changing diapers and playing. Or washing laundry. I will be at family dinner with the newest addition to the Kane family. Everyone this is Tessa Lynn
>
> MERC D
>
> I have so many questions
>
> BROOKY
>
> You can direct those to my lawyer
>
> TOBES
>
> I KNEW YOU KNEW SOMETHING E!

LENI ROSE

I'm sorry are you having a stroke? Is that an actual baby in your hands? Is it yours? Have you secretly been dating someone? Wait ARE YOU MARRIED?

E-MAN

He literally just said he's not answering any questions

LENI ROSE

I don't give a fuck what he said I need answers

MA

Leni dear language.

MERC D

I happen to agree with Leni...poor language aside of course

LENI ROSE

🤷

ADDY

WHAT. IS. HAPPENING?

TOBES

Brooks had a baby

ADDY

But how?! He's only been off work for four days. Don't those things take time to bake?

BROOKY

You're an idiot

She's fucking gorgeous Brooks.

Leni's head whips in my direction when my text comes through. I shrug. "What? Look at her."

"I know, but still, are you not shocked?"

"Flabbergasted, actually. But don't you think he might need

our support right now? However this came about Brooks has a baby. He's gotta be scared shitless."

Leni looks equal parts turned on and mushy when she looks at me. I can almost see hearts in her eyes. Her phone pressed to her chest like she's holding herself together with it.

My phone vibrates in my hand, making me look back down at the group chat.

MA

She's perfect

TOBES

Need anything big bro? I'll stop by later so Tessa can meet her favorite uncle.

LENI ROSE

I have so much shopping to do! Hello baby girl, Auntie Leni cannot wait to meet you! 😍

MERC D

Oh like hell you'll be the favorite uncle Toby. You barely even have a real job

BROOKY

Hey...

ADLER

Obviously I'm going to be the favorite fun uncle.

What's legal drinking age again?

BROOKY

Yea you're never being left alone with her

What do you need Brooks?

BROOKY

For now I'd settle for help on the ranch. I'm interviewing nannies this week hopefully.

E-MAN

Done

ADLER

Done

TOBES

Done

MERC D

You got it.

MA

LENI ROSE

This is so wholesome. I can't even. Guess I'll be home this weekend for family dinner. I can't let you guys turn her against me already.

MERC D

Are you serious? All we had to do to get you home was have a baby?

ADLER

Shiiit. I could have done that years ago

TOBES

You'd actually have to find someone that wants to sleep with you first

ADLER

I pull way more than you bro

MA

Boys there are some things that do not belong in this chat

LENI ROSE

I shake my head as the boys continue to argue about who

gets more pussy, and who will be the best uncle. Leni looks happy and sated. She's snuggled back into the bed, arms stretching up above her head.

She looks so fucking sexy with her hair a mess, my marks on her skin. I could stay here and get lost in her over and over again. "We should tell them."

I blurt it out before I even know I want to say it. I need them to know that she's mine. I need them to see what she is to me. Because this is it for me.

She's *it* for me.

Chapter 23

Flannel Daddy Vibes

Leni

"Yes," I breathe, and I mean it. It's one thing for me to be here, hiding, lying to my family. It's another thing to make Clay continue to lie, but I need a little bit more time. "Just not today."

I hate myself as soon as I say it, wishing I could take it back when Clay's smile falls. It's only a fraction, but that smile tips down and my heart strains in my chest.

"I don't want to take away from Brooks' big news. Otherwise, I'd text them right now. I swear it. Let's let Brooks have today."

Realization dons on his face, and the smile that blooms reaches all the way up into his eyes. "You're so good." He kneels on the bed, crawling toward me across the sheets. "Too good for me."

"Hardly," I whisper, hating that it was only half true. That I absolutely would not have texted them right then. Even if Brooks hadn't announced a mystery baby. While this might have been ten years in the making, this is still too new. Too fresh. Too unsettled. I'm moving back to Benson. My life is there. Clay just moved home; his life is here. There's too many variables, too many things that need to be worked out before we can tell them.

He kisses me long and slow, shattering the last little bit of defense I've built around my heart, putting back together some of the pieces that broke ten years ago.

I'm aching between my legs by the time he pulls away. I've never felt so needy in my life. I don't know if I could handle another round of Clayton right now, even if he did have time. I mean, I'd make it work, but still, I have a feeling I'll be good and sore today as it is.

"I have to go, gorgeous. I'll see you later?"

I can't help but chuckle. Where would I go? I have tons of online shopping to do for my niece anyway. *My niece!* "Anything you want me to order for Tessa?"

Clay looks at me like I'm speaking a foreign language. "Am I supposed to have an answer for that? I have no idea what babies need."

"Do you want some? Babies, I mean."

"With you as their mom? Yeah, I'd take a whole brood of little Eleanors, if that's an option."

I bite my lip, peeking at him through my lashes. "Sounds like we'd better get busy then."

Clay chokes on saliva, banging at his chest to try and get air back in his lungs. "Christ, you're going to kill me."

"I better not! We're just getting started." Leaning down, he pecks me on the lips one last lingering time.

"You bet your fine ass we are. Order whatever you want." He slips a credit card out of his wallet and hands it to me.

"You don't have to pay, I'm doing okay."

"Can we gift them from you and me?" he asks. His eyes are wide and puppy-dog-like.

"Yeah, we could do that."

"Then I absolutely can pay for them."

"Fine." I toss a pillow at his head, laughing when he dodges it and almost topples down the stairs. He chucks the pillow back, sending me a wink before he heads downstairs. I can hear him shuffling around, but if I'm honest, I have no desire to get out of bed and see him off. Plus, I think if I walked down there naked, he'd have to call in and tell them he isn't going to make it today.

A few minutes later, the smell of coffee wafts into the loft. I stay quiet, listening to the sounds of Clay getting ready for work.

"Bye, Leni. Have a good day!"

"Be safe, Cowboy!" I call down the stairs, already pulling open the girl's chat.

BEST BITCHES GROUP CHAT

> I have news! huge news and somewhat less huge news.

PEPPER

Oh no is his dick small?

MIYA

Jesus Pepper…you have no chill

PEPPER

Isn't that why you love me though?

> Unfortunately I also have news. Though it's of the bad variety.

Flipping onto my stomach, I rest my phone against the headboard and make sure all my nakedness is covered before I start a video chat with the group. Pepper pops up on my screen first, and she looks like a hot mess. Her hair is pulled in a messy bun, but not a cute one. One that suggests it might have been in the same bun for several days now. Makeup is smudged down her face, and I'm pretty sure there's Cheeto dust on her nose. She sighs when Miya joins the chat and gapes at her.

"I know," Pepper moans. "I'm in mourning."

"Let's start there. No offense, Leni."

"None taken." I shift my eyes to Miya, hoping Pepper doesn't notice the worried glance we share.

"Ugh." Pepper flops onto her back, holding her phone up above her face. "I did something stupid, and it got me fired."

"Oh no." I fill in an awkward gap of silence because Miya is trying to hide a face that plainly reads, *saw that coming.* "What happened, Peps?"

"The tiki bar had a wet t-shirt contest and wanted it filmed to be put up for advertisement. My manager asked if I wanted to join in on the promo, so I did. I didn't really see the harm in it, you know? But the school board called me in and told me a parent had alerted them to the videos, and they didn't think I was a good fit to be teaching kindergarten."

"Can they fire you for doing something outside of work?" Miya looks annoyed.

"Yeah," she sniffs. "There's a code of conduct I agreed to when I signed my contract."

"Shit, babes, I'm so sorry." I give her my best sympathetic look before I smile like an evil maniac. I sit up suddenly, forgetting for a second that I'm naked and covered in hickeys. "Oh shit, fuck!" I squeal before falling off the bed, flashing my two best friends my entire body.

The girls are howling with laughter, and I can't help but join in. Lying on the floor for a solid minute, my abs ache from laughing so hard. Popping my head over the bed, I reach for the blanket and wrap it around myself before getting back onto the mattress.

"You know," Pepper wheezes, still trying to control her laughter. "I'm feeling so much better now."

"Girl," Miya wipes tears from her eyes. "We saw *everything.*"

"How did I not know you had like, the best boobs?" Pepper winks. I can feel my cheeks heat at the compliment. This was so not a conversation I ever planned on having with my best friends.

"I kind of feel like we should flash you now, make it even." Miya surprises the hell out of me, taking a sip of coffee and giving us the most innocent-looking face.

Pepper shrugs before ripping her tank down, showing us her small, perky tits. "I've got nothing to write home about, but feast your eyes, ladies."

I fall over laughing, gasping for air, before squealing at my phone screen because no-nonsense Doctor Park is flashing us, and there's *JEWELRY* on her boobs.

"And now I'm bi," Pepper says, bringing her phone closer to her face so all we can see is her forehead. Miya laughs, shaking her head as she rights her shirt and sits back, like nothing weird just transpired. "Did those hurt?"

"A little, but it really wasn't that bad."

I'm staring at the phone, shocked. Growing up, Miya and I did everything together. We snuck our first beers together, had our first kisses at the same bonfire. She called me when she lost her virginity, and I called her when I lost mine. Hell, we even went and got tattoos together when we turned eighteen.

"Len, why do you look like someone kicked your puppy?" Miya scrunches her forehead in concern.

"I feel like I don't know you anymore. Nipple piercings? Flashing? Who even are you?"

"I'm still me, Leni, or...at least trying to figure out who me is. You might have been right about me focusing too much on work. I'm not sure I even know who I am."

"Ahh, you guys, we're having a moment!" Pepper says

seconds before ruining said moment by dropping her phone onto the bridge of her nose. "Ow, goddammit!"

"Okay, back to Leni now, it looked like you had an epiphany when Pepper was talking about work, but before we get to that, I need to know about those hickeys, because the ones on your shoulders look like bite marks."

My face is red again, and I realize that I really should have put clothes on before trying to video them. "Ugh, yes." I hide my face in the blanket, peaking out only when they are finished laughing.

"That's hot." Pepper fans her face.

"It kind of is, isn't it?"

"Dammit," Miya whines. "Do I have to move back home to have hot sex?"

"Hell no!" I wag my finger at my phone. "The only single guys worth dating out here are my brothers, and I love you, Mimi, but you can't."

She gives me an evil smirk that makes me narrow my eyes. "Jeez, I'm kidding. Leni, your brothers are hot, but I don't want to bang them."

"I do." Pepper sticks a sucker in her mouth before tapping her chin like she's thinking. "Which one is the one who never smiles in any of your photos?"

"Brooks!" I squeal, pretty sure I'm sick to my stomach now. "No, take it back, please."

"What? He's got flannel daddy vibes written all over him."

"Oh my God, please."

"Help me out, Mimi..."

"Sorry, I'm definitely not into Brooks. Once you meet him, I think you'll understand. The guy could look at crops and have them shriveling up because he's so intense."

"Okay, but you said her brothers are hot, plural. So if Daddy Brooks doesn't do it for you, then who does?"

"Please, for the love of God, stop." I rub my hands over my eyes, trying to scrub the vision of Brooks and Pepper out of my mind before it can fully take form. The girls become suspiciously quiet. I peek around my fingers and catch Miya mouthing Adler's name. "Jesus Christ, Mimi, leave my baby brother out of this."

"What? He has that bad boy thing to him, and Ethan...in a suit. God." Her shoulders shimmy like a shiver worked its way down her spine.

"Like, business suit, or swimsuit?" Pepper pops the sucker out of her mouth with a loud noise. With anyone else, the gesture would almost be vulgar, but it's just Pepper being Pepper.

"Take your pick there, hon. Shit, maybe I should come back to visit this summer."

"Stop fantasizing about my brothers!"

"Fine." Pepper pouts. "I thought you'd want me to be happy, Leni."

"You can be happy without fucking one of my brothers. Plus, unless you want to be called mommy, you definitely want to take Brooks off that list."

"I'm sorry, what?" Miya spews her drink across the table while Pepper shrugs. "He could call me mommy any day."

"Pepper Cinnamon Basil, keep it in your pants for five Goddamn seconds. What do you mean, Leni?" Miya triple-naming Pepper gets the younger woman to shut up, leaving me with the perfect opening.

"First, I have no details because he isn't talking, buuut...Thursday morning, he was just Brooks, and then this morning, he texts us a picture of him with a baby, and tells us she's the newest addition to the family."

"Oh my God." Miya sits back in her chair, looking absolutely horrified by this revelation. "He barely takes time to sleep. When the hell did he knock anyone up?"

"I don't think he did," I say, because I honestly don't think that's what happened. "I won't know for sure until he tells us, but I'm not entirely sure she's his. Biologically, at least."

"Color me intrigued." Pepper sits up, propping her phone against something on her coffee table as she adjusts her camisole.

"That's where my idea comes in, Pep. He's looking for a nanny."

Miya snorts, but Pepper sits up straighter, her eyes brightening. "Wait, really?"

"Yeah! So, you should totally come to the ranch this weekend. You can meet him, and we'll convince him to hire you. Then you can live here with me, and I wouldn't have to miss you."

"Stop," Miya whines. "What do you mean, live there with you? I thought that was just talk? I thought you were delirious because Clay is good with his tongue."

"That's not the only thing he's good with..." I hide my face again, barely holding back a smile as Pepper giggles in the background. "I haven't decided yet, but Pepper could come for the summer. I'm probably stuck here until fall anyway."

Miya grumbles something under her breath, then flips me the bird.

"Do you really think he'd hire me, though?" Pepper looks down at her apparel. It's true, Pepper isn't the most grown-up adult I know, but she loves teaching, and she's great with kids. And selfishly, I want at least one of my best friends nearby. I miss them.

"I mean, would it hurt to try? Worst case, you come spend some time with me here until you find something to do. Best case, he gives you a trial for the summer and decides to hire you forever."

Pepper snorts. "Gosh, hopefully not forever, but at least for the summer would be nice. I still have the tiki bar job, but it's not going to pay my bills."

"I hate you both." Miya squints her eyes at us, then down at her work phone. "Shit, gotta go."

She disappears from the screen before we even get a chance to say goodbye. "Damn," Pepper whistles. "I would really hate her job."

"I know, right?"

Chapter 24

Are Girls into That?

Clay

"I'm not answering that!" Ethan's snapping at Mercer when I walk into the Sheriff's office.

"He said to direct any questions to his lawyer. Last I checked, *you're* his lawyer."

"He also said you can go see him yourself, or you can wait for Sunday and ask him then."

"But you're right here with all the juicy details."

"I don't have time for this, Merc, go see Brooks."

Ethan bumps the side of his fist with mine as he walks by, then makes his way out of our office, heading toward his.

"I don't know how to change a diaper," Mercer whisper-shouts after his brother.

I chuckle, throwing my fist up to bump into his before settling down in a chair across from his desk. It's pretty rare that we sit in here. Mercer is almost always on a call or an investigation, or bothering the other deputies in the deputy room instead of sitting in here. Solitary creature, Mercer is not. It's a wonder he hasn't found himself someone to settle down with yet.

"You could probably look it up online," I offer, taking a sip of my coffee, trying not to grimace. Patsy must have made the coffee today. This shit is hearty enough to put some chest hair on a grown man. I don't know how she drinks the stuff. Mercer gives me a knowing smile before reaching beneath his desk and pulling out coffee creamer. The same kind I picked up for Leni on Friday.

"Just trust me," he nudges it towards me.

I pour a healthy amount into my mug, watching as the pitch-black coffee turns into something much less manly. I try a sip and give him a nod because damn, that is so much more palatable.

"I swear," he lowers his voice, like Patsy might be lurking around a corner listening to him. "If she put any more coffee in that filter, we'd be chewing it instead of drinking it."

That pulls a laugh out of me, one I'm only starting to get used to hearing again.

"I don't know who you're sleeping with, but I'm glad you're happy, Clay. I missed this."

"Me too." I try not to cringe. An epic amount of guilt weighs me down as I think about how hurt he's going to be when he finds out I'm sleeping with Leni behind his back. Don't get me wrong, he'll be thrilled we're finally together, but he will not be happy that we kept it from him. Even if it is fresh, Mercer is the kind of friend who expects an update about a date the moment you finish kissing her goodnight.

"Seriously?" He throws his hands up in frustration. "You're not going to tell me who it is?"

"It's still new," I lie. It was new ten years ago. Now it's official. Or it should be. Shit, I'm not even sure what to call her. I never even asked her if she wanted to date me. I sort of bit her like an animal and called her mine. Fuck, are girls into that? She seemed into it.

"So?"

"So, we agreed we were going to wait a little bit before we talked to other people about it."

"Clay, brother, I can count on both hands the number of single women our age in town. Most of them have fucked either me or one of our brothers, so please, for the love of God, tell me who it is."

"Sorry, man."

I push up from the chair, biting the inside of my cheek to keep myself from spilling all my secrets. Another talent of Mercer's. I'm not sure he even has to interrogate people; he starts talking to them, and suddenly they're telling him exactly what he wants to know, without even realizing it.

"Well, that's bullshit. First, Brooks is keeping huge life-altering secrets, and now you."

"You're being dramatic, Merc." I lean my shoulder against the doorframe. Not surprised I didn't make it any further.

"Gasp! I would never." He rests a hand on his chest, like the delicate little flower that he is, before shooing me away with the same hand. I shake my head, chuckling as I push myself off the door frame and head to the back.

Sitting at the deputy desk, I find myself making a list of things I might need for a date instead of doing any actual police work. There are a few calls out for the fire department, wild-fires cropping up here and there. We haven't had nearly enough rain this season. The whole county is under a red flag warning, meaning no open flames whatsoever. Not even a tiki torch or citronella candle can be lit right now. Shit, half the wildfires we get are starting on the side of the road where some jackass tosses a cigarette butt out the window.

The ranchers and farmers hate years like this. Our dry climate and wide-open spaces are like a tinderbox waiting for a spark.

It looks like those calls are all being taken care of by our rural fire crews; they haven't requested any assistance out there, so I do a quick perusal of the night shift's calls and pretend to work. Without any actual calls for service to attend to, I'm sitting here planning out the perfect date so that I can ask my girl to make it official.

Is going steady still a term the kids use these days? Because that's what I want. I want Leni, and nothing else will do.

THE DAY IS DRAGGING ON, there's hardly anyone out on the roads to run traffic on, and I find myself a little bit jealous of how busy the night guys stay. Granted, I have no desire to work nights myself, but I wouldn't mind a little bit of the action on the day shift. No one wants to start a bar fight at noon, so I'm stuck writing elderly people parking tickets and counting down the minutes until I get to go home to Leni.

When three o'clock rolls around, Ethan scares the shit out of me, rapping on the window of my truck. Some cop I am, not even noticing him walking up on me like that.

"Jesus Traeger, you should really have more situational awareness."

"Yeah, yeah." I damn near hit him with the door as I shove it open, stretching out my back as I turn to face him. "What're you doing sneaking up on me anyway?"

"We need to talk."

"Okay..." I drag the word out, noting the way he's standing, wondering if I'm about to get KO'd. I've seen him hit bigger guys than me and knock them out. It wouldn't take much.

"What the hell is going on with Mercer?"

"What do you mean?"

"I mean, he's not being his usual annoying self, and that

means that he's hiding something. Something he doesn't want everyone to know."

"How should I—"

"Save it, Traegs, you and Nate are his best friends. He tells you everything, so I know you know what's going on with him."

"I don't, honest to God."

"Oh, really? Is that why shit got weird on the ranch over the weekend? Do you think we're all stupid? Because it was pretty obvious he was pissed at you, and I've never seen him pissed at you."

I squeeze the back of my neck, looking out over Main Street, willing some kind of accident or fire alarm to get me out of this situation. I told her it wouldn't work. I can't lie to these guys. They see *everything*.

"I knew it." Ethan's eyes narrow, his right hand wrapping around the left as he cracks his knuckles. I honestly don't know if it's a habit or a tactic. Right now, I'm not sure it matters. "Spill it, Clay."

"I don't know what he's up to," I muse, trying to figure out the right words.

"Then start with why he was pissed off at you, and we'll go from there, yeah?"

"Fuck, you're scary."

His eyes pinch even further, and if I weren't me, I think he'd actually take a step closer.

"I told him something that wasn't necessarily mine to tell."

Ethan sighs, taking a step back, he undoes the button on his sports coat, and fuck, is everything this guy does a threat? Because it feels very much like a threat. "I swear to God, Clay, if you don't get to the point and tell me what happened..."

"Jesus, fine. Ten years ago, when Leni turned eighteen, she found me. She came to see me, and I trashed a hotel room and scared the shit out of her. That's why she was on that bus alone in the middle of the night."

Ethan's body freezes; the only motion visible is the muscle in his jaw that feathers, slowly. His eyes flash to mine, nostrils flaring as he takes a deep breath.

"She said she never found you."

"I know," I sigh. "I didn't know she never told you guys."

"You never told us." He jabs a finger at my chest, right into my vest.

"I thought you knew! I thought she told you."

Ethan turns his back on me, one hand resting on his hip as the other messes up his perfectly styled hair.

"You sent her away? You let her leave and get on a bus in the middle of the night?"

"No...I, yes. I didn't send her, but I couldn't stop her either. I passed out and ended up in the hospital because the hotel staff didn't know what else to do with me. But yes, I'm the reason she was out there."

His fingers flex in and out as his foot taps out a rapid beat. "She was mugged because of you."

The words slip under my skin, hitting a little too close to home. They don't know it wasn't a mugging; they don't know how much trauma I'm to blame for.

"Yes," I manage to grit out. All of that guilt and anger surging back into me.

"I need to sit with this." Ethan storms off, leaving me with my heart hammering in my chest. My breath ragged, painful.

I get back into my truck, white-knuckling the steering wheel as I think about how much I'm responsible for. All the things I put her through. My vision starts to tunnel, and all I can think is that this is going to blow up in my face. The lies of omission are piling up, eating me alive from the inside out.

I don't remember grabbing my phone, don't remember

dialing her number, or listening to it ring. The only thing I'm fully aware of is the intake of oxygen the moment her voice hits my ear.

"Hey, Cowboy," she chirps, her warm sunshine-soaked voice washing over me.

"Hey," I choke out the word, my voice strained.

"Clay." Her tone changes instantly, fixer Leni on the line now. I never wanted this for her. I never wanted her to have to deal with this.

"I was supposed to be better."

"I know," she answers quietly. "So was I."

I blow out a breath, trying to get my shit together, trying not to tell her that not one but two of her brothers are now much more aware of the past than they were three days ago. A heaviness sits on my chest like a bad omen. A warning of how close I am to losing everything. "I can't shake this feeling, that everything is going to fall apart. There's too many lies, too many secrets."

Silence on her end of the line has me gripping the steering wheel even harder. The vinyl creaks in protest.

"You want to tell them I'm here."

"I want to tell them you're mine," I bite back. Ideally, she'd tell them everything, but starting with her being here. Not having to hide that she's here, with me, would be everything.

"Clay..." Her voice drops low, a warning.

"I can't—I can't go back. There is no future for me without you." She sucks in a deep breath, releasing it with a puff of air before she replies.

"Hear me, when I say this one time, and one time only, Clayton Traeger...I need you to be the one person who takes me at my word. I need you to trust that I know what I need, that I know what is best for me. I need you to believe me. To wait until I say I'm ready. Please." Her voice breaks at the end, desperation bleeding through her tone, and I know this is a make-or-break moment. If I can't meet her here, if I can't give her this, she won't wait around for me to figure it out.

"Okay," I whisper, air returning to my lungs in a natural rhythm. "I'm not trying to pressure you. I just—"

"I know. I know I'm not being fair to you, asking you to keep this secret, to keep all of my secrets. I need more time. You're healing parts of me that I thought would never be whole again. I need you on my side."

"Always. I will always be on your side."

"Then stop second-guessing everything. Stop looking for reasons why this won't work."

I hold back a groan. I can't exactly tell her why it came up, but I feel like I'm balancing on a tight rope. One wrong move and everything is going to come crashing down.

"I'll do my best."

"That's all I ask. I'll see you in a couple of hours, yeah?"

"Yeah. See you soon." Leni's line disconnects, and I force myself to breathe. Everything is fine. It's all going to be fine. Once Leni tells the family she's here, we can tell them about us, and there won't be a need for any more secrets.

Hopefully, she won't hate me for telling them. Hopefully, she'll understand.

I hit the main drag through town, writing several more parking tickets that I know are going to get thrown away and forgotten about. I don't even file them in the system; it's just something to make me feel like I'm working. And before anyone asks, yes, Mercer did tell me to do it. Something about police presence and all that.

When five o'clock rolls around, I'm already halfway home. I radio into dispatch that I'm done for the night and clock out on my phone. We might have our office in an ancient building, but the county is surprisingly high-tech for our small town community.

Turning into the driveway of Leni's cabin, I start to get antsy. First date jitters take over my body. Which is stupid, because I literally had sex with her this morning, taking her on a date should be the least scary thing I do today.

I transfer my date night supplies from my work truck into my personal, then take a deep breath and head inside to find *my* girl.

Chapter 25

Leni, Baby

Leni

I'M STANDING BY THE KITCHEN SINK, STARING AT MY parents' house, when strong arms wrap around me. Clay's familiar scent fills me with a sense of rightness, a sense of home. He kisses my neck before looking out the window to follow my gaze.

"You miss them, don't you?"

I lean back into him, snuggling deeper into his embrace as I sigh. "I do."

"You could always tell them you're here, walk over, and surprise the hell out of them." He grins, a goofy kind of smile that's tight around the corners. He's joking, but only partly. The part of him that feels responsible for the rift between the family and me is dying a little on the inside. I can see it.

"I will, I mean, I'm expected back for family dinner to meet Tessa, so I have to tell them. I just...I need to do things at my own pace."

"I know, I respect that. It doesn't feel right hiding." He turns me around, one hand caressing my face as his other slips through my waves. "You aren't something that should ever be hidden."

I feel my cheeks blush, heart skipping a beat in my chest.

"I want you, however, and wherever you are. If that's here for the summer, just the two of us, or over in Benson, I'm yours if you want me. There's no walking away from this, you're it for me."

"Clay," I breathe his name. My hands grip his neck and slide into his hair, swaying us back and forth a bit. I could certainly get used to this. Get used to Clay coming home to me every night, used to him whispering sweet nothings in my ear. It's hard to picture him in an apartment in Benson, but I don't hate the idea. I could take him with me. We could start a life out there, together.

The thought sits wrong because there is no separating Clay from this place, not permanently. He's as much a part of this ranch as I was, and I'm starting to wonder if the two of us ending up back here was inevitable.

"Go get changed. We're going out."

"Out?" My eyes widen, excitement pulsing through me. "Where are we going?"

"It's a surprise."

"Clay...I don't—"

"We're going somewhere private. No one's going to see you." He smiles, pressing a tender kiss to the tip of my nose. "Go grab whatever it is girls need for a date night, and we'll head out in ten. I'm going to take a quick shower and change my clothes."

I squeal and race up the stairs, looking through the shelves in the closet for something cute to wear. I've only been dreaming of going out with Clay since I was ten years old. Now that it's here and happening, I can barely focus on getting myself ready. My stomach is a mess of nerves, and my heart feels like it's fluttering, pumping all kinds of nervous hope and mushy feelings into me.

I decide to keep it casual, since we still haven't told anyone I'm home. I assume a restaurant isn't likely. So I select a pair of jean shorts. They're light wash stretchy denim that do all kinds of things for my ass. For the top, I pick a lavender corset tank with spaghetti straps. It's edgy and feminine, with the right amount of see-through material to tease him. I opt for brown sandals that have a bit of a platform to them, hoping they might help even out our height difference.

Ten minutes isn't nearly enough to do a full beat and hair, so I swipe on some mascara and glittery eye shadow before separating my thick waves into two sections. The top gets twisted up into a cute little messy bun. My curtain bangs are finally coming in clutch to work with me, instead of against me, as they frame my face and make my eyes pop.

I'm swiping on some soft pink lip gloss when Clay emerges from the bathroom. He's pulling a forest green t-shirt down his torso. His abs and deep V cut enough of a tease to send liquid heat straight to my core. His belt is hanging open off his hips like an unholy invitation to explore exactly what he's got under those jeans.

Holy shit, my cowboy is hot. He's in a pair of dark wash Wranglers, the kind that hug his ass and thighs within an inch of their lives. He's still wearing socks, but cowboys have a thing about their boots. They don't need a million pairs of shoes, only one good pair that they wear with everything. Because once they're broken in, they're basically a part of you.

That's what this feeling is, when I look at Clay. A well-worn pair of boots that fit just the right way. I never want to try another pair on, because they'd never feel this good, this right.

Clay stops dead in his tracks. He gives up trying to thread his belt through the buckle, his pupils dilating when he looks me over. Giving a low whistle, he swaggers his way towards me, pulling me to him with a hand on the back of my neck. It's possessive, strong, and oh God, I should have worn panties. I'm going to make a mess of these shorts by the time the night is over.

"Leni." He kisses the corner of my mouth. "Baby." Another kiss on the other side. "You." Kiss. "Look." Kiss. "Edible." Kiss. The way he says edible is sin personified, his voice dripping with sex and need, that same need vibrating down to my very bones.

"You trying to get me out of this cabin, or into that bed, Cowboy?"

"Both." He shoots me a wolfish grin before taking my mouth in a knee-buckling kiss. Clay kisses me like he's drowning, like he's been lost at sea, and I'm the first sign of land he's seen. Clinging to me like his life depends on it, and I am here for it. I'd be his life raft any time, if it means being kissed like this. Like I'm the only person on this planet. Like I'm the only thing he needs.

"Date night first, then?" I giggle, pulling away from him before we end up staying in for the night. I swipe a new layer of lip gloss on before following him down the stairs. He keeps a warm palm on the small of my back, and I can't help but wish we were going out in public tonight. I'd love to hit up the Rusted Rail and have Clay's hands all over me, claiming me in front of everyone. The thought sends a shiver straight through me.

I am so gone for him.

~

WE TURN off the highway onto a lease road, and I know exactly where we're going. The swimming hole is on our ranch, though it's usually easiest to get to on horseback. There aren't any roads that lead directly there, but there's a well-worn path from the lease road, thanks to the countless parties we had out here growing up.

I can barely contain my grin when we stop at the head of that path, Clay getting out to open my door. He surprises me when he opens the back door and pulls out a picnic basket, like an honest-to-God, wicker picnic basket. He also has a reusable shopping bag that looks like it's filled to the brim with supplies.

"Clayton Traeger, did you—did you plan an actual date for us?"

The tips of his cheeks are pink, but he gives me a little head dip. He shuffles the bags off to one side and offers me his hand. I take it, interlacing our fingers as we walk the quarter mile inland to our private swimming hole. It's not a natural spot. Mercer and Ethan got tired of having to drive all the way to the lake or into town to swim. So they'd taken the tractor and skid steer into the field and dug our very own swimming hole.

They'd neglected to ask dad's permission, but he'd been pleasantly surprised by how well it had turned out. Of course, he had to punish them for the insanely high water bill they'd accrued trying to fill it. They'd spent that summer rerouting the fences around the swimming hole so we didn't have to worry about cows and manure dirtying up the water. I've seen my parents drive down with their side-by-side to sit by the water many nice summer evenings.

The swimming hole was very well thought out, actually. There's a gradual incline that leads into the deeper parts, making it perfect for littles, but also fun enough for the teenage boys who dug it. Brooks built a little dock in the deep end, and I can't be sure, but I'm fairly certain they get it stocked with fish every year so they can come down and fish. Toby commandeered an old telephone pole that the boys stuck into the ground at an angle. He built a little platform and hung a rope swing that will fling you off into the deep.

There's a natural little grove of trees that surrounds it, and it's honestly one of my favorite places in the world. Clayton lays out a blanket near the shallow end, setting out a couple of towels as well. Opening the picnic basket, he sets out plates, like actual ceramic plates, two wine glasses, a bottle of Moscato, and a full-blown meal. There are sandwiches from Winnie's, a cute little cafe in town that shares my mother's belief that sandwiches do not have to be boring. There's a little tub of potato salad and some chocolate-covered strawberries. I don't even know where he would have gotten them, but I don't care. This is the nicest, most romantic thing anyone has ever done for me.

I sit down on the blanket, crossing my legs as I take the glass of wine he offers me. It's sweet and fizzy, and exactly what I like. "Clay, this is..." I look away from him, out over the water as emotion threatens to take me. "It's too much," I whisper.

"This is the bare minimum. You deserve so much more than a little picnic at the swimming hole. It's a start, though. The first of many dates that I intend to take you on."

I turn back to look at him, and I can practically feel the stars in my eyes. This is perfect. Reaching up to cup his cheek, I pull him into me, hoping I can convey all the love and gratitude I'm feeling in this kiss.

The moment his hand slips into my hair, tugging gently to angle my head and take the kiss deeper, I know we're not getting into the food. At least not right away.

Clay pulls away from me when we're both breathless. Taking our wine glasses, he sets them carefully on the picnic basket that he somehow transformed into a little table. When he turns back to me, the hunger in his eyes is palpable. He looks like he wants to eat me alive, and I can only hope that I look like I'd let him. Because the things he can do with that tongue are just the right amount of wicked.

"This top," he whispers into my neck, running his fingers along the thin straps of my crop. His fingers slip under one strap, letting it fall down my shoulder. He trails them across my breasts to the other side, lowering that strap too. This shouldn't be that erotic, but I can barely breathe; it's so good. "I like that it shows off my marks."

I bite my lip, looking up at him through my lashes. "Not second-guessing them now, are you, Cowboy?"

Pressing an open-mouth kiss to the bite mark on my shoulder closest to him, I feel his tongue lave at my skin, shivers erupting over my whole body.

"Nah, baby, you like them, so I like them."

"Yes." My voice is breathy and quiet, and we've barely even started. I reach for Clay's shirt, but he grabs both my wrists and holds them up above my head. In one swift motion, he has me lying on my back, arms stretched up above me, Clay straddling my middle. He shifts his grip so one hand is holding both of mine and reaches into his back pocket. He drags a pair of hand-cuffs up my stomach and over my chest, dangling them off one finger in front of me.

"Eleanor Kane, you are under arrest."

"For what?"

"Interfering with a police investigation."

"What are you investigating, Deputy?" My voice dips low and sultry.

"How fucking sexy you look in this getup. I'm going to put you in cuffs now. Do you understand?"

I feel a rush of moisture between my thighs, a resounding yes pounding through my body. I nod frantically, not sure I can get the words out. Clay tightens his hold on my wrists, eyes narrowing.

"Words, Leni," he demands, his voice rough.

"Yes, I understand."

"Good girl." He tightens the metal around one of my wrists, then soothes his free hand back down my arm. "Am I going to be able to take this top off with your wrists tied up, or do we need to take it off now?"

"Now." Clay moves back onto his heels, giving me the space to sit up. My hands go to the bottom of my top, but Clay gives a gentle tug on the handcuffs, pulling my hands away. I still, staring up at him through my lashes. His eyes are dark, burning with lust so intensely that I feel like I could catch fire from looking at him.

"Arms up, baby." I do as he says, sucking in a breath as his warm fingers trail up my body, pulling the top up over my head. "Fuck me." He's still sitting above my hips, looking down at my breasts as my chest heaves. His hands slip beneath them, lifting them and pressing them together. His touch is soft, reverent. The whole thing feels sweet until he leans forward and whispers in my ear, "Someday, I'm gonna fuck these perfect tits of yours."

I whimper, the ache in my core burning a path through my body. I need him inside of me. Now. Clay snaps the other handcuff in place, using the chain between the two to slowly lower me back onto the ground.

"Are you sure this is okay?"

"Yes," I nearly cry. With anyone else, the panic would be setting in. The idea of being held down, unable to be in control, has always scared me, but here? With Clay? I want nothing more.

"Can you keep your hands up here? Or do I need to find something to stake them in?"

I gulp at the thought of being fully restrained, at his mercy. "I'll be good," I whisper.

Heat flashes through his eyes at my answer, before he moves himself lower down my body. Hooking his thumbs into the waistband of my shorts, he slides them down my legs, so fucking slowly. He sucks in a breath at the sight of my freshly shaved pussy, fingers slipping through my folds in a light, teasing touch.

"Oh Leni, such a naughty fucking girl. Where are your panties?"

I can't answer him. My mind isn't working anymore, heart in my throat, and I'm going to pass out from how badly I need him inside of me.

He takes his time exploring, hands sliding up and down my legs, lips pressing kisses into my skin, alternating between little bites and soothing touches. He makes his way between my thighs, sinking his teeth into my inner thigh as his fingers pinch my nipples. I cry out, the little bite of pain and pleasure swirling around me in a dangerous vortex.

"What do you want tonight? Do you want to ride my face? Let me eat this sweet little pussy until you come on my mouth? Or do you want to turn over and take your punishment for forgetting to wear all your clothes?"

Chapter 26

FDAU

Clay

A SEXY LITTLE WHIMPER ESCAPES HER LIPS AS LENI squirms beneath me. Personally, I'm good with either option, or both, really. I want to keep touching her. Want to keep pushing her, watching as she eagerly follows my commands and lets me take the lead.

"The—the second one," she stumbles over her words.

"Stay here, love," I command, pushing myself up to stand. I take in her naked body, arms outstretched, the silver metal of the handcuffs shining in the evening light. Pulling my shirt up over my head, I kick off my boots, then tuck my socks into them. Leni's watching me, her eyes never leaving my hands as they discard random items of clothing. Once I'm fully naked, I stand over her. Fisting my cock I give it a few rough pulls, from root to tip.

Her eyes widen, tongue darting out to lick her lips. Her muscles start to shiver, like it's taking an effort to do as I said, to stay where she is.

"Such a good girl for me." Her eyelids flutter closed, back arching off the ground. Yeah, my girl likes that a lot. "If you turn over," I say, voice gruff as I jerk my dick again, hard enough to hurt. "I need you to know that I won't be able to hold back. It's going to be hard and fast. Do you want that?"

Her eyes pop open, glazed over with lust. "Yes."

"If I take you from behind, I'm going to leave my handprint on your ass. Do you want that?"

Her teeth sink into her juicy bottom lip as she nods her head eagerly. I quirk an eyebrow, prompting her to open that pretty mouth again. "Yes, Clay."

"Then turn over, baby. Face down, ass up."

She scrambles to her knees eagerly, pressing those perfect tits into the blanket, her arms stretched out in front of her head, giving me the perfect view of the handcuffs she still has on. Thank God I need to get on my knees for this, because standing is no longer an option, not when she peeks over her shoulder and flutters her eyelashes at me. Not when she's so open and trusting.

Lining myself up behind her, I smooth my hands over her ass and up her back. Drawing my hand away, I pause. I've done this with other partners, but it feels different with Leni. I've spent my entire adult life trying to prove that I am not my father. I don't find pleasure in hurting people, but I do like control in the bedroom. I like to punish and praise, and that's all I want in this moment.

Leni senses my internal battle, turning to look over her shoulder, she gives me a coy smile. "I didn't wear panties all day," she croons. "Took me until after lunch to convince myself I could shower you off."

I groan, smoothing my hands over her ass as I watch that grin turn into something feral on her face.

"Then I touched myself in the shower, thinking about the way you fucked me with your fingers."

"Fuck." I squeeze her hips, kneading my fingers into the soft skin. "So fucking naughty."

"So naughty." She bites her lip, fluttering her lashes at me. "What are you going to do about it, Deputy?"

I pull my hand back and send it flying into her ass cheek. A satisfying crack sounds, a sting biting at my own skin before I soothe the mark on her.

Leni moans, pushing her needy little cunt into my dick that's fighting to get between her cheeks. "More?"

"Again, Clay." I smack her again, spreading my fingers and hitting the same spot. Satisfaction washing over me as my handprint begins to show on her soft, tan skin. She screams this time. "Yes, again."

I raise my hand to smack her again. Lining myself up with her entrance, I brace her with my other hand on her hip. The moment my hand connects with her skin, I slam myself into her, hard and deep. Leni nearly collapses beneath me, choking on a sob.

"Shh." I soothe away the sting with my hand. "You're doing so good, baby. Look how well you take me." I grip her hips properly and pick up a rhythm that is as brutal as I warned her it would be. She's sobbing beneath me, chanting my name over and over again as our skin slaps together.

"It's too much."

"You can do it, Leni girl. I wish you could see how well you're taking me."

She moans, pushing back into me.

The position feels almost too good for me, but I can tell it's not quite enough for her. Sliding my hand into her hair, I grab a fistful and pull her up. Fitting her back to my chest, I slam into her from the new angle, and she cries out again. It's the best feeling in the world, to be balls deep in my girl, knowing I'm the one making her scream like this.

I look down over her shoulder, mesmerized by the way her tits bounce with each of my thrusts, the way the handcuffs clink as she brings her hands up to play with her nipples. Sliding my hand down her middle, I find the spot where she needs me. The second I put pressure on her clit, Leni falls forward, her orgasm too powerful to allow for any words. I'm not even sure she's breathing as her pussy clenches around me, like she's trying to suck my dick even deeper inside of her. I break, following her into oblivion as my own release destroys me.

We sit for a moment, both of us needing a minute to come down from that. I have never ever had sex like this. I've had good sex, sure, but this? Being with Leni? It's the closest thing I've found to heaven on earth. The way her body fits into mine, like she was made for me. Like we were made for each other.

Eventually, Leni slumps into me, her body spent. I settle her back onto the blanket. She stretches her arms up high, her hip curving up with the stretch, showing my handprint on her ass.

"Fuck baby. If I could take a picture of you right now, looking like that."

She sucks that bottom lip between her teeth and gives me a coy little shrug.

"So do it." I feel my dick jump between my legs at her compliance and the way her voice is strained and sexy. Leaning over, I snatch my phone from the pocket of my jeans and do just that. By the time I get us cleaned up and get my boxers back on, I realize Leni is still in handcuffs, still lying there like a model with her arms stretched above her.

"Give me your hands." Slowly lifting her hands, she tries to hide a wince, which makes me pause. "Did I hurt you?"

"No." She gives me a knowing grin, rolling her wrists out

when I remove the cuffs. "Not hurt, I'm just sore. The good kind of sore."

"There's a good kind of sore?"

"Of course there is." She sighs when I rub my fingers over the little red marks the cuffs made.

"I wasn't too rough?"

"No, Clay." She brings a hand up to my face to pull me into a kiss. "That was perfect, it was amazing. You're amazing."

I peck her lips once, then on the tip of her nose, before fishing through the picnic basket to pull out a sandwich for her.

"Should I get dressed to eat?" She bites her lip again, clearly picking up on the way it affects me. Leaning back, I take in her sweaty skin, that freshly fucked glow in her cheeks.

"No, I don't think so." I wink before taking a bite of my own sandwich.

"Ah, rats," she giggles, not at all disappointed by my answer.

Chapter 27

Warpath of Avoidance

Leni

Days fly by, and I realize that time is not on my side. It's Friday already, which means in two days I have to face the entire family for a family dinner. Thank God the focus will be on Brooks and his surprise baby. I'm not ready to admit that I'm technically jobless and homeless, though at this point, there doesn't seem to be any other option.

It will take all of one second for them to clock the way Clay looks at me, like I hung the freaking moon. I'm not complaining, but there's no way to hide what's going on between us.

I don't know what to do yet. I have the interview at the prep academy on Tuesday. Yesterday, Ranch Life reached out to let me know they want to publish my article, and then proceeded to ask if I had ever considered writing as a career. We emailed back and forth throughout the day, and I have a phone interview with them next week.

I didn't tell Clay, because I'm afraid he'll get excited. A job with the magazine would mean working remotely. I could live anywhere to write articles for them. I wouldn't have to move back to Benson. I could stay here, with Clay.

It sounds like a dream, but I know this bubble we've created will burst the second my family finds out we're together. Which, I think we are? We haven't really had a talk. It seemed like that's what Clay was offering, the other night when he took me to the swimming hole. We never really discussed it.

On the one hand, the family is going to be thrilled that Clay and I are...whatever we are. On the other hand, I don't want to hear Ethan's self-righteous "I told you so," when he finds out why I'm here.

I think, maybe, it'd be worth it though. Sitting through a big brother lecture might not be half so bad if I'm sitting there with Clay beside me.

I'm running through all the potential scenarios when Pepper's face pops up on my screen. How she always calls at the perfect moment, I will never know.

"Hey, Peps," I sigh into my phone.

"Damn, not exactly the welcome I was expecting. What's up, buttercup? Sex with the hot cowboy not as great as you thought it would be?"

I snort. If Pepper got a gold star for anything, it would be for being inappropriate at the exact right time. "No, that is most definitely not a problem."

"Well, that's good to hear. One of us needs to be getting railed. I'm clearly not getting any."

I laugh, throwing myself back onto the bed.

"I was wondering if you still wanted company this weekend. We never made any official plans, and I should probably consider letting the tiki boss know."

"Actually, I have an interview on Tuesday. I was thinking you could come back with me then?" There's an awkward pause until Pepper sighs.

"You still haven't told them you're home, have you?"

"No," I whine. Last time I came home without a job, they

took it upon themselves to schedule interviews for me around the county. I had to call not two but five local businesses and tell them I didn't need a job. I mean, I did, but I can get my own fucking job. "I want to spend some time with Clay before we blow the whole thing up."

"You keep telling yourself that, Leni. Personally, I feel like you're a little harsh on them."

I groan, rolling onto my side so I can push myself back into a sitting position. "You haven't been around long enough, Pepper. My mom literally told me not to come back if I left. I was eighteen. The boys have driven all the way to Benson, on more than one occasion, to yell at me because I refused to answer my phone."

"Leni," Pepper sighs. "I love you, I really do, but I've heard you talk with your mom on more than one Sunday. She loves you, and you miss her. I know she hurt you. I do, but I need you to remember how lucky you are to have a mom who cares. To have a whole ass family that cares."

"I know that," I bite out, trying to reel in my Kane temper.

"Do you? Because you act like having a family who cares about you is the worst thing in the world, and I can tell you, there are a lot worse things out there."

Shame builds up in my chest, choking my throat as my phone vibrates with incoming text messages. "I'm sorry, Peps. I shouldn't complain."

"No, you should. You're allowed to complain," she sighs. "I think it might be time for you to have some conversations. You're all adults now. You can set boundaries, and if they can't respect those, then maybe you continue this warpath of avoidance."

I snort. "Warpath of avoidance?"

"It sounded good in my head," she chuckles. And we make plans for traveling back to the ranch together on Tuesday after my interview. I'll be going back to Benson to stay with Miya on Monday.

I check my messages, a smile taking over my face as I see the group name.

THE ACTUAL BABY BROTHER'S GROUP CHAT
ADLER JAMES

Where are you staying this weekend?

When do you get in?

TOBIAS RUSSEL

wdym where is she staying? She has a cabin here.

ADLER JAMES

Yea...one where Clay is staying

TOBIAS RUSSEL

Oh shit.

Where are you staying?

I can clean up my guest room

ADLER JAMES

She's not staying with you, why would she stay with you?

TOBIAS RUSSEL

Why wouldn't she stay with me?

MERCER DUANE

Boys. Boys. Boys.

You already know she's staying with me. Her favorite brother

ADLER JAMES

That's it! I'm buying a new phone!

TOBIAS RUSSEL

What kind of hacker app do you use that you are somehow in ALL of our group chats?!

I want to answer and tell them I'm staying with Clay. Wouldn't that be a way to tell everyone what's going on?

> I haven't decided yet. Probably be home in time for dinner.

ADLER JAMES

Dinner? You're coming for dinner and that's it?

MERCER DUANE

That's completely unacceptable Leni.

You can spare a weekend for us can't you?

ADLER JAMES HAS SENT A PHOTO TO THE GROUP CHAT

I sigh, looking at the photo of my two younger brothers. Both looking up at the camera, bottom lips hanging out, big ole puppy dog eyes begging me to come home for longer.

MERCER DUANE

Damn. If that doesn't work on you I don't know what will

No wonder you guys take girls home all the time

> Fine. I'll come back tomorrow.

MERCER DUANE

And stay with me...right?

> We'll see.

Chapter 28

I Just Lost Everything

Clay

"Do you really have to go?" Leni pouts her bottom lip, tugging at my t-shirt, trying to entice me to follow her into the bedroom.

"Unless you want your brothers showing up here, I really need to get on the road."

"When did Mercer even start poker night? It sounds dumb. I hate it."

I chuckle, pulling her into me, taking my time to kiss her breathlessly. She hums into my mouth when I start to pull away.

"He started it last year. It's only once a month and I'll be back before midnight."

"Toby still the best poker player?"

"Damn right. I don't know why we still invite him to play."

She grins, that smile that makes me weak at the knees. My whole heart expands when she looks at me like that. "Wait up for me?"

I watch, a lump growing in my throat, dick jerking to life as she pulls off her t-shirt. Underneath is a lacy, see-through lingerie body suit that hugs her curves in all the right places. Just the right amount of skin peeking out through the straps, teasing me, making me rethink poker night entirely.

I watch as her hand slides down her stomach, fingers dipping below the waistband of her shorts. She slips it lower, sultry hooded eyes looking at me through her lashes. Teeth sinking into her bottom lip, a gasp follows.

"Hurry back," she whispers, drawing slick fingers out. She's about to wipe them on her shorts when I grab her wrist and suck them into my mouth. My eyes close, a guttural moan ripping from my chest the moment her arousal hits my tongue. "This outfit is crotchless." Her sexy voice whispers in my ear, breath warm and inviting against my skin.

"Fuck me," I breathe. My voice is closer to a whimper than it's ever been in my entire life. My cock presses into my zipper, so hard it physically hurts. I grab the back of her neck, hauling her body into mine, our eyes meeting. "You're going to pay for that, Leni. So fucking naughty."

Heat sparks in her eyes, and she gives me a feral grin. "Looking forward to it. Get out of here so you can get back sooner."

I press a quick kiss to her lips, then pull myself away, slipping on my boots, so I don't say fuck it and end up in bed with her. I wasn't joking, her brothers would absolutely find their way here if I don't show up.

Unlike the Main house, the only way to get to Mercer's is to take the highway around. All the boys live on the ranch. Adler still lives at home, but the rest of them have their own spots. Brooks, naturally, is the furthest from town. Ethan lives the closest, and Leni's cabin would be second. Then the main house, and then, depending on which direction you want to travel, you'll get to either Mercer's or Toby's place next.

Mercer has the nicest lawn, something you can credit to his

use of community service. It's not actually court-ordered, but when kids get into trouble. He uses manual labor on the ranch or at his own place to get them to pay their time. Keeps their records clean and their parents happy. Most of the time.

He has a little ranch-style house with a wrap-around porch. A small lean-to shed tucked in with a horse pasture and a small round pen. He doesn't take much time for himself these days, but I know he tries to ride at least once a week. Fabio, as always, is looking like a fairytale horse, with his long flowing black mane and bougie tail bag. It's practical, and I know that, but it looks ridiculous on a ranch horse.

I got photos a couple of years ago when a group of girls did some landscaping after teepeeing the school. Mercer came home to Fabio covered in glitter, his hair braided and bedazzled. That motherfucker strutted around the paddock like he was God's gift to horses. They say dogs match their owners, but I wonder if the person who created that saying ever met horse people.

I park outside of Mercer's house, not entirely surprised to see Ethan sitting outside on one of the wooden rocking chairs. A beer in his hand, resting bitch face on display. I know he's waiting for me; all the other guys' trucks are here. In Adler's case, his horse, Sir Percival, is tethered to the hitching post outside the house.

I grunt when I pull myself out of the truck, mentally preparing myself for another Kane brother's confrontation.

"Ethan." I stop at the steps, giving him a weak smile that he returns with narrowed eyes. We stare at each other for an uncomfortable amount of seconds before I break. "Spit it out already."

"I'm pissed at you. You should have called us the moment she showed up on base."

"Fair," I say. The thought had crossed my mind, sure.

Twenty-one-year-old Clay wanted at least a little bit of time with her, even knowing it wouldn't last.

"Why didn't she tell us what happened?" Ethan stands up, draping his forearms across the banister. His eyes distant, brow furrowed, like this is a puzzle he can't quite figure out.

"I don't know, E." I dart my eyes to the door, willing someone to come out before I admit that I'm lying and I do fucking know.

"Guess I'll ask her this weekend then, because that's fucked up."

"She's going to be thrilled, I told you guys," I mumble, the weight of all this guilt gnawing at my insides. I walk past Ethan, shouldering open Mercer's front door to the loud arguing voices of the three youngest Kane brothers and one stoically quiet Deputy Clark. He makes eye contact with me, nodding his head in my direction before going back to observing the boys.

"They're doing a hot wings challenge," Ethan says, standing next to me. "And she'll get over it. If we have to deal with her telling lies all of a sudden, she can deal with the consequences."

My chest tightens. This is why Leni moved away and hates coming back. Ethan sounds a hell of a lot more like an angry dad than a hurt older brother.

"Ahhh." Adler taps the butcher block counter, his face turning beet red, tears steaming down his face. "No, more. Please." He slams back a glass of milk, Mercer following suit behind him. Toby, the bastard, is sitting there completely unbothered, tearing into a wing.

"It's not that bad." He grins at the other two, who look like they're regretting their choices.

"I love it when he eats spicy food." Ethan can't take his eyes off Adler, who looks like he's about to bawl like a baby. "Good to see he's actually human." He snickers before moving into the kitchen to help himself to another beer.

"Ah!" Mercer grins. "The final member of the party, seeing as Daddy Brooky won't be making it."

"Can we not call him that?" Toby screws up his face.

"Yeah, no." Adler coughs, chugging milk between breaths. "No, Daddy Brooky."

Nate chuckles from his spot at the island. I've only been to one other poker night, and while he doesn't talk much, Nate seems to be the only person who can actually best Toby. It's interesting to watch the struggle. The rest of us are here for fun; these two are out for blood.

The boys do one last round of wings before we move down to the basement. Toby and Adler murmuring some kind of plan to best the new guy. Whatever they cooked up didn't do them much good. I don't know where he came from, but Nate can play poker.

"For fucks sake." Adler tosses his cards down, pushing his last pile of chips across the green felted poker table to Nate. The rest of us all grumble similar sentiments while the asshole smiles. His arm draped over the back of the chair, free hand moving a chip across his knuckles.

"Good thing ya'll stopped playing for money." He chuckles, showcasing how badly he took us all by stacking his chips in obnoxiously straight lines.

"I think he cheated." Toby eyes the growing stacks in front of Nate. His gaze moves from the chips piling up in front of Nate, turning a knowing smirk at Adler. One of those looks that means they're having a private conversation with their eyes.

Nate glares a narrowed-eyed stare at him, a look most people might shy away from, but not Toby. At six-five, he's built like a bear, the biggest of the Kane boys by far. Toby is a solid wall of muscle, and he doesn't flinch when Nate glares. Nah, he just smiles.

"I do not cheat," Nate growls, leaning forward. The dark corner of Mercer's basement feels twice as small when he crowds the table.

Toby's grin only widens, completely nonplussed by the action. He shrugs, brushing Nate off entirely, which succeeds in pissing him off more. Nate's nostrils flare as he leans back in his seat, arms crossing over his chest.

"On that note." Ethan chuckles, pushing up from the table. "I'm heading out. See you guys Sunday." He cracks his knuckles against his chest. "Nate, you comin' for family dinner?"

"No." Nate, for the first time tonight, looks uncomfortable. I know that feeling, the overwhelmingness of the Kane family and all their goodness. It's hard to handle when you're used to having a shit family yourself. "Thank you, though, for the invite."

"We're going to get you there eventually." Adler smiles at the newest member of our group. I'm surprised no one has added Nate to the group chat yet. Mercer sure is close to him, and it seems like the rest of them have adopted him, too. Maybe they're waiting for him to make it to family dinner first. Seems to be the official welcoming into the family.

Nate doesn't answer, giving Adler a jerk of his head with a signature grunt before grabbing his jacket and heading up the stairs. We all file out the door. Adler takes off, hopping on his horse, and rides into the night as he whistles. Toby and Nate walk toward their trucks, voices low and rumbling about something, probably more cheating accusations. I'm about to head for my own truck when Mercer taps my arm and nods his head toward the rocking chairs. He has that *"I'm The Sheriff And We're Having A Chat face."*

I sigh, but drop my ass down onto one of the wooden seats. Planting my feet on the deck, I settle into the seat and rock. "What's up, Merc?"

"I did a little more digging." He drops into the extra chair, watching as the boys take off down the driveway. My muscles tense, fingers flexing as I try not to show the discomfort. "I called the police department and asked for the files on Leni's mugging. A detective sent me that picture I showed you." His fists ball up at his sides. "They said there wasn't a mugging." He shakes his head, eyes turning toward me. "They wouldn't tell me anything else over the phone. I won't have any paperwork until Monday, but I need to fucking know what she's hiding."

"Maybe you should ask her, instead of digging for answers behind her back."

"You really think she'd tell me? After ten years of lying about it? What's to stop her from lying again?" His brows furrow, the thought of asking Leni so far out of his mind that he can't imagine it.

"I don't know, Merc. Maybe because she's an adult now? Maybe she had a reason for it."

Mercer's eyebrows go up to his hairline. His body leans back into the chair as he appraises me. "You know something... what do you know, Clay?"

"Nothing," I scoff, looking out over the empty drive, wondering if he would follow me if I made a break for my truck. Anything to avoid this conversation.

"Nah, that's not going to work tonight. You know something, but how?" His index finger taps his chin, eyes watching me, in a way that leaves me feeling exposed. "How do you know something? When's the last time you talked to Leni?"

"Before I got here," I mutter, my eyes widening in disbelief.

I didn't even realize I was saying it until the words came out. Fuck my life.

"Excuse me?" Mercer leans forward, his eyes bright with excitement. "You're talking again? When did you start talking again?"

"I—fuck, I don't know Merc." My fingers pick at the seam of my jeans, eyes looking anywhere but at him right now because I'm so goddamn uncomfortable.

"Holy shit." Mercer stands, walking to the railing of the porch, where he turns around to face me. Leaning against the banister, he crosses his ankles, then his arms, glaring. "She's home right now, isn't she?"

I gulp, looking at the roof of the porch. Maybe if I stare at it hard enough, it'll collapse and take me out with it.

"I swear to God, Clay, if you don't start talking right now, I'm going over there."

"Fuck, yes. She's fucking home. Okay?" I meet his eyes. The idea of him going over there and accosting her sets my teeth on edge.

"Home, as in her cabin, right? Just to clarify, my sister is in the little one-bedroom cabin that you are also occupying."

"Yes," I growl, fingers gripping the chair's arms. This is such a huge violation of Leni's trust. She told me that the one thing she needed was for me to trust that she knows what's best for her. That she will do things in her own time, and here I am, not allowing her that privilege.

"She's the girl you're fucking." Mercer uncrosses his arms, running a hand through his hair before it scrubs down his face. "Great. I mean, I'm not mad about that part; I've been saying it for years. But what the fuck, Clay? I've been talking non-stop about getting her home for the summer, and you're what? Playing house with her?"

"It's not like that. She asked for time to figure stuff out."

"Figure what out? You and her? How did this even happen? One minute, she told me she wasn't coming home all summer, and now she's here, and you're fucking. That didn't happen overnight, so how long has she been here?"

I sigh, leaning forward, burying my face in my palms, shoulders shrugging in reply.

"You know why she lied back then, don't you?"

"Yeah, Merc, I know."

"This is bullshit." Mercer marches off the porch, heading straight for his beat-up green Dodge pickup. I beeline to intercept him, putting myself between him and the truck door.

"You're not supposed to know she's here. You're not even supposed to know that she found me that night. She didn't tell you that, remember?"

"Oh, I fucking remember Clayton. So what? You're hiding her from all of us? What does she have to figure out?"

"She feels like a failure," I blurt, the words tumbling out of me faster than I can stop them. "You guys closed ranks on her after that summer. She didn't want you to know she's back because she feels like she proved you all right."

"How? By being super successful? By putting herself through school and doing it basically alone?" Mercer looks completely baffled. Jesus, does no one realize how alienated she feels? I know that she keeps them at arm's length, but do they not see why?

I lean against his truck, gut churning as my mouth keeps moving. "None of you wanted her to go."

"Of course we didn't!" Mercer shouts, his temper getting the best of him. He takes a step back, his shoulders creeping up toward his ears. "She's our sister, our only sister. How were we supposed to protect her all the way in fucking Benson?"

"She didn't need your protection, Merc. She needed your support, fuck, anyone's support."

"We have been nothing but supportive."

"Right." I shake my head, rolling my eyes at him. "That's why Brooks told her she'd never make it, right? Why she avoided coming home for over a year. Because of all the support?" I wrap air quotes around support, my voice edged with a challenge.

Mercer shoves my chest, slamming my back into the pickup before he jabs a finger toward my face. "You don't get to fucking talk. You weren't here. Where was your support, Clay? Where were you when we got a call from a hospital in the middle of bum fuck nowhere saying she'd been hurt? Huh?"

My fingers ball into fists at my sides, heart pounding painfully in my chest. "You know where I was." My voice comes out steady, calmer than I feel.

"That's right," he sneers. "You were in the hospital after you threw a tantrum so bad you scared my baby sister into getting on a bus in the middle of the night. Is that why she lied, Clay? Did you beat her up? She's so fucking good, she wouldn't tell us so that we wouldn't turn on you. Is that what happened?"

"I would never hurt her, and you know it, Mercer." A knife slices through me; he knows I wouldn't hurt her. He has to know I didn't do that.

"Do I? Because the Clay I knew wouldn't lie to me. He wouldn't hide my sister from me and keep secrets. He would't go off half-cocked and confront his dad while he was on a fucking work call and then forget to tell me about it. So how am I supposed to know what you're capable of, Clay? Huh?"

"Not that!" I bellow, shoving him back a step. I need space to breathe. "I wouldn't fucking do that!"

"Then tell me what happened, Clay, because the evidence is stacked against you." Mercer steps his feet apart, arms crossing over his chest, eyes bore into mine.

"It's not my story to tell, Mercer."

"Well, I'm asking you to tell me, Clay. Enough with the secrets, man. What did you do?"

The open anger in his eyes takes the wind right out of me. He's supposed to be my best friend, my brother. "You're supposed to fucking trust me," I manage to calm my voice, the tenor shaking as I speak.

"How can I do that when you keep fucking lying?"

"I'm not lying now, Mercer."

"Just go," he spits out, disgust on his face. He starts to walk back toward his house. "I can't even look at you."

"Some asshole tried to *rape* her." I spit the word out, knowing it's going to hurt him, using it like a weapon, hitting my mark with expert precision. Mercer turns slowly, his eyes wide with disbelief. "Yeah, she was attacked in that bathroom, and she didn't want you to know. Didn't want any of you to know."

The words taste bitter in my mouth. The flavor of betrayal coats my tongue. I did the one thing she asked me not to. Delivered it in such a way that I knew it would do the most damage to Mercer. *Fuck.*

"You need to leave." Mercer's voice comes out low, deadly.

I don't look back at him as I storm to my truck. I hit the highway at a dangerously fast speed, racing against a clock I know I can't beat. I pull up in front of Leni's cabin, tires spinning so fast that the front porch and the woman standing on it are wrapped in a cloud of dust as I fling open the door.

When the dirt settles, it takes one look into Leni's eyes to know that I just lost everything.

Chapter 29

Don't Leave Me

Leni

I wander to the kitchen, making myself a cup of tea for the night, when I see an envelope on the kitchen table, my name written in Clay's handwriting. An old familiar thrill rolls through my body, the excitement I used to feel when I'd get a letter from him, makes my chest squeeze. I take the letter to the couch and open it, smiling at the heading.

DAY 8 OF FOREVER
DAY 1 OF CHUCKING THE RULES

ELEANOR,

YOU KNOW I'M SHIT WITH WORDS BY NOW. I DON'T KNOW WHY IT'S SO HARD TO TELL YOU WHAT I'M FEELING IN THE MOMENT. I'M TRYING TO GET BETTER AT IT, I SWEAR, I AM. I'VE SPENT TOO MANY YEARS TRYING NOT TO THINK ABOUT YOU, TRYING NOT TO WANT YOU. THEN YOU BURST BACK INTO MY LIFE AND TURNED EVERYTHING UPSIDE DOWN AGAIN.

I KNOW I'VE SAID IT BEFORE, BUT I NEED YOU TO

KNOW, LENI, THAT THERE HASN'T BEEN A DAY IN THE PAST TEN YEARS WHERE I DIDN'T THINK ABOUT YOU. WHERE I DIDN'T ALMOST PICK UP MY PHONE TO CALL YOU, JUST TO HEAR YOUR VOICE. GOD, I'VE FUCKING MISSED YOU. NO ONE MAKES ME FEEL THE WAY THAT YOU DO, AND I KNOW YOU THINK IT'S SIMPLE. THAT THE CHOICE IS BLACK AND WHITE, BUT IT'S NOT FOR ME.

I HAD NOTHING BEFORE YOUR FAMILY TOOK ME IN. NO ONE CARED IF I ATE, IF I WENT TO SCHOOL, IF I MADE SOMETHING OUT OF MYSELF. THEN MERCER CAME ALONG AND SUDDENLY I HAD A FAMILY. I HAD BROTHERS AND PARENTS WHO CARED ABOUT THE SMALLEST, MOST SIMPLE THINGS. I'VE BEEN TOO SCARED TO RISK THAT. SCARED THAT I'LL FUCK EVERY-THING UP SO BAD THAT THEY'LL FINALLY REALIZE THEY MADE A MISTAKE IN TAKING ME IN.

BUT IT WASN'T JUST THEM THAT I GAINED, IT WAS YOU TOO. I FOUND MYSELF LOOKING FOR YOU AS SOON AS I WALKED IN THE FRONT DOOR. YOU WERE MY FAVORITE PART OF EVERY DAY, NO MATTER HOW SHITTY IT WAS, I KNEW YOU'D MAKE IT BETTER. I LOVED YOU THE MOMENT I MET YOU.

IT HAS ALWAYS BEEN YOU FOR ME. I WANT YOU, ELEANOR ROSE KANE. WITH EVERY FIBER OF MY BEING. MORE THAN I'VE EVER WANTED ANYTHING ELSE, I WANT YOU.

I'LL CHOOSE YOU, IF YOU'LL LET ME. BECAUSE EVEN WITH THE RISK OF LOSING EVERYTHING, I COULD NEVER WALK AWAY FROM YOU.

TAKE WHATEVER TIME YOU NEED, ASK WHATEVER QUESTIONS YOU WANT TO ASK, BECAUSE I'M NOT GOING ANYWHERE.

YOURS FOREVER,

CLAY

P.S. IF YOU HAVE TO LEAVE, I HOPE YOU KNOW I'M COMING WITH YOU. I WASTED TEN YEARS WITHOUT YOU. WISHING I COULD SEE YOU, HEAR YOUR VOICE, KISS YOU. I WON'T SPEND A SINGLE DAY WITHOUT YOU AGAIN. SO IF YOU DO HAVE TO GO, THAT'S FINE. JUST DON'T LEAVE ME BEHIND.

I almost reach for my phone to call him. To tell him that I love him too, because I really fucking do. I have always loved him. I don't know what my future looks like, but I know who I want to be in it. No matter what happens with the interviews, I don't want to give him up. I know nothing other than the fact that I feel safe and loved and whole when he's with me. The way he believes in me, listens to me, and supports me. The fact that he offered to move again, for me. To follow me means something.

It means everything, really.

I haven't had that kind of support in ten years. Maybe Pepper has a point, maybe I'm responsible for that. I haven't exactly given them a chance to be supportive recently. Not that all of them would be, if anything, Brooks and Ethan have gotten more grouchy over the years, but I know my parents miss me. My voicemail sits just shy of full every week. I leave enough room for up to two new voicemails, but I hate deleting the ones from my dad. He was the only one who supported me leaving, even if it was quietly.

THE CORNERS of my eyes sting from how much I've been crying. I can hear Ma in the kitchen, banging around in the cupboards while the boys all watch me pack my Jeep. Standing around in their Wranglers and cowboy hats, arms crossed over their chests, they watch me struggle with boxes and bags, none of them offering to help. The two younger boys took off, Toby, as adverse to conflict as Pa is.

I'm about to get into the Jeep, watching as, one by one, each of my older brothers shakes their heads and walks away. No goodbye, no good luck. Just mutual disappointment in their little sister. My dad is at my side, pulling me into a giant bear hug, his big arms wrapping me up like they used to when I was little. I let his hug swallow me whole, the last of my tears soaking into his shirt.

"You wipe your eyes now, Eleanor." He pulls away enough that I can do just that, rubbing my already tired eyes on my hoodie sleeve. Then he tucks an envelope full of cash into my pocket and puts one big hand on the side of my face. "You will always have a place here, sweetheart. Always."

I nod, chest heaving with a shaky breath, before I slip into the driver's seat.

"She'll come around, Leni. I won't minimize what you're feeling by trying to justify her words. But don't give up on them, alright? We love you. All of us."

"Love you too, Pa." I strap my seatbelt across my chest and give him a nod. I never expected to do this next chapter alone, but at least I have Miya. At least I know my dad isn't disappointed in me.

THE MEMORY of fighting with my mom always sets me on edge. I'm her only daughter; we used to be inseparable. We might be better now, might be talking, but it's nothing like it used to be. We probably could have used a few more joint therapy sessions, but I hated making her drive all the way to

Benson to sit and cry in an office together. We both had things we regret, but we can't change that now.

Maybe moving back would start to heal some of those cracks. Some of the pieces that aren't quite right yet. I'm agonizing over the implications when my phone rings. Mercer's goofy smile lights up my screen.

"D, you will be the first one to know when I decide where I'm staying."

He's silent for a full minute, making me pull the phone from my face to see if he's still on the line. When he speaks, his voice is low, angry, and I'm instantly on guard.

"Leni, I need you to tell me what happened ten years ago, and before you lie and say you were mugged. I need you to know that I'll have the police report on Monday."

"What?" I nearly choke, sitting up on the bed. I try to put my thoughts in order. "Why would you request the police report?"

"Because Clay told me you did, in fact, find him on that trip, and I got to thinking, what else could Leni lie to me about?"

"Clay told you what?" My head starts to spin, thoughts racing faster than I can sort through them. If Mercer had already requested the report, Clay would've had to have told him before now. Meaning he told him and didn't tell me.

"I need to hear it from you, Leni, because if what Clay told me tonight is true, then I don't even know you. I'm not sure I ever did."

"He told you more?" I whisper, heart fissuring in my chest. He promised. He told me he respected my need to do things at my own speed. He said he was on my side.

"Leni," Mercer breathes, some of the anger draining from his voice as he sighs. "Tell me what happened."

"Why? You can read about it, can't you?"

"I don't want to fucking read about it. I want you to tell me what happened."

"If you wanted that, you would have asked me first, Mercer. You wouldn't have gone behind my back and used it as blackmail. How fucking dare you!"

I'm shaking, completely blindsided by this conversation. He didn't even bother to ask me, just went straight to the source. Bile rises in my throat as panic sets in. If he knows, everyone is...they're all going to know, and I'm going to have to explain it. I'm going to have to tell them what happened and relive every last detail.

My lungs start to riot, not enough air getting in. The walls feel like they're collapsing. Like I'm running out of time, running out of choices.

"Leni, if we had known, if you would've just told us what happened back then—"

"You would have been even more crazy!" I'm shouting, pacing the bedroom. "God, imagine if you guys knew back then. You would have locked me in my room and thrown away the key. You guys didn't care what I was going through, only that I made a mistake."

"That's not true. You scared the shit out of us. Do you know how terrifying it was to find out from Miya that you left? That you took off across the country and hadn't checked in with her in days? All we cared about was finding you, about making sure you were okay."

"And what did you do when you found me? None of you even questioned the story. All anyone cared about was making sure I knew I'd made a mistake. You never let me live it down. I know what I did was stupid, but you guys never saw more than that."

"Leni." Mercer's voice softens, but I'm done with this conversation. Done with him. Done with all these men who think they know better than me.

"Don't," I whisper. My voice is thick with emotion, tears welling in my eyes. I hang up the phone and move around the room, packing up what little I brought into the cabin. I can't be here. Not anymore. I was barely ready to tell them I'm home. I can't have this conversation with them either. I won't.

Clay.

My heart feels like it's being ripped into shreds. Eviscerated as the idea of us starts to crumble. I told him what I needed, and he promised. I really believed that he wouldn't tell them. I really thought he would wait and let me decide. But he's just like them, taking away my choices. My tears start to fall, and I'm overcome with the need to leave. To put this place in my rearview and never come back.

I try to get everything together and out to the Jeep before he gets back, but I don't make it. His truck slides to a stop in front of the cabin as I'm standing on the porch.

"Leni," Clay pleads, his strides eating up the distance between us. I hate myself, but I flinch, body jerking backwards when he reaches for me. The hurt in his eyes breaks my heart. "Baby," he tries again, keeping his hands down at his sides.

"No." I step towards the trees, shaking my head at him. "No, I told you what I needed. I told you, and you said you were on my side."

"I am. I swear, I am on your side. Mercer—"

"God, you're just like them." I shake my head. "I can't be with someone who makes all the decisions for me. I needed you to wait. I needed it to be my choice."

"He was going to figure it out."

"Why, Clay? Why did you have to say anything? Why couldn't you leave things alone?" My voice comes out broken, desperate. I wanted *this*. I wanted him.

"He kept pushing me to call you, to work through the past

and make things right with you, but he didn't know all the pieces. He deserved to know that I'm the reason you got hurt. He deserved all the information."

"No, you needed to absolve yourself of the guilt. You wanted him to know so that he'd finally see you the way that you see yourself. To give you one more reason to think you're not good enough for me, another excuse to walk away like none of this mattered...like I never mattered."

"That's not true." Clay's head drops, hands stuffing into his jeans' pockets. "Not anymore," he whispers, cloudy grey eyes meet mine. "I want you, Leni. I've always wanted you."

"That's not enough," I whisper, tears spilling out over my cheeks.

"Please don't leave me." His voice cracks, feet taking tentative steps in my direction. "I can make it right. I can fix this."

"There's nothing to fix." I turn on my heel and march toward my Jeep, whipping around when I hear him step toward me. "Don't follow me." I take one last look at him, turning on my heel, I walk away from him. Again. Willing myself not to turn back.

When I get to my car, I text Miya to let her know I'm coming back and need a place to crash. I don't know why I thought things would be different this time around. Things will never change for us. My family will never see me as more than a child who needs their protection, and Clay...*Clay* will never think we're worth the risk.

My tears make it hard to see the road. An entire season of rain has suddenly erupted from the sky, not helping my case either. We were heading into summer with a drought for the record books, and now it's like Mother Nature is trying to catch up in one night. I slow down, trying to dry my eyes enough so that I can see where I'm going.

Halfway back to Benson, I'm driving the freeway by pure

memory. It's so damn hard to see. The highway is a ghost town. It's going to take forever to get to Miya's at this rate, with how badly it's pouring down. I drive in silence; the radio in my Jeep hasn't worked in years. I turned my phone off, chucking it in the back seat when the notifications wouldn't stop, everyone trying to reach me. It was too much to explain and rehash while I'm trying to drive through a tsunami.

The rain finally lets up enough for me to drive at highway speeds. My chest feels heavier the further away from the ranch I get. I don't know why I thought things would work this time. They would have gotten worse, especially once they all knew everything. I wouldn't be surprised if they showed up in the next couple of days and tried to get me back home. For the first time since leaving home at eighteen, I'm wondering if maybe Benson isn't far enough away. Maybe I need states between us. Maybe I need to completely start over.

The idea starts to take root, of driving on through Benson, not stopping until there is enough space between us. I wouldn't have to deal with overbearing, disappointed family members again. It's tempting, until grey eyes pop into my head, heat shining in them, as calloused hands map my body. The feeling of rightness washes over me as I remember exactly what it feels like to be loved by Clay.

An all-consuming love that didn't judge me when I told him everything. Love that was so big, he didn't want to hide it. Love that I pushed to the sidelines, in favor of hiding my own secrets. I accused him of looking for excuses when I was doing the same thing all along.

I told him he wasn't enough when all he ever asked of me was not to leave him.

Fresh tears fall from my eyes as I pull onto the shoulder. When I left the ranch for the first time, it felt freeing, like I was on the cusp of something great. This time, I feel like I'm losing part of myself, that I'm leaving home behind me, and it's not the ranch. It's Clay.

Flinging my seatbelt off my body, I wiggle around the wheel to search the back seat for my phone. I need to fix this before he leaves. Before that dark place takes him again, and I lose him forever. The past doesn't matter or my family knowing about it. Nothing matters if he can be mine.

Turning on the overhead light, I lean back over the center console, shuffling through my things, looking for a needle in a haystack with how cluttered it is. The black of my screen flashes as a spotlight shines through the window, illuminating things better than the dome light ever could.

I turn toward it, my tired brain taking too long to process where the light is coming from. My world blurs in slow motion as headlights smash into the side of my vehicle, the world shattering around me.

We Need Leni
Updates Group Chat

MIYA PARK
2 YEARS AGO

Again. I will not be doing that.

MERCER

Don't think of it as spying Mimi. Just think of it as you keeping tabs on Leni

BROOKS

For us...

ETHAN

Fuck it. Call it what it is. We need you to spy for us Miya.

MIYA PARK HAS LEFT THE WE NEED LENI UPDATES GROUP CHAT
MIYA PARK HAS JOINED THE WE NEED LENI UPDATES GROUP CHAT

MIYA PARK
2:56 AM

Leni was brought in by life flight.

BROOKS
3:45 AM

Are you serious?

MIYA PARK

I don't have time to call. On shift. Get here.

BROOKS

Fuck

Chapter 30

I'm Not Going Anywhere

Clay

> Please come back and talk.

> Just…at least tell me where you're going. Please Leni.

> I know I fucked up. I need to know you're okay.

> Baby. Please tell me where you are.

> I love you.

I STARE AT MY PHONE, WILLING A TEXT FROM LENI TO come through. Even if it was just her telling me to fuck off, I need to know that she's okay. I've been waiting for something from her all night. I haven't slept. She should have made it to Benson by now, if that's where she was headed. The more time that passes, the more anxious I can feel myself growing.

I don't know if she's okay or if something has happened to her. It downpoured half the night, meaning driving wasn't exactly safe. If she had been crying, she could have driven off the road. Or worse, crashed. She could be out there, some-

273

where, sleeping in her car. I don't fucking know, and it's killing me.

It's almost nine a.m. when I decide to stop rotting in my dirty clothes and head for the shower. It's the fastest shower I've taken since being out of the military, too worried that I'd miss a call from her. I rush back to my phone, catching it on the last ring of a call from Brooks. I set the phone back down, a heavy sigh echoing through the empty loft. Barely a second passes before he calls back again.

"Hello?" I sigh, the exhaustion weighing me down as I wonder who all Mercer might have told by now. I can't think of another reason why Brooks would be calling me this early.

"Where the hell are you?"

"Huh?" I sit up straighter, clutching the phone to my face, fear stirring in my chest. If Brooks is looking to fight me, I won't stop him. Nothing could hurt as badly as watching her leave, *again*.

"Leni is in the ICU in Benson, and you're not here. Why the fuck not?"

"What happened?" I launch myself off the bed, fumbling around for clothes as Brooks barks into the phone.

"Miya texted us, *fuck*. I forgot. I saw her jeep in the trees; no one else knew she was home. No one knew to call you." I hear him murmuring something in the background. I knew he'd figure out she was home. Brooks and Orson Kane know everything that happens on their ranch, but Mercer...he didn't call me. Not even a single fucking text. I knew I'd lose them all eventually, but part of me always hoped it wouldn't happen. I don't know who I am without these guys.

"Brooks!" I shout into my phone. Whatever he's doing on the other end is taking too long. "What the fuck happened?"

"She was in a car accident. They had to life flight her here.

Get here, Clay, she's..." Brooks pauses, his swallow audible over the line. "She's hurt bad, brother."

"Fuck." I don't bother saying goodbye, slamming my phone into my back pocket, I rush to my truck, spitting gravel at the cabin as I tear out of the driveway. "Fuck!" I scream into the cab, ramming my hands into the steering wheel.

I checked my phone a couple of times throughout the drive, expecting notifications in the family group chat to keep everyone updated on Leni's condition. But there's nothing, at least not on my end. Lead drops into my stomach as I realize they must have started a new group chat. One that doesn't include me.

I provide my ID to the nurse at the ER check-in, and she gives me a visitor pass before pointing me in the direction of the ICU waiting room. I look wrecked, with big, dark bags under my eyes, hair no longer curly, some spots sticking straight up where I've run my hands through it too many times. I haven't heard back from Brooks, and I don't have Miya's number to call and try to get more information.

The gal who checked me in wouldn't give me any information either. Only that I can sit in the waiting room and get my updates from actual family members.

She might as well have stabbed me in the chest with those words. The way I haven't been able to breathe, wondering if she's okay, praying she's still alive. That I still have time to make things right.

I make it to the waiting room and find absolute chaos. There are Kanes everywhere. The whole room seems to have been turned into a camping area. Half the brothers are passed out in chairs; hospital blankets pulled up to their chins. A perky blonde girl is lying on a blanket next to the baby Brooks sent a photo of, making faces at her phone while Brooks' baby stares blankly at her. Brooks is watching them, only glancing up when I clear my throat.

"Finally." He gets up to make his way toward me, drawing the attention of the family members who are awake. Ma and Pa both link hands and walk toward me. They look exhausted. Ma's eyes are puffy from crying.

I'm about to bump my fists to the one Brooks offers when I'm ripped backward. Landing on my ass, I skid out of the waiting room, slamming into the wall. Mercer stands over me, his face a mix of exhaustion and rage.

"Get up," he spits. His fists ball up at his sides. It's stupid, I know exactly what is going to happen if I stand, and yet, I do it anyway. I don't even try to stop him when he swings, his knuckles splitting open my lip as my head whips back. Another fist lands a blow to my ribs, knocking the breath from me before he's being pulled back. Brooks pins Mercer's arms behind him as Mercer tries to lunge for me again.

I slump against the wall, wiping blood from my lip. "Mercer, what the fuck?" Toby comes to help Brooks manhandle Mercer back into the waiting room. Pa makes his way over and offers me a hand. I shake my head, leaning back against the cool concrete.

"You can walk in there on your own, or with my help, son. But you're coming in. I don't know what that was about, but I intend to."

I peek an eye at the man who raised me, the only true father I've ever known, and I wonder if I'm about to lose him too. I nod, pushing myself off the wall. I square my shoulders and follow him into the room.

"He knew that whole time." Mercer's voice is gravelly, like it might be on the verge of becoming hoarse.

"Is that true?" Ethan turns to me, his fingers dancing at his side, itching to crack his knuckles or maybe to punch me.

"Is what true?" Pa asks, moving to stand behind Marcy. Big hands resting on her shoulders.

"Leni wasn't mugged," Toby mutters, voice low and heartbroken.

"Someone tried to rape her, and he knew," Mercer spits out, bouncing on the balls of his feet, like he wants to come at me again.

"I didn't know. Not until last week." My answer doesn't seem to make things better.

"But you knew she left in the middle of the night, and you didn't think to call any of us?" Ethan is fuming, his jaw clenched so tight, you can see the muscles grinding.

"I—" I'm no longer sure if we're talking about a decade ago or just last night. Guess they could take their pick, maybe it's both. I don't know. I look to Mercer out of habit, hating the way I don't get the reassurance I need, the backup I've come to expect. "If you're talking about ten years ago, I had a panic attack and ended up in the hospital. She wasn't answering my calls, so I thought she blocked me. I thought she made it home. I didn't know anything about this until a few days ago."

"What do you mean, last week?" Ma's green eyes, so much like Leni's, meet mine full of hurt and doubt.

I blow out a breath, gripping my ribs when they expand a little too far. I think he might have cracked a few. "She's been back at the ranch since last Thursday."

"Excuse me?" Ethan's seconds away from finishing what Mercer started, betrayal clear on his face.

"It's true," Brooks pipes up, from where he's sitting with his baby, who's still staring at the blonde-haired stranger. "I saw her Jeep. I knew she was home."

Mercer growls, throwing his hands up in the air, shaking his head.

"Why didn't she tell us?" Ma looks close to tears. I'm not

sure I've ever seen her cry. She's the backbone of this family, the one who helps to hold us all together.

"She didn't want you to know," Miya says from behind me.

"That's bullshit." Adler is standing next to her, arms crossed over his chest. Miya cuts him a look that has him stepping a couple of feet away from her.

"Why? Why did she keep so many things from us?" Ma's voice chokes, tears falling down her cheeks.

Miya and I share a look. It's not our place to fix this, not our place to intervene. Neither of us says anything. Instead, we nod, an understanding passing between us.

"You'll have to ask her that, Ma. It's not my place." I grip the back of my neck, hating this. Hating the way I feel like I don't fit. As if I'm an intruder here.

"She can have two more visitors now," Miya says to me.

"Great." Mercer shoulders past me, snapping his fingers at the woman with Tessa. "You and me, blondie. Let's go."

"Um, I think maybe Clay should go. He needs to see her." The blonde chews her bottom lip, looking entirely uncomfortable with the whole situation.

"That's Pepper," Miya whispers, as the blonde gives me an awkward wave.

"You're not going in there." Mercer points a finger at me before storming off. No one says anything to contradict him. Ethan follows Mercer. I look at Miya, the desperate plea obvious in my eyes when she moves closer.

"She looks rough, Clay, but she's going to be okay. It'll take some time. She has a lot of broken bones, but she's going to live."

I nod, feeling a thousand pounds heavier now that I'm here, and there's nothing I can do to help Leni.

"Come on." Miya pulls me toward the corner where Brooks

and Tessa have carved out a space for themselves. "Rest, Clay. Okay?"

I nod, trying my hardest to keep my eyes open. A little snort escapes me when Pepper's phone slips out of her hands, landing on the bridge of her nose. Her gasping groan pulls a little smile from the otherwise expressionless Tessa.

"And you're done here." Brooks steps in, scooping the little girl off the ground. He gives me a curt nod before tossing a blanket at me, turning all of his attention to Tessa.

I DON'T REMEMBER FALLING asleep, but it's after dark by the time I wake to Miya shaking me. Sheer exhaustion makes it hard for me to open my eyes.

"Come on," she whispers. I realize then that most of the Kanes are tucked away and sleeping. Brooks is the only one sitting up, a bottle in one hand, Tessa in the other. He gives me an encouraging nod before gesturing his head toward the door.

I nod, eyes opening wider when I realize I'm going to see Leni. With Mercer and Ethan both passed out on the opposite side of the room, I get up, eagerly following Miya as we sneak out of the visitors' section.

"Technically, visiting hours are over, but she's still in a medically induced coma. They don't want to try to wake her up yet, so I don't think it'll hurt for you to sneak in. At least for a minute. The nurses already know you're coming."

"Thank you, Mimi."

"She talked about staying." Miya's bright blue eyes meet mine. "She wanted you more than she wanted to avoid them. I hope that counts for something, Clay."

I swallow hard, trying to work the emotions back down. "Yeah, Mimi, it does."

"Do you love her? Like, really love her? Not like before."

"I do."

"Good. I know they mean well, and I know she's pushed them away, but she really does need someone who's hers. I know Mercer's your best friend, Clay, but she needs someone who takes her side, someone who thinks of her first."

"I know," I whisper, breath wheezing a little as I try to ignore the pain in my side.

"You should get that looked at." Miya points at my ribs, then my face.

I shrug. "I've had worse."

"I bet." Whether she's thinking of my childhood or life on a ranch, I don't know. I suppose it doesn't really matter.

"What am I walking into, Mimi?"

We stop outside the door, my palms sweaty, heart racing.

"Hell," Miya says. "She doesn't look like Leni. She broke six ribs, broke her pelvis, fractured her spine in two places, snapped her radius, and got her face bashed in. She's on a vent right now. Her right lung collapsed due to the accident. We don't know what happened, but she wasn't buckled in when she was hit. The car that hit her spun out on the highway and t-boned her. Paramedics said it looked like she was parked on the side of the road. She has a long way to recovery ahead, Clay."

"Jesus," I groan, ripping my hands through my hair.

"Give the family some time. She knew they wouldn't react well to the news. You're still one of us." Miya smiles, her hand resting on my arm. "They need to realize this isn't on you."

"Isn't it?" I pin her with a look that says *bullshit*.

"It isn't. Someday you'll learn that. They're not even mad at you, Clay. They're mad that it happened. Just give it time."

I nod as a courtesy. It doesn't matter if they do, not anymore. Leni is my family, and as long as she wants me around, I'm not going anywhere.

Chapter 31

We Forcefully Declined

Clay

GRAVITY NEARLY TAKES ME TO THE FLOOR WHEN I SEE her. Leni's lying in the hospital bed, wavy locks splayed out around her head. Half her face is blocked by cords and tubes; so many wires are attached to her body. Her eyes are swollen, soft, creamy skin is darkened with bruises.

The ventilator chimes every time it takes a breath for her.

"Hey, baby." I take her hand gently, bringing my lips down to press a kiss on her knuckles. I can't stop the tears, because this is too much. I shouldn't be holding her like this. We should be tucked into bed at the cabin, snuggled into each other. "It's me, Leni. It's Clay. I don't know if you can hear, but I am so sorry, love. I'm so fucking sorry." I drop my head to the bed near her shoulder and lose it completely.

When the tears are all dried up, I scrub my face on the scratchy blanket and turn back to Leni. She looks so serene, so peaceful. I don't know what she'll hear or remember, but I need to get this off my chest.

"I can't believe I wasted so much time with you. You have

always been it for me. Did you know that? I fell in love with you a little more with every letter you sent, and then, that summer, I knew I'd never love anyone the way that I loved you."

Sitting forward, I swipe her bangs off to the side, wishing she were awake. Wishing she could tell me that everything is going to be okay. I need to hear her voice. I need some kind of sign of life in order to take a full breath in.

I need her.

"I think about that last night all the time, Leni. Do you remember it? The first time we kissed? I'd been at war with myself all day, wondering what to do about you. Part of me wanted to ask you out, part of me knew it was a bad idea. That we couldn't go there. I was scared things would blow up between us, and I'd lose my family. But I was more scared that I was losing myself and that I'd take you down with me."

My fingers rub up and down her forearm, trying to avoid the many, many bruises she's covered in.

"I'd all but convinced myself that I was going in there to tell you goodbye, that it was going to be the last time I saw you, talked to you. Then you smiled at me when I walked in that door, and I was lost to you all over again. I was spiraling, lying in that bed with you. The thought of losing you was shredding me apart, and I let myself wonder what it would be like if I didn't let you go. Maybe we could have worked something out. Maybe it wouldn't have all fallen apart. Maybe I needed regular sleep, and I would get better. I wouldn't have to worry about putting my issues on you or hurting you again. Then you turned around and looked at me, and you asked me if I thought I would need you. That you would find a way to get to California, and you'd take care of me. You laughed when I said you needed to graduate. Laughed, Leni. I knew then that you would have done absolutely anything for me, and I couldn't let you destroy yourself. At seventeen no less."

I'm staring at her face, trying to recall the way the light shines in her eyes when she smiles, trying to remember what it sounds like when she laughs. Everything feels too big. It's been less than forty-eight hours, and I can't even summon those things to my mind.

"Please, Leni." I take a deep centering breath, forcing myself to choke the emotion back, to be strong for her. "When I didn't answer you, about coming with you, you blushed so hard. The deepest blush I'd ever seen on your face. I thought you looked so damn cute...blushing at me like that. You thought my silence meant I didn't want you. Assumed that I was going to try and let you down easy. But when you faked a smile and tried to turn around, I couldn't let you go. I didn't want my last memory of that summer to be of you faking a smile, so I kissed you, and it ruined me."

"Fuck did it ruin me, Leni."

"I broke my own goddamn heart sneaking out of the house that next morning. The selfish part of me was glad that I'd kissed you. Glad that I would have that memory to take with me wherever I went. It nearly killed me, thinking about how badly I was going to hurt you. I wish we could get that time back, Leni, just attach another ten years onto the end of our lives so that we could make up for everything. I'd give it all up if I could go back to last Friday and turn you away. I'd tell you to go; if I could somehow go back and prevent you from being here, I would do it, Leni. Because I can't fucking live without you in this world. I need you alive, baby, even if it's not with me. I need you to live. We all do. Your whole family is camped outside in the waiting room. Pepper's here, Miya. Everyone is here waiting for you. So please, Leni, you have to wake up, okay, baby? I need you."

Emotion clogs my throat, and I can't speak anymore. I hold her hand and stroke her arm until I somehow fall asleep next to her. The sound of the ventilator lulls me into a restless sleep.

I WAKE with my neck aching from the angle I slept in. Miya is standing next to me, her hand on my shoulder.

"Glad I got here first. Brooks is trying to stall Mercer. You better get out of here, Clay."

I look at Leni, and she looks the same as when I first came in. I know she's being kept in a coma to encourage healing, but it's discouraging to see her looking exactly the same, small and fragile. Vulnerable.

"I don't want to leave her."

"I know." Miya squeezes my arm. "I'll be here. They're going to run some tests to see how she's doing this morning. See if we can get her breathing on her own."

"Will she wake up?"

"It all depends on what they find. If it's safe to take her off the vent, we can back off the anesthesia. It can take time for people to wake up, but we'll let you know if we start that process."

I sigh, pushing up from my chair, feeling heavy and not at all rested. Leaning down, I press a kiss on her temple and whisper, "Time to wake up, baby girl. We're waiting for you."

I slip out of her room as a line of doctors makes their way in. The sound of the ventilator pulsing in my ears as I walk down the hall. I don't make it very far before my legs give out. I slide down the wall and bury my head in my hands. Everything hurts: my body, my heart, *everything*.

"How is she?" Toby slides down next to me, his long legs stretched out in front of him as he sighs.

"I don't know." It's the only answer I have right now, because I can't form into words what it's like to see her like that.

"Sorry, about..." He gestures to my face, where my skin feels a little too tight, a dull throbbing ache in my jaw. "I've never seen Mercer like this."

I sigh, leaning my head against the wall. I glance at him. It's still weird seeing the Kane boys in sweats. These guys live in their jeans and boots, or suits, in Ethan's case. They might be dirty half the time, but they're always put together. Right now, they're a mess. Completely undone, and it's jarring to see.

"So you and Leni, huh?"

I smile, for the first time since everything exploded with Mercer. Leni is the one thing I am absolutely sure about. Now I just need her to wake up, so she can tell me if she wants me to go or stay.

"Yeah."

"It's the real deal then?"

"Yeah, Tobes. She's it for me."

"Damnit," he complains.

"Don't tell me you bet against us." I nudge his shoulder with mine, wincing when the motion jostles my ribs.

"Oh, right." Toby tosses me a bottle of Ibuprofen, then hands over a shopping bag. "Those are from Miya. She had some in her locker." He points at the bottle of Ibuprofen. "And that Pepper chick went out and got us all a change of clothes."

"Oh, well, that was nice of her."

"And fuck yeah, I bet against you. Ten years is a long time, man. Too long. She could have moved on, bro." He gives me a pointed look before offering to help me off the floor.

"I know," I groan. "I'm not even sure she'll want me here when she wakes up."

"Well, here's to hoping then." He winks. "Also, I think you'll appreciate the fact that Pepper likes you, because Adler might have hit on her one too many times, and the clothes she got him...well, you'll see."

Throwing back the ibuprofen, I swallow them dry, then follow Toby back to the waiting room. "They tried to tell us to leave," Toby chuckles.

"We forcefully declined," Pa says, coming up to wrap me in one of his famous bear hugs. Whenever Pa hugs me, I feel like that scrawny little kid that he saved. He pats me on the back a few times before pulling away to look at me. "You okay, son?"

"Good as I can be."

He nods and moves back into the room, headed for the window where Ma is standing, looking out over the parking lot. Warm morning light is shining into the windows, and Ma has her head tilted toward it, like a sunflower in summer. Leni does the same thing on nice days. She did it that day on the lake. When we were all messing around on the boat, Leni was sitting near the front, eyes closed, head facing the sun.

I remember how my breath caught in my throat, seeing her like that. A fucking vision. So alive and at peace. I couldn't help but go to her, like I'd been sucked into her gravity, helpless to the pull between us. I guess some things never change, because I'm right back in that same spot. Helplessly drawn to her, eager to borrow even a fraction of her light. Her peace.

I find myself a seat toward the back of the room. The perfect spot to witness whatever shenanigans go on, but not actually close enough to have to participate. Mercer is glued to his phone, shooting daggers at me. If he wasn't putting out proverbial fires in the county, he'd probably come over for round two.

I can't stifle the laugh that bursts out of my chest when Adler walks in with to-go bags from a fast food joint. He's dressed head to toe in hot pink, and while Pepper might have thought she was pulling a pretty good prank, he's owning the outfit like it was made for him. Because, of course, Adler can pull off pink. He looks like a human highlighter; it's so bright.

Brooks drops into the chair next to me, tossing me a breakfast sandwich before rubbing his face with calloused hands.

"How are you?" he asks, staring at Ethan, who's somehow juggling Tessa and eating. I mull over the question, wondering which answer he wants to hear.

How do I tell him that I feel like I'm bleeding out? That every second Leni spends unconscious, I feel like tiny pieces of my soul are being ripped away. I'm so scared I can barely breathe. That I've been holding my breath since we got here, or that I'm not sure if this is survivable. How do I tell him that my heart is lying in that hospital bed? That her life is on the line, because I am nothing, nothing without her. I'm about to give my standard bullshit response when Brooks lifts his hat, setting it on his knee, his hands pulling at the ends of his hair.

"I knew." His voice comes out hoarse and thick with emotion. "I knew something else had happened. She came back a different person, Clay. You don't change that much from someone stealing your bags. I was so focused on my shit with Kate that I didn't dig in. Didn't ask more questions. I just doubled down. My whole life felt out of control, so I tried to control hers instead. She was always so easy, so agreeable before. We never fought. She'd bend over backwards to take care of all of us, and I'm not saying that was right, but that's how it was. When she came back, she was harder, more withdrawn. I thought if we could keep her here, we could draw her back out. But I pushed her away." He can't finish the sentence before his words are choked off.

Brooks isn't the kind of man who will sit and cry in front of just anyone. Seeing him like this, the mirror to my utter agony inside, I can finally take a tiny sip of air into my lungs. Finally, let a little bit of these walls crack, to feel everything I've been trying to lock into a neat little box in the corner of my mind. Because if Brooks Kane can cry about feeling guilty, then I sure as shit can too.

Chapter 32

I Need Clay

Leni

Everything hurts. My whole body feels like it's on fire, and for a second, I think I'm still in my car, listening to the horn blare, unable to move my body at all. There's a deep voice speaking in a familiar cadence, my hands heavy with the weight of being held.

It takes a minute before I can sort out the sound being Ethan's voice. He's talking to someone, Mercer, I think. Telling him about one of his cases, lots of legal jargon I don't understand. There's a stabbing pain in my head and chest. My ribs feel like they're on fire, and all I can do is wonder where Clay is. Is he here? Did he come? Would he have left? Why isn't he here now? I wish it were his hand in mine, glued to my bedside.

I must whimper, and the two go quiet around me. One hand squeezes mine tighter, while the brother on my other side leans forward and moves my bangs off my face.

"Hey, Leni girl." Mercer's voice is low and warm, softer than it was when I spoke to him on the phone that night. "Can you open your eyes, sweetheart?"

I want to shake my head. It hurts too much.

"Eleanor," Ethan commands, using his lawyer voice on me. "Try." That strong voice cracks a little, emotion clogging his throat. "Just try, please."

I focus on taking little sips of air; anything more sends my lungs into a full-blown riot. When I finally peel my eyes open, I'm relieved to find the lights dimmed. Mercer and Ethan sigh in relief.

"There you are." Mercer relaxes into the chair beside me. Ethan's shoulders lose their tension. The scruff on his face is the longest I've seen since he went off to law school.

"How long?" I ask, noting that Mercer also has a few days' worth of hair on his face.

"Three days," Ethan croaks, kissing my knuckles. My other arm is in a cast. A brace around my neck makes it impossible to move my head and assess the rest of me.

"Where's Clay?" The boys look at each other and choose to ignore me. A stone drops into my stomach with the words they're not saying. He isn't here. He didn't come.

Ethan gets up and shouts down the hallway, "She's awake!"

Adler flies around the corner, launching himself into the room. He runs past Ethan and nearly slams into the hospital bed. Eager eyes take me in, before he leans down and kisses my cheek.

"I'm good, I'm okay." *I'm here.* I want to say. *I'm alive.* Adler nods, then makes room as more people pile into the tiny recovery room. Ma wiggles her way between Adler and me, hands squeeze both of my feet. Ethan's on one side, Toby's on the other. Dad's standing next to Mercer, his big hand wrapping around mine. Adler sits next to my leg, one warm hand resting on my shin.

"Jesus Christ," Miya says from the doorway, and Pepper gives me an awkward little wave. "Leni needs to rest! You guys are practically crushing her. AJ, get the fuck off the bed."

Adler peeks up at me, a sheepish grin on his face. "I think she likes me." He winks, then slides off the bed.

"Seriously, Leni, I'm glad you're awake and alive, but your family are animals. You should see what they've done to the waiting room."

Her voice sounds serious, but she's smiling at everyone, and I know she's as relieved as they are. "But really, two visitors at a time unless you're nine months old, then you may have three."

I would squeal if my throat would allow it because somewhere between fighting with Clay and waking up here, I'd forgotten that I have a niece now. I wiggle my fingers out toward Toby, who I only now realized is holding a tiny little squish in his arms. I get lots of toe squeezes as people start to file out of the room. Toby leans the sweetest little bean towards me, letting me take a look at her. I kiss her cheek before Toby pulls her away and passes her off to Brooks, who moves to the seat on my right, Mercer staying in the chair on my left.

Toby leans down to kiss my forehead, moving his lips closer to my ear when he whispers, "Clay's in the hall. Him and Merc are fighting. But he's here."

My heart skips a beat on the monitor, too many sets of eyes whipping around to look at me when they hear it. Toby pulls away quickly and heads out the door with the rest of them.

Miya shoves a lingering Adler out the door, closing it behind the rest of the crew. Mercer pulls his chair closer, wrapping his hands back around my cast.

Miya squeezes past Brooks, leaning over to hug me, her inhale shaky. "Do you need anything, Leni?"

"I'm hurting," I whisper, hoping the boys don't hear.

"How bad?" Miya's eyes crinkle in the corners, concern etched in the crease of her brow.

A few more tears slip down my face because now that the excitement of waking up alive has worn off, the pain is debilitating. She looks down into my eyes and nods, not needing me to say it. "I'll get your doctor, okay? Anything else?"

"I need Clay," I say, looking between Brooks and Miya. Mercer's fingers tighten around my hand, making me take a sharp breath. Pain spiking through my chest and ribs.

"Leni." Mercer's voice pleads with me, but I keep looking at Miya. A silent conversation passes between us. She nods, then looks at Brooks, who gives her a tilt of the head. He's got her back on this one.

"Come on, Mercer." She wiggles her hands at him. "Let's go get some food."

"I'm not a child, Mimi." Mercer glares. "I'm not leaving her." He sits back further into his chair, shaking his head.

"Yeah, you are." Brooks' deep voice snaps.

"Brooks, come on. He lied to us. He's not—" Brooks quirks an eyebrow, his mouth set in a hard line.

"You've seen him, Mercer. That man is wrecked. If she wants him in here, then he needs to be in here." Brooks nods at Mimi, then gives Mercer his own fierce glare.

"Fucking ridiculous." Mercer shoves up from his chair, stomping out of the room, muttering more curse words as he goes. Miya shoots me an apologetic look before following him.

I glance at the most perfect little squishy cheeks and take in my niece for the first time. She looks a little bit like Kate, but mostly takes after her dad, whoever that is. He must have red hair, I guess, because I don't remember anyone in Kate's family having red hair. Tessa stares at me, one chubby little hand coming up to touch my cheek. She has that same giant pink pacifier in her mouth, but it tips out a little when she starts to smile. "Care to share?" I ask Brooks.

"Kate showed up out of the blue with her. Said she wasn't cut out to be a mother and asked me to take her." I raise an eyebrow, asking more than one question with that gesture. I'm surprised that Brooks would have taken in a child that wasn't his, surprised she had the guts to show up and ask it of him. "She put my name on the birth certificate. She might not be mine, but Kate hadn't even named her, Leni. She's been calling her baby girl Kane for nine fucking months. I couldn't let her leave with her. Who knows what she went through."

Brooks glances at Tessa in his arms, snuggling her deeper into his chest when her hands reach up to pat his face. "I took one look at her and knew she belonged here. With us. So yeah, dad mode activated."

I laugh, pain lancing through my chest, lungs sucking in air through my sore throat.

"Okay." Brooks leans forward, swiping my bangs back off my face. "No more laughing, you're supposed to be resting."

"Then stop being funny."

Brooks cracks a rare grin before looking down at Tessa with so much love and adoration in his eyes. I almost can't stand it. "She might not be blood, but I'm sure she'll learn to deflect with humor too."

"I can attest," Clay speaks from the doorway. My heart rate spiking on the monitor draws another grin from Brooks. "It's absolutely a Kane trait that can be learned."

Brooks turns a serious face at Clay, something sad and resolute in his eyes. "You're the reason I agreed to take her in. Do you know that?"

Clay shakes his head, looking as shocked as I feel.

"You came from shittier circumstances than she did, and you turned out okay. I almost told Kate to get lost, but then I remembered that day we came after you. The way you looked around the table that night, like you were the luckiest kid in the world, and I knew we were her best bet." He looks down at the baby in his arms with a soft smile on his face. "That she will be the luckiest girl in the world. So I signed the papers, and here she is. I thought I was going to have to wait longer for the two of you to figure things out, but since you're both here, and we know things don't always go to plan, I was kind of hoping you'd agree to be her godparents."

I can't stop the tears from streaming down my cheeks, chest growing tighter the more I cry. For Brooks and Tessa, for little Clay who needed a family. For this man who's standing before me, losing the only family he's ever known because he fell in love with someone as selfish as I am. God, he thinks he doesn't deserve me, but it's the other way around.

"Brooks, you asshole, the one time you choose to monologue and look what you've done to me." It takes an embarrassing amount of effort to bring the scratchy hospital blanket up to wipe my eyes.

"Sorry," Brooks croaks, wiping at the corners of his own eyes. "Fuck, this whole, you almost dying and me becoming a dad thing has made me mushy."

"It's okay, it's actually helping. I thought someone put sandpaper in my eyes earlier." Looking at Clay, I tilt my head. "Godparents?"

Clay's eyes darken, recognizing the question for what it is. Less about being godparents, more about us. Are we still an us? "Hell yeah." He walks into the room and pulls Brooks into a hug. "I—we, would be honored, Brooks."

"Good," he sighs. "Now I have to break it to the guys."

"Eeeh, I don't envy you with that." I try to grin, but judging by the look on their faces, it must look more like a grimace.

"How bad is it?" Brooks asks, pushing to stand from his chair.

"It's not great," I whisper, leaning further into the bed.

"Get some rest, we'll be here as long as you need us." Brooks gives my hand one last squeeze.

"You sure the ranch isn't falling apart?"

"Nah," Brooks says, looking between Clay and me. "The whole town's banded together to take care of things. Turns out you're kind of a big deal."

I gasp, closing my eyes as I feign horror. "You're just now finding this out."

Brooks chuckles as he leans down and kisses my forehead. "Love you, Leni."

"I love you too, Brooky." My voice chokes, more tears slipping through.

Brooks makes his way out the door, and I'm finally left alone with Clay. He's standing at the end of my bed, looking haggard. I wonder if he's slept at all the past three days. If he's okay. I've never seen Mercer mad at him, much less mad enough to throw punches. Clay looks like he's taken at least one fist to the face.

"I'm so sorry," I whisper, reaching my unbroken arm toward him. Clay rushes to the side of the bed, dropping down to his knees as he buries his face in my hand.

"I was so worried, baby." His voice is muffled in my palm.

"I'm sorry. I'm so sorry. I was trying to find my phone to call you. That's why I stopped because I needed to tell you that I was wrong. The things I said..."

"It's okay," he whispers. His lips press to my hand before he stands up, grey eyes boring into mine. "It's okay."

"It's not. I didn't mean those things. You are enough. You're everything. I'm the reason Mercer is acting like this, I—"

"Baby," he whispers, leaning down towards my face, one hand sweeping hair back behind my ear. "Do you want me here?"

"Yes," I whimper. The thought of him leaving, of being even a minute without him, makes my chest ache.

"Then I don't care about Mercer or his feelings. I don't care if they all decide to hate me tomorrow, because I'm not leaving you."

"I love you," I whisper, my lips moving against his. He pecks me once on the lips, and my eyes flutter closed.

The silence feels loud between us, but I'm too tired to open my eyes, too tired to try and figure out how to fix what I've broken. Instead, I scoot over and tug his hand.

"Leni," he warns, keeping his big body right where he planted it. "I don't want to hurt you."

"Please? I need you to hold me. I thought..." I manage to peel my eyes open as they fog over with a fresh batch of tears. "I thought I'd never see you again."

"Me too," he whispers. He toes off his boots and climbs into bed beside me, carefully turning me so that I'm resting on him. "I hope you know that I'm never letting you go. Ever."

"Good," I whisper. My eyes fall heavy as sleep drags me back under.

Chapter 33

Just Another Lie
Clay

"Get out." I wake to Ethan's voice hissing in my ear. The weight of Leni's body partially on top of mine, grounding me. It's tempting to pretend I didn't hear him, but I can feel his angry presence behind me, and another set of eyes watching close by. I don't doubt that it's Mercer.

"I told her I would't leave her," I hiss back, trying not to wake Leni. She tried to hide it, but I could tell the pain she was in before a nurse came in to administer pain meds through her IV.

"Just another lie you told. Now get the fuck up."

I sigh, there's no point. Ethan would have dragged me out of this bed by now if he weren't worried that it would hurt Leni. I slip out from beneath her, surprised to see Ma in the room and not Mercer. She's not looking at me with animosity, but she's clearly not here to change Ethan's mind either.

Smoothing her hair back, I lean down to kiss Leni's head before I shuffle past them. Mercer is waiting on the other side of the hospital door, a warning in his eyes.

"Shouldn't you be at work?"

"I put in for time off." I shrug.

He huffs a mirthless laugh. "Yeah, that got denied. Should've checked your app."

"Then I resign, Merc. Effective immediately."

He gapes at me, mouth opening and closing as his eyes widen.

"I'm not leaving her. Not when she needs me, not ever." I stand to my full height, voice shaking a little.

"She doesn't need you. She needs her family."

"She's it, man." I take a deep breath and lean against the wall, tipping my head back as exhaustion settles deep into my bones. "She's all I have. She's my family, and I'm not leaving her."

"You are," he growls. "I'll fucking make you."

Mercer reaches forward, grabbing my shirt with his fist.

"Are you kidding me?" I glare at him, hands shaking at my sides, itching to grab his shoulders and shake some sense into him. "She pushed you all away because you decided everything for her. Do you really think...you know what? You should at least ask her what she wants." I feel a lump rise in my throat. "If she wants me to go, then I'll go."

His eyes simmer with disdain, upper lip curling back. He doesn't hit me or scream anymore. His fists tighten as he ducks into Leni's room. I stay in the hall, listening as voices get louder. My body itches to go in there, to back her up, to be on her side, when Mercer and Ethan clearly aren't.

To my surprise, it's Ma's voice that raises above the rest.

"Don't you think you two have done enough?"

The murmured responses are too low for me to make out.

"No, I don't want to hear anymore. I've watched the two of you overstep Leni's boundaries over and over for the past ten years. You don't get to make any more choices for her. You don't get to tell her your opinions, and you don't get to keep the one person that she wants here away from her. As far as I'm concerned you need to get out of this room and get back to fucking work."

Ma sends both the boys sulking down the hallway. She gives me a tight, closed lip smile before closing the door behind her once more. Their voices are too low for me to hear now. When she opens the door again, she nods toward Leni.

"Take care of our girl, Clay. I think it's time these other yahoos get back home."

I nod, taking the hug she offers.

"They'll come around. You'll see."

Her eyes are free of tears today, something lighter in the way she's carrying herself, too. I guess I feel that myself. Having Leni conscious, knowing she still wants me, makes all the difference in the world.

Chapter 34

You're on Narcotics

Leni

THREE EXCRUCIATINGLY LONG WEEKS LATER, I'M FINALLY discharged. Miya practically lived at the hospital with Clay and I. He never left. He bought a few changes of clothes and showered in the room.

When I asked him about work, he told me it didn't matter. My gut says it definitely does matter, but I couldn't get myself to ask him to leave. From the moment I woke up, he was the only person I needed to see. The one I needed to tell me that everything was going to be okay.

He's the steady hand I need when I try to stand. The one I want washing my hair or changing my clothes because I can't do it myself yet. I never felt like I'd left home behind, because the ranch is just a place without him. Now that I've had a taste of life with him, I don't know how I could ever go back to life without him.

Today we're heading to the airport. Adler, of all people, surprised me by telling me he would charter a plane when I was released, so I wouldn't have to ride all the way home in the car. I tried to tell him it was ridiculous, but he insisted.

300

I didn't even know Benson International had private hangars, but that's where we're headed to board a jet and fly back to the ranch. They can't land a plane on the ranch, so we'll be flying into Halfor County's airfield, but that's only a thirty-minute drive home.

I can't wait to get back to my little cabin. I want to soak in my tub and sit in my reading nook. I want some actual alone time with Clay where we don't have to worry about someone walking in. He refuses to have sex with me, convinced he's going to do more damage than good, but I'm hoping being back in our home will put that fear out of his mind. Hospitals are scary places, and I'm so ready to be out of there. Not to mention, Brooks stole Pepper and took her back to the ranch to be his nanny. I miss *my* Pepper. Neither Clay nor I have gotten around to replacing my phone, so aside from a handful of FaceTimes with Miya, I've had zero contact with her since she left.

"Holy shit." I whistle as Clay carries me up the stairs into the plane. "Damn, this is nice. How does one even charter a plane?"

"The hell if I know," Clay grunts.

"How did Addy know how to book it?"

"He's not an idiot," Clay chirps into my hair as he settles me down into a seat. His tone harsher than I think he meant. "I mean, yeah, he pretends to be one. But I think there's a lot more to Adler than we see."

"Hmm." I give him a suspicious look. Clay snorts and gets up to rummage through the minibar stocked with expensive-looking alcohol. "Can we afford any of that?" I whisper-shout at him.

Clay turns around, a bemused smile on his face. "You're on narcotics, Leni. I'm not getting alcohol for you." Looking at the bottle of water in his hands, he twists the cap off before handing it over. "Maybe they'll put it on Adler's tab. I never gave anyone my card number."

He winks, settling down next to me.

"I still don't understand how he knew about these planes. It's not like he's ever ridden in a private jet. Has he? How much money did Nana leave him?"

Clay shrugs. "I guess enough to charter a plane? I can't believe she really left nothing to the rest of you."

"I can." I chuckle, my jaw cracking with a yawn. "Nana spent most of the time in the hospital with him when he was younger. Ma was needed here, so Nana was always the one with him. They were super close."

"I wasn't around for most of that," he muses.

"No, he only had that one bad injury after you came around."

"Mhm." He threads his fingers through my hair, his nails scraping against my scalp gently.

I lean into his hand. Letting his fingers lull me toward sleep as the medicine starts to kick in.

"Uhm, Leni." Clay tweaks my big toe, getting my attention. "You might want to rethink that whole *Adler's-never-flown-on-a-plane-like-this* idea."

"Why?"

He tosses me a notepad with a gold-foiled plane in the letterhead, the tagline reading, 'Adler Aviation.'

"What the fuck?" I look at Clay, eyes wide as he shrugs his shoulders.

"I told you, more than he lets on."

"Did you know about this?" I'm gaping at Clay now.

"No, I swear to God. I don't think anyone knows about it."

Jesus, how out of touch have I been these last few years? "How the hell did he manage to keep this big a secret?"

Clay tips his head, arching an accusing eyebrow.

"Shut up." I slap his chest before leaning my body back into the seat. "How much do planes even cost?" I wonder out loud as the engines roar to life.

"No fucking clue." He looks around the jet like he's seeing it through new eyes, and damnit, so am I.

~

ETHAN AND MERCER pick us up from the airfield in the Expedition. The rest of the boys, Dad included, are busy trying to put things to rights with the ranch.

The car ride home is incredibly awkward; neither of the boys speaks to us. Clay sits in the captain's chair next to me, his fingers wrap around mine. I don't think he's left my side for longer than ten minutes since I woke up, and if I'm being honest, I don't mind it at all. Even those ten minutes made my skin itchy with nerves. The last time I went somewhere without him, I woke up with more than ten broken bones. I'm not ready to face that head-on again.

Part of me is happy he doesn't have to go back to a real job. I know he's going to have to work eventually, whether that be at the ranch with Brooks or back at the Sheriff's office, if Mercer ever gets his head out of his ass. But I'm hoping for a few more days with him. Days to settle in, to keep my mind from wandering too far into the what-ifs. I need him to keep me grounded, keep me present. The same as I did for him all those years ago.

Clay asked me if I remember the crash, and the truth is, I do. Not the actual crash itself, but I remember waiting for the firemen to cut me out of the car, the way I could smell the gas leaking, feel the rain on my skin, how I couldn't feel my legs. There's more to process than I want to deal with right now.

When we pull up around the horseshoe drive at the main

house, Ethan stops the car, goes around the back, and opens the hatch. Mercer opens the side door, a soft smile aimed in my direction. "Ready?"

"Huh?" I glance at him, then out the window at the main house. This house hasn't been my home in years. I guess I thought we were dropping something off, then we'd go back to the cabin. That little piece of paradise I carved out of the ranch. Somewhere for Clay and me.

"You can't stay at the cabin." Mercer stands there, looking at me like I'm dumb.

"Excuse me?" I rear back, blinking, wondering where he gets the fucking nerve.

"Baby." Clay soothes his fingers down my arm. "You're still in a wheelchair. The cabin isn't big enough, or accessible enough."

"Oh." I look down at my legs. They work fine, if only my pelvis weren't still broken. Speaking of said pelvis, I am suddenly very aware of how long I've been sitting. Everything is beginning to ache. "But it's my home," I whisper to Clay with sad eyes. "Our home."

"I know," he whispers, pressing a kiss to my hair.

"It isn't fair," I whimper when Mercer scoops me out of the vehicle, his face flinching when he hears the noise.

"Sorry, sweetheart." Mercer sets me down gently. "I didn't mean to hurt you."

"I'm okay, just sore."

"Aren't you glad you didn't drive?" Ethan comes around the Expedition, taking up a post on the other side of me, blocking Clay from me. I sigh, my heart heavy as the boys wheel me away from him. I can't even turn back to make sure he's coming. My neck is still locked in this stupid brace.

Mom is waiting for us when we make our way into the entryway.

"There she is, our little pincushion." Adler grins down at me.

Ethan's nostrils flare, hand curling into a fist at his side. It might be a little too soon to joke, but I chuckle. If there's one thing Adler is a pro at, it's getting a rise out of someone, especially once he learns which buttons to push.

"How was the flight?" Adler asks, around a mouthful of food.

"It was enlightening, Mr..."

Adler's eyes widen as he shakes his head. I guess I'm not the only one who doesn't know that he owns an aviation company. I narrow my eyes at him, a silent demand for a conversation in the near future.

He nods, looking relieved when I don't say anything else.

"Weird..." Mom reminds us that she's there. "I've prepared your old room for you, Leni."

"Thanks, Ma," my voice croaks out. My throat is a mess from the extubation; it feels like fire most nights, and Miya said it will probably feel dry for a while as it heals.

"Do you need a room as well, Clayton or..."

"He's not staying here," Mercer cuts in, arms crossing over his chest.

Clay's shoulders droop, the look of utter defeat on his face.

"Excuse me?" I scoff at the same time Ma says, "I beg your pardon?"

She looks at us, her face drawing into a tight expression. One that has Mercer relaxing his stance. A form of surrender.

"He can't stay here, Ma. Not after everything." Mercer spreads his fingers wide, lifting his hands out in front of him.

"He can, and he will. If that's what your sister wants. This is my home, Mercer Duane, you'd do well to remember that."

"Of course, he's staying with me. In my room." I glare at Mercer. "This whole over-the-top, trying to make decisions for me thing is the reason I never came back before. You're lucky, I have nowhere else to go. Lucky that Clay is willing to be here with me, because if he weren't here, I wouldn't be either."

Mercer shakes his head, crouching down to my level, which makes me feel even more like a child, stuck in this goddamn wheelchair. "That's not fair."

"Don't," I cut him off. "Save it. Ma, can you call a family dinner tonight? If we're going to be back, staying here, there's some shit we need to work out."

Ma gives me the biggest smile, her eyes brightening as she nods. Whipping her phone out, I grin at the fervor with which she types out her message.

Tonight should be really fun for everyone.

Rain pelts my face as I stare up at a pitch-black sky. I can't feel my legs. Every other part of my body is screaming in pain. Something thick and warm drips down my forehead, into my eyes, tinging the world around me an eerie red.

My car's horn, or maybe it's the other car's horn, is blaring, like the driver is stuck there, pressing on it. Suddenly, the heavens open and the rain begins to pour. It rises on the street, filling my car. Ice cold water that feels like daggers pricking my skin as it continues to rise.

Move. I tell myself. Please move. But I can't get out. I can't feel my legs. I'm going to die here. I'm going to drown.

Please! I beg.

"Shh, baby. Leni girl, you're safe. You're safe, baby. Wake up, love." I wake sobbing. Clay holds me to his chest as he strokes my hair, arms wrapped tight around me. "You're safe, Leni. You're safe."

I can't form words coherently, as I cling to him. The only thing I can say is his name; it comes out broken, and I keep saying it like I'm begging. Begging him to take the nightmares and the pain in my body. Begging him to make it all better again. To erase the last few weeks and make me whole again.

"The rain," I whimper, when my sobs have subsided enough to speak. "I thought it was real. I thought I was going to drown." I choke back tears again, trying to get my words out.

"You're safe. You didn't drown. You're safe."

"It felt so real. It was cold. I could feel the rain. I could smell the smoke."

"I know, baby." He wipes my face, smoothing my hair back before he looks me in the eye and says, "I *know*."

He's been here, waking from nightmares that feel like real life, and I suddenly realize how horrible all those years must have been for him.

"Tell me that it goes away. Tell me that it gets better. Please."

"It does, love. It gets better. They get less real, and as time goes on, you stop dreaming about them altogether. You start to dream new dreams. Better ones."

"What were your better ones?" I whisper, snuggling back into his chest, pulling the blankets under my chin.

"You. You were in my better dreams. Every single one of them. Sometimes we were on the boat, and you'd close your eyes and turn your face up to the sun. Sometimes we were here in your room, and you'd hold me through the night, so I'd feel safe again."

"All that time?"

"From that very first night when you snuck in to help me.

That was the first night I dreamed of you. Eventually, the bad dreams became less, and when I could sleep, I always dreamed of you."

Chapter 35

We All Lost the Bet

Clay

ONCE LENI SETTLES AFTER THE NIGHTMARE, I HELP HER shower, getting her cleaned up and ready for battle as she says.

Family dinner can be intense on a good day and tonight seems like it might not be a good night. I've never felt more like a stranger in this house than I did this morning. It's weird, being here and feeling like I don't belong. This place was the first place I ever felt wanted. The first place I ever felt safe enough to let my guard down.

Tonight, it feels like I am going into battle. Probably the most important one I'll ever face, considering my entire future is sitting in that wheelchair. Brown wavy hair pulled up into a messy bun, soft curves interrupted by the casts and braces.

"I love you," I breathe into her, dipping down at the waist to kiss her lips. "No matter what, I'm here for you. I'm on your side."

"I know," she whispers, pulling me closer and kissing me deeper. "I love you too, Clayton Sue Traeger."

I groan at the nickname. Shaking my head, I move around to the back of her chair. "You ready, love?"

"No," she whines, slumping into her seat, before quickly jolting out of the position. "Ow, remind me not to do that again."

"You okay?" I lean around her, assessing her, ensuring she doesn't sugarcoat her answer.

"Yeah, my ribs aren't quite ready for slouching yet." I help her settle into the chair more comfortably, trying to ease some of the tension I can feel that's built up.

"Alright, baby, here goes nothing." I press one last kiss to her temple, before we head into the lion's den.

Dinner starts out with quiet conversations. Two or three people chatting together, Ethan and Mercer avoiding my gaze at all cost. Making it clear I'm not welcome here tonight. Brooks has his hands full with Tessa. Pepper steps in where she can, grabbing things Tessa throws on the floor. She's giggling when Pepper slams them back onto her tray in a dramatic fashion. That quiet little baby I met at the hospital is so different around the two of them now.

Adler and Toby are more concerned with forming a poker strategy for next month's game than they are with anything drama related. Ma and Pa oscillate between mooning over Tessa and Leni, like they can't decide who they're more excited to have at their table.

Half way through, I can tell Leni is getting tired. Today is the most she's sat in the three weeks since the accident. It's wearing on her and I wish I could clear the place out, take her to bed, and let her rest, knowing that she needs it. She wouldn't want me to do that, so I move myself closer, positioning my body so she can lean on me. Her body sags into me, a breath blowing out when I take some of the weight for her. Her head tips up, as much as it can in the neck brace, with a small smile on her lips.

"Thank you," she whispers. I lean down and peck her cheek, moving those cute little bangs off her face again.

"Gross." Adler screws up his face, then winks at us.

"Can we get this over with?" Ethan finally turns to me, with much less animosity in his eyes than I expected.

Leni sighs, trying to sit up again, but I hold her to me. "Let me hold you, baby," I whisper into her ear. "You tell them what you're feeling. I got you."

She nods into my shoulder, her hand reaching down to find mine, our fingers interlacing. "Fine." Her head tips into me, leaning to the left so she can look Ethan in the eyes. "Where do you want to start?"

"Why were you hiding in the cabin?" He taps his fingers on the table, leaning forward.

"The school cut my program, so I lost my job. Edna's son sold her house and moved her to a nursing home, so I lost that, too."

"Why didn't you tell us you were home, though?" Toby tips his head to the side, hurt flashing in his eyes. I catch Ma glance over at Pa, squeezing his hand once, while everyone else keeps their eyes trained toward Leni. Towards us.

"Because I know how you guys are," she sighs. "I knew it was going to be a big deal. I didn't want to deal with all the lectures."

"We're not that bad," Mercer groans.

"Ehh," Adler chimes in, scrunching his nose. "You kind of are."

"Shut up, Adler!" Ethan snaps. "Leni, we would have helped you. You don't have to do everything on your own."

"I know." She sinks deeper into me. Her head moves to look across the table at Mercer. "But at some point, it became less about helping me and more about you guys deciding you knew best. Even when you didn't have all the information, you still tried making decisions for me."

"We worried." Ethan shakes his head, still digging into the idea that they're not to blame for any of it. "We're allowed to worry."

"Yes, you can worry. Of course, you can worry," Leni sighs. "You don't get to decide that what I'm doing is wrong."

"When did we ever do that?" Mercer sits straighter.

"You sure you want to know?" Toby leans forward, looking around Adler to get his eyes on Mercer.

"You guys remember Aspen?" Leni asks. I even remember the name. Mercer and Ethan wouldn't stop texting about how much of an asshole the guy was. They did not like him at all. The few sneers let me know they do remember him. "I was living with him." Leni taps my arm, silently asking me to help her sit up, so I do. I gently lift her, so she's sitting tall. "He asked me to move out, gave me until January third to be out of the apartment."

"Fucking prick," Adler mumbles. Ethan taps the table with his index finger before cracking it with his thumb.

"I didn't know you were living with him." Mercer's brow furrows.

"Well, I was."

Mercer looks at me briefly, but I shake my head. I didn't know. I only knew what they told me about Leni back then.

"So we ran off a few boyfriends." Ethan crosses his arms over his chest. "That hardly makes us the villains you make us out to be."

"No, I know. I pushed you guys away. I know I played a part in that, but you guys always took it too far."

"What else?" Pa asks, when it's clear the boys are going to sit there and sulk, instead of actually listening to what she has to say.

312

"Someone called Patty's and got me fired," she complains. Her voice is hard, edged with annoyance.

"Yeah, not gonna apologize for that one," Brooks finally joins in the conversation. A hint of humor in his eyes. "It's funny you think we'd let you work at a strip club, Leni."

"I was bartending, Brooks. I had thirty dollars in my account, and my rent was due the week after you got me fired. My last check didn't cover it."

Brooks flinches. Pepper gives him a disapproving glare over Tessa's head.

"Fuck, I'm sorry, Leni. I didn't know." Brooks holds eye contact with her.

"Thanks," Leni whispers, leaning herself back into me, shoulders caving a little under the strain of holding herself up. "That's the point, though. You guys never bothered to ask what else was going on in my life. You saw something that I did as wrong and tried to fix it."

"So what?" Mercer chimes back in. "We're supposed to turn off twenty-seven years of being big brothers?"

"No." Leni rolls her eyes, turning at the waist to look at him. "You can stop telling me what to do, though. Stop assuming you know what's best for me and stop blaming Clay when you're really mad at yourselves."

Ethan scoffs, but Mercer looks down at his empty plate. "It's our job to protect you."

"And you did," she says. "For eighteen years, you guys were always there for me, you took care of me. Showed me how to take care of myself. I'm practically middle-aged now, leave me the fuck alone. Who cares if I make mistakes along the way? That's what you're supposed to be here for. To pick me up when those mistakes happen. Not preemptively stopping me from living life."

Brooks sighs, scooping Tessa out of her highchair when she starts to fuss. "She's right."

"I disagree." Ethan uses his thumb to toy with the class ring he wears on his right ring finger. "I still think Clay is partially, if not fully, responsible for what happened ten years ago, and three weeks ago. He shouldn't have let you drive like that. Should have called one of us and told us to go look for you."

"Clay wasn't the only reason I left." Leni squeezes my arm when she feels my muscles stiffen.

"You didn't have to leave," Mercer mutters, toying with the fork on his plate. Avoiding looking at her.

"Mercer," Marcy starts, her voice low, warning. "What did you do?"

He sighs, long and deep, before looking to Ma, avoiding everyone else's gaze. "I requested the call logs for the incident."

Ethan's eyebrow shoots into his hairline. "That's how you found out? I thought you talked to her about it."

"Not exactly," he mutters.

Adler whistles, a long, low note.

"Damn, that's brutal, bro." Toby looks from Mercer to Leni, and then back to Mercer when Leni quirks an eyebrow at him.

"I might have blackmailed her into talking about it then."

"Holy shit." Adler sits back in his chair, eyes wide.

"Mercer, what the fuck?" Brooks pinches the bridge of his nose, shaking his head.

"I needed to know what happened." Mercer groans into his hands, scrubbing them down his face before he looks at Leni and then me. "You weren't talking. Either of you. And then Clay drops this bomb that you did find him, but you didn't tell us—"

"You don't have a right to every single thing in my life, Mercer." Leni's good hand balls into a fist.

"But I did. I used to know everything about you, Leni. It

was always us, you and me." His voice cracks, full of emotion. "I've been so fucking pissed at you for shutting me out, leaving me behind. I thought, if I could get to the bottom of this big secret, that maybe things could start getting back to normal. I wasn't..." Everyone is quiet at the table. I knew the family was hurting the second I got back; I could feel it, like there was this fracture straight down the middle. "I didn't mean—you know." He turns to look at Leni, eyes sad, and his shoulders heavy. "I think maybe I was trying to hurt you a little."

I glance around the table, catching Adler mouth, "Oh my God," to Toby before Ethan sits back in his chair.

"That's fucked up." I pin Mercer with a glare.

"Yeah, I know, Clay. I never claimed to be perfect." He rolls his eyes, the corners softening when they drop down to Leni. I wish I could see her face, so I could read whatever it is that has Mercer sighing. His eyes meet mine. "I might have over-reacted."

Pepper snorts, every single head at the table whipping around to look at her. She's been so quiet this whole time, I kind of forgot she was here.

"Sorry," she huffs, trying to hold back more laughter.

Brooks gives her a glare that only really succeeds in making her laugh harder.

"Are all families this intense?" She whisper-shouts at him. Brooks shakes his head; the corners of his mouth tipping up before he resumes his regular scowl.

"Leni might not be in that chair." Ethan's voice cuts through the comedic break, shattering any sense of peace that might have started to build. "If you hadn't done that, Merc."

"I know," Mercer mutters, looking at the ceiling.

"I think we all have things to be sorry for," Pa cuts in, deep voice filling the room. "The things you all have been through, I never wanted these hardships for any of you. We're better as a unit, stronger. Leni, I won't tell you what to do, who to forgive or when, but I am sorry."

"You don't have to apologize, Pa. I just...I want to come home."

The air shifts immediately, almost every back at the table snapping to sit straighter.

"What do you need to feel like you can?" Ma leans forward, reaching for Leni's good hand.

"I need you guys to let me make whatever mistakes I'm going to make. The only one who gets to give me unsolicited advice is Clay."

My arms grip around her a little tighter, my lips pressing into her hair.

"You guys finally realize you're soulmates then?" Mercer crosses his arms over his chest.

"Something like that," Leni answers at the same time I say, "Yes."

He sighs. "I'm sorry about your face, Clay. And your ribs. I uh, probably shouldn't have taken all that out on you." He squeezes the back of his neck, looking pained as he says, "Also, I need you to get back to work on Monday."

I startle, my spine stiffening as I stare at him.

"I couldn't go through with actually firing you. Not if you're that invested in my sister. Someone has to take care of her, and you're gonna need money to do that. A bunch of the guys pitched in their time, so you wouldn't have to worry about being without leave."

"Are you serious?"

"Yeah," he sighs. "Listen, I'm still pissed about all the secrets," he raises a hand to stop Leni from cutting him off. "But you put her first, and that's all I've ever wanted for her. For any of you assholes." He looks around the table, some of the tension draining from his face. "Thank you for that."

Orson grins from his seat at the head of the table, lifting his beer bottle. "Hear, hear."

We all raise our glasses, and while there's still tension we can feel in the room, it's significantly less than it had been at the start of the meal.

"To fresh starts," Marcy adds her own toast. "Fresh starts, and family."

AFTER DINNER, I convince Leni to let me take her to bed. She was practically falling asleep in her chair. Once I get her tucked in, she's out like a light, painkillers knocking her into oblivion.

I take that as my chance to sneak out for a few minutes. The boys were all heading out back when I left with her. I get the feeling there's more that needs to be said between us. Things they wouldn't say in front of Leni.

Pa claps my shoulder when I walk by, stopping me at the door to the deck. "I'm proud of you, son. Proud of the man you've become."

I swallow the emotions down, giving him a quick nod before I let myself onto the deck. The four younger Kane boys are sitting around the gas fire pit. Adler is the only one sitting right by it, roasting a marshmallow.

"How long was she home?" Ethan asks, cracking his thumbs before taking a swig of his beer.

"She was home that whole week before the accident." I wander closer, taking the beer Toby holds toward me.

Adler's eyes widen, his gaze shooting to Toby's.

"Oh my God, she was home the day you tried to break in!" Toby bursts into laughter.

"Me?" Adler spits. "You were there too!"

"Yeah, but it was your idea. She probably heard us talking." Toby grimaces.

"Oh, she definitely heard you." I chuckle, plopping down into an empty Adirondack chair.

"How is she?" Mercer asks, sinking deeper into his chair.

"Doing okay. She's in a lot of pain, pretty much all the time." I splay my legs out, picking at the seams on my jeans. "She has nightmares sometimes. She woke up some time after the crash. She sat and listened as they cut her out of the car. Couldn't move her legs."

"Jesus," Adler mutters, marshmallow dripping off the skewer into the fire pit.

"Damnit, Addy, those rocks are a pain to fucking clean." Toby's growl turns into a chuckle when Adler realizes he lost his snack and starts to pout.

"Damnit, that was a good one!" He sighs, grabbing another marshmallow and putting it on his stick.

"I was a dick," Mercer huffs, lolling his head to the side, glancing at me.

"Yeah, man. You were."

Ethan snorts, shaking his head. "I'm always a dick." He says by way of apology.

"Yeah, you are." Alder grins, ducking at the right time to avoid the beer bottle Ethan lobs at him.

"Shut up, Addy, no one asked you."

"Rude." Adler waves a flaming marshmallow toward Ethan, sending the fireball straight toward his feet.

"Jesus Christ, and you wonder why no one wants to hang out with you." Ethan stomps it with his boot, cursing more as the fiery mess clings to the sole of his shoe.

"Everyone wants to hang out with me, thank you very much. I'm a delight."

"Sure thing, bro." Toby steals a marshmallow, popping it into his mouth before Adler can take it back.

"So you and Leni, huh?" Adler bites his bottom lip, making everyone else groan.

"Fucking hell, Traeger. Three months. You couldn't have waited three more months?" Mercer digs out his wallet, pulling a hundred-dollar bill, and passing it to Adler.

"You're kidding me, right? There's no way, boy wonder guessed the exact date."

"Nah, we all lost the initial bet. Ten years was fucking ridiculous." Toby pulls a hundred dollars from his wallet.

"Started a new one when you moved back. Adler gave you a week and a half, from when Leni was supposed to come home." Ethan grimaces when he passes his own bet over to Adler.

"Damn." I settle back into my chair, grateful I'm not out a hundred dollars. "I don't know if I should be insulted by that or not."

"Just take it as a compliment, Clay." Adler winks, three hundred dollars richer, as he digs into his s'mores.

Chapter 36

Loved & Well Fucked

Leni

Monday comes sooner than I'm ready for. Clay's alarm startles us out of a dead sleep. The nightmares are still happening, though they never fully take root. Clay is always there to wake me up.

When my nightmares wake him, he wakes me with playful little nips and kisses. It's the best way to wake up from a bad dream and an almost sure-fire way to make sure another doesn't come back. I wonder if Clay's getting enough sleep, but he isn't complaining either. He takes care of me, the way I've always wanted him to.

Today, when I wheel myself to the kitchen, I'm surprised to find Pepper and Miya sitting at the island.

Ma's kitchen is made for making huge meals. It's large and functional, but with an adorable farmhouse feel. She redid it several years ago. The original was covered in ugly blue tiles, a green fridge and orange gingham curtains. Papa Kane was not an interior decorator, that's for sure.

"Well, that's a look." Miya raises an eyebrow at my cropped One Direction t-shirt that barely covers my breasts. High school Leni was flat as a pancake. I'm also wearing a tiny pair of Sofee shorts that might as well be a thong at this point. There are pretty slim pickings in the clothes department right now, seeing as no one has bothered to gather my stuff from the cabin when they made the decision I couldn't stay there. I get that it makes sense, but I'm still salty at being stuck here, especially without my clothes.

"Ugh, don't make fun of me. I'm working with a limited wardrobe."

"Oh, I know." Miya points to the kitchen table that's laden with reusable grocery bags. "You owe me big, by the way. I had to leave extra early so I could go by the cabin and pack up all your stuff. Well, most of it. Pepper mentioned she was questioning your wardrobe lately, so I thought I'd help."

I grin. "You're an angel."

Sorting through the bags until I find my favorite oversized hoodie and a pair of sweatpants, I slip the hoodie over my head, Miya helping me into the pants. "So much better." I make my way to the island, locking the brakes on the wheelchair when I park next to Miya and Pepper.

Miya looks down at me, eyes narrowing at the little wheeze from my lungs when I take a deep breath, trying to hide how winded I am. Standing up, she takes a stethoscope from the tote bag hanging off her chair, pressing it to my chest and then my back.

"So, Pepper, I've barely seen you since I've been back. How is it working for Brooks?"

Pepper chokes on the massive bite of pancake she shoved into her mouth, holding a finger up at me while she works it down. "Oh God," she gasps, taking a gulp of orange juice. "Shit, shoot, fuck. Sorry." She rubs her face before dropping her forehead to the counter, narrowly missing the plate full of maple syrup.

Her hand swings toward a pack-n-play I hadn't noticed tucked over into the corner. Tessa is belly down on the mattress, her little fleece-clad booty sticking up into the air as she sleeps. "This is where we're at. She has decided that daytime sleeping is more fun than nighttime. I'm starting to think that maybe baby care was not my strongest idea."

"At least she's sleeping right now." Miya pulls the stethoscope from her ears and tucks it back into her bag. Patting my knee, she gives me a smile and nod, which I think means...I'm good?

"Yeah, but, like, what about nighttime?"

"Sometimes babies get their sleep periods mixed up. It's pretty normal." Miya shrugs.

"Brooks is really having you watch her at night, too?" I quirk an eyebrow. "Jesus, he must be shelling out a fortune for twenty-four-seven nanny care."

"No, I mean, I'm not supposed to, but one person can only take so much. One time, she screamed for three hours in his room. I heard him curse and slam a door. When I went in there, he was locked in the bathroom while Tessa was crying in her crib. I took over then, and eventually we got some sleep, but please don't tell Brooks because I put her in my bed."

Miya grins at Pepper. "Let me guess, Brooks won't let her sleep anywhere but a crib?"

"Yeah, basically."

"But it worked?"

"Yes, and I looked it up. There are ways to safely co-sleep. I dressed like a nun so I wouldn't need any blankets. I've literally never slept with so many clothes on in my whole life. Plus, it's not like she's a newborn. The girl moves around in her sleep more than I do!" Pepper glances over at Tessa, her face softening. "She's so fucking cute, though. Like, how the hell is one baby so damn cute?"

"I bet he loves your potty mouth, too," Miya chirps, swiping a piece of bacon off Pepper's plate.

We laugh. Around here, there is no such thing as too much cussing. Even Mom has been known to drop a few f-bombs. She likes to tease me about being a lady. It's never been enforced. When you're raising your kids alongside transient ranch hands, it's kind of a given. Knowing Brooks, Tessa's first words will likely be God and dammit.

"How are you?" Miya asks, her eyes searching mine with sincerity.

"I'm okay," I whisper, pulling the hoodie sleeves over my thumbs, tucking my hands into my lap. "The nightmares are still pretty bad, but Clay's really good about helping me through them. He knows what it's like, you know?"

"Yeah," Miya sighs. "I'm glad, Leni."

"Thanks, Mimi." I bump her side with my elbow and look at Pepper, who might be sleeping sitting up. "Peps, go take a nap. We've got her for a minute."

"Seriously?"

"Yeah, go on." Miya waves her hand dismissively.

"It's my job, though. I'm not getting paid to nap."

"Well, she's napping. So go lie down. We'll wake you when she wakes up."

"Bless you both." Pepper slips off the barstool and heads for the couch. She's barely lain herself down before she's snoring.

"I can't believe he hired her," Miya whispers.

I grin because I can believe Brooks hired her. Brooks is desperate, but he's also a good judge of character. Pepper might be a little immature for a twenty-five-year-old, but she's got a heart of gold. "I wonder if they'll bang."

"Wait, I thought the brothers were off limits!"

"Adler is, for sure. She can't fall for my annoying little brother, but Brooks could use a little wild, don't you think?"

Miya eyes me suspiciously, like she can't quite believe what I'm saying.

"We could die at any second, Mimi. Better it be loved and well fucked than lonely and horny."

"Cheers to that." She raises her coffee mug before taking a sip.

~

A KNOCK at the door has me looking up from the book I'm engrossed in. Wheeling myself around isn't exactly ideal with the cast still on my broken arm. I spend a lot of time in my room, not wanting to bother anyone with my need for help doing pretty much everything. Clay keeps me comfortable when he's here, but he's back at work now, leaving me to my very boring devices throughout the day.

"Come in!" I call out, not surprised to find my mom peaking around the corner.

"Leni dear." She smiles. "This package came in the mail for you." She sets a small box on my lap with a pair of scissors.

My eyes widen at the label, a squeal coming out before I can stop it.

"I uh, I'll let you..." Ma stands, giving me space like she has for the last ten years. Only, I don't want it anymore. I want her here. Want a new normal.

"Wait." I catch her hand. "Stay, if you're not busy."

"I am never too busy for you."

I smile, because that's exactly how it used to be. Ma would run herself ragged trying to make sure everyone had what they needed. She might have had six of us, but I don't recall a single time as a kid when I was jealous of her time with my siblings. There was always enough of her to go around somehow.

She settles on the bed next to me, tucking her legs to the

side, shoulder bumping into mine. I can't remember the last time we sat like this. Slumping my body down, I rest my head on her shoulder, the cumbersome nature of the neck brace making it hard to do so.

"Brooks really got you fired from a job?" She asks, one hand smoothing my hair away from my face.

"He did," I sigh. It was probably for the best in the long run. Patty's was not a great place for a twenty-something to work. Though it was supposed to pay my bills. I still don't know how Brooks knew I was working there. I don't know how they had half the information that they did. Sometimes I wonder if Miya was a double agent, but then, I think it's more likely that she told her mom things by accident, and Miss Iva took things into her hands a time or two.

"I'm sorry I stayed quiet. I was trying to let you handle things. I should have seen that you needed help with the boys. I should have asked more questions, especially about that boyfriend they ran off."

I chuckle. "I'm not mad anymore. Imagine if I were still dating him, it'd be pretty awkward considering Clay is kind of the love of my life."

A warm laugh bursts from her chest. "Your dad and I knew it after the first time Mercer brought him home. There has never been anyone else for you, dear."

"I think I get that now," I sigh. "We wasted so much time." I glance at her, sorrow building in my chest. Not only Clay and me, but all of us. I wasted so much time pushing my family away, building up walls when I could have had them on my team this whole time.

"We won't waste anymore, will we?"

"No." I smile, catching the tears that are trying to sneak out.

"Well, what's in the package, Leni? I thought Ranch Life

was a magazine. Do they have subscription boxes now? Like those smut boxes I see all over the facebook?"

I cackle, holding my ribs to minimize the pain that flares when I laugh. "Please tell me you are not subscribed to any of those."

"Not yet." She grins. "There's one that offers toys in each box. I've considered that one a time or two. Your Pa's not really—"

"Uh-uh." I lift a hand, cutting her off. "Nope, that's as far as I need that conversation to go, thank you."

Ma gives me a sheepish smile before nudging my hand that's holding the scissors. I take a breath, giving myself a second before I slice through the tape and open the box. There's a note inside from Karina, my new boss.

Leni,

I hope we did your article justice. Our focus groups loved it. I think this issue is going to be a bestseller. I can't wait to learn more about your family, and hear what you have to say about...well, anything really. Be in touch soon.

- Karina

P.S. I hope I counted right (there's a lot of you to keep track of), but I sent an issue for each of your brothers, and one for your parents. They should be really proud of you!

Ma reads over my shoulder, her body tipping back before she looks at me. "Leni, what is this?"

I bite my bottom lip to keep from squealing again. Tears fill my eyes when I see the cover. Beneath the title of the magazine is an old photo of the Kane Ridge Ranch sign. I stole it from Ma's website, and Karina did the work to get the license from the photographer who took it originally. The subtitle makes those tears fall like rain.

KANE RIDGE RANCH: HOW ONE FAMILY TURNED AN EMPIRE INTO A LEGACY OF LOVE AND ABUNDANCE.

I flip to the middle of the magazine, staring at the article with my name in bold underneath it. A note from the editor at the top, before my words begin.

"Enter the world of Kane Ridge Ranch, an honest-to-God cowboy dynasty full of back-breaking work and the kind of love we all dream about. Immerse yourself in the story of how one of America's largest cattle ranches came to be, and how it's continued on its legacy to the next generation, and the one after that. All through the lens of one of the Kane's very own. Eleanor Kane's take on her family's ranching business is a breath of fresh air. Raw in a way that makes you want to find your way to their spot in the world to enjoy some of the magic she's infused into this article."

Ma digs out her own copy of the magazine, eyes darting over the pages as she devours my article. *Our* article. The one about us. Us ten years ago. The us that I've been missing.

Her eyes fill with tears, some slipping down her cheeks. She lifts the magazine, avoiding letting the tears drip onto the pages.

"Leni," she breathes, the same green in my eyes reflecting back at me. "This is incredible."

I can't help the pride that swells in my chest. "They hired me to write more." My voice sounds small. My inner child is desperately needing this validation from my mother.

"How could they not, Leni?" She stares down at the pages,

one hand smoothing over the words, like they're something tangible. "I'm so fucking proud of you, sweetheart."

"Thanks, Ma." I lean onto her shoulder, taking in a deep breath of her scent. It's warm and sweet, and she smells like every happy childhood memory. "They want to do an article on you next. If you're willing."

"You'll be the one writing it?"

"Yes," I say. She gives my hand a gentle squeeze.

"Then yes, I'd love to do an article with you."

"They want to bring cameras in. Pa will hate it."

Ma chuckles, shaking her head. "Pa will get over it."

"And maybe, I could help with your retreats too? If you'll have me?"

Her face lights up, a smile beaming at me. "Of course I will!" She wraps me in a side hug, pressing a kiss to my hair.

We sit in silence for a minute, Ma reading the article again while I flip through the rest of the magazine, taking note of the tone and voice of other pieces. My article doesn't sound like a competition piece, but one that was meant to be there all along.

I snap a photo of the cover to send it to Clay, when I think better of it and start a new chat.

Kane Siblings Group Chat

> YOU SENT A PHOTO TO THE KANE SIBLINGS GROUP CHAT
>
> TOBIAS RUSSELL
>
> Holy shit
>
> ADLER JAMES
>
> Is that about us??
>
> MERCER DUANE
>
> I thought I was the only one allowed to create new group chats

ETHAN TODD

Shut up Mercer

Who wrote an expose on us this time?

BROOKS ELLIOTT

Bet if you looked at the picture you'd know

You at the house Leni? I need to read it

Now

ADLER JAMES

wait for us man

I want to read it too

COWBOY

It's good 😊

Really good

MERCER

Any other secret publications we should know about...

Eleanor?

Nope.

But I'll sign these for free if you want

ETHAN TODD

These?

My editor sent me enough for each of you

TOBIAS RUSSELL

Hell yea

There's a five-minute pause before three of my five brothers burst through the door. Adler grins at the sight of Ma, and I snuggle up together. He's always been a mama's boy. Squishing into her other side, he picks up a magazine, a low whistle coming out when he takes in the cover.

Toby sits beside me, grabbing for his own copy.

"Can I?" Brooks looks at the end of the bed, almost like he's not sure I'd want him here. Guess that's my fault. It's going to take some time, but eventually, we will get back to how we all used to be. I hope.

"Of course." I offer him a copy. He smiles, the soft one that, until Tessa arrived, hadn't made much of an appearance after Kate.

We sit in silence as the boys all read the article. Adler finishes first, setting the magazine down on his lap, his eyes staring at the cover. There's so much written on his face that I want him to share. Toby is wiping quiet tears out of the corner of his eyes. Brooks glances at me, one sharp exhale before he stands up and walks for the door.

"It's really good, Leni. Really good. I..." He stops, his voice choking on emotion, and I know he won't say more. That's not really his style. Instead, he tips his hat at me and walks out.

There's a pause between the four of us still here, holding our breaths before Brooks marches back in and snags his copy off the foot of the bed.

"It's allergies," he grumbles, swiping a thumb under both eyes.

"Sure." Adler shrugs, no cocky smile on his face.

"Asshole," Brooks mutters, turning on his boot heel, leaving the room again.

Toby looks at Ma and me, making eye contact with Adler before they burst into laughter. Ma and I join in, my whole body aching by the time we manage to pull ourselves together.

"Fuck, that hurts." I clutch my side. Toby's smile drops instantly.

"You okay?" He swipes my bangs off my forehead, eyes full of concern.

"Just laughing with a couple broken ribs, I'm fine." I bat his hand away.

He grimaces. "I forgot about those. That sucks."

"You guys are whiny babies," Adler shakes his head, popping off the bed. His copy of the magazine is tucked under his arm.

"Not everyone gets to avoid pain," I pout.

He grins. "True. When was your last pill?"

"Yesterday," I grumble.

Toby sighs, shaking his head. "We'll go get you one. Need anything else, Leni?"

I bat my eyelashes. "A sandwich? Please?"

"Oh my God! She's back for less than a week, and we're already catering to her!" Adler shuffles out the door, carrying on about how much of a nuisance I am, while Toby presses a kiss to my head.

"It's really, really good." Toby grins. "I'm glad you're back for good, Leni."

"We all are." Ma presses a kiss to my cheek. "I'm going to go make sure they don't destroy my kitchen, making you a sandwich. I'll be right back, sweetheart."

"Sounds good." I smile, wincing at the pain. "I'm not going anywhere."

Chapter 37

You Can Go For a Ride

Leni

The rest of the week slips by with little to nothing going on. I'm so fucking bored I decide to have my mom show me Annie's office. It's in a little cottage style building that's set off from the main house. This is where guests register and meet the staff before getting their room and chore assignments. That's right. The big city corporate types come in and pay to muck our stalls or groom the horses. It's a trip.

Annie was meticulous and well organized, two traits I don't possess but can absolutely appreciate as I set up to take over everything she'd been working on. At mom's request, she's left all the logins and passwords for the business accounts. There's a smartphone left on the desk, too. It must have been a work phone. When I turn it on, the notifications go off for a straight minute before the buzzing settles down.

As far as I know, Annie didn't manage the inquiries about the retreats. From the looks of it, these notifications are all from social media and comments on the website. I sort through the comments, replying when appropriate, and making sure to like them all. We haven't posted anything since Annie left, so I scroll through the photos on the phone, looking for something fun to post.

I've been following the Ranch Retreats profiles since they started, so I know exactly what vibe I'm going for. I find a photo of a tall woman, with red curly hair, and brand new fancy clothes, beaming at the camera as she bottle feeds a lamb. Selecting the photo, I go with a couple of heart eye emoji and the company's slogan. "Rest your heart, feed your soul."

The likes come almost immediately. A few comments about being excited for their upcoming retreats, and I can't help but smile. This is what being a Kane has always been about. Helping people, far and wide. Dad used to tell us all the time, "We've been blessed with what we have, and our goal should be to bless as many people as we can."

I like that philosophy.

I find several more photos and a few notes from the red-haired woman's retreat. Pulling open the web developer app, I start a blog post. I get so wrapped up in the story I'm weaving that I don't even realize Clay is standing in the doorway. He clears his throat to get my attention, and I squeal.

"How long have you been there?"

"A minute." He grins, stalking toward me like a predator on a mission. He leans down to take my mouth in a hot, messy kiss that leaves me breathless and wanting more. "So, are you taking the job then?"

"Yeah, I think so." Swiveling back to the desktop, I double-check my article and hit post, hoping it's not too late for the SEO to do its thing. Clay wheels my chair away from the desk, heading for the door.

"It's well past quittin' time, Leni girl, and I've got plans for you."

A little shiver works its way down my spine as I smile at him. "Oh, do you now?"

"I do. So, get your fine ass out of this chair and let's go for a drive."

He tucks me into his pickup. Heaviness fills my chest at the thought of all I lost in that wreck. Everything I still had in my Jeep from moving out of my apartment in Benson is gone. My clothes, laptop, and phone. Everything but what I left in the cabin. I was planning for a fresh start, but I never planned to start with nothing.

Clay drives us toward the sevens, turning off the highway onto a prairie trail. This little parcel of land is one of the only sections that's not connected to the rest of the ranch. We don't use it for cattle, but do occasionally keep the broodmares out here.

He drives around the pasture until we're sitting in front of an open plot of land. It's gorgeous out here. I can't remember the last time I was here. There's a little lean-to just outside of the pasture, a paddock attached to it, and two horses grazing within the gates.

"Is that—"

"Calypso? Yeah, he's been waiting for you."

I wait for Clay to get me out of the truck, my fingers itching to pet my old horse. He's got to be at least twenty years old now, and it's been far too long since I've seen him. He nickers a greeting when I call his name, prancing over toward me. He nudges my shoulder, then lowers his head, sniffing my lap, looking for treats.

He's a palomino gelding that Brooks trained for me. Well, originally, Brooks had purchased him to train and work cattle on, but Calypso preferred easier trail rides. To Brooks' horror, some light barrel racing, too. I love him. Every chance I got, I was riding Calypso. Next to him, a blue roan stands swishing his tail, nickering his greeting to Clay.

Clay croons at him, reaching over to give him rubs on his

muzzle. "Hey Mako." Clay fishes a sugar cube from his pocket, and Calypso ditches me without hesitation to go sniff around Clay. "Here you go, Cal."

"Clay." I look out at the land before us. It's flat, open, and perfect. "Where are we?"

"The broodmare pasture." He grins, knowing that I already know that. He sighs, scratching Mako under his chin. "This is my spot. Haven't really needed to build yet, but this is where I chose when Pa asked me what I wanted. It's part of the land but..."

"Separate," I whisper. Just like Clay always seems to feel, part of the family, yet somehow outside it. An outlier we never saw as one.

"I thought maybe you'd want to help me figure out the best spot for a house?"

I turn slowly, eyes wide. "A house? You're going to build a house?"

He shakes his head, leaning down to press a kiss on my lips. "We are going to build a house."

A tear slips down my cheek, heart in my throat, because hearing him say that is everything. "I'd like that."

"Good, and I just have one more question," he says. I pull away, and my heart starts to bang against my chest. I swear to God, if he gets down on one knee while I'm stuck in this goddamn wheelchair, I am going to smack him. "When we do get married, because we will, can I take your last name?"

My heart soars as I launch myself into his arms, knocking him onto his ass as I spill out of the wheelchair. "Yes," I whisper, smothering him in kisses. "I love you, Clayton 'Someday' Kane."

He chuckles into my mouth before scooping me into his arms. Heading back for the truck, Clay sets me on the tailgate, pushing my hair back from my face. "I can't wait until I can go for a ride with you." I'm eyeing the horses, but Clay only has eyes for me.

"I talked to Miya," he says quietly. His voice dripping with sex and promises.

"Oh? About what?" I bite my lower lip, already knowing what he talked to her about. I've been begging him to at least try having sex with me.

"If we're slow and careful, it might work. She said it all depends on the patient."

"What are you saying?" I squeeze my thighs together, my pussy ready and waiting for him.

"I'm saying that if you want, you can go for a ride, baby. The horses will just have to wait."

"Yes, please." I help him shimmy off my pants. Clay drops his pants to his knees, not even bothering to take them off before he brings me to the edge of the tailgate and notches himself at my entrance.

"You sure? Because I can wait. I'm really good at that."

I chuckle, slapping his shoulder before I dig my nails into his t-shirt. "No more waiting. I need you."

"I love you, Eleanor Kane. I'm yours," he breathes as he slides inside of me.

"I'm yours," I whisper. Wishing I could tilt my head back, wishing he didn't have to be so gentle. "I love you too."

Epilogue

Clay

Six Months Later

LENI ISN'T IN BED WHEN I WAKE UP. IT'S A SATURDAY morning and we're supposed to be doing our weekend ritual of sleeping in and snuggling until one of us breaks down and we make love. Only she's not here, and I'm not appreciating the deviation in our routine.

She's finally back on her own two feet, using a walker on the bad days. A cane when she's feeling better. Her arm is healed. The neck brace is long gone. The worst break by far was her pelvis. It's taking its sweet time healing, but she's almost well enough for us to move back into the cabin. I know she's itching to get out of here.

I joked that we might as well stay until the house is built. The contractors plan on breaking ground in the next couple of months, and we will hopefully have our own house by winter. She didn't laugh, her fierce independence is hating relying on everyone else for help.

Light seeps through the bathroom door, the muffled sound

of a shower running behind it. She's supposed to shower with help, preferably mine, if she can wait until I'm around.

Letting myself into the bathroom, I take a minute to appreciate my girl. She's standing under the spray, her head tipped back, body on full display. I can't believe she's mine. Can't believe we're really here, finally together.

I thought we'd have a tougher time getting back into the family's good graces after that first family dinner, but it turns out the Kanes had a harder time working out Brooks' new situation than dealing with ours.

Things are still awkward with Mercer at times. We aren't the same as we used to be, but at least he hasn't tried to punch me again. He might be a romantic, but the dude can throw down as hard as any of them. I'm hoping to never repeat that again.

Slipping out of my boxer briefs, I let myself into the shower as quietly as possible. Leni gasps when I grab her hips, eyes flashing with surprise before they fill with heat. I duck my head to find her neck when she swats me away. "No marks today. We have the magazine shoot!"

That's right. My Leni and her mama are going to be featured in Ranch Life Magazine. Turns out, you can make a living from blogging, and people have been eating up Leni's monthly articles about cooking with her mom. The extra posts on her mom's business page have become so popular that the magazine reached out and asked to start photographing their sessions. Today is their first professional shoot. Ma is over the moon excited, even if Pa grumbles about having camera crews in his house. I know he's really proud of his girls. Just like I am.

"No marks," I promise. Keeping my teeth to myself, I pepper kisses down her neck before dropping to my knees. "At least not where they'll see." I grin at her with a devilish smile before I sink my teeth into her inner thigh. She moans, fingers digging into my hair to stabilize herself.

"Such a naughty girl. You're not supposed to shower alone," I murmur as she spreads her legs further apart, giving me access to exactly what I want. "What kind of punishment do we think you deserve today?"

"You can spank me later. If you're going to use that wicked tongue of yours, you'd better do it quick. I have a schedule to keep."

I chuckle, then swipe my tongue up her slit, teasing her.

"Yes," she mutters, her nails digging into my scalp. "More, Clay. Please make me come."

"See? Now you're being such a good girl, Eleanor." Carefully, I haul her closer to me, dipping my tongue inside of her for a taste, before I pull it out and find her clit. My fingers dip inside of her, fucking in and out as she begins to ride my face.

"God, yes, keep doing that," she cries, using my hair to keep my face flush with her core. My tongue laps up everything that seeps out around my fingers. When her walls start to flutter, I press my tongue back into her clit, crooking my fingers inside of her in just the right spot. She doubles over top of me, legs shaking as she chants my name. When she comes back down, I stand to my full height, pressing a gentle kiss to her lips.

"Better get going, baby. You don't wanna be late for your big day."

"Uh-huh," she mumbles, rinsing something out of her hair before smacking my ass and slipping out of the shower.

"You'll pay for that!"

"Hopefully." She winks at me from outside the glass doors before heading to the vanity to start getting ready for the day.

~

SOME DAYS, I still beat myself up for waiting so long to claim her. For pretending that I didn't need her as much as I do. But every kiss, every touch, makes it all worthwhile. Because regardless of whatever we've gone through in the past, we're in this for the long haul. The sparkly princess cut diamond that's sitting in my underwear drawer proves it.

Leni Kane is going to be my wife.

An Excerpt From
Don't Forget About Me
(Kane Ridge Ranch Book 2)

Brooks

Two Weeks Ago

I open the pasture gate when my Buckskin mare, Shine, turns her head. Her ears pricked forward toward the house. I follow her gaze, eying the dust as it climbs up the horizon.

When I picked my plot to put a house on, we reworked some of the gates, creating an easy path between my homestead and the main house. I'm close enough that I can grab a side-by-side or horse to be in the hub of the ranch quickly, but far enough from town that I don't get many visitors.

Especially when I'm not expecting someone. And I'm not. That cloud of dust tells me I have an unwanted guest coming up my driveway. I finish turning my favorite horse, Whiskey, out into the pasture. His bright white mane flies behind him as he chases his girl around. Hanging his halter in the barn, I make my way toward the house.

My gated backyard isn't much. A small patch of grass that

leads to a concrete deck where I have a patio set and hot tub. There's not much for landscaping around here. I tried my hand at it a few times, but all the plants I got in the ground died from being ignored.

Deciding to greet whoever has come to infringe on my sanctuary and solitude without giving them the option of coming in, I walk around instead of through the house.

When I turn the corner, I see a brown, rusted-out Sedan, the front bumper hanging on for dear life. A donut of a tire on the back; the front door panel caved in like it got head butted by a buffalo.

Jet black hair and sunken eyes turn toward me with a paper-thin smile. There's makeup on her teeth, and I shudder when she pats her hair down, like she's worried she won't impress me.

She doesn't.

"Damnit," I grumble. I was having such a good day. I went to check on a friend, who's more like a brother, only to find my sister was secretly at home sharing a cabin with him. The last time I saw Clayton Traeger looking well rested, he was sneaking into her bed, and we all pretended like we didn't notice. Like we had no idea that Leni was the only thing helping him sleep after his first tour as a Marine.

We had a bet running that they'd end up together once she turned eighteen, but it's been ten years since we've seen them in a room together. Guess that streak is over now.

I sigh, pinching the bridge of my nose as I try to prepare myself for whatever my hurricane of an ex-fiancée has to say. I'm about to open my mouth when I realize there's a car seat sitting on my porch, a grocery sack next to it. A little hand sticking out, fingers twirling in a sunbeam.

"Kate," I bite out her name. My tone brooking no question of warmth or familiarity.

"Brooks, hey." Her voice has always been one of my favorite things about her. She has a slight southern drawl that's both sweet and sexy.

"What are you doing here?"

"I need to ask you something." She flinches, bony shoulders curving in. This isn't the villain I've built up in my head over the years. That Kate is larger than life, and as destructive as a tornado. This Kate is wrecked, small, and helpless. A twinge of guilt surges through me before I remember all the shit she put me through.

"The answer is no, Kate, whatever it is."

"God, you're such an asshole." She rolls her eyes, then shoves the car seat aside to sit on the porch. The baby inside doesn't make a noise. Kate's long legs stretch out in front of her. They're bony and bruised, pockmarked and sickly white. I take in her emaciated frame and wonder how I ever found her attractive. Of course, she wasn't always an addict. She wasn't always like this. "You won't even listen to what I have to say?"

"What could you possibly have to say, Kate? I told you last time I never wanted to see you again. I thought I made that pretty clear."

"I know that, but things have changed."

"Not that much."

"Brooks, I have a daughter."

"Congratulations," I deadpan.

"I need you to take her." She shoves her fingers into her pockets, gnawing on the side of her cheek. "I got sober for the pregnancy, went cold turkey, and it nearly killed me. But I'm not a mother, Brooks, you know that."

"That's not my kid." I jab a finger at the car seat that's still sitting on the porch by itself.

"Obviously." She rolls her eyes. "I'm not cut out for this,

Brooks. And you're the best person I know. She'd have a better shot at a good life with you."

"Where's her dad?"

Kate drops her eyes, looking down at her dirty tennis shoes. "I don't know. I don't even know who he is."

"Fuck," I mutter, rolling the brim of my hat between my hands. I told myself I was done cleaning up Kate's messes, but this mess doesn't just affect Kate. There's a baby in that car seat who needs care and love. Two things Kate is incapable of giving to another human being. "What the fuck, Kate? You think you can just pull up here and drop off your kid? Like I'm a fucking daycare?"

"No, I know you. I know you won't take her unless I give her up completely. So, call Ethan and write up whatever you want. I'll sign over all my legal rights, put it down in writing that I'll never come back. I just need you to take her."

"I can't just take your kid, Kate. There are laws. It takes months to adopt a child."

"You don't have to adopt her, Brooks. I put your name on the birth certificate."

"Jesus fucking Christ." I scrub a hand down my face. What the hell did I ever see in this woman? "Get in the house, Kate."

She shrugs and ambles her way through the front door, leaving her infant on my porch.

I pace back and forth, gravel crunching under my boots as I stare at my house. My safe haven. My one place that I can drop the facade that I'm fine.

I drop my gaze to my boots, toeing the dirt beneath me. This is the spot where I brought Kate when I proposed. We camped out in the bed of my truck and planned a life together. I used to sit here, in a camp chair, picturing exactly what the house would look like.

I pictured Kate, glowing as she stood on that porch, barefoot, and pregnant. I pictured little dark-haired children running around, screaming, and laughing. God, there wasn't anything I wanted more. I nearly broke my back paying for the house, for all the upgrades Kate said she would need if I moved her so far away from town.

She lasted two weeks here. Two weeks before, she started driving into town for parties. Staying with whoever would let her crash. Sleeping with whoever happened to be around.

I excused it all. I gave her second chances, time and time again. I don't even know how many times I got a call from a friend or the hospital. How many times I had to bring her back here and help her through a hangover, or the withdrawals when she'd try to get clean.

I had a whole fucking protocol to deal with Kate. Going through the motions, because I was clinging to that dream in my head.

The dream I had all but given up on.

I learned a long time ago that I don't get the girl. I don't get the cozy family life I once thought I'd have.

"You can't love me the way I deserve," she spat out that final night. *"Don't you get it, Brooks? You drove me away. You're the reason I had to go looking for more. You and this stupid fucking life in the middle of nowhere. You were never good enough for me. You have nothing I want."*

I drop to the porch steps, head falling into my hands as I struggle to breathe past the ache in my chest.

My entire life, I had a plan. I was going to take over the ranch, marry my high school sweetheart, and be the unicorn couple that I see in my parents. Build a family. Have a life.

All of that shattered the second Kate first put a needle in her arm, and I've been running from it ever since. I don't do failure. I don't make mistakes. Not anymore.

A little squeak from my left has me looking over at the car

seat. One little hand is lifted up again, fingers still twirling in a sunbeam. I hook a corner of the seat and turn it towards me, peering down at the sweetest little face. There's a wisp of red hair on her head, big blue eyes staring up at me, and stubby little fingers reach out to touch my beard.

Shit. I breathe out. I will never have the life I planned for with Kate, but this little girl won't have any kind of life with her either. Not one I'd wish for anyone, especially not someone so tiny and vulnerable. Her little head cocks, a tentative smile crossing her face. She doesn't fuss, doesn't try to get out of the battered car seat she's strapped into.

Staring up at me, those blue eyes seem to take in everything. I stroke a finger down her cheek, her smile blooming wide, nose scrunching. I know then, at that moment, I'm not letting her leave here. Not with Kate and not to go into foster care.

"Holy shit." I blow out a breath, fishing my phone out of my pocket to dial Ethan's number.

"Hey," Ethan says, shuffling something around in the background.

"You home?"

"Nah, just packing stuff up at the office."

"What paperwork do you need to sign over your rights as a parent?" Ethan's side of the line goes so quiet I can practically hear the gears in his brain moving.

"I beg your pardon?" Leather squeaks, and I'm almost certain he had to take a seat.

"I'll explain more later. For now, I just need to know what's needed."

"Family law isn't exactly my area of expertise." I hear his computer booting up in the background.

"Give it your best shot then."

"Uh, sure. We'll have to file a petition with family court, and you're gonna need cause."

"Well, she's a drug addict who doesn't want the kid, so I think we have cause."

"Fucking hell. I knew she was going to come around. What the fuck, Brooks?"

"Don't get your panties in a twist. I didn't invite her here." Big blue eyes widen when my voice raises, her little body shrinking back into the dilapidated car seat. "Hey," I lower my voice, crooning like I would at a scared horse. "It's okay, sweetheart. You're okay."

"Please tell me you're talking to a colt," Ethan groans in my ear.

"Nope, not quite."

"Fuck. Listen, I think we can get the process expedited, but adoptions take time."

"She put me on the birth certificate."

Silence. Then, he blows a breath out loud and obnoxious in my ear. "Of course she did. It's not yours?"

I laugh a dark, humorless noise.

"Right," he sighs into my ear again. "I'll text Judge Reinhardt and see if he's free tomorrow."

"'Preciate you." I loop my arm through the carrier, then opt to just scoop it up from the bottom when the handle pulls clean off. I leave the plastic bag and whatever she has inside it on the porch. Not at all surprised when I find Kate going through the fridge, probably looking for alcohol. Sucks to be her, though. I gave that shit up when she left.

"I see you're just as fun as ever," she spits, leaning back against the counter with a can of soda in her hands.

"What's her name?"

"Dunno, I never gave her one."

"How'd you file the birth certificate?"

347

"It just says Baby Girl Kane." She shrugs like this is a totally acceptable answer.

"How old is she?"

"Eight...nine months maybe? I don't know. I took the pain meds at the hospital, and that was that."

Meaning the second those drugs left her system, she went looking for another high. It's a wonder the baby even lasted this long. I don't know the first thing about babies, but she's tiny. The tiniest little thing I've ever seen. Ignoring Kate, I pull my phone back out and shoot a text off to Pa and my foreman, Destin.

Acknowledgments

First and foremost, I want to thank you, the reader. This book was incredibly healing for me to write, and I can only hope that it was something you enjoyed. Thank you for taking a chance on a new author. I hope you loved it. P.S. There's so much more in store!

I have to give a shout-out to my boys. To my incredible husband, who made this possible. I wouldn't be here, in this place, without you, Love. Thank you for sticking by my side, for encouraging me, and for helping me pursue my dreams. I am so grateful for all the work you do, for the way you support us. To my baby guy, Tato. Thank you for inspiring me to be a better human every single day. These stories aren't for you. Please God, never read them. But I hope these show you that you can do the things you dream of.

Thank you to my editors. Sara and Zara. Sara, thank you for seeing the potential in this book and for giving me tough love to make it what it is. I am so incredibly blessed to have worked with you! Zara, thank you for being exactly what I needed in an editor and mentor.

Carolyn, thank you so incredibly much for being the gracious human being you are. I was so close to calling it, and then you told me to be proud of this book, and damnit, I am.

To Callie, one for providing the name Benson. And two for being the first person who willingly read my book. Thank you for your feedback, encouragement, and indignation. I swear, all the drama will be worth it! I can't wait to serve you Toby's book on a platter.

Thanks to Soph for providing the name Hillcreek for our little town!

There will never, ever be enough thanks to give my in-laws, who are constantly helping us out here on the farm. Whether it be in my kitchen or hanging with my kiddo. Endless, endless thanks! But especially to Debbie, who will sit and let me yap about my books.

Thank you to my sisters for always being willing to hear me chat about my stories and my books. Thanks for putting up with my traumatizing story lines, Sara. Appreciate you. ;)

To my parents, who purchased me no less than eight million composition books in high school. Bet you never thought it'd go this far!

To my girls. The ones who stuck by me through some of my hardest days. My best friends. Thank you for constantly encouraging me to keep going. For cheering me on and rooting for me. I love you guys!

About the Author

Bailey Johnson is a contemporary romance author who loves all things coffee and baked goods. She lives in rural North Dakota with her husband, son, obese dog, three cats and an ever growing flock of chickens.

If she's not writing you can usually find her exploring the farm with her son or out riding a borrowed horse. She's obsessed with all things cowboy and is really enjoying returning to her ranching roots. Even if it is only in fiction.

Find out more about the Kane Ridge Ranch Series on her
website
www.authorbaileyjohnson.com

Also by Bailey Johnson

Sign up for Bailey Johnson's newsletter to receive a free copy of Pillow Talk. A Kane Ridge Ranch Novella that follows Ma and Pa Kane throughout the years as they raise their children leading up to the epic love story of Don't Leave Me Behind.

www.ingramcontent.com/pod-product-compliance
Lightning Source LLC
Chambersburg PA
CBHW051945240626
47153CB00005B/1637